Burke's Samovar

Bob Burke Suspense Thriller #4

a novel by

William F. Brown

PROLOGUE

Helmand Province, Afghanistan

You can say it started three years before on that Op up in the mountains...

"See anything down there?" "Ace" asked.

"No, and that bothers me," "the Ghost" answered as he continued to scan the small village below through the Leupold telescopic sight on his Mk-110 sniper rifle.

Ace had a pair of M-22 Steiner binoculars and was doing the same thing, looking for movement or any sign of life down there, but there was none. They were sent here because Intelligence said there was to be a meeting of five of the local Taliban khans and their lieutenants in the small village this morning. That would be at least a dozen enemy soldiers and their leaders. So far, nothing. No one was there. Or, it was meant to look that way.

It wasn't much of a village, or "Vil," as they called it, to begin with: eight dilapidated mud-wall huts sitting between the main north-south valley trail and a dry stream bed. Not much else: no activity, no people, not even any goats or chickens.

The Ghost was Major Robert Tyrone Burke, team leader. Ace was Master Sergeant Harold Randall, Bob Burke's #2, his top-ranked NCO and best friend, but never to be called Harold or even Hal under penalty of death. Their team of ten Delta Force "operators" had flown out of Kandahar in two Black Hawk helicopters at 8 p.m. the night before and dropped off five miles south. They double-timed it up the valley along a narrow goat trail that wound along the mountainside in order to be in position in the rocks above the Vil before the sun came up. They were hidden, but the site didn't afford much cover. That was never a good thing, especially in the heart of Helmand Province, the deadliest place in Afghanistan for Americans.

"Where did this Intel and Op Order come from, if I may be so bold?" Ace asked. "Tell me it wasn't from that dumbass new Light Colonel in G-2."

"Okay, I won't tell you it's from that dumbass new Light Colonel in G-2."

"And a bad op is a bad op."

"Copy that," Bob said as he looked at his watch. It was already after 10 a.m. "Well, Master Sergeant, we can't sit here in the middle of Indian country much longer," he said as he swept the Vil with his scope one last time.

"A rolling stone gathers no bullets? But if we're going down there, we should light it up first – a little recon by fire to see if Haji pops out of his rabbit hole."

"That's what I was thinking, but I didn't know you went to West Point too."

"Me? West Point? No, just Uncle's School of Scars and Hard Knocks. And I'll tell you, after six tours I'm getting a little old for this shit."

"Copy that. Only my fifth, but it takes a handful of Motrin to roll my ass out of the rack in the morning."

"And harder and harder to tolerate fools."

"Roger that. No wonder we get a bit cranky from time to time," Bob replied as he looked around the valley and up the hill behind them.

"Something bothering you?"

"Probably nothing; but ever since the sun came up, I get this weird feeling somebody's watching me. You ever get that?"

"Depends who I'm dating and whether her ex-husband is still around, but I'll tell Lonzo and Herbie to keep an eye on your Six. You never can tell."

Bob had placed Sergeant First Class Vinnie Pastorini fifty meters up the trail to the north and left Sergeant Joe "The Batman" Hendrix to block the trail behind them to the south. They kept the heavy weapons group in the center, consisting of Sergeant Henry "Lonzo" Hardisty, Sergeant Herbert "Herbie" Jacobs, and Sergeant Miguel "Toro" Torez. He activated the mic on his PRC-154 Rifleman squad radio and said, "Wake up gentlemen, siesta's over, folks. Time to go to work. "Lonzo, on my mark, hit the Vil with your SAW," referring to their squad M-249 light machine gun. "Herbie, you and Toro drop some 'thumper' rounds in there too." Those were the accurate and lethal grenade rounds they fired from the M-203 grenade launchers attached under their M-4 carbines. "Let's see what we flush out. All right, light it up. Now!"

The Army's Delta Force has three peculiarities that distinguish it from other units. First, membership in the elite infantry unit is top-secret. Other than wives, its members tell no one, not even their mothers or girlfriends, for their protection. Second, like undercover cops, Delta "operators" were not required to adhere to the Army's normal physical appearance standards. Long hair, beards, tattoos, and earrings were not only the norm, they were needed to rid them of that telltale "Army" look so they could blend more easily into civilian populations. Except in formal military settings with other soldiers around, they usually used their tactical radio names or "handles" in normal conversation, regardless of rank. It was a sign of unit cohesion, exclusivity, and even affection.

While Bob Burke was a major, the others were senior sergeants in their mid to late 20s and 30s, all seasoned professionals, and older and far more battle-weary than the average soldier at Kandahar or Bagram. Most were on their second, third, or even fourth tour in Afghanistan plus a couple in Iraq, always out in the field on Special Operations that ended up kicking everyone's ass. But soldiering was their choice. They got what they had bargained for. Now they were trapped in it. Get out? To do what? Private security work? Hire out as a mercenary? Or stay in and go back to Bragg or Benning as an instructor or a goddamned supply clerk? There was nothing else they could do that gave them the camaraderie, the sense of mission, or the incredible high that this did.

In the States, they dressed like a motorcycle gang – trendy, hairy, and Jim Beam "country." Ace Randall usually wore a long, tightly braided ponytail, a Fu Manchu moustache, and a tattoo on each forearm. One read, "Been There, Done That," and the other said, "Kill 'em All. Let God Sort It Out." But when you are six feet two inches tall, a muscular two hundred and ten pounds, and ruggedly handsome, camouflage was essential.

On a deployment like this "to the desert," which meant anywhere in the Middle East, be it Iraq, Afghanistan, or parts unknown, their appearance went "native." They wore the same unkempt hair, scraggly beards, earth-colored baggy pants, shawl, and flat "pakol" hat that the Afghans wore.

The firing lasted no more than thirty seconds, but neither the half-dozen gold-tipped high-explosive grenade rounds nor the bursts of machine gun fire flushed out any response from the Vil. All they accomplished was to knock the corners off a couple of buildings, pockmark the walls with bullet holes, cave in a roof, and kick up a large cloud of dust. As the last of the echoes died away, the Valley became dead quiet again.

"Damn," Ace said as he scanned the Vil again, "looks like we'll have to go down and kick in some doors."

"Take 'Chester with," Staff Sergeant Festus Blackledge, "and The Bee," Sergeant Jimmy Beemaster, "and Crispy," Sergeant Jamil Johnson, "We'll cover you from here."

Keeping low, Ace and the other three men leapfrogged down the hillside from boulder to boulder until they reached the valley floor. They paused behind some large rocks to recon once more. Still, nothing. But as soon as they left the cover of the rocks and were out in the open, all hell broke loose. Bursts of automatic rifle fire drove them back to the rocks, where they took cover as best they could, but Crispy was down and The Bee was hit trying to drag him away. He managed to get them both to relative safety behind one of the boulders a hundred meters short of the Vil, as Ace, Chester, and the six men up on the hillside trail all opened up on it with supporting fire.

Unfortunately, that wasn't the end of the morning's surprises.

"Ghost, Vinnie, I have Hajis coming down the trail from the north," he heard Sergeant First Class Vinnie Pastorini say over the tactical net. "Squad strength at least. Am engaging."

Before he could reply, he heard a second radio call from the south end their line. "Ghost, Batman, same-o, same-o, a half-dozen, maybe ten. Am also engaging."

Fortunately, the trail was very narrow, forcing the Talis to come at them in column and making it easy to stop them where they were for the time being. Bob rolled over and looked up the mountainside to see if there were any more enemy troops getting in position above them, but he saw nothing. Reaching under his shawl, he pulled out his handheld AN PRC-154 field radio. It was about the size of an old-fashioned walkie-talkie, but much more powerful, which he used to communicate with the fixed-wing, forward air controller usually circling northern Helmand Province when operations were ongoing.

"Sky Bird, Ghost..." he called, hoping the guy hadn't gone back to Bagram to refuel. "Sky Bird, Ghost," he called again, knowing reception was worse the further north they got.

"Ghost, Sky Bird," he finally heard the scratchy reply. "What can we do for you this fine morning?"

"Not so fine at the moment, Sky Bird. We need fire support and an extraction, ASAP."

"I have two F-16s north of Kandahar I'll vector them in. Should be over you in five minutes. Call sign 'Hoosier-15.' "

"Sooner would be better. It's getting a tad toasty up here."

"Copy, that, Ghost. I'll also send in two Black Hawks for extraction and two Apaches for fire support, but they're at least fifteen minutes out."

Fifteen minutes, he thought. The gunfire from the Vil was increasing and his four guys down there were seriously outgunned. At the same time, activity was increasing at both the north and south ends of their position. So, while he was talking, being the best shot in the unit as well as its commander, he took shots at anything that moved or even looked suspicious down in the Vil with his M-110 sniper rifle.

"Lonzo," he called out, "reposition north and support Vinnie with the SAW. Herbie, take your Thumper and support The Batman."

"Ghost, Sky Bird. What are the targets?"

"We have enemy infantry with automatic weapons dug in a small Vil. Eight mud huts and a reinforced squad at least. Also, we have enemy in the open on the trail at each side of our positions. Priority to the Vil and tell him to put a rush on it."

"Copy, Ghost. Hoosier-15 and his wingman are toting Mark-82 500-pound 'dumb' bombs. They should be perfect to flatten your huts. Then they can come around and hit the trail targets with guns or rockets. Hoosier-15 will want you to mark the friendlies with smoke and vector him in."

"Roger that," Bob told Sky Bird and switched to the squad tactical net. "Ace, we have two fast movers coming in and we need to mark your position. What color smoke do you have?"

Ace rummaged through his rucksack and said, "Ghost, I have an orange smoke grenade, I say again, an orange."

"Roger that, Ace, go ahead and mark."

Feeling like a one-armed paperhanger with two radios and three firefights going on simultaneously, he finally heard the slow drawl of the Air Force F-16 pilot come online.

"Ghost, this is Hoosier-15, starting up the valley. You marking with smoke?"

"Roger that, Hoosier-15. We marked friendlies with an orange, I say again an orange. Your target is 90° and 100 yards east and across the valley from the smoke."

"Copy that, Ghost, commencing run. I see an orange... No, I see two oranges."

"Damn!" Bob swore. The last thing they needed was a confused F-16 pilot with 500-pound bombs. "Abort, abort!" He said as he looked down into the valley and saw a second cloud of orange smoke beginning to waft over the Vil.

"Look like Haji's learned some new tricks," Ace said as he dug in his rucksack and pulled out a yellow smoke grenade. "Ghost, I'm dropping a banana," he said as he popped it downwind from their position. "I say again, a banana."

"Hoosier-15 come on around. My guy's put out a banana, I say again, a banana." But no sooner did the jet pilot acknowledge and start a second run than Bob saw a second cloud of smoke in the Vil. Naturally, it was also yellow. "Hoosier-15, Abort, Abort. Looks like the bad guys have a well-stocked supply room. But come on around one more time."

"Ace," Bob told him, "the bastards are matching your smoke to confuse the FAC. What else you got?"

"Purple. I'll toss a purple." As Bob watched, the purple smoke drifted away from Ace's position, but that was all he saw.

"Ghost, this is Hoosier-15 again. I have a grape... Lo and behold, just one grape. Target in view, with some leftover orange and banana, just like Carmen Miranda."

"Hoosier-15, you best take Carmen out, 'cause we're fresh out of fruit down here."

In a matter of seconds, the two F-16s rolled in and put four Mark-82 500-pound bombs into the cluster of mud huts. The explosions rocked the valley, sending rock and debris into the air and columns of choking dust.

"Hoosier-15, Ghost. All good, but we still need some help up on the hill. We are being pressed at each end of our line by enemy infantry."

"Well, Ghost, if ya'll think you can get the smoke right, from today's menu, the chef recommends our 20-millimeter Vulcan Gatling gun for that particular application. It ought to clear off that trail right quick for you."

"Vinnie, Koz, mark your positions with smoke." Bob saw yellow smoke pop from Vinnie's position and orange smoke from Koz's, and then called pilot again. "We are on the inside of those two markers, a banana and an orange – I say again, the inside – bring it on in."

"Ghost, Hoosier-15. I see one banana and one orange. I say again, only one each. Commencing our runs, I'll come in from the south and strafe the north target, and my wingman will come in from the north and hit the south. But Ghost, we saw their positions from the muzzle flashes last time around and the Tali are 'danger' close to your guys. You sure you want us to do this? Or would you rather wait for the Apaches?"

"No time, Hoosier-15. Take 'em out or we'll die here."

"Roger that, Ghost. Tell your boys to get their heads down."

Bob tried to locate the two jets, but the sky was too bright. "Vinnie, you and Koz shoot everything you got down the trail, then get the hell away from there and take cover."

Perhaps ten seconds later, the first F-16 Eagle screamed directly up the valley, drifted up the hillside, and flashed over the American positions, low and hard. It opened up with its Vulcan Gatling gun and strafed the trail, beginning exactly where the smoke grenade spewed a bright orange plume of smoke. The Vulcan had six barrels that rotated like a Gatling gun and fired up to six thousand 20-millimeter cannon rounds per minute. It sounded like a high-pitched, shrieking chainsaw when it was fired, but even that loud, grating noise was drowned out by the roar of the F-16's engines as it passed right over their heads. It is a devastating weapon. The burst from the 20-millimeter cannon couldn't have lasted more than three or four seconds, but Hoosier-15 fired it with pinpoint, devastating accuracy. Hundreds of 20-millimeter rounds shredded a 300-yard long by 10-yard wide stretch of the trail and hillside, slicing and dicing every living thing in its path with the high explosive rounds and flying shards of stone. It was both terrifying and exhilarating.

As he turned off and soared out over the valley, his wing man swept in from the other direction and did exactly the same thing to the trail beyond Koz's position, beginning at the spot where his yellow smoke canister lay. Again, another three- or four-second burst and the hillside trail erupted in dust, flying rock, and shrapnel before he too powered out over the valley and was gone. Their day was done.

"Hoosier-15, Ghost. Right on target. Thanks for the help."

"Your friends up here in blue always aim to please, Ghost. Now, ya'll have a good day ya hear," he said, no doubt headed for the bar at the officers' club for a beer, a steak, and a hot shower in their air-conditioned hooches at Bagram Air Force Base over the mountains to the east. Yes, Bob thought, it was one hell of a war.

The Taliban, or what little was left of them, vanished as quickly as they had appeared, and Bob was able to quickly reposition his men down on the edge of the Vil. They commenced treating their wounded as two Black Hawk helicopters swept up the valley for their pickup. Two Apaches circled above them, providing high cover, but there was no need. The short, sharp fight was over. It was impossible to come up with a hard body count; but from a quick scan of the body parts and weapons strewn about the rubble that had been the Vil, he figured they'd killed eight or ten there, plus another dozen or more between the two ends of the trail.

In the process, however, Bob had lost two good men KIA: Sergeant Crispy Johnson, who died from bullet wounds in the initial attack on the Vil, and Specialist Herbie Jacobs, who died from Taliban rifle fire up on the south end of the trail. In addition, Lonzo, The Batman, The Bee, and

Toro all sustained one or more minor wounds, but none were life-threatening.

As they flew back down the valley, Bob sat next to Ace in the open door of the Black Hawk, legs dangling out on the struts as it flew down the long valley and headed for the field hospital in Kandahar. As he looked out across the desolate rock-strewn countryside, he couldn't help wondering about this country and its people.

Helmand was home to dozens of fiercely independent hill tribes. The truth was, they harbored no more dislike of the Americans than they had for the Russians, the British, the Persians, the Mongols, the Arabs, or the Greeks under Alexander the Great. Nothing personal, but they just didn't like foreigners of any kind coming in and telling them what to do; and they had kicked everyone's ass who tried, including ours. That was the reality of Afghanistan. So were the two bodies lying on the floor of the helicopter behind him, and the four men sitting on the benches, bandaged and glassy-eyed from painkillers.

It was 11:30 when they landed at the Kandahar Military Hospital. As Bob and his remaining men stood silently watching, the medical staff rushed his wounded off to triage. After they came back and unloaded his two KIAs, Ace looked over and said, "I don't like that look in your eye, Ghost. Tell me you ain't gonna do what I think you're gonna do."

Bob turned and stared at him with those hard, black eyes and an expression hot enough to burn through steel. "Me? I'm a pussycat. What's wrong with stopping by and saying Hi to the new Deputy G-2?" he asked as he threw his gear over his shoulder and set off at a brisk pace toward the Special Operations Command – Central compound, or SOCENT, a quarter mile away. Ace signaled Vinnie, Koz, and Chester, and they did their best to keep up.

Kandahar wasn't a large base. That made it an easy place to walk and a hard place to keep secrets. Bob and his unwanted entourage of babysitters were only halfway to the SOCENT compound when he saw a very large black man in crisp, fresh-off-the-plane camo BDUs and clean boots coming toward him on the dusty road. No need to walk much further, he thought. It was Lieutenant Colonel Jefferson Adkins of the Adjutant General Corps, the new Deputy S-2 in Plans and Ops. At 6' 7" and 270 pounds with an in-grown, angry frown, the man was hard to miss.

Adkins's sullen attitude was perhaps understandable. A former All-Big 10 offensive lineman and son of a GM auto worker in Detroit, his prospective professional football career ended when he blew out his knee at the end of his junior year of college. Instead of the New York Giants or the LA Rams, he ended up with a Physical Education degree and an Army ROTC commission. Still, when it came to important staff jobs in Special Ops, where guys lives are on the line every day, one hoped they would plug someone in who had plenty of combat time in a branch whose emblem shot something, like the crossed rifles of the Infantry, the cannon of the Field Artillery, or the tanks of the Armor Corps. Seeing those Adjutant General emblems on the collar of his BDUs in a war zone did not inspire confidence. Word was someone in higher authority thought it would be a good idea to put him in the Deputy S-2 Military Intelligence slot in SOCENT in Kandahar, albeit temporarily, to help pad his resume for the upcoming promotion board.

Given the time, Adkins was probably headed to the officers' mess, which was around the corner, and an early seat at the General's table, when Bob cut him off. Burke was a little guy, only 5' 9" and maybe down to 150 pounds after weeks in the field, so the Colonel towered over him. Dirty, haggard, and still dressed in his Afghan hill tribe attire with no name or rank, as opposed to his dress uniform which bore a 75th Ranger Regiment and a chest full of medals, it was no surprise that Adkins didn't recognize him. Still, Bob Burke was already a Special Ops legend and the field pack over his shoulder and the long M-110 sniper rifle in his hand should have given Adkins a clue.

Adkins went to his left and Bob stepped in front of him. He went to his right and Bob did it again. Finally, the Colonel stopped and glared down at him. "You playin' games with me?"

"That intel you gave us last night was bullshit! It got two of my men killed this morning, because you sent us right into an ambush."

"I didn't do shit, boy!" Adkins glared down at him, as the other Deltas gathered around. "I guess you must be Burke," he said as the lightbulb must have finally come on. "Yeah, I heard there was a firefight out there. Too bad! But don't blame me just because you screwed up the op. Now get the hell out of my way, *MAJOR,* 'cause I'm late for lunch."

Adkins put the palm of his huge hand on Bob Burke's chest and stepped forward, intending to shove him aside and continue on to the officers' mess. Big mistake, and the last thing Jefferson Adkins remembered for a while. A lightning fast straight right caught him on the button, lifted him several inches off the ground, and dropped him on his back on the dusty road, out cold, with a broken nose and minus one front tooth.

All this happened on a busy street in the middle of the base in broad daylight. When Adkins came to some minutes later and tried to file a report with the MPs, it was amazing how they could find no witnesses who saw anything other than him push the Major, slip, and hit his head as he fell to the ground. Funny how things work out sometimes. It didn't take long before everyone in the headquarters knew what happened. Most just smiled, figuring the big guy had it coming.

Bob never regretted it, but that was one more big straw on the camel's back. From the direction the war and the Army were headed, he soon realized it was time for him to get out. What he didn't realize was that this was not the last time that he and Jefferson Adkins would cross swords.

CHAPTER ONE

Moscow, on a Bright Spring Day

Oleg Shurepkin couldn't help himself. He hid his eyes behind his hand, if only for a second, to glance outside through the ornate conference room's floor-to-ceiling windows. It was early April. The weather in the city had finally broken and spring was in the air everywhere. The meeting was in the top floor conference room of the Four Seasons Hotel: safe, neutral territory. Its windows looked out over Red Square, the red and white Nikolskaya Tower, Lenin's Tomb, halfway between the red brick wall of the Kremlin and the KGB's old Lubyanka prison several blocks behind them. Well, perhaps not so safe, he reflected. Beyond the windows, the city was turning green. The dead gray and muddy brown of winter and early spring were finally fading, and the forest was budding and greening up. Nothing improved a Russian's psyche after a long, bitter winter more than these first, precious days of spring.

The eight old men sitting around the long, polished mahogany conference table with him were the "Vor" Council, the loose confederation of organized crime bosses which the international press liked to call "the Russian Mafia." Like the others, Shurepkin was a Zek, a former Gulag inmate, who had spent far too many years in the KGB's slave labor camps above the Arctic Circle. That was why he couldn't resist a quick peek at those gorgeous trees on the horizon. They would always be more important to him than these constipated old men.

How ironic, he thought. This room had the finest view in the city. With its French windows, crystal chandeliers, and gold-framed landscape paintings on the walls, they could be sitting in the Peterhof, the Ekaterininsky, or one of the Czar's other palaces. Imagine! A tableful of decrepit thieves and murderers sitting in these palatial surroundings with the blessing of the new "Czar," Vladimir Vladimirovich Putin. The world was upside down.

"Oleg!" Yuri Paretsky sniped at him. Shurepkin sat at one end of the long table and Yuri Paretsky, his old nemesis from Kazan, sat at the other. "You have not been listening to a goddamned thing poor Kuryakin's trying to tell you, have you?"

"But I have, Yuri, every word." Oleg kept a straight face as he turned away from the lovely spring day outside and focused his powerful, coal-black eyes on the hunched-over old man at the other end of the table. "Every goddamned word."

There were snickers around the table that Paretsky ignored. "That is crap, Oleg," he challenged. "If you really were listening, you would have jumped to your feet, pulled out your pistol, and shot him on the spot."

"And I still might!" he said as the others laughed. "But we all agreed there would be no guns in here, did we not? Besides, Kuryakin is from Yaroslavl. I figure it was safer to let him bore you all to death. Then I shall shoot him." The laughter from the others broke the tension, which was good.

Oleg Shurepkin always felt out of place in these meetings. The others would drink vodka and draw naked women on the pads of paper the hotel placed at each seat, occasionally mumbling an obscene joke to the man sitting next to him. Shurepkin always kept his gnarled, broken hands in his lap; but no matter where his eyes or hands were, he listened. The others sat with ties down and shirt collars unbuttoned, looking like what they were: peasants and leg breakers with thick necks and barrel-shaped chests. Shurepkin, tall and rough-hewn, had a rugged handsomeness about him with sharp angles and chisel marks, like a hastily carved avant-garde statue. While the others looked like they had stolen their clothes from the basement clearance rack in the GUM department store on Red Square, Oleg wore a perfectly tailored, pin-striped Savile Row suit, complete with a rich maroon tie and matching handkerchief.

Each Vor had his own territory and his own family or gang, and each was fiercely independent. Technically, they were equals and their incessant challenges and insults were but one more part of the normal power games they played, but times were changing. Oleg Shurepkin was the Vor or Boss of Moscow, the seat of all real money and power in the country as far back as Ivan the Terrible. While all Council members were equal in status, being the Vor of Moscow made Oleg Shurepkin more equal than the others. He was the wealthiest, most sophisticated, most devious, most powerful, and most ambitious of the lot. He knew it, and they knew it. They didn't trust him, and he didn't trust any of them.

There was a tottering balance of power on the Council. For self-preservation, no member would allow a move against any other or against the council chief for fear it would all unravel. Better the bastard you know, unless he made a catastrophic mistake, was costing the others money, or had put the organization in peril. Unfortunately, that was the precise position Shurepkin found himself in today. He had not called this meeting; they had, because he had done all three and that did not bode well.

When the Soviet government finally collapsed of its own dead weight in 1991, the crooked policemen and spies of the former KGB suddenly found themselves out of work, let go by the new reformist government. Perestroika! But it didn't take long for the KGB, the secret police, and the Russian Mafia, the "Bratva," to realize they could rob the country blind much easier if they worked together than if they fought over its bones. That was Vladimir Vladimirovich Putin's unique contribution to the development of the Russian state. He reorganized the KGB and the civilian and military police and brought them under his thumb. He did the same to the criminals. He directed Oleg Shurepkin to impose structure and discipline on the rag-tag underworld gangs who were now overrunning the country. When you go to work for "the Czar," however, you soon learn everyone is replaceable. Men were only "useful" as long as they were "useful" to *HIM*, and everyone knew it.

"Putin is squeezing us again, Oleg," Paretsky continued. "He wants another 10%! You have all the banks and all the ministries and businesses here in the city to fall back on," Paretsky said as he swept his hand toward the windows, "but my little family cannot absorb many more of his 'cash calls.' "

"Neither can mine," Leonid Makarov joined the chorus. "When I go home to Obinsk and Voronovo, it is like trying to make soup from a shriveled old turnip. My people only have so much to give, you know."

"*YOU* were the one who talked us into it, Oleg," Lutarski from Volgograd in the Crimea, spoke up. He rarely said anything at these meetings, and for him to side with the malcontents was an alarming sign. "But we were neither fools nor virgins. The President's power and protection are seductive. But look at us now. The fellow treats us like serfs and picks our pocket any time he pleases."

"Perhaps you should tell him that," Shurepkin answered too quickly.

"You are supposed to be our leader, our 'Boss.' Well, act like one!" Paretsky pounded his fist on the table as his face turned an angry red. "It is your job! The 'Czar' does not care to hear anything from the rest of us."

"The 'Czar?' I would be careful what I call him," Shurepkin chuckled as he looked up at the chandeliers and flicked his ear. "Vladimir Vladimirovich does not like it."

Paretsky's eyes narrowed. "You told us you had this room swept, you bastard!" he growled and snapped his fingers at a large man standing behind him.

"Relax, Yuri. I *DID* have the room swept. I was merely making a point," Shurepkin answered as Paretsky's man pulled out a small black box and quickly circled the room, staring at a small screen. "Besides, we have all brought enough signal jammers to crash a 747. So what? The FSB can hear whatever it wants to hear, but that is not your point, is it?"

"Unfortunately, no," Kuryakin answered, glaring at Shurepkin. "I am told the man does not need listening devices, that he already has a pair of ears and a tongue in here."

"What is that supposed to mean?" Shurepkin sat forward and locked his cold, dark eyes on the smaller man. They say when you get that treatment, it is like staring down the twin barrels of a sawed-off shotgun, and as intimidating.

Barely fifteen years old, Oleg Shurepkin became one of the nameless prisoners in one of the hundreds of nameless forced labor camps that once dotted the Soviet Arctic Circle. Like the other inmates, he remained alive at the sufferance of the "Czar" of that day: Comrade Josef Stalin. Perhaps they forgot about Oleg. Perhaps his execution order got lost. No one ever knew, and there was no explanation for why he was allowed to live. The inmates were cyphers, names in some dusty ledger book long since lost, sentenced at a trial they were not allowed to attend, if one was held at all, and never even told which crimes they were charged with. That was the random nature of the terror.

When the NKVD arrested him, Oleg Shurepkin was the exception in that he knew exactly what they were charging him with. The Communist mayor of his village at the foot of the Ural Mountains thought his father insulted him. It was a personal matter regarding a cow, but that did not matter. The mayor had the NKVD arrest his father in the middle of the night for spreading "defeatist rumors and anti-Soviet thoughts." They hauled him away in one of their "Black Maria" vans, never to be seen again. Oleg was only fifteen, but he stole a neighbor's revolver, broke into the mayor's house, and put three bullets into the man as he slept, then two more into the mayor's fat wife. There was no proof Oleg did it, but that didn't matter either. Fifteen or not, they sentenced him to five years in a "hard regime" labor camp. That was a death sentence, but they soon extended the five years to seven for insolence and bad behavior. The seven was in turn increased to ten and finally to twelve for his continuing anti-Soviet attitude.

They dropped the full weight of the Soviet system on Oleg time and again, but they never broke him. He was a tall, muscular young man who spent his early years in the camps chipping coal and iron ore from the frozen ground, bent over with nothing but a dull pickax, a steel bar, and his bare hands, but he had an indomitable will to live and fists like sledgehammers. It was jungle rule there, gang rule. He killed three men with his bare hands in the first few years. One tried to steal his food. One tried to steal his coat, and one came after him in the dark. But it was that reputation that made the others fear him, and it was the man who was the most feared who became the Vor, the Boss.

CHAPTER TWO

Fort Bragg, North Carolina

If Bob Burke had one major character flaw, it was that he couldn't tolerate fools. It didn't take long after the end of that tour in Afghanistan for him to decide he'd had his fill of the Army's incompetent senior leadership. He had been on track for much higher rank and probably stars on his shoulders, which was why it came as a shock to everyone when he resigned his commission, filed his papers, and got out after twelve years for a blonde he met at Hilton Head and a lucrative job with her father's growing software company in Chicago.

For Bob, it meant no more idiots, no more fighting battles they wouldn't let him win, and no more losing good men in wars that never made any sense. In a way, he could thank Jefferson Adkins for his sudden reverse epiphany. The solid right he landed on Adkins's chin may have put the Lieutenant Colonel out cold in the middle of the road in Kandahar, but it woke up Bob Burke and turned his life around.

Other than the tooth, Jefferson Adkins hadn't done badly either. They promoted him to full colonel to shut him up, and he spent the rest of his tour safely away from the Taliban finding his true calling as a staff bureaucrat in the Inspector General's Office where he excelled as a petty bureaucrat, conducting inspections and ensuring that his Army operated "by the book." But he never forgot the noticeable bend in the cartilage of his nose, compliments of the right fist of Captain Robert Tyrone Burke. He hated him, hated the Deltas, and particularly hated all of Burke's "Merry Men." He never said it in public, but he kept thinking, "Sooner or later, I'm gonna get ya, sucka, all of you!"

His chance came a year later in Iraq when they sent a squad of Burke's former Delta Force troops to support an Iraqi unit attacking an ISIS headquarters in western Syria. It was a trap. They slaughtered the Iraqis, except for their two officers and a sergeant who no doubt sold their men out. Those three knew what was to happen, so they fled and sneaked on board the second of two American Silent Hawk helicopters carrying the Deltas back out. The first American helicopter was downed by the ISIS in the ambush with the loss of its crew and several Deltas. For some unknown reason, as that first helicopter crashed in flames on the rocky desert below, the three Iraqis must have decided to join it and "disembarked" from theirs at 3,000 feet. Later, when their battered bodies were found, the four Deltas aboard the helicopter were accused of tossing them out the door.

Weeks afterward, Jefferson Adkins managed to worm his way into a full colonel slot as the IG, or Inspector General, of the Joint Special Operations Center at Fort Bragg. JSOC coordinated the military's special operations assets, from the Army's Delta Force and 75th Ranger Regiment to the Navy's SEALs, Marine Corps Recon and Raiders, and the Air Force Special Operations squadrons. During the subsequent ISIS attack on the post, Adkins again crossed swords with Bob Burke, face to face, and again ended up out cold on the floor with another broken nose and a missing tooth. The former major was only half Adkins's size, but he was a martial arts master and had been one of the most elite killing machines the US Army ever created. You'd think Adkins would have learned, but he didn't.

It was shortly afterward that the word came down that the IG's office was beginning an investigation into the helicopter incident in Iraq. From the beginning, it was the word of four Deltas, four of Bob Burke's Deltas, against the helicopter's co-pilot. He had initially reported that he thought something happened in the seats behind him that night, but soon thought better of it. He kept trying to withdraw his statement, but that was all Jefferson Adkins needed. Those were Burke's men. Like a pit bull with a bone, the big Colonel wasn't about to let go.

But after three years, Bob realized the time had come to put an end to their war, too.

CHAPTER THREE

Moscow, The Four Seasons

When he sat at a conference table like this, the others never saw Oleg Shurepkin doodling on a pad of paper or drumming his fingers on the table. He kept his hands discreetly folded out of sight in his lap, because one hand had only three and a half fingers and the other only four. Both of his arms were covered with scars and prison camp tattoos that ran from his fingertips, up the back of his hands, under the crisp French cuffs of his silk dress shirt, to his shoulders, which bore particular eight-pointed star-shaped tattoos. Like business cards or an Army uniform, those tattoos showed a man's gang rank, number of kills, and prison record for all to see. So, despite his impeccably tailored $10,000 suits from Henry Poole and Richard James on London's Savile Row, it was the tattoos, the scars, and the missing fingers that described the man. Like all the others around that table, he was a Zek. They would never pass for gentlemen.

Yuri Paretsky spoke up to calm the waters. "Oleg, we know Putin will take anything and everything he wants. But when we funded those big plans of yours to expand our operations into America – and I would remind you that *WE* funded them, not you – those operations were to buy Putin off. Of course we knew he would take his split of the profits, but we were told he would be content with that, content with the upside cash from America and the intelligence he would garner. There were to be no more levies."

"Why are you explaining it to him, Yuri," Avram Abramov from Vladimir questioned. "It was Oleg who sold the deal to us and then sold it to our 'illustrious' President. They were *HIS* terms!"

That opened the floodgates, and the others around the table took turns whacking at him.

"Oleg, as I recall, you were also to 'rein in' those pissant little Russian street gangs in New York, Boston, and Miami and bring them under our 'umbrella.' "

"And how did that work out?" Aleksander Zinoviev chuckled.

"Pocket change! You told us and you told *HIM* that your sons had a foolproof plan to hack into the Pentagon's computer systems. Ransomware? Espionage? Real time intelligence on their military planning and their new equipment? That is what Putin wants. *THAT* is what he is expecting."

Shurepkin knew he couldn't let this go any farther. He was the boss, but the ice under his feet was cracking. He could hear it. He could feel it. "My friends, my friends," he rose and looked around at each of them. "We have made great progress in America, Viktor, but you are talking about some very complicated software. Worming our way into the Pentagon computers takes time."

"You promised Putin this would work, and you promised us, Oleg. You may have forgotten that, but we have not, and he has not. That is what his new levy is all about. It is 10% this month and 20% next. Then he will come for your head. And after that he will come for ours!"

"I understand, Yuri. Patience. We are almost there."

"Almost there? Where? We have been bankrolling those two sons of yours in Brooklyn, have we not? Well? What have they been doing?" Paretsky rose to his feet and looked around at the others, each of whom was now nodding in agreement.

Oleg Shurepkin realized he was in a position he rarely found himself in. Someone was pointing the sharp end of a stick at him for a change. "I assure you that my two sons are handling this, and everything is in motion."

"In motion?!" Valeri Kandarsky, a thick-bodied former steelworker, laughed at him. "Your older boy, Piotr, is out until dawn every morning making his rounds of the discos, the bars, and private poker games in Manhattan with his entourage, his 'posse.' They drink top-shelf Champagne by the case and tip the waitresses with $100 bills."

"Poker?" Sergei Dimitrov questioned.

"An American card game at which Piotr has yet to demonstrate any skill," Paretsky shook his head and laughed. "The boy has lost a lot of money, a lot of *OUR* money, a lot of *MY* money!"

"Even the Italians are laughing at us, Oleg," Kandarsky went on. "And the only thing your son has 'in motion' is in his pants."

Even Sergei Dimitrov from Mozhaisk, an old friend whom Shurepkin had always relied upon, chimed in. "Oleg," Dimitrov said, almost sounding embarrassed. "You are not the only one who has eyes and ears in New York. We are not your enemies, but these issues must be dealt with and corrected before it is too late for all of us."

Paretsky sensed Shurepkin's growing isolation and went for the kill. "While that boy of yours, Piotr, is out partying and dancing with his whores, his brother, the 'strange' one – what is he? Seventeen years old? He sits alone in the back booth of that club you bought for them, bent over a laptop, giggling and mumbling to himself like a little child."

By this time, Shurepkin's forced smile vanished as those hard black eyes glared down the table at Paretsky. "My younger son's name is Evgeni. And yes, he is only seventeen and Piotr is twenty-eight. Evgeni is a brilliant young man. He is autistic, not 'strange,' and considered a savant, a software engineer, and a genius with computer programs. You can ask the people at the University if you don't believe me. He is smarter than all of us put together, and he is the one who is writing the programs we are using. While some of his mannerisms may be unusual, he is no more… 'strange' than you are, Yuri. So, I warn you, aggravate me no further by insulting my son like that."

That was a warning sign to Paretsky that he may have finally gone too far. Personal attacks between them were nothing, but a man's family was out of bounds even though this was an unusual situation and his sons were part of the equation. "All right, all right, Oleg," Paretsky backpedaled and raised his hands in mock surrender. "I meant no insult or offense to the young man. He is autistic, not strange, but you must get your house in order. You made promises, and not just to us."

Shurepkin rose to his feet, his back ramrod straight, and glanced quickly around the table at the others. "Agreed. I shall correct whatever needs correcting. And I believe that concludes our business for today," he announced. "If there is nothing else, we are adjourned."

"Not so fast. You say those matters will be attended to?" Valeri Kandarsky dared ask.

Shurepkin paused, glaring at him, but holding his anger in abeyance. "You have my personal assurances," Oleg finally answered.

Slowly, the others got up and their noisy conversations broke into small groups. One by one the others all left the room, motioning for their bodyguards to follow, until Oleg found himself alone with his own man, Dema Kropotkin. He stood near the door with his back against the wall. Dema's hands remained folded in front of him, calmly waiting for orders. Like a large, muscular robot, he could remain like that for hours until he was told to do something else.

Shurepkin leaned back in his chair and stared out the windows again, suddenly feeling exhausted, waiting for his mind to clear. He was getting too old for this, but the others were right. He had a major problem in New York that he could no longer ignore. It could undermine everything he had spent a lifetime building and bring his entire empire crashing down around him. Oleg would not let that happen, however. He would fix it.

He pulled a cell phone from his inside jacket pocket and pressed the top number in his speed-dial list, which connected him to the direct line of his administrative assistant.

"Tatiana, there is a 2:15 direct flight to New York this afternoon, as I recall? And a return flight around midnight?... Yes, that's it. Book two first-class seats, for me and Dema. He will go with me," he added, looking over at his bodyguard. Despite his stone-face, Oleg knew Dema had heard every word.

"We'll swing by the office and pick up our passports on the way out," he continued. "And call Sergei Tarasov at Aeroflot. Tell him I shall be on those flights with my bodyguard. We shall both be armed, and I expect no problems from the authorities here or there. Also, arrange a limo to pick us up at JFK. It is to remain with us for the evening. Got that?"

He listened for a moment as she read the notes back to him and asked him a question. "Are you to tell my sons we are coming?" he asked, repeating her question. "No, no, my dear. This will be a 'surprise' visit."

Stone-faced or not, even from across the room, he saw a flash in Dema's eyes and the slightest hint of a smile.

CHAPTER FOUR

Fort Bragg, North Carolina

It was a lovely afternoon in late April, the perfect time of the year in the North Carolina Piedmont. The sun was shining, the dogwoods and azaleas were coming into bloom. Colonel Jefferson Theodore Adkins could be excused for taking a more leisurely lunch than usual in the senior officers' dining room in the officers' club. In the opposite corner of the room was the table where the four-star Commanding General of JSOC held court. There were many high-ranking officers stationed at Bragg. Colonel Adkins was as far down the pecking order from the Commanding General as you could get, yet he occupied an identical table in the opposite corner. Rank had its privileges, but the mere thought of a surprise IG inspection produced stark terror in Army officers worried about their careers. With carte blanche to meddle into almost anything he felt like meddling into, Jefferson Adkins had power well beyond his rank. That was why the other officers gave him and his corner table a wide berth, if that was what it took to keep the big man happy and keep his attention someplace else.

They set the JSOC building back in the woods, invisible from surrounding roads. It could only be reached by a long, circuitous driveway with three increasingly rigorous checkpoints, requiring a few extra minutes when you returned from lunch, no matter who you were. Still, the MPs on the gates knew exactly who Adkins was – that pain-in-the-ass full bird Colonel in the IGs office on the second floor who would write them up in a heartbeat if they didn't follow every security procedure to the letter. So that's exactly what they did. They studied his papers and pass, searched his car, and looked under it with a mirror and camera. He would then pass on to the next checkpoint where the next guards made the same checks all over again. But rather than piss Adkins off, watching them work brought a satisfied smile to his face. Power. Don't you just love it, he thought!

Unfortunately, his warm after-lunch glow only lasted until he reached his second-floor office, punched his security key code into the electronic lock on the door, and stepped inside. As was his habit, he tossed his Army dress hat like a frisbee onto the top rung of the coat rack in the corner, and smiled. He never missed, but as he turned back, he saw Bob Burke sitting in his custom-made ergonomic desk chair behind his big mahogany desk reading his crisp copy of the *Army Times*. The hat bounced off the hook and fell on the floor, and his smile vanished.

"What the hell are you doing in here in my office, Burke?" Adkins glared. "And get your ass out of my chair!"

"No offense intended, Colonel, but it was the only open place to sit," Burke answered as he motioned to the stacks of papers on the other chairs and small couch along the far wall.

The only thing the two men would ever agree on was that the other was a classic example of everything wrong with the Army. They hated each other, but it was a standoff. Burke was a lowly major, and a retired one at that, but he still walked on water here at Fort Bragg, which was probably how he got into Adkins's office this afternoon, despite the keypad and locks. Adkins might be a proud "full-bird" colonel, but Burke had been a highly decorated Special Operations and Delta Force commander. On the rare occasions he ever wore a dress uniform, it bore rows of ribbons and badges that Adkins could only dream of. If Adkins closed his eyes, he could picture the Distinguished Service Cross, three Silver Stars, Bronze Stars with "Vs," a Purple Heart with five Oak Leaf Clusters, Air Medals, that damned sacred Ranger tab, and others too many to mention. While Burke couldn't care less about any of them, Adkins did; and he obsessed on it.

Fortunately, Burke had only worn blue jeans and a plaid flannel shirt that morning, because Adkins' green, size-50 dress jacket, large enough to have been sewn by Omar the Tentmaker, only carried two paltry rows of inglorious "I'm in the Army ribbons," about what you'd expect from a career pencil pusher. Burke, on the other hand, had every ribbon and medal Adkins coveted and would never receive, got away with cold-cocking him twice, and then threw his own career away, which only made the staff colonel jealous and very angry.

Adkins might obsess on Burke, but except for the incidents in Afghanistan and the post commissary, Burke didn't think about Adkins much at all. To him, the big man was more like a nasty case of crotch rot. You deal with it when you must but wish it would simply go away.

With most normal human beings, Adkins would have reached over the desk, yanked this insolent major into the air by his shirt front, and thrown him out the door. However, Bob Burke had twice put him out cold with apparent effortlessness. Worse, Adkins had never even seen a set of hands move that fast. They were a blur. So Adkins kept his attitude, but he also kept his distance. "How the hell did you get in here, anyway?" he demanded to know.

"In here?" Burke asked innocently enough. "Oh, I was just saying 'Hi' to a few old friends down the hall and thought I'd pop in and say hi."

"Stop by? Pop in? Bullshit! I have a high-security mag lock on that door."

"Really?" Burke looked over at the door and shrugged. "Maybe it wasn't working." He then neatly refolded the Army Times and rose to his feet. "Well, I thought it was time that you and I have a little face-to-face, Colonel."

"Face to face? You don't even have clearance to get into JSOC any longer, and that door was sure as hell locked! I personally had your Creds pulled, and Stansky isn't around to pull strings for you anymore, is he?" referring to Major General Arnold Stansky who had been Deputy JSOC Commander and Burke's "godfather" for years, until he was killed by a car bomb during the terrorist attack the previous year. Adkins's open disrespect of the General was a sure way to piss off the younger man.

Burke stepped around the desk, looking for another place to sit. He reached down to move a tall stack of folders from one of the chairs, but Adkins stopped him.

"Don't touch that stuff. You won't be here long enough."

Burke looked down and saw they were 201 files, personnel records, and official operational files. "A new hobby?" Burke asked until he saw several of the tabs.

"Hobby?" Adkins answered with a bitter laugh. "Take a closer look. You'll see they're the personnel files of everyone who served in your unit, the after-action reports on every operation you were in, and inventories of every bullet, canteen, M-4 assault rifle, and pair of boots you requisitioned during your last five years on active duty. I'm gonna nail you, Burke, you and your 'Band of Merry Men'… Yeah, I know all about that too."

Burke shook his head in disbelief. "You're certifiable, Colonel. I did six tours in Afghanistan and Iraq. There was a war going on over there, whether you knew it or not."

Adkins's eyes flared. "Certifiable? No, those are unofficial files and folders, *Mister* Burke. That's *MY* war zone, where I'm the 'King of Battle,' and I will nail your ass with them. You accused me of giving you bad intel for that op *you* screwed up, not me, and it damn near ruined my career!"

"No, it was bad intel, and you gave it to me. Simple as that."

"That didn't mean it was mine! You sucker punched me."

"I don't give a rat's ass where you got it, Colonel. You gave it to me and that made it yours. Take some responsibility."

"You son of a bitch!" Adkins sputtered. He took a step closer but stopped.

"And I didn't sucker punch you, I was standing right in front of you, face to face, like we are and it was a straight right... well, not straight, because you're nine inches taller than me and I had to punch up."

"And they let you get away with it that time too, didn't they?"

"Guilty as charged, Colonel."

"Guilty? But they never charged you, did they? That's my whole goddamned point!"

"Well, you got me there, but admit it. That punch did you a big favor, Colonel."

"Favor my ass!"

"When I decked you, it muddied the waters just enough to save you from being fired for incompetence and malfeasance."

"What do you mean I didn't get fired? I *DID* get fired!"

"Yeah, but there's 'fired,' like getting your ass kicked up to a paper-pushing admin slot in the Green Zone in Kabul; and then there's 'fired' like finding yourself on the first plane out of Bagram dressed in civilian clothes headed for a 'Meet the Vet Job Fair.' "

"Oh, you did me a favor? I suppose your guys putting that stolen Iraqi museum gold jewelry in my suitcase was another of your 'favors?' It took me two months to clear that up."

"That wasn't me," Bob tried to sound innocent. "I had nothing to do with that."

"But your guys did. Don't lie to me."

"You brought that on yourself. Every officer learns you never piss off a clever NCO, much less a bunch of them. Personnel records, pay records, baggage? Sooner or later, they'll get you."

"You're a fraud, Burke. The Iraqi gold? How much did you keep? That big estate of yours across the river. What do you call it? Sherwood Forest – your little 600-acre estate – how the hell did you afford that on a major's retirement pay?"

"My wife and I are just the caretakers. We work for a..."

"Bullshit! I couldn't even begin to untangle all the title and tax records down at the county recorder's office, but I know you own it. And I suppose you can explain that big software firm of yours in Chicago?"

"Toler TeleCom? I inherited that from my first wife. It was her father's company, Ed Toler's. We develop and sell inventory and business integration software to the Army. If you don't believe me, ask your little brother Charles. He knows all about us."

"Charles? What's he got to do with all this? And how in *THE* hell do you know him?"

Burke turned toward the framed photograph sitting on the Colonel's credenza of another African American Army officer, a major in his dress blues, but much smaller, and smiling. "Your brother does software acquisitions for DoD in the Pentagon. He's the Deputy Acquisitions Manager for the PX and Commissary data systems, stuff my company excels at. He and I have been working together for a couple of years now. That's how I know him."

Adkins stared silently at him, not knowing what to say.

"Charles is a talented guy. He's fair, and he does his homework, but you two are like Mutt and Jeff. He's half your size, and I always figured he had to be your half-brother. But that is what I do now. I run a software company."

"You trying to con me again, Burke? What the hell does a Delta Force Tier-One Operator know about websites, virtual reality, and all that Cloud stuff?"

"Nothing when I started, but a smart guy hired me, and I hire even smarter ones."

"Commissary data systems? Really? I never saw a Delta get much farther than the display cases of beer on sale that week in the Commissary." Finally, he reached out and pointed to the VIP plastic security badge hanging around Bob's neck. His eyes narrowed when he saw that the Provost Marshal had signed it and the Commanding General had countersigned. "All right, why'd you come here today? To piss me off again?"

"No, I'd like to talk about those," Burke motioned toward the stacks of personnel files. "It's time you and I buried the hatchet. Leave my guys alone, Colonel. If you want to come after me, have at it. I'm a big kid and I can take care of myself, but those guys are heroes and deserve better. How about you and I just forgive and forget, huh? Besides, you know those won't go anywhere."

"Forgive and forget?" Adkins said as he walked around his desk and plopped into his oversized leather desk chair. "Your guys tossed those two Iraqi officers and a sergeant out of a helicopter at 3,000 feet. Is that the way you trained them?"

"If you'd done a proper investigation, you would have learned that they led a Delta team into a trap and sold out a platoon of their own infantry to ISIS. Maybe they fell, or maybe they decided it wouldn't be healthy for them to return to base with the Americans and jumped. If my guys threw them out, you might arrest them for littering, Colonel, but that's about all."

"Littering? It was murder and you know it! Eventually, I'll nail them for it, and I'll nail you too, *MISTER* Burke."

"Jefferson, you've already tried to nail me three times before."

"It's *COLONEL* to you!"

"And if you continue with your little vendetta against Delta…"

"Not Delta, just you and that private army you have working for you."

"There's no evidence that my guys did anything wrong. I wasn't even in Iraq or Syria then, and you can't make a case against any of us."

"Only because your pal General Stansky destroyed the evidence. Well, he's dead and gone now, and there's nobody here to cover for you or your men anymore. You're mine!" he said as he leaned forward and pointed a finger at Burke.

Burke shook his head. "Look, we're having a Saturday afternoon barbecue and late-night poker party out at Sherwood Forest this weekend. Come on out, I'll show you around and introduce you to the guys, and you might even enjoy it."

"I doubt it, but would some of them explain the strange stories I keep hearing about you and 'little dustups' with the Chicago Mob and the Gambinos in New York?"

"The Chicago Mob? The Gambinos? Do I look Italian to you?"

"You son of a bitch! How can you say that stuff to me with a straight face?"

Burke sighed and turned to the door. "Well, I guess this was another wasted trip, wasn't it? Too bad. Not that I didn't try," he said as he pointed to the stacks of files. "But go ahead, strap on a fresh tank of air and keep right on deep divin', Jefferson. Go all the way to the bottom, if you can, but there's nothing down there to find, like I told you."

"My ass!" Adkins seethed as he pointed to a patch of bare wall over his couch. "See that spot up there? That's where I'm gonna hang your head when I'm done, *Mister* Burke. Right up there where I can look at it every damned day."

"Maybe, Jefferson, but I take care of my friends. Someday, you might want to remember that."

"Get out of my office!"

CHAPTER FIVE

Brighton Beach, Brooklyn,

The United States has been a melting pot since it was founded. Same for New York City. Brooklyn? Perhaps. Brighton Beach on its south coast? Not so much. It was still a tight-knit community of Eastern European Jews. Mostly farmers and tradesmen driven out of their dirt-poor villages in Russia, the Ukraine, and what was now Belarus around the turn of the 20th century by one pogrom after another. They packed up, carrying most of their belongings on their backs, and headed for America. Some went on to Philadelphia, Boston, Cleveland, Detroit, and Chicago, but many never got past New York City and found themselves crammed into the narrow tenements on Manhattan's Lower East Side. It was their children who moved up and out to the promised land of Queens and Brooklyn, into neighborhoods like Brighton Beach between the wars in the 1930s.

After WW II came new waves of Holocaust survivors. During the 1990s, with Glasnost, Perestroika, and the break-up of the Soviet Union, Brighton Beach saw new, largely Jewish Russian immigrants. Unlike the previous waves, they might have been Jewish by lineage, but most were non-practicing and had grabbed the chance to get out of Russia. They didn't speak Yiddish or Hebrew. They spoke Russian and the area quickly became known as "Little Odessa." Flat-brimmed, black hats, untrimmed beards, and side curls of earlier generations made way for tailored track suits, gold chains, and black leather coats. They drank cheap Smirnoff and Sobieski vodka, Baltika beer, and bottles of cheap Abrau-Durso Champagne when celebrating almost anything. Rather than assimilate and scramble for jobs, many brought with them the same old crooks and corruption that had ruined their lives in Moscow and Kiev.

There were Russian tearooms all across the old neighborhood, especially along Brighton Beach Boulevard under the rumbling steel girders of the overhead elevated-subway line which covered the street from curb to curb. Most of the tearooms were over-priced tourist traps. Like the gift shops, they sold "authentic" Russian nesting dolls made in China, lacquer boxes from Vietnam, Russian figurines from the Philippines, bad food, and Lipton's tea. A few tearooms remained pleasant family restaurants catering to locals and serving authentic Russian food and desserts, but you had to look down the side streets to find them.

And then there was Kalinka's. It stood in the center of the Boulevard retail strip and was a "clubhouse" for the local Russian mob. Mob? That had been an accurate description until the Shurepkin brothers took over, and crime became more "organized." Unlike the Italians, the Colombians, or even the Jamaicans, Russian "gangs" were little more than loose associations of nasty street thugs, each loosely affiliated to one of the criminal gangs back home, usually run by younger brothers, cousins, or former gang lieutenants who had emigrated. Now and then, one group would bash its way to the top, but those periods of one-gang primacy didn't last long until Piotr Shurepkin came over with his Moscow muscle and pounded organization and discipline into them.

Even in New York, Russian gangs operated with the same brutality and "jailhouse" criminal culture they sprang from in the Gulag work camps. A "full" member or "made man," as the Italians would say, was called a "vorami v zakone," a "thief in law" or "vory," distinguished by the eight-pointed star tattoo on his shoulder. But the only law they paid any attention to was gang law. After the brutal KGB-run prisons in Russia, they considered American jails, the police, and even the FBI to be little more than minor annoyances. Like a horde of ravenous locusts, when they saw something they wanted, they devoured it.

Still, they remained little more than petty criminals, with petty squabbles and petty profits from the usual rackets: strong arm "protection," murder for hire, drugs, arson, loansharking, extortion, hijacking, stealing from JFK airport, terrorizing immigrants, stealing checks from old people's mailboxes, credit card fraud, and identity theft. Unfortunately, back home in Russia they viewed America as the "land of milk and honey" and the bosses up the food chain wanted bigger and bigger pieces.

In Brighton Beach, they were easily spotted: young men, never women, 30-somethings in black leather coats, with trendy light beards, dark sunglasses, diamond earrings, gaudy rings on their fingers, shirts unbuttoned halfway down their chests, and a half-dozen gold chains around their necks. They would rise around noon, make their collections, and head to Kalinka's in the early evening to get a buzz on before they headed into the city to party until dawn. Some wore wedding rings, but the young women draped all over them in their short skirts and thick makeup weren't their wives. Hardly. The wives were home with the kids, while their husbands hung out with their posse and girlfriends.

Most nights around 8 p.m., after the chicken Kiev and pelmeni dinner crowd had cleared out, the lights inside Kalinka's would dim, the canned Russian folk music would switch to loud, metallic, Euro-rock with the bass turned up. The owner liked it loud enough to make his fillings rattle. The bouncers outside the front door politely turned away any strangers who tried to get in after 8 p.m. and told them the tearoom was closed for a private party. Inside, between the empty bottles of vodka and overflowing ashtrays, you could often see a thin residue of white powder on the black Formica tabletops.

It might look like a party, but there was a rigid social structure to the place, reflecting gang rank and influence. The lowest rung of petty criminals, the strong-arm, "muscle" men, and "wannabees," sat at a semicircle of small tables near the front door. The booths and tables behind them went to "friends," "business associates," mid-level crew chiefs, and "guys who knew guys." The back rows behind them were the exclusive domain of the "made men" underbosses and lieutenants in the brotherhood. Finally, there were the two semi-circular booths in the rear corners of the room. They were the exclusive domain of Kalinka's owners: Evgeni and Piotr Shurepkin.

Evgeni, the younger brother, was only seventeen: young, shaggy-haired, and autistic, he was a genius with numbers. He sat alone in the large booth in the far-right corner, hunched over his laptop computer, pounding down cans of Diet Mountain Dew, and completely ignoring the surrounding chaos. His older brother, Piotr, twenty-eight years old, was the Boss. He sat in the large booth in the opposite corner and it was always the busiest, loudest spot in the room, covered with Champagne and vodka bottles, and faint traces of white powder. Like an eagle in full flight, his arms spread wide across the rear cushions of the booth and folded around two glassy-eyed, very young women, always blondes, snuggled up against him. Like a king with his court, there would also be a constant parade of brash young men coming and going from his table, laughing and joking. From time to time, he would disappear down the rear corner door to his back office with one of the girls, returning in ten or twenty minutes. The girl would still be straightening her skirt when he passed her off to another member of his "crew," and she would be as quickly replaced in the booth by still another young blonde.

Where his booth joined the side hallway, Pavel Bratsov, his musclebound, ex-weightlifter bodyguard, stood like a troll guarding the bridge. Three blondes later, around 9:30, as the noise from the crowd began to compete with the pounding bass from the oversized speakers, Piotr motioned for Bratsov to lean in closer. "Bring Gennady Kremoy over here," Piotr whispered. The big man nodded and walked away as Piotr lifted his arms off the current pair of glassy-eyed girls' shoulders. "Go powder your noses girls, I have business to attend to, then you meet me in office," he told them. "Go." The two girls grumbled but squeezed out of the booth, walking away down the hallway on unsteady legs toward the restrooms and then his office.

A moment later, Bratsov returned with one of his oversized paws on the shoulder of a thin, older man. He was half Bratsov's size. The big bodyguard shoved him up against the front edge of Piotr's table and then loomed over him like an avalanche racing downhill. Kremoy wore the same trendy leather jacket and gold chains the other men in the club wore, but on him none of it seemed to fit. Perhaps it was the bad dye job on his hair, but he was too thin and too old by at least ten years to pull it off.

Piotr let him stand and sweat for a moment, before he looked up at him and then leaned forward, staring deep into Kremoy's eyes. "Well?" Piotr finally asked impatiently and held out his hand. Kremoy reached his out, thinking Piotr wanted to shake it. "No, you fool!" Shurepkin slapped it aside. "The envelope! It is 'pay day,' Gennady. Where is your envelope?"

Fumbling, Kremoy reached inside his jacket and pulled out a business envelope. He tried to hand it to Piotr, but Pavel Bratsov snatched it away and tossed it to Evgeni at the other table. The boy had not even appeared to be watching, but his quick hands caught it, opened it, and pulled out a stack of American bills. He raised the stack to his ear and lightly fanned it with his thumbnail.

"Light, light, it's light..." Evgeni said in a singsong voice. "Not enough. No, no, light... 150,000 rubles light. Yes," he fanned the stack again. "151,200 rubles light," Evgeni said proudly, like a child.

Piotr never took his eyes off Kremoy. "Gennady, Gennady," he shook his head hopelessly. "This is three times in the past two months. What has it been now? Six months since I took over. Your old bosses, Markov and Tsvetskoi long gone now, I hear they 'retire' to the soft life in Miami Beach... Or maybe it was bottom of Sheep's Head Bay in two oil drums. I never keep those straight," he laughed. "You do not want to adapt to the new regime, Gennady, do you? So is your choice, which do you prefer? Miami Beach, or Sheep's Head Bay?" Piotr asked with the cold, thin smile of a mortician, an expression he had learned from his father.

"No, no, I... I'll get the rest, Piotr. I'll get the rest," the older man stammered.

"You know baseball, Gennady? That game the Americans play?"

"Uh, no, I uh... not really."

"They say, 'three strikes, you are out,' " Piotr told him as he looked up at Bratsov, who promptly slammed Kremoy's face onto the hard,

Formica table. "Understand now, Gennady? I want rest of my money, here, on table by 7 p.m. tomorrow night, plus another 20% Vig, that's the interest, and to cover my aggravation. You got that?"

Kremoy straightened up, woozy, and bleeding from the nose and mouth. "Piotr, Valery Kandarski on Council was going to talk to your father for me and..."

"Wrong answer, Gennady," Piotr said and Bratsov slammed his face on the table again. "That will cost you another 20%. Get him out of here!"

Bratsov only needed one hand to drag the thin, semiconscious Kremoy down the center aisle through the restaurant and toss him out the front door onto the sidewalk. The visible humiliation and brutality of the punishment were as much for Kremoy's benefit as a "teaching point," as Piotr's father liked to call it, for everyone else. Piotr continued to sit there for another long minute, rigidly upright, staring at every other face in the room with a withering scowl, knowing they were all watching him and still testing him. In this business, his father also told him, bloody lessons needed repeating as often as possible.

Finally satisfied, Piotr leaned back in the booth and pulled a small silver vial from his pocket. It had a tiny spoon attached, which he dipped into the vial. He filled it with some white powder, bent over the table, snorted the powder up his left nostril, refilled it, and did the same for the other one. The rush was sudden and overwhelming. He went limp, waiting for the warm glow of the cocaine to course through him. The vial dropped from his limp fingers, spilling some white powder on the tabletop, but Piotr was completely unaware and couldn't care less. Soon, Pavel Bratsov returned from "taking out the trash" and resumed his protective position at the side of the booth, legs spread, hands clasped together, guarding the entry to the table and the office like the Colossus of Rhodes.

Piotr did not know how much time passed. As his eyes focused, an icy chill suddenly ran down his neck. He snapped awake and sat upright, eyes wide open, staring at the restaurant's front double doors. He saw the black silhouette of a large man, backlit by the glow of the streetlights and neon signs outside. Piotr could not make out the man's face, but he appeared to be scanning the crowded room, looking at each face, waiting for his eyes to adjust to the dim light. Finally, the eyes settled on Piotr's back table and the man set off at a measured pace across the room, heading directly for him.

Impossible, Piotr thought as he finally recognized the man. It was likely that no one else in the room even knew who he was, but Piotr did.

His eyes went wide, and he felt a burst of uncertainty overtake him. It was Dema Kropotkin, his father's bodyguard and hit man, the deadliest man in Moscow.

Kropotkin wore a black, knee-length overcoat from Berluti, or Piana, or one of the other expensive Italian tailors and perfectly cut. Perhaps it was the many years he spent in the labor camps wearing rags, but his father always insisted on dressing well and the people around him doing the same. "We may be thugs, but we should not look the part," he often said. Kropotkin's was unbuttoned and hung perfectly from his shoulders. His hands hung at his sides, empty, but Piotr knew he would have at least one pistol, a knife, and a garrote in easy reach. Not that he needed a weapon. His bare hands were deadly enough.

Piotr's own bodyguard, Pavel Bratsov, was also tall and muscular, perhaps even more so, and accustomed to having his way with anyone. As trained killers do, he sensed a threat in the air and placed himself directly between this stranger and his boss's table without being told. Still, Kropotkin's cold, confident expression, and athletic stride should have given Pavel ample warning that he was in an altogether different league.

The Moscow killer stopped directly in front of the table; his eyes locked on Bratsov's until he turned toward Piotr. "Does your man have a death wish?" he quietly asked.

"Pavel, move aside, you fool," Piotr snapped at Bratsov, suddenly flustered. "This is Dema Kropotkin. He... works for my father."

When Bratsov heard the other man's name he quickly did what he was told and allowed Kropotkin to approach the table. Piotr pushed the glasses and bottles aside until his hand touched the vial of cocaine he had dropped. "Someone must have been partying," he mumbled, quickly picking it up and shoving it in his pocket. "Sit, sit down, Dema, please," he motioned to the seat next to him. "But why on earth are you..."

Kropotkin stared at the clutter on the table, especially the thin streaks of white powder, and glanced at his watch. "No time for this bullshit, Piotr. Your father is outside, and..."

"My... my father?" Piotr stammered.

"Yes, he is finishing a phone call. Then he will..."

"My father?" he repeated, wide-eyed, as his surprise turned to panic.

"Why else would I be here, numb nuts?" Kropotkin answered as he leaned forward on the palms of his hands and glared down at the younger man, who suddenly felt much smaller and much younger. "My best guess is you have sixty seconds to get this crap cleaned up… and get yourself cleaned up!"

Piotr scrambled across the leather bench seat and shouted at Bratsov, "You heard him! Get this cleaned up. All of it, now!" and dashed down the hallway to the restroom, trying desperately to wipe away any remaining white powder on his face.

When he came rushing out minutes later, still drying his hands and face with two handfuls of paper towels, he looked over at the tearoom's front door and recognized his father's tall, distinguished form, backlit by the streetlights. Like Kropotkin before him, his father glanced around the club with an expression of disdain before he began walking toward the rear of the room. Eventually, his eyes adjusted to the dark and locked on his eldest son, but the facial expression did not change. Piotr quickly stepped forward to greet him, arms spread wide, waiting for a paternal bear hug, but his younger brother Evgeni beat him to it.

"Papa, Papa!" Evgeni screamed like a child, which he still was in many ways, and threw both arms around his father's waist. In the blink of an eye, Oleg's expression changed from anger and disgust to fatherly affection as he wrapped his arms around Evgeni and gave him a big hug back. Only then did he turn his eyes back on his older son, and Piotr could immediately feel the icy chill wash over him.

"Father! What on earth are you doing here?" Piotr asked with a forced smile, still stunned to see him here. In the pit of his stomach, he realized that whatever his father's reason for coming unannounced like this could not be good. "Come, sit, please! We will order drinks and food," he said, motioning toward his booth. "You must be…"

"I ate on the plane," Oleg brusquely dismissed the offer.

"Then sit, please. We will talk," Piotr offered. "I will have them bring a bottle of…"

"No!" Oleg cut him off as he looked around the now silent room. The crowd may not have recognized Dema Kropotkin, but after a few hushed whispers, they all knew who Oleg Shurepkin was, even in a dark room. He had not set foot in Brooklyn for well over a year, not since there had been that "change of management," and he placed his two sons "on the throne."

"Outside," Oleg said as he motioned toward the door. "We shall walk."

Oleg went out the door and turned west, walking down the sidewalk with a son on each arm and their two bodyguards trailing behind. Finally, he stopped and turned back to take a long look at Kalinka's. "I only have one question, Piotr. When I burn that circus of yours down to the ground, should I leave you and your pit bull inside with the others, or should I allow you to stand out here and watch with the rest of us?"

"Papa, I…"

"Silence! I do not blame your younger brother, Evgeni," Oleg went on, ignoring him. "He does what you tell him to do, and I saw him working on his laptop. But I hold you responsible for him, Piotr. And you," he said as he turned his wrath on Bratsov, "you I hold responsible for both of them."

"Yes, yes, Father," Piotr tried to explain, "we are proceeding with our plan to muscle our way into the Pentagon supply program, and Evgeni is…"

"Proceeding? With your plan?… In all this time, is that all you have accomplished? A… plan?"

"Papa, it is not as easy as…"

"Easy?" Oleg turned and poked his son in the chest with his index finger. Coming from the old Zek, it was like being hit on the sternum with a ball-peen hammer and drove Piotr back a foot. "Not as… easy? Nothing I ever did was 'easy,' Piotr, and I did not have to put white powders up my nose to make them happen."

Piotr stood there, shoulders slumping like a whipped dog, and began to tremble.

"People in Moscow are watching you – people on the Council and in the Kremlin – watching every tentative misstep you made since you arrived. Your head is on the block, you naïve fool, don't you understand that, and so is mine!"

"Yes, yes, Papa, I understand. We shall do better, we will…"

"Do you? Do you really understand?" Oleg moved closer and glared at him. "Fail me at this, Piotr, and I will personally come back, take one of those broken Champagne bottles you are so fond of, and turn you into a eunuch… then I'll burn that place down, with you in it… That is, if they haven't killed me first. This is your one warning. Your only warning. Do it! Get this done! Now!"

CHAPTER SIX

Fayetteville, North Carolina

Bob Burke usually began his mornings early, around "O-Five-30," or 5:30 a.m. to normal people, sitting alone in the breakfast nook at the rear of the big house with a cup of strong, black coffee. He enjoyed listening to the birds and seeing the first hints of dawn rising through the mist off the river, as men had done on this spot for hundreds of years. His wife, Linda, wouldn't be up for another hour to get Ellie off to school. That would put an end to the day's peaceful solitude. But in the predawn darkness, the only light in the room came from his laptop as he caught up on his e-mail and watched the sun come up over the tree line at the edge of the fields. Infantrymen, even retired ones, are accustomed to the pre-dawn hours, and old habits die hard, especially old Army habits.

After West Point, Ranger school, the 82nd Airborne Division, and the 75th Ranger Regiment, they selected him for the elite 1st Special Forces Operational Detachment, or "Delta Force," as the writers in Hollywood liked to call it, although the unit has many other names. He frequently vanished on "off book," black ops assignments with the CIA and other "alphabet soup" joint operations during his career in Iraq and Afghanistan, plus more "week-enders" than he cared to think about. He'd fought over useless rocky deserts and barren mountain peaks in Iraq and Afghanistan and dodged enough RPG rockets and IEDs buried in every road, and enough well-aimed bullets from AK-47s, to last a lifetime.

Still, after a dozen years of trackless jungles, inhospitable mountain ranges, and parched, uninhabitable deserts fighting people who didn't want us tromping through their garden patches telling them what to do any more than we'd want them tromping through ours telling us what to do, and losing a lot of good men in the process, Bob wondered. Doesn't anyone in the Pentagon read history? Good questions, and when he stopped asking them, he knew enough was enough.

In the end, after that one particularly bad Op in Afghanistan, he knew it was time to get out. A month after he rotated back to the States, he walked into Personnel and filed his papers. That amused no one, not the Army and not his father or grandfather. But with his record, he didn't need to apologize to anyone, not even them.

Bob's farm, which his wife Linda named "Sherwood Forest," comprised 600 acres of former North Carolina tobacco fields and dense woods on the west side of the Cape Fear River across from Fort Bragg. It could pass for the set of the old Earl Hamner *Waltons* TV series. All you can see from the road is the central façade of the main house. A row of tall oak trees ran down each side of the drive, forming a low arched canopy over the paved surface, reminiscent of the opening shot of Tara in *Gone with the Wind*. It blew Bob and Linda away the first time they saw it. When the previous owners, a Connecticut insurance company, decided to sell, he had all the cash they "liberated" from the Chicago Mob, so Bob had the property titled in the name of "The Merry Men, LLC." The house wasn't a grand antebellum Georgian with white columns like you see in Gone With The Wind, but it gave Linda ample opportunity to say, "Frankly, my dear, I don't give a damn!"

The house was two-and-a-half stories tall, a big, white Victorian with white gingerbread, pointy-top cupolas, and a handsome forest-green, raised-seam tin roof, and eight bedrooms. There was a covered porch around the front and sides, deep enough to hold two dozen white Adirondack deck chairs. Out back and out of sight were the façades of an old barn and several other farm buildings that had been converted into two dozen luxurious, individually appointed guest rooms. Bob had added a state-of-the-art satellite communication system, a theater, two multimedia "man caves," a to-die-for spa for the women, several modern kitchens, three fully stocked bars inside and out, an indoor pistol range, a running track, a Ranger-level obstacle course through the woods, a helipad, electronic fences, and perimeter motion sensors. And before they moved in almost two years earlier, he brought down some information technology staff from Toler TeleCom in Arlington Heights, Illinois, to install a state-of-the-art internet and telecommunications system with the latest Defense Department security standards.

Like most men of a certain age, Bob Burke got his management education from reruns of *The Godfather*. Whatever organizational, personnel, or political problem you ran into, Vito Corleone had the answer. Take security. As the Don said, "Women and children can afford to be careless, but not men." As usual, as recent history proved, the Don was spot on. They had created some serious enemies in recent years. With over six hundred acres, nine buildings, and several gates to cover, security for Sherwood Forest was a challenge. He invited some old CIA and Special Ops friends from Langley and Fort Bragg. Based on their recommendations, he installed an embassy level system of invisible wire, laser fencing, sensors, motion detectors, silent alarms, infrared and optical cameras, magnetic locks, and emergency lighting.

"The Merry Men" was an eclectic group. It grew from an initial half-dozen of his Delta Force sergeants to a group of over twenty, the Geeks, Chicago Police Detective Captain Ernie Travers, the late Major General Arnold Stansky, Command Sergeant Major Pat O'Connor, Dimitri Karides, the world's best pickpocket, a Royal Dutch Marine Lieutenant, the FBI Agent-in-Charge in Trenton, New Jersey, a New Jersey State Cop in their Organized Crime Division, a CIA agent in Cyprus, two Fayetteville police detectives, an Army CID detective on post, Bob's wife Linda, her daughter Ellie, and Godzilla the cat. Membership was by invitation only, limited to those who went on their first Op, facing off against Tony Scalese and his mob gunmen in the woods north of Chicago, or later to Atlantic City and Donatello Carbonari's thugs from Philly and New York, and finally on the most recent "dustup" against Islamic terrorists who attacked Fort Bragg the year before. So some of what he told Jefferson Adkins was true. He took care of his friends. What he didn't tell him was they stole from the crooks and gave most of it away to people who needed it and to veterans' charities.

The Sherwood Forest complex was owned by a very murky string of investment companies that ended in a private philanthropic institution located in Zermatt, Switzerland, and everyone knows how uncooperative Swiss government and banking officials could be. On paper, Bob and Linda were employees of one of the shell companies three or four rungs below Zermatt to manage the estate on a long-term contract. After all, how could a simple, retired Army major possibly afford a spectacular $13 million complex like this? Adkins could try all he wanted, but he wasn't even close to figuring it all out. As "da boyz" in Brooklyn and Cicero would never admit, the few that survived anyway, they didn't have a clue what happened to them.

"We wuz robbed." Indeed! And to the tune of over $23 million.

With the Geeks running his computer operation, neither could the New York or Chicago Mafia, or ISIS. But Bob knew not to underestimate Gumbahs or Islamist radicals. Both have long memories. The Calabrese and Sicilians were as well known for their blood feuds as the Sunni, the Shia, the Ghilzai, or the Pashtun he fought in Iraq and Afghanistan. Eventually, the wrong people would come after him, his family, and his friends. If they had to "go to the mattresses" like the Corleones, then Sherwood Forest was the perfect place to hunker down.

After they moved south, Bob remained president and chairman of the board of Toler TeleCom, but he had a great staff and the operation ran itself. True, he had to show his face every so often for staff meetings and there were house calls to be made on the Pentagon to keep the procurement colonels in Washington in line, but all that commuting soon got old. That was when he had an epiphany. He promoted Maryanne Simpson, Ed Toler's and his long-time executive assistant, to the presidency, gave her and a half-dozen other key employees large blocks of stock incentives, and stepped aside from day-to-day operations. The one duty he continued performing was the obligatory monthly visit to the Pentagon to renew old ties and "press the flesh" with the procurement colonels and other assorted "REMFs," or Rear-Echelon Mother... well, you get the idea.

Next to a Barrett M-82 sniper rifle, the Geeks had become Bob's favorite secret weapon. They were the Berkeley-trained computer techies that Bob brought down from the Chicago office, where they developed the high-level logistics software Toler TeleCom sold to the Army. In stark contrast to the muscular, well-tanned Deltas in the outbuildings who prowled the grounds during their crack-of-dawn workouts on the running track and obstacle course, the three Geeks were pale, long-haired, nocturnal creatures.

They had converted most of the third floor of the main house into "The Geekdom," their data center and personal "cribs." Their "days" usually began in mid-afternoon and ran well into the wee hours of the morning, so they rarely saw the Deltas and vice-versa. When they weren't bent over the keyboards in their custom-made, state-of-the-art cubicles in the data center, they battled each other "to the death" in intense video game wars. Their arguments ran loud and long into the night, forcing Linda, their den mother, to install soundproof doors and carpeting and wall coverings throughout their high-tech suite, for everyone's protection.

Jimmy Barker and Ronald Talmadge were the two techies Bob brought down from the Chicago office to ferret through the New York Mob's bank accounts and computers. When they added Sasha, a Russian classmate of theirs at Berkeley, the set was complete. Sasha was reportedly a former KGB hacker from the bowels of "the Center" in Moscow. Patsy Evans, Jimmy's main squeeze since Atlantic City, completed the foursome by providing some desperately needed "adult supervision" up there. They were in charge of the computers, and Patsy was in charge of them. It was a full-time job.

Bob picked up his coffee cup and headed back to the kitchen for a refill. He didn't have an elaborate, stainless-steel Italian espresso machine or even a Keurig with those cute little pop-in plastic cups. He made his coffee the old-fashioned way in a cheap percolator with four scoops of plain old Maxwell House on the back burner of a gas stove. He had just refilled his cup when he heard the shuffle of fluffy pink, "Bunny Rabbit" slippers approaching down the hall. It was Linda, in a set of baggy flannel pajamas, a thick, terrycloth bathrobe hanging open from her shoulders, and her hands jammed in the pockets.

"Sex-y!" Bob grinned at her.

"Could have been," she shrugged, "maybe at 10:00 p.m. last night, but you and Ace sat out back and drank with the guys instead, didn't you?"

"No guys, just me, Ace, and a few of them."

"Of course, so Dorothy and I got in our jammies, opened the last bottle of that primo Chardonnay the insurance company left in the wine cellar, and watched a chick flick."

"Got a little hangover, do we?"

"Yeah, but to your credit, you didn't wake me up when you came in." She saw him looking down at her pink Bunny Rabbit slippers, grinning. "Stop that. Ellie gave me these for my birthday when you were off in Iraq, or Syria, or some damned place. She put your name on the wrapping paper, but you completely forgot about it, didn't you?" He opened his mouth to say something, but she cut him off. "Don't even try. You should give her a big hug, but I liked these slippers a lot more than I liked you that morning. They're comfortable, they're warm and fuzzy, and I always know where I can find them… right next to my bed."

He raised both hands in surrender. "Guess I deserve that."

"Any more coffee in that thing?" she motioned toward the coffeepot.

"It's strong. You usually don't like it that way."

"It's 6:00 a.m., Burke. That's the middle of my night and sometimes strong is good."

As she poured a cup of very hot, very black coffee and sat down across from him he told her, "You'll be happy to know that last night wasn't a total waste."

"No?" she looked up at him over the steaming cup with a suspicious eyebrow.

"Ace and I got talking. We both decided we're done, no more getting ourselves involved with Special Ops, private little wars, and other 'dust ups.' "

She stared at him for a moment, stone-faced, trying to understand. "You and Ace? You decided you're hanging it up?" she asked as her skeptical voice rose in pitch. "And I'm supposed to believe that?"

"I'm serious. The truth is, it's a young man's game now. We're too old. Hell, he's two years older than I am, and we've got too many responsibilities now."

She took a sip of the bitter coffee and grimaced. "I couldn't be happier if it's true, but that commitment's only going to last until somebody kills somebody, blows up one of your friends, or somebody throws somebody out a window. You know that as well as I do."

"All true. But we don't need to be the ones to lead the charge. We've got a lot of young, hard bodies we can call on or hire to do that."

"The trumpets will sound *To Horse!* The blood will rise, and the Merry Men will come thundering out of the woods like the *Ride of the Valkyries.*"

"Opera? You're dropping opera stuff on me now? Look, I know something can always come up, but it will take dynamite to get me out of here again."

"Dynamite? Nah, that's old school, Bob. They use plastique now, remember? Like when they blew up the PX and half of Fort Bragg last year... and our front hall."

"I'm serious! No more."

She looked at him again. "And what are you going to do with yourself, Bob? Without that high-octane rush you'll shrivel up, and I'm not sure I'd like that Bob any more than I like the one I've got right now."

"I've been thinking I need to spend a bit more time on Toler TeleCom business, anyway. With my contacts, there are some great new business opportunities for us to expand our offerings with the Navy and Air Force. You know how I can sell, and expanding the business will be a full-time job, more than enough to keep me busy."

"Sell? When you do go up to Chicago, all you do is sit in those staff meetings cracking jokes. That's what *YOU* said, not me. And those Pentagon 'sales' meetings? You hated them. Trying to impress those procurement clowns with your war stories? What do you call them? REMFs? Rear Echelon something or others. That's what you want to go back to doing?"

"For your information, I'm pretty damned good at impressing staff colonels with my war stories."

"You seem to forget that you turned the day-to-day management of Toler over to Maryanne Simpson. She runs the place now, and the last thing she needs is you up there rattling around the offices like the Ghost of Christmas Past."

"That was the ghost of Jacob Marley, not..."

"Wow! Correcting me on English lit now? Really? What about the Geeks? And what about Sasha and the 'KGB Spymaster Data Center' upstairs?"

"They should be back in Chicago; we both know that. There's plenty of work for them there, but they can be on the far side of the moon and do what they do."

"Maybe, but it won't be nearly as much fun around here without them."

"True, but they'll get by. So will we."

CHAPTER SEVEN

Falls Church, Northern Virginia

They say you can tell a lot about a man by the books he keeps in his bookcase and the things he leaves lying on his desk. If he's in the Army, it's much simpler. Soldiers carry their resumes sewn on the front of their uniforms: their rank, branch, their unit, any skill badges they have earned, like marksman, pilot, parachute jumper, medic, not to mention all of their accomplishments in the colorful rows of ribbons on their chests. Some are for bravery in combat, but most are "atta-boys" for doing their jobs passably well or serving in whatever war was going on. Throw in the color of the beret on his head and you have the complete picture, including his name on a black plastic tag above his pocket.

A simple military rule of thumb says if the soldier's uniform has over three rows of ribbons, crossed rifles on his lapels, or there is a maroon, tan, or green beret on his head, reflecting the various flavors of Special Forces, it's a good idea to be polite. On the other hand, if he has two or fewer rows of ribbons and a brass branch insignia of something that doesn't shoot bullets, he probably spent his tour in Afghanistan or Iraq in an air-conditioned trailer inside the "Green Zone" pushing papers or writing reports. You can put money on that.

Army Lieutenant Colonel Steven Weathers was one of those. At 6' 2" and a trim 180 pounds, Weathers still appeared boyishly handsome despite his 41 years of age, as he politely waited in line at the McDonald's just off Arlington Boulevard at Route 50 in suburban DC. He had a fresh "white-wall" haircut and perfectly tailored uniform, but all it showed were two meager rows of "I did my job" ribbons, a green Pentagon staff officer badge, and a pair of diamond-shaped Finance Corps branch insignias on his lapels. They told the tale. With a black beret and a bulging leather briefcase in his hand, he was what the good citizens in the District called a "shiny-ass killer," a "Potomac River warrior," "a Pentagon desk commando," or a "PX Ranger." The less charitable called them "POGs" or "Pogues," "backseat bean counters," or "REMFs."

None of those things bothered Steven Weathers any longer, if they ever did. He knew who he was and what he was. His eighteen-year career, which once looked so promising, had slowly, slowly faded to mediocrity. As the Peter Principle suggested, he had precisely risen to his level of mediocrity. Then again, he had not been shot, blown up, or sent home in a flag-draped box, at least not yet. To him, that more than balanced the scale. Unfortunately, Weathers had bigger problems on his mind today. He recently had a "career-planning session" with the Finance Branch career planners. They advised him to begin looking for a civilian position he could be mediocre at, because this one in green was quickly coming to an end. When he completed his twenty years, he would be out on the street.

Many people would be content with the retirement pay a lieutenant colonel received, but they didn't have Weathers's house payments, three kids in private school, one of whom would start college in the fall, or a mountain of credit card debt that did not include over $70,000 in gambling markers his wife had run up in the Live Casino, the Horseshoe Casino, and the Hollywood Casino over in Maryland. The woman had a sweet tooth for Texas Hold 'em, and there was nothing he could do to stop it. Worse, if the word got out on those, he would never even see his twenty.

Weathers glanced nervously at his olive-drab "tactical" wristwatch and stepped up to the counter. It was 6:10 a.m., the precise time he always arrived here, to the minute. That was just early enough to be ahead of the worst of the rush-hour traffic, to be here when the line at the counter was dwindling down, and just late enough for the food and coffee to still be fresh and hot. Steven Weathers was a precise man, and he had it down to a science.

The young girl behind the counter smiled up at him and said, "Good morning, Colonel Weathers. I know, the usual, right?"

"Roger that, Lucy. I guess I'm in a rut," he answered proudly. Well, perhaps not a rut. It was just that Weathers was a man of well-developed habits. Two Egg McMuffins, a hash brown, and an early cup of coffee were his perfect breakfast.

He lived ten minutes away on the other side of Falls Church, and this McDonalds was right next to the on-ramp to Route 50. The remaining drive to his office in one of the big private office buildings in Pentagon City, a mixed-use complex south of the real Pentagon, was just long enough for him to finish the two breakfast sandwiches, the hash browns, and the medium coffee, and find a parking space. Perfect. Give or take a minute or two, he would be sitting at his desk precisely at 6:45 a.m.

The office was in one of the big suburban steel and glass buildings filled with the likes of the TSA, the DEA, and a hundred other alphabet federal agencies on the periphery of power. The actual Pentagon was across the Interstate. He could look out his window at the massive structure as a priest might look at the Vatican, knowing he would never quite be part of it. That's how it had been every day for the last seven years, minus the two "short tours" when they sent him "down range" to "Rag-head land." Look, but don't touch, but that was the professional trade-off, he guessed. He had his own little empire over here, but being forced to stare across the expressway at the big leagues every day didn't do much to enhance loyalty, self-esteem, or motivation. The Finance Corps had told him more than a few times that he wasn't up to their career standards, and he concluded this was their way of making sure he never forgot the message.

Lucy slid his bag and Styrofoam cup across the counter, and he handed her a $10 bill. "Keep the change, Lucy," he said with a fatherly smile. "For your college fund," knowing all too well that $2 or $3 every day for the rest of her life wouldn't scratch the surface of what she would soon need.

With the paper bag and briefcase in one hand and the cup of hot McDonalds coffee in the other, he turned and headed back to the side exit and his car. But halfway to the door, two large men stepped into his path. They were in their mid-thirties, with black leather jackets and an unshaven, rough-cut look. One of them placed his left hand on Weathers's chest to stop him, while the other stepped behind him and he felt something nudge him in the back. The man in front nodded toward the side aisle and in heavily accented English said, "Go... You take seat and have coffee with Boss... Go."

Weathers's eyes followed the man's as he looked down the aisle. At the corner booth, a younger man in an expensive business suit sat watching him. He smiled and motioned to Weathers with a crooked finger, which was when Weathers also noticed that the two goons boxing him in had their right hands inside their side jacket pockets.

Weathers didn't know what to make of this. There were other people in the restaurant, plus the staff, but they were all too busy to notice or to help him even if they did, so he did what he was told. The man in the booth motioned for him to take a seat on the other side. The two goons, or bodyguards, or whatever they were, then backed away and sat at nearby tables, making sure none of the other customers got any closer and assuring them of privacy.

"How nice to meet another morning person, Colonel Weathers," the young man said in formal, if slightly stilted English. "That is most commendable for a professional man like you. My compliments, sir." He had a cup of McDonalds coffee in front of him too. He picked it up, took a sip, and scowled, muttering something in a foreign language. "Terrible! Is bitter bathwater! In future, we meet at Starbucks, someplace I can get civilized coffee like double-decaf caramel cappuccino. Ah, America!"

"Double decaf...?" Weathers stared at him, getting irritated. "Who the hell are you?"

"Ah! You must excuse me, Steven, if I may call you Steven. I am being rude. My name is Piotr Shurepkin, your new best friend."

"My new...?" Weathers began to get rattled. "What the hell are you...?"

Shurepkin gave him a thin smile, leaned closer, reached inside his jacket, and pulled out a stack of folded letters. He carefully laid them open on the table between them. "Recognize, Steven? Are what you Americans call 'markers,' your *wife's* markers, ones Erica left at Horseshoe Casino in Baltimore. They are notes, loans, all executed, notarized, and 'legally binding' as lawyers say. Maybe she thinks Baltimore is too far away and nobody notice, eh? Maybe she pretend nobody care? Women can be so silly, Steven. Well, I hate to tell you, Horseshoe is owned by Genoveses in New York City. They are more best friends of ours, and they do care. People give them 'bad paper'? They care, Steven, they care."

Shurepkin then peeked inside his jacket again and pulled out several more sheets of paper before he looked back up at Weathers. "More markers, from Hollywood Casino and Live Casino. Total is $65,700 which your lovely wife Erica now owes three casinos, not counting $3,000 each week in 'Vig.' You know what Vig is? It is interest. And more bad news. It is accumulating, and accumulating, and accumulating. Maybe wife thought no one notice that either, eh?"

Weathers slumped back in his seat and stared at the paper, getting sick.

"That is a lot of money for anyone to owe, no?" Shurepkin asked as he leaned forward and bored in. "For an Army officer living in very wealthy DC suburb in house he should never buy because he never could afford, mortgaged 'to hilt,' as bankers say, all done to please his pretty wife... Not a good idea, Steven. Wife Erica is very pretty but has bad head for cards. Ah! And you have son going to Georgetown in September. Congratulations. Plus two daughters in The Congressional School, most expensive private school in town. Steven, Steven... what can I say? You have really big problem."

"What? How do you...?"

Shurepkin reached in a pocket and pulled out photographs of three teenagers walking off a soccer field. "Talented children can be curse, yes? My father tells that to my brother and me all the time, but schools back in Russia are free... to right people, of course. But here! My friend, all those tuition bills that will soon be dropping on your head like big bricks. Maybe your wife thought casino was good place to raise big money. Is that what she thought, Steven?" he asked as he placed another photo of a very attractive woman at the pool in a two-piece bathing suit on the table. "Yes, lovely children and very lovely wife, very lovely."

Weathers turned beet red and tried to get out of the booth until one of the goons placed a large paw on his shoulder and shoved him back down, effortlessly.

"Relax, my dear new best friend," Shurepkin laughed. "This is not Army Board of Inquiry or Court-Martial," he said as he reached inside another jacket pocket, pulled out another envelope, and pushed it across the table to Weathers. This one was much thicker. "For you, my friend. Open."

Weathers frowned, but his curiosity got the best of him. Inside, he saw a thick stack of one-thousand-dollar bills. He slowly fanned the stack. There were thirty of them. "What is this supposed to be? A bribe?" he demanded to know.

"No, no! You are worth much more than that, Steven," Shurepkin shook his head. "Is not a bribe, is an act of friendship: enough money to pay off tuition you owe today, to bring your mortgage up to date, and perhaps a bit to start paying credit card bills. We know how unforgiving those headmasters and Monsignors are, don't we? Almost as unforgiving as Genovese guys in New York... almost, but not quite. Then there are the Shylocks at the bank too... So do not think of this as bribe, Steven. Is down payment on long-term partnership with us," Shurepkin smiled again.

"You're out of your mind," Weathers quickly answered. "I'm not taking..."

"Of course you will, my friend. Why? Because you have no choice. None," Shurepkin said as he tapped his finger on the envelopes with the casino markers and leaned forward, his smile now long gone. "$65,700 is a lot of money. How else you pay them off? It is work with us or drive car into bridge abutment on expressway, so wife Erica gets life insurance. I can't think of anything else. Can you?"

Weathers stared at him, stunned. "You bought the markers?" he managed to ask.

"Not exactly, Steven. I have them 'on consignment' from another dear 'friend,' Gino Curci. He runs Horseshoe for the Genoveses, and from others. My brother and I will purchase them and get Gino off your back, if you cooperate... Otherwise, we give them back to him, he will get more angry, and that will be doubly bad for you."

"But I can't pay them off, you told me so yourself," Weathers laughed helplessly.

"With us, you not have to. In fact, we pay you money. But if you say no and we give them back to Gino... Well, he has no use for you, but he does have places up in Baltimore where an attractive woman like wife Erica can work off gambling debts. Please believe me, Steven, Gino is not man who takes no for answer. You understand what Piotr is telling you? Meanwhile, Army will boot you out, you'll lose nice house, and children will be in lousy public schools. Well, maybe not two cute daughters. I am afraid Gino would put them on wife's payment plan too. Not nice people, Steven, and $67,500 is big money. Take long, long time for wife to work that off. Erica not like it. Pretty soon, she not so pretty, eh? So, like I say, Steven, you have no choice."

"What do you want?" Weathers whispered as he saw the trapdoor to hell opening beneath his feet and felt the flames licking up his pants legs.

"Is very simple. We in software business. Startup company, new to States. We want Army contracts. We do good work, but we in hurry. No time to go through Pentagon red-tape bullshit. We need help from new best friend. My brother and I solve your big problem; you solve ours. Simple, no? You give us contracts we want; we pay you money for bills and tear up markers. Then everybody happy."

"You're out of your mind, I can't do that."

"Of course you can. Just consider alternative." Shurepkin looked at his watch. "We meet you here tomorrow, same time. I give you proposal for new Army PX inventory and ordering system which you were about to contract to... let me see," he said as he pulled a slip of paper out of his shirt pocket and read the name. "Ah, yes, Toler TeleCom in Schaumburg, Illinois. Instead, you give that contract to us."

"Toler...! Now I know you're nuts! Look, I'll have a much larger one coming up in maybe two months. Take that one, because you have no idea who..."

"No time, Steven. Focus!" Shurepkin said as he tapped the sheets of paper and leaned in closer, his eyes growing even harder and a harsh Russian accent coming out. "No time. Two months, Army will boot you out and wife and daughters working in Baltimore by then. We want Toler contract, *AND* we take other one too, maybe several more. Then you start getting your wife's markers back... on installment plan, like at Sears. What do you Americans call it? Light at the end of tunnel? So be here tomorrow morning. If not, Gino come see your pretty wife."

"What if I go to the CID or the FBI? That'll put an end to all this nonsense, and to you."

"I think not," the Russian smiled and shook his head. "First, they have no reason come after us. We are programming shop, pure as Russian winter snowstorm. But you? You still have Gino and mountain of debt. Do what I tell you and it all disappears before you retire in two years. You and family have bright future. You go watch son graduate at Georgetown, watch girls graduate from Smith and Wellesley.... or they all go see Gino. Your choice."

They stared at each other, and Shurepkin saw that Weathers was hooked. He reached into another jacket pocket, pulled out a third envelope, and slid it across. "Here financials and professional credentials for you to set up file. Tomorrow I give you contract and the rest."

Weathers flipped through the sheets of paper. "Is any of this true? I'm putting my career at risk here, you know. For what?"

"For a lot of money, Steven. And not to worry about your career. It wasn't going nowhere, anyway. You retire in two years. Nobody care then," Piotr laughed at him. "Nobody care. My brother Evgeni is programming genius. We work offshore. All good stuff. And who knows, Steven, maybe we even better! But nobody going to care. Trust me."

Weathers looked at him and turned serious. "You're wrong, Bob Burke will care."

Piotr frowned. "Burke? Who is Burke? He is the man who owns this Toler? Not to worry about him."

"I'm not going to worry. But you have no idea who..."

"I said not to worry," Shurepkin cut him off. "I send my two large associates behind you, Gennady and Zurab. They reason with him."

"You're making a mistake."

"No mistake. Won't be a problem. You worry about contract and all that money that pretty little wife of yours owes Mafia casinos... Oh, and you tell her, no more gambling. If we hear she so much as goes to bingo game or buys scratch-off ticket at gas station, after they visit with this Burke, Gennady and Zurab, will visit your wife. They would like that. Erica would not."

CHAPTER EIGHT

Sherwood Forest

Bob Burke had two reasons to resign his commission and cut the cord with the US Army. The second was his first wife, the late Angie Toler. They met during a torrid long weekend in Hilton Head, where he went with his best friend, former Master Sergeant "Ace" Randall. Ace declared the weather forecast was running "partly cloudy to drunk." He also said that "met" was a very polite way to put it. Angie picked Bob up in a riotous beach bar, drove him to her condo in her new Corvette, and returned him three days later wobbly-legged and badly hung over with a permanent dopey grin on his face.

After a blowout wedding in suburban Chicago, that nearly destroyed a posh private country club, her father Ed's job offer to join his software firm in Schaumburg eventually sealed the deal. Bob "pulled the pin" and filed his retirement papers. He didn't know much about software or telecommunications, although he was technically a Signal Corps Officer and had gone through their training when he was a new second lieutenant. What he had was common sense and the ability to manage and lead people, which was exactly what her father was desperate to find. The rest of the stuff he could teach him. Ed put him through a non-stop, rotating training program in finance, sales, micro circuitry, bench repairs, customer support, and warehousing, and he became a 90-day-wonder vice president. When the cancer Ed had been fighting finally got the best of him the next year, Bob found himself president and responsible for the jobs and futures of over 90 employees.

The staff he inherited in Schaumburg was first-rate when he got there. The worst-kept secret around the office was that Maryanne Simpson, who had been Ed's and then Bob's executive secretary and then office manager, was the one who really ran the place. After the "dustups" in Chicago with the DiGrigoria Mafia family and later in Atlantic City with the Gambinos and Luccheses, Bob set up a clever stock plan that distributed the company stock and ownership to the employees and promoted her to president.

The last piece of advice he gave Maryanne was, "Don't call me unless the building's on fire."

That morning, he got the call. The building was on fire.

Bob drove his Ford 150 pickup truck around back to the kitchen door so he and Ace could unload all the boxes of food, beer, and booze for the weekend's pending barbecue. It was the second anniversary of the big "dustup" near O'Hare that got it all started. All the Merry Men plus their significant others were invited, so it would be a big blowout. That meant dozens of bags of chips, corn on the cob, tubs of slow-cooked baked beans, assorted deli items, and desserts. Boxes of hot dogs, hamburgers, steaks, and cases of beer filled the rear cargo compartment of the pickup truck.

Linda came out the back door, wiping her hands on a kitchen towel. He told her to look around inside and "grab some guys to help us unload this   stuff."

"Strong backs and weak minds? I know just the ones," she said as she pivoted on her heel and went back into the kitchen. Two minutes later, she came out herding the three Geeks toward the pickup truck, snapping them in the butt with her dishtowel.

"I caught them in the pantry trying to sneak that chocolate cake upstairs," she said. "I told them they could either help you unload the truck or put on their boots and help the guys pumping out the septic tank. I'm not sure why, but they picked you."

"I am truly honored," Bob answered as he pointed to the back of the truck. "Besides, sunshine, exercise, and fresh air is just what those three need."

"I think that's why they chose you over the septic tank." At that point, Linda's eyes went wide, and she smacked herself in the forehead with a 'dopey slap.' "Sheesh! Maryanne!" she suddenly said. "You've got me so rattled cornering these three I forgot why I came out here to see you."

"Maryanne Simpson?" he asked, suddenly getting a bad feeling.

"She called this morning just after you left for the commissary. I forgot."

He pulled out his cell phone and tried to turn it on, but the screen was unresponsive. "Damn!" he swore. "The battery must be dead."

"Yeah, she said she couldn't get you, so she called the house."

"Guess I forgot to recharge it."

"No kidding. And here I figure you dropped it in the toilet at the Roadhouse Café."

"Nothing that dramatic. Do you know what she wanted?"

"She didn't say, but she sounded pretty upset."

"That's odd, I just talked to her early this morning," he said as he went inside and grabbed the house phone off the wall. He had Toler TeleCom and Maryanne's direct number on speed dial. He pressed that key and she answered within seconds.

"Maryanne, I understand you...?" he tried to ask.

"I don't know what to say, Bob," so flustered that she cut him off. She was usually the unmovable rock everyone else hid behind when the fiercest Chicago winter gales got blowing. Not today. "We received a letter today from Software Procurement in Washington, and... they aren't renewing the PX and commissary automation contract. I'm so sorry, I have no idea what I could've done wrong."

"I doubt you did anything wrong, Maryanne. I just talked to those clowns last week."

"But we're twenty-four months into that job. All of a sudden, they tell us they're not renewing us. In the middle of the job? That's a third of our people and almost half of our project profits this year. I don't know what to say."

"Who signed the letter?"

He heard some papers rattle, and then she came back on and said, "Weathers, Lieutenant Colonel Steven Weathers, Software Procurement, Officer in Charge."

Burke frowned. "Yeah, that's him. But what else did it say, did he give any reasons? They've got to cite the reasons."

"Yes, there are some bullet points in the letter. It's only one page long, but he says our 'interim products no longer meet Army standards'... 'substandard coding verification'... 'inability to meet current quality control initiatives'... and 'failure to comply with current DoD foreign labor eligibility document criteria.' I have no idea what any of that means, Bob. I've never seen things like that in any of the contract specs or the procurement documents. You have any idea what he's talking about?"

"No, and I don't think he does either. Tell you what, scan that thing, shoot a copy down here to me, and then send one to George Grierson, our attorney. I'll be up there as soon as I can get a flight."

"I don't think it makes any sense for you to come up here, Bob. You'll have the letter in a minute or two. The problem's in DC."

"You're right. I'll phone Weathers and get in to see him first thing tomorrow. I'll talk to you later when I know more."

Ace Randall had wandered into the kitchen from the garage with two bottles of beer, one of which he handed to Bob as he asked, "Road trip?"

"Yeah, DC. Somebody screwing with us."

"Screwing with us? Those dorks in procurement? They're Finance Corps, or Quartermaster, and wouldn't know how if they tried."

"That's what concerns me. I'm gonna fly up there, knock some heads together, and see what falls out."

"Fly? To DC? We can drive up there in five hours, four if we go up I-95 tonight with me behind the wheel. It'll take you longer than that to mess around with two airports, a commuter jet, and a rent-a-car counter. Besides, you need company. I'll grab some Country and Western CDs and you gas up the Ford 150. If we leave about midnight after we put everyone to bed, we can be sitting outside Weathers's office when he opens in the morning."

Bob thought about it for all of a second or two and nodded. "Sounds like a plan." He looked at his watch; it was only 2:30 in the afternoon. "Meanwhile, I'll make a few phone calls."

"DC, huh? You want me to pack some 'gear'?" Ace asked.

"By 'gear,' I assume you mean of the exploding or bullet firing variety?" Bob asked, considering the idea for a moment before he shook his head. "No. If I go up there carrying a weapon, when I see that moron Weathers, I'm likely to use it. Besides, he may not be in the Pentagon, but that's an Army office and it wouldn't be a good idea to go in there packing."

"You sure? DC can be a dangerous place… all that street crime?"

"True, but you and I are usually the ones doing the committing."

Bob walked down the hall to his office, flipped open his laptop, and found his address book. Weathers's number in Army Procurement was easy to find in the W's at the bottom of the list. His dead cellphone was of no use, so he used his computer, clicked the Area Code link in his address book, and let the software do the work.

On the fifth ring, a confident female voice answered. "Software Procurement, Sergeant First Class Goss, sir, how may I help you?" Bob liked that. It had taken more than a few years, but female career soldiers now ran the administrative end of the Army, much as their male counterparts had run the field operations for years. They were better at it, and the ones like Stephanie Goss, who he had run into when she served two tours in some of the less popular places in Afghanistan and one tour in Iraq, were the best. Having been in that office many times, he always found it amusing that she usually worked in shirtsleeves, with her service uniform jacket hanging on a rack behind the door. She never showed it off, but she had far more ribbons and skill badges on her jacket than "the boys" did, but she knew it wasn't smart politics to embarrass them. Unfortunately, she blew out a knee in the mountains of Afghanistan, her infantry days were over, and she ended up being put out to pasture in the Finance Corps.

"Sergeant First Class Goss, this is Bob Burke. Is the Colonel in?"

"Oh, I'm afraid not, Major, he *said* he was in a meeting."

He was good at reading people, but he didn't need to be a rocket scientist to figure out what she was telling him. Stephanie was lying. He knew she was lying. And she wanted him to know she was lying. She knew exactly who Bob Burke was and what he used to wear on his uniform, and like two consummate professionals who had spent serious time "downrange," neither cared if the other knew what they thought about the situation.

"He's in a meeting, huh? You're sure about that, Steph?"

"Bob, I am *absolutely* sure. Colonel Weathers personally told me he was in a meeting, so that must be where he is. Was he expecting your call?"

"Oh, I'm pretty sure he was. Tell you what, how about Major Adkins, is he in?"

"No, the Major left at O-dark-30 for a two-week IBM class in Atlanta."

"I just talked to him a couple of days ago and he didn't mention anything like that."

"I talked to him late yesterday and he didn't mention anything like that to me, either. But gone he is. Now, I'm supposed to be running the damn place!"

"I don't suppose you have his cell phone number, do you?"

"You know I'm not supposed to give those out, sir."

"Not even to your very favorite ex-Delta who gave you those two box seats to the Nationals' playoff game last summer because my wife was due, and she wouldn't let me get up to DC to use them and they were going to go to waste? Not even then, Steph?"

"I'm so sorry, Bob, but you know I could get in a lot of trouble if I told you his number was 697–8215. I'm sure you understand... By the way, how's the baby?"

"Nine months old and taking over the place. Thanks. And tell Colonel Weathers I'll be in his office at 0700 tomorrow. He can count on it."

"I'll be sure to come in early. That sounds like fun."

"You read the letter?"

"Read it? I typed it for Christ's sake."

"You have any idea what's going on?"

"Not a clue, but the way he suddenly sent Major Adkins out of town, something is up, and I don't like it."

"You have any idea who he's giving the contract to? He wouldn't be dumb enough to pull the rug out from under us unless he knew where he was going with it."

"You'd think. He had some files on his desk yesterday and what looked like a contract in a blue binder. I saw a return address, New York City, Brooklyn. I didn't give it much thought at the time; but whatever that stuff was, it didn't come through me."

"Strange. The Army just doesn't work this way."

"You got that right. I'll see what I can find out. If he leaves and I can get a peek at his desk, I'll give you a call. Otherwise, I guess I'll see you in the morning. Don't worry, I'll have the coffee on. Should be quite a show."

"Just don't go selling tickets. The fewer witnesses the better."

Bob dialed the number she gave him and let it ring, but Charles didn't answer. If Stephanie was right and he was driving to Atlanta, that could explain it. When the call shifted to voicemail and Adkins's polite recording came on, Bob said, "Charles, this is Bob Burke. I understand you're on your way to Atlanta. Give me a call when you get a chance. Thanks."

Charles Adkins was as different from his older brother Jefferson as a cheetah was to a rogue elephant. He was average height and runner-thin, pleasant, polite, funny, thoughtful, and all the other good attributes. He was also a very good software systems engineer; and if he was going to a class at IBM, he should teach it, not waste his time sitting in the student seats. Charles always told Bob that he and Jefferson never got along because neither man took the time to get to know the other. Bob always replied, "You two are brothers from another mother, no doubt about it."

CHAPTER NINE

Washington, DC

While he was waiting to hear back from Major Charles Adkins, Bob put in a call to his congressman in Washington. He didn't expect to find him in either, and he wasn't, so Bob left a message there as well. He didn't expect to find the congressman to be of much use, since North Carolina was going through one of its periodic, fiercely partisan redistricting battles that left Fayetteville and Cumberland County split between three congressional districts. He wasn't even sure who would be representing him in the fall, but since he'd given all three congressmen some money, there was always a dim hope that he could call on one of them later, after he knew more.

He also put in a call to George Grierson in Schaumburg, Illinois, the attorney who had represented Toler TeleCom ever since Ed set it up years before, even through the dark days dealing with Consolidated Healthcare, the city of Indian Lakes, and the Chicago Mafia. George was the first call Maryanne made that morning after she couldn't reach Bob, so he had already read the letter from Weathers. Since then, George had dug out the Army contract and got up to speed on all its terms. He had been expecting Bob's call.

"This letter's all fluff, Bob," George began. "His 'grounds not to renew' are BS – that's the technical legal term – there's nothing specific and nothing you can hang your hat on, but he manages to touch all the bases for default and non-performance stated in the contract. In fact, he is simply reciting the 'such as' requirements it sets forth. Can you beat the weasel in court if he doesn't have anything more substantive than this crap? Of course, you can. But you'll spend two or three years and a lot of money doing it. That's the problem with Federal Government contracts. They're always one-sided. You can usually make good money off of them while they last, and their checks don't bounce, but you're working entirely at their pleasure and they can be as arbitrary as hell... But something tells me you already knew all of that."

"Yeah, but we both know I had to ask."

"Let me know if there's anything else you want me to try."

"What kind of contacts do you have with the congressman up in Schaumburg?"

"He's a pretty average stooge, no better or worse than the rest of them, but I know he was an old crony of your buddy Hubert Bloomfield, the Mayor of Indian Lakes."

"Is he still serving time?"

"No, they let him out for good behavior and he's back selling used cars."

"No help there, either."

"No, but I'll put in a call to the new mayor and at least let the congressman know about the situation. It's jobs in his district, so it can't hurt."

Bob hung up the desk phone and noticed the light blinking for an incoming call on his now powered-up cell phone. The screen said it was Charles Adkins.

"Hey, Bob, what's up?" the other man asked. "You sounded pissed in your voicemail."

"Are you aware of the letter your pal Weathers sent me... well, sent Toler TeleCom?"

"Weathers is a lot of things, but he ain't my pal. What's he want?"

"He doesn't want anything, Charles. He's pulling the plug on us. He's not renewing the Toler TeleCom contract."

"What? That son of a... He can't do that. It's my project!" Adkins sounded as surprised as Bob had been, and every bit as angry. "I mean he can *do* it, but that's not the way things are done. We have procedures, rules, laws, for god's sake. You know that, I know that, and for damn sure he knows that too!"

"Is that why he sent you to that IBM course in Atlanta? To get you out of town."

Adkins was silent for a moment, and then he said, "You could be right. I've got over two years of my life invested in that project, and he knows what I think."

"So this training class wasn't your idea?"

"Hell no! He sprang it on me last night at close of business, told me a slot in the course opened up, and it would look good in my 201 File for the Promotion Board."

"He knows what buttons to push."

"Yeah, well, I'm gonna push some of his buttons as soon as we get off the line."

"You have any idea who he's giving the contract to?"

"Man, when I left the office yesterday afternoon, as far as I knew this was just a routine renewal. The papers were already down in legal for final review. We never talked about doing anything else. You know as well as I do, every time any DoD contract comes up, we get those vultures in

Congress trying to stick in a proposal for some contributor or for his cousin Larry. I can't blame them for trying and some are legit, but a hell of a lot of them aren't, just more hogs trying to belly up to the federal trough."

"Do you ever remember getting a proposal from a software shop in New York City, in Brooklyn, for the kind of work we do?"

"We've used plenty of companies in New York, but I can't recall any in Brooklyn, not for inventory control systems. Besides, don't you guys know who your competitors are? Most software companies know theirs by heart."

"Sure, but I don't know any shops up there who do what we do either. Not in Brooklyn. And if you don't know them and we don't know them, who the hell are they? But somehow, I'm not surprised. Ace and I are driving up to DC tonight, and we'll be sitting outside Weathers's office when he opens up."

"And I'll be right there with you, brother."

"No, I don't think I'd do that if I were you, Charles. You're on TDY orders. All you'll accomplish is get your own ass in a bind, and you know it. Let me talk to Weathers and then I'll take it up the chain of command if I have to. If it all blows up, you're gonna need to be away from the blast zone, so you can come in and pick up the pieces."

"Yeah, you're probably right, but call me when you learn anything. I don't know who got to him, but this ain't right."

Lieutenant Colonel Steven Weathers was on the phone at the same time. He wasn't calling Atlanta, his call went the other direction, to Brooklyn.

"I told you this wasn't going to work! Burke called here and he'll be here on my doorstep first thing tomorrow morning. And my project manager called. He isn't very happy either. I won't be able to duck Burke forever. He has too many connections, and if it gets over to Legal it's all going to hit the fan. Like I said, you need to wait for the next one."

"You are the boss. No waiting. Tell them all to piss off and do your job."

"And I thought you were going to take care of this!"

"Colonel, like a lame horse, do not become more trouble than you are worth."

"You have no idea who you're dealing with," Weathers continued to mumble.

Shurepkin fumed for a moment, then said, "Okay, okay, I will send Gennady and Zurab down tonight. They will take care of this Burke for you. And be careful they don't take care of you, too," he said as the line went dead.

"Oh, Christ," Weathers stared at the receiver as he put down the phone.

Bob and Ace weren't leaving for DC until after midnight, so at 7 p.m. he threw some steaks on the barbecue grill outback for them, the wives, and Ellie, popped the tops on two bottles of Harp and grabbed a chair on the deck. Ace soon joined him, and they sat watching the local herd of deer meander through the evening mist along the tree line.

"One of these days, we need to thin out the deer herd, you know," Ace commented.

"You want to suggest that to Linda and Ellie, be my guest."

"I ain't but so dumb, Ghost. I figured we could get the State Game Commission to come over, do a little survey, and have them tell us that's what we need to do."

"You'll need a lot more cover than that if you want to go shoot Bambi."

"Yeah... so I guess Simba is out of the question too."

Fortunately, Bob's cell phone rang, forestalling any further discussion of wildlife management and Disney cartoons. He didn't recognize the number on the screen, but Area Code 703 was probably from the Pentagon.

"Bob, this is Stephanie Goss," he heard when he answered.

"Hey Steph, learn anything?"

"After you and I talked, Weathers had several angry phone calls and then dashed out of the building about twenty minutes ago. One was from Major Adkins..."

"I talked to him earlier and I suggested he stay out of it. Bucking his department head won't do him any good, not until we know a whole hell of a lot more."

"Good advice, but it didn't sound like he listened. Then the Colonel made an outgoing call on his direct line. I don't know who to, but he was the one doing the yelling this time," she told him. "He finally left the office a little while ago and I got into his office. He'd locked his door, but I have keys to everything."

"Learn anything?"

"Not really. He's not a neat freak, but this time Weathers's desk had been swept clean. He didn't even leave a paperclip out, and it looks like he locked that new contract and all the papers in the office safe."

"I don't suppose you know the combination."

"No, but SOP is for all new contracts to go over to the Judge Advocate's Office for vetting and a quick review. We aren't supposed to keep them here. Colonel Weathers made one mistake, though. He was in such a big hurry that he left the envelope in the trash can. It was all crumpled up and ripped in half, like he was really pissed, but I put it back together. The return address says it came from Matryoshka Software Alliance, 415 Brighton Beach Boulevard, Brooklyn, NY 11235. Ever heard of them?"

"Matryoshka Software Alliance?" Bob replied. "We've butted heads with a lot of software shops over the years, lots of startups, but that's a new one on me. You?"

"No, I checked the DoD contractor directory and they're not in it. Not that it means all that much. It's never up to date and everyone and his brother have tried to sneak one under the door and get in here. But I don't suppose you know what a matryoshka is, do you?"

"Russia's not my usual area of operations, but it's a nesting doll, isn't it? One of those wooden things with a bunch of dolls, one inside another? Babushkas they call them?"

"That's the cruise ship tourist view, but I have an aunt in Bethesda who collects them... and lacquer boxes, which really are nice. The matryoshkas do symbolize women, particularly grandmothers, but it is the doll within a doll within a doll that adds the mystery and surprise to it. Like peeling an onion. In fact, that's what the lawyers and crooks over there call their multi-layered shell companies and complicated tax evasion schemes – a matryoshka."

"A matryoshka, huh? So you think they're Russians?"

"Not a bad guess, 'Ghost,' not a bad guess at all."

"Can you leave a pass for Ace Randall and me downstairs, so we can get inside in the morning?"

"Why not, Weathers didn't tell me not to."

The Ghost? Great! Stephanie called him Ghost, which means she knew all about the late, great, former Delta major force of nature who could disappear when he was standing right in front of you in an open field. The Ghost. Bob had hoped those days were far behind him by now. Guess not, he realized.

He wasn't just retired Army; he had been a Delta Force commander, a master sniper, an expert in small unit tactics, guns, knives, or his bare hands, one of the most finely-tuned killing machines the US government had ever created. "The Ghost" was his Special Ops radio call sign. Over the years it had morphed into a nickname he'd love to forget.

In the nine months since he and Ace Randall returned from their personal 'Operation Payback" in Syria, his life, his business, and Sherwood Forest had quietly returned to normal. That's what he thought he wanted, but sometimes you have to be careful what you ask for. When you're 41 years old and a retired Delta Force major, quiet, semi-retired, and "normal" ain't what they're cracked up to be, especially when combat is "in the blood."

His grandfather had jumped into Holland with the 82nd Airborne in 1944 and fought his way across Holland and Belgium into Germany as an infantry sergeant, retiring after 30 years as a crusty, highly decorated sergeant major. His father had also been a career infantryman, rising from a plebe at West Point to full colonel. His ties to the 82nd were also long and hard, and he had been a company commander in the 3rd Brigade at Chu Lai during the Tet Offensive, among many other assignments.

After also graduating from the family "finishing school" on the Hudson, Bob drew the Signal Corps for a permanent branch, a subject he knew nothing about and had even less interest in. Not that it mattered. They detailed him to the Infantry for the first few years. And since that was what he wanted in the first place, he had no intention of letting it be temporary and never left. They let you do that if you volunteer for the toughest jobs and do them well. He spent twelve years in Special Ops around the world, which, as it turned out, he was one of the very best at it.

Oddly enough, though, it was those matching red-and-white "surrender flags" of the Signal Corps they made him wear that proved the most useful. They drew loud guffaws from both his father and his grandfather, but they were the perfect cover for a Special Ops and Delta Force officer, and they got Ed Toler's attention when he was trying to lure Bob into the telecommunications business after he married his daughter and got out. It was that telecommunications stuff that ended up giving him his other hideous nickname, "the telephone guy."

1.

CHAPTER TEN

Pentagon City, Arlington

The Pentagon, with the Defense Department, the Secretary, the headquarters of all five US military branches, and about anyone else who can squeeze in, occupies twenty-eight acres on the west side of the Potomac River. It's across from the Tidal Basin and the Lincoln Memorial in the District, nestled between three expressways south of Arlington National Cemetery. Colonel Leslie Groves built it in record time during the height of World War II. He did such a great job that he went on to bigger and better things like running the Manhattan Project and building the atomic bomb. This behemoth five-sided monster of a building contains 6,500,000 square feet, with five stories above ground and two more below ground (plus several more below that which they don't admit to), housing over 26,000 employees. Now, unlike 1944, if you work there and don't have stars on your collar, trying to find a parking space is almost impossible.

Fortunately or unfortunately, the ever-expanding Defense Department blew through even that mind-numbing amount of office space years ago, and only the absolutely "mission important" offices continue to be located in the Pentagon itself. The rest of the "ash and trash" administrative departments – likened to the guys who buy the horses as opposed to ride on them – were relocated to leased space in the huge private office complexes which have sprung up in Arlington, Crystal City, Reston, Silver Spring, and all the other stops around the Virginia and Maryland Beltway. It was a "bad/good" thing. On one hand, not being in the Pentagon itself seriously dents a lot of mid-career egos. On the other hand, you can find a parking place out there, a seat in a reasonably priced restaurant with better food, and you can slip out of the office to play golf with much less chance of being noticed.

Lieutenant Colonel Steven Weathers found each of those little perks attractive when they relocated his software contracting office to the fourth floor of "Pentagon Towers," as the locals call it, a large commercial building in Pentagon City directly across I-395 or Shirley Highway from the real Pentagon. Combat soldiers like Bob Burke and Ace Randall had never worked at the Pentagon and never wanted to. Not having to put up with headquarters was one of the few perks they got from spending so much time out in the jungle, desert, or the mountains of Afghanistan, where they could "go native" and let their hair and beards grow.

With Ace driving, the Ford 150 pulled into the Pentagon Towers parking lot before 6 a.m. Without the monstrous security issues involved in getting on the Pentagon property and inside the building itself, they even found a space in the middle row of the visitors' parking lot reserved for bigger vehicles, and parked between an SUV and a panel delivery truck. With the visitor passes Sergeant First Class Stephanie Goss left for them in the lobby, they were sitting on the floor outside the software procurement office when Stephanie arrived at 6:17 a.m. toting a box of Dunkin' Donuts.

"Hi, Major," she beamed. "It's so unusual for us to get the right kind of visitor up here – by which I mean real soldiers – that I stopped and bought a box of my favorite morning carbs, with plenty to share," she smiled and shook the box. "You all locked and loaded?"

"Normally, Ace and I would devour that entire box in three or four bites, but we stopped at a big truck stop about an hour south of here and had their 'Long-Haul Trucker' steak, eggs, and grits breakfast special. So, we're probably set for the week."

She entered the security code in the door's keypad and waved them in. "Take a seat and get comfortable while I make coffee," she said.

In addition to Stephanie's desk, the reception area had the couch and three chairs. Ace plopped down on the couch while Bob looked around. There were five rooms that opened onto the lobby. One contained a bank of file cabinets, supply shelves, and copy machines, while the others were side offices. From the nameplates on the doors, one was for Weathers, one was for Charles Adkins, both of which had windows looking out on the Pentagon, and one had no name.

The door hung open to Weathers's office, so Bob stepped inside. "Looks like nobody is home," he commented.

"No," Stephanie answered. "If he was here, the door would be closed and probably locked, because he never leaves it open. But he never gets here quite this early, either, usually at 6:40 on the dot with a McDonald's bag in one hand and a briefcase in the other, unless there's an accident out on I-95 somewhere, which there usually is."

Bob walked in and made a quick recon of Weathers's office, immediately taken aback by how sterile it looked. Other than a DoD standard office array of framed prints from Civil War battles, the kind you find in every Army office, standard GSA-issue furniture, a bookcase partially filled with official manuals, and a credenza, there was almost nothing personal to be seen anywhere. That was unusual. Military officers always had their walls covered with a collection of crests and "goodbye" plaques from the units they had passed through, but Weathers had none of those on the walls. On the desk, Bob saw a photograph of what he assumed was Weathers's wife and three teenaged kids in private school blazers: two blonde daughters, and a blonde son. No books, no awards, and no sports stuff, making it hard to get a read on the guy. Then again, he thought, maybe it wasn't so hard.

"Are these his wife and kids?" he called out to Stephanie.

"I guess. I've only seen her once, but she seems nice enough. So are the kids – a typical Fairfax County family, as far as I can tell. He has spent very little time overseas, and he's mostly been stationed right here in DC. I think they've sunk roots."

"Just like my family," Bob laughed. "I don't think my Dad was stationed anywhere longer than eighteen months."

"I was an Army brat too; tell me about it."

"Builds character, or so they kept telling me."

"Bullshit," she laughed, "what it builds are scars and calluses."

"By the way, thanks for the passes and the coffee," he told her. "But don't do anything that's going to get him pissed off at you. I don't want your career to take a hit because of me."

"I'm high enough up and know enough people that whatever he thinks won't make a damn bit of difference. Trust me."

They were into their second cups of coffee a half hour later when the front door opened, and Steven Weathers stepped in. He paused in the doorway for a moment, taking in Bob Burke and Ace Randall, before he gave Stephanie Goss a dirty look.

She looked at her watch. "A long line at McDonald's this morning, sir?"

"What's this man doing in here, Sergeant First Class Goss? He doesn't have an appointment, and I don't recall requesting a pass for him."

"Customer service, sir," she quickly answered with a smile. "He's one of our contractors, he requested to see you, and if there's a problem, you never read me into it."

Bob stood, and Ace followed. "You and I need to talk, Colonel," Bob said.

"About what?" Weathers snapped, doing everything he could to avoid looking at him. "I assume you received the department's letter," he added as he quickly headed for his office. "I have nothing further to add. The contract is not being renewed, as the result of a quality control audit which revealed some serious flaws in the work product. If you have anything further to say, I suggest you put it in writing, through channels per Appendix D of the contract, which you should make yourself familiar with."

Bob followed him, and as Weathers attempted to close the door behind him, Bob blocked it with his foot. "Colonel, you don't seriously think you can get away with this, do you? I don't know what you're up to, but that letter's garbage, and you know it."

Rather than look at or try to reply to Bob's statement, he looked back at Stephanie. "Sergeant First Class Goss, call Security and have these people removed from my office immediately. That's an order. Is that clear!"

"Like I said, you won't get away with this," Bob told him as he pulled his foot out of the door and let Weathers close it behind him. Stephanie slowly picked up the phone on her desk. "No need, Steph," Bob said. "We'll go peaceably."

"I figured you would," she said as she set it back down in its cradle with a sympathetic shrug. "And if I hear anything, I'll let you know. I suspect Charlie will too."

CHAPTER ELEVEN

Office Parking Lot

"**That went well**," Ace commented as they walked down the long corridor to the elevator, the main exit, and parking lot. "So what's 'Plan B?' " Ace asked.

"We'll start digging and find out what he's really up to. That stuff about a quality control audit is laying down smoke. That works to hide things until it doesn't."

"All you have to do is tell the Geeks that the Army thinks their programs have 'serious flaws in their work product.' That's all it'll take to get Jimmy and Ronald going," Ace laughed, "and you'll need to chain Sasha to the wall."

Bob looked at his watch. "Too early to call them. We'll be back in North Carolina before those two get up. And I want them nice and rested before I turn them loose. Once they get going, they won't stop until they hit gold."

A dozen years of continuous training interspersed with violent bursts of anti-insurgent combat had left both men constantly aware of their surroundings. It was basic Delta training. Like two sharp-eyed hunting hawks, there wasn't much they missed: something out of place, a slight movement, or maybe a reflection off window glass. As they neared the truck, they saw two large men standing in the shadow between the panel truck and Bob's Ford 150.

"Looks like we have company," Ace said calmly.

"I'd have been surprised if we didn't."

"And disappointed. They look like rejects from a sumo wrestling team."

"You hang back, I'll see what they want."

"You know, it would be nice if you left something for me every once in a while. Just holding your coat gets boring."

Bob didn't slow down. Instead, he sped up and walked directly toward the two men, his hands swinging easily at his side. In his experience, nothing confused a dimwit faster than a victim who didn't act like one. As Bob reached the front of the Ford 150, Goon #1 stepped in front of the other one in the narrow gap between the two vehicles, blocking Bob's way to his truck door. He was big, weightlifter big, like a beer barrel on legs, with his chest puffed out to intimidate the uninformed. Bob figured he was maybe 6'2" and close to 300 pounds, twice Bob's size. He was probably used to winning by scaring the crap out of people, but that would not happen this morning. Another weightlifter! Those were exactly the guys Bob loved to take down. When it came down to skilled, precise speed versus slow weightlifter muscle, it was never much of a contest.

These two clowns had made four cardinal mistakes. First, it was a little after 7 a.m. The sun was coming up behind Bob and Ace, and directly in their eyes. Bad tactical planning there. Second, the space between the trucks was narrow. The front guy was standing in the way of his partner, so Bob could take them down one at a time. Third, the front goon had let Bob get way too close. And fourth, if you're going to war, do some research on your enemy. They hadn't done that, nor had they any idea who they were dealing with.

Bob Burke was normally a mild-mannered guy who didn't go looking for trouble. After that letter, the phone calls, the long drive up here, and his verbal confrontation with Weathers, he had some serious pent-up aggression wanting to vent; and it wouldn't take long for it to come out. Bob had no bulging Gold's Gym muscles and hardly looked intimidating, but he did extreme daily workouts and was in peak physical condition. As his lead NCO, Ace Randall, once commented, he was a man with a lot of "sharp edges." Whether he was using his hands, feet, or a knife he was incredibly fast, precise, and well-practiced. That was why he walked right up to Goon #1 and stopped exactly three and a half feet in front of him: the perfect distance to block, get inside a punch, or use a dozen different moves with his hands or feet.

Goon #1 looked over Bob's shoulder at Ace. "You stay out, you know what's good."

"Me?" Ace laughed. "Bubba, I'm just here to watch the show," he answered as he crossed his arms and leaned back on the fender of the truck, where he had a ringside seat.

The Goon frowned but didn't take the hint and turned his attention back to Bob. "Mees-ter Burke," he smiled down at him. "Cor-o-nel Weathers not want see you anymore. Here, anywhere. Never. You understand?"

Bob returned the smile. "Where are you two guys from?"

"None of your beez-ness," the Goon answered.

Bob shrugged. "I just wondered, because I've never seen two guys as big and as dumb as you two. I heard that in Russia, parents put the really dumb ones out in the woods so the wolves will eat them, or they smother them with pillows, so they won't have to admit they're part of the family."

The Goon frowned for a moment as Bob's words sunk in, then he growled, took a step forward, and tried to poke Bob in the chest with the index finger on his right hand. Fast versus slow? No contest. Bob was lower, lighter, and quicker. His right hand shot out and he grabbed the Goon's index finger from below. He bent it backward until he heard an audible "Snap!" like the neck of a dead chicken. The Goon screamed and took a step backward, wide-eyed, bringing his hand back and cradling it to his chest; but Bob didn't stop there.

As he was always on the small, light side, his father had started him out with boxing, Karate, and Judo classes in sixth grade, not YMCA stuff, but training from Asian masters. As the years went on, he added Aikido, Tae Kwon Do, and many others, choosing the techniques that seemed to work best for him. Over the past five years he concentrated exclusively on Krav Maga, the lesser-known hand-to-hand system developed by the Israeli military. There was no "art" or anything showy about it, nor was it in any way defensive. Some called Krav Maga "street fighting with an attitude." It was a violent, aggressive style of hand-to-hand combat that taught brutal all-out attacks and counterattacks. You get in the first punch, the last, and everything in between, with the intent to incapacitate or kill an opponent in seconds, regardless of his size.

Bob continued toward the Goon and got inside his reach, "up close and personal." As he did, he spotted the automatic pistol the Goon had tucked in his belt. At first glance, it looked like an old Russian Makarov 9-millimeter. It was a cheap street gun a thug might carry, not that a bullet cares. Even a cheap piece of crap handgun can kill you, and this guy would never have that chance.

Before the bigger man could react, Bob twisted the Goon's broken finger again to get his attention, and then drove his right elbow into the center of the Goon's face, flattening his nose. Nothing was more painful or stunned a man quicker than a hard blow to the nose. At the same time, he followed up with his left knee, driving it into the Goon's groin: second place on the quick incapacitation list. That drew a painful grunt and a loud burst of air. The Goon's eyes opened as round as hockey pucks and his hands went to his crotch. That was when Bob brought that same sharp elbow down onto the man's right clavicle, snapping it and putting his gun hand out of commission.

For all intents and purposes, the first half of the fight was already over, but Bob didn't wait for the second half to start. As Goon #1 stumbled backward, Bob grabbed the Makarov out of Goon #1's belt. Even assuming he was the boss and the smarter of the two, which was hard to believe, Bob knew the second guy would react and join the battle sooner rather than later, so he shoved Goon #1 backward as hard as he could into Goon #2.

He had been reaching inside his overcoat, fumbling for his own pistol; but he was the same size, give or take, and no more fleet-of-foot. There was no room for him to move between the two vehicles. When 300 extra pounds crashed into him, he went down hard. His head bounced off the asphalt with the "Thump!" of a Halloween pumpkin landing in the street, and he let out a loud "Oomph!"

By the time Goon #2's eyes cleared, Bob was standing over him with Goon #1's Makarov pointed at him. Bob's dark eyes drilled holes in the bigger man as he bent down and pressed the barrel of the automatic onto the tip of his nose, watching him go cross-eyed as he stared up at it.

"Now, like I asked your pal, nice and polite," Bob said as he pressed his forearm down on Goon #1's broken shoulder blade until the man howled, "Where are you two from?"

CHAPTER TWELVE

The Pentagon Parking Lot

"**From taxi...** we come from taxi..." Goon #2 said, gasping from the weight of Goon #1 plus Bob pressing down on him.

"No, you dumb ass!" he asked as he pressed down harder on the Makarov. "Where did you come from before that, where d'you fly here from?"

"No fly, ride train... train."

"You came here on the train? To Union Station? All right then, where did you take the train from?"

"New York, New York... Brooklyn."

"Who sent you?" Bob's eyes narrowed as he pressed harder.

"Piotr, Piotr!" he answered between clenched teeth.

"Piotr who? Goddamn it!"

The guy was about to answer when Goon #1 jabbed him with an elbow and said something in what sounded to be Russian that was clearly threatening. Once that happened, despite more prodding with the pistol barrel, Goon #2 said nothing more.

"Brooklyn? You know, that's the second time that place has come up today," Ace said as he looked around, scanning the big parking lot. "But we need to get out of here, Ghost. Security will be coming around soon, and this monkey pile's gonna be hard to explain."

"Yeah, while I screw this thing onto his nose, see what they've got in their pockets. And check the bottom one out first, he's probably got a weapon somewhere."

Ace began digging into the guy's pockets. "Them taking the train and a cab makes sense," he said. "No security checks or IDs, and it's easy to carry one of these," Ace said as he reached into the guy's shoulder holster and pulled out a small, semi-automatic pistol. He held it up by the grip with two fingers, like a dead rat. "Look at this antique piece of crap: an old 7.62-millimeter Tokarev TT-33."

"Maybe his grandfather carried it on his hip when they rode into Berlin in 1945. Definitely 'Old School.' "

"And definitely the B team. Almost a shame to waste the energy on them," Ace added as he started on the guy's pockets, pulling out a wallet, a train ticket, cigarettes, lighter, and a set of keys.

"Take everything and throw it in the truck, including their shoes... and their belts," Bob told him.

"Oh, you really are nasty," Ace laughed as he jerked their shoes off, pulled out their belts, and threw them, the wallets, papers, tickets, pocket money, and the old revolver on the passenger side floor of the Ford 150.

Goon #1 glared up at Bob. He was obviously in pain, with sweat pouring off his forehead. "You are dead man, Mees-ter!" he said through clenched teeth.

"You're out of your league, Pal," Bob answered. "When you get back to Brooklyn, if you get back to Brooklyn, and if your boss doesn't dump you two out in the Bay first, tell him I'm coming up to see him." Bob then pushed himself up to his feet, leaning heavily on the Goon's upper left chest. The guy's eyes went wide, and he screamed from the pain until he passed out. Bob and Ace got back in the pickup truck with Ace driving again, leaving Goon #2 to wiggle out from under his friend.

"You're getting old, Ghost. I'd have put the second one out of commission too," Ace commented dryly as they drove slowly away through the big lot, heading for the exit. "I thought they taught you at that boarding school up on the Hudson. 'Never leave a viable enemy force to your rear.' "

"I'm sure they tattooed that on your ass down at the 'NCO boys' camp' at Fort Benning," Bob said as he began going through their wallets. "But 'viable' is the operative term here. It's gonna take everything they've got to figure out how to get out of the parking lot, barefoot, with no IDs, cell phones, or money, and one clown half-carrying the other."

"Maybe they'll try to call Weathers, because I can't see them making it back to Union Station on their own," Ace said.

"No, the rent-a-cops or the DC cops will pick them up long before that. I'd love to stick around and watch, but that isn't something I want to get caught up in." Bob was making a small pile of plastic cards and slips of paper on the floor of the truck as he quickly flipped through the two wallets.

A few minutes and several quick turns later, Ace turned onto Route 1 South. At this time of the morning, most of the traffic was headed north, into the District, and the Pentagon soon disappeared in the rearview mirror. "Find anything interesting?" Ace asked.

"Not as much as I had hoped. A couple of large wads of cash, their return train tickets to Grand Central Station, no credit cards, no Kiwanis Club, Moose, Elk, or health insurance."

"No Soviet 108th Motor Rifle Division Alumni Association cards?"

"No, and no Georgian Greco-Roman wrestling booster club card either, but they both have Green Cards."

"Or they used to."

"Very true. And New York State Driver's Licenses."

"How nice of the Empire State."

"Goon #1's name is Gennady Orlov. It says he's thirty-seven years old, from Brooklyn, with that same address, 415 Brighton Beach Boulevard as was on the envelope in Weathers's office. The photograph's butt ugly, like a freshly dug potato, but it's him."

"The flattened nose and two black eyes might improve the look, then."

"Couldn't hurt... well, it probably did hurt, but that's what you get."

"Like you always say, sometimes you bite the bear and sometimes the bear bites you."

"The other guy's Zurab Baratashvili, twenty-eight years old, same address."

"A Georgian boy, and not from Atlanta."

Ace continued south until they hit the I-95 Beltway, took that around to Springfield, and got off on I-95 South to Fredericksburg, Richmond, and Fayetteville, North Carolina. When they reached Colchester and the long bridge over the Occoquan River, Bob rolled down the passenger-side window and tossed the two Russian handguns as far as he could into the muddy, brown water. When they hit the next state rest stop, Bob stuffed the shoes, the empty wallets and most of the miscellaneous scraps of paper into several trashcans, but he kept the two driver's licenses, their green cards, and the cash. Next Saturday night their contribution would help defray the cost of the weekly Merry Men blowout.

At Sherwood Forest, the first floor of the main house contained the parlor, main dining room, lounges, recreation rooms, and a huge kitchen. They had converted the second floor into two large suites. Bob and Linda took the one to the left for themselves, including bedrooms for Ellie, Linda's daughter, and her overweight attack cat, Crookshanks — or Godzilla as Bob preferred to call him when Ellie wasn't listening — and now a third bedroom for James, their infant son. The large suite on the right was reserved for Ace Randall and his new ex-Air Force pilot-captain-wife, Dorothy, now that they had both retired.

The entire third floor was the "Geekdom," the "Sovereign State of Geek," and a dozen other things, depending on the mood he or Linda was in. It was the exclusive territory of the Geeks: Jimmy Barker, Ronald Talmage, and Sasha Kandarski, their recent addition, who had been a classmate of Jimmy and Ronald at Berkeley. While they were thin, pale, non-athletic American couch potatoes, Sasha was a large, hairy, overweight bear of a Russian. Jimmy and Ronald had worked for several of the top US hi-tech firms before Toler TeleCom, while Sasha's credentials supposedly stretched back to the KGB's espionage "Center" in suburban Moscow. When Sasha joined the North Carolina group they equipped and built out the third-floor suite at Sherwood Forest. He was the one who christened it "The KGB Spymaster Data Center," and wrote the specs for their vast array of telecommunications and computer gear inside.

The Data Center wasn't all work, of course. They built an entertainment center and video game area, and there were bachelor pads for Sasha and Ronald on one side, plus a third room, with a softer touch, for Jimmy and Patsy. She was the most mature and sensible voice of the group; and then there was Linda, their Den Mother. No doubt, the Geeks were high maintenance, but they were the ones who had cleaned out $23 million in New York City mob money from the Genoveses and Luccheses without leaving a fingerprint or even a sniff of where it went, much less that it had ever been there. The mob money vanished in the blink of an eye, making the Geeks worth every penny Linda kept spending to keep them happy and somewhat under control.

Bob waited until 10:30 a.m., when he and Ace were an hour north of Fayetteville to call the house and get Linda on the phone.

"You never called to get bailed out, so I assume you two are coming back in one piece?" she asked.

"Us? Did you seriously doubt it? We did some clog dancing with two Russian weightlifters, but nothing that Ace and I couldn't handle."

"Russians? Now we've got the goddamn Russians picking on us. Sheesh! Who's next?"

"Not so loud, dear, the baby might hear you. We don't want to scare him, now do we?"

"He's sleeping. And just like you, when he's doing that, he doesn't hear a thing. When are you going to be home?"

"We should roll up the driveway in about an hour. What I'd like you to do in the interim is roust out the Geeks. I want them bright-eyed, bushy-tailed and 'standing to' at their cyber 'battle stations' at 1200, ready to go to war."

"1200? You think the Geeks will understand that?"

"Tell them it's when Mickey's hands are both pointing up to 12 on their watches."

"Cute. You know they were up playing computer games all night, and Jimmy and Patsy's room is right above ours. Obviously, they don't embarrass easily, because I know exactly what they were doing after that... and after that... and after that... "

"We talkin' the same Jimmy, here?"

"We talkin' the same Patsy, let me put it that way."

"Lucky Jimmy."

"Could've been lucky Bob too, but you weren't here."

"Point taken. Tell Jimmy and Ronald that a Lieutenant Colonel Steven Weathers with the US Army says that their programming work sucks. Tell them it 'no longer meet Army standards' and has... 'substandard coding verification.' "

"Wait a minute! Do I need to write that down?"

"Nah, you can ad lib, just say an 'inability to meet current quality control initiatives'... and 'a failure to comply with current DoD foreign labor eligibility document criteria,' et cetera, et cetera, ad infinitum. That ought to get them going."

"They taught Latin at West Point?... and I'm supposed to remember all that?"

"No, and no. And Weathers's name should be enough. Tell them he's their new project. Tell Jimmy, 'I want to know what he's got under his fingernails.' "

"Who? Jimmy or Luca Brasi?"

"Ah, you're catching on. Either one," Bob laughed. "I want to know everything there is to know about Steven Weathers, and they don't need to wait for me to start digging."

"What about Sasha? You want him on it too?"

"No, tell Sasha '415 Brighton Beach Boulevard, Brooklyn.' That should be enough of a hint for him."

CHAPTER THIRTEEN

Washington, DC

After Burke left, Steven Weathers spent most of the morning at his desk staring at one of the cheap framed prints on his office wall, fuming, trying to breathe and to think. The print was a colorful copy of the Remington painting of Custer's Last Stand at the Little Big Horn. At the end of the battle, the Indians trapped him and a handful of his troopers on a low hill being circled by hundreds of screaming Sioux on horseback. That was exactly how Weathers felt at that moment, barely holding down his own overwhelming panic, and he didn't even have a long-barreled Colt Army revolver like old George did. That was when his desk phone buzzed. He had told Stephanie he wanted no interruptions and was so wired by that time that he almost jumped out of his chair.

"What, what!" he pressed the intercom button and screamed. "I told you…"

"It's Major Adkins on line #1, sir. He's called twice and says he'll keep calling until you talk to him."

Weathers fumed and took a couple of deep breaths. "All right, all right!" he said and picked up the phone. "What do you want, Major? I left instructions that I was not to be disturbed. Besides, I thought you had class this morning."

"It can wait. I understand you canceled the Toler TeleCom contract, Colonel. Since it is *MY* project, do you mind telling me why?"

"Operational needs, Major. I reviewed all the contracts myself and I felt it was time to prune the deadwood. However, and to be precise, I did not cancel it. I decided not to renew it. A fine point, I must admit, but the correct one."

"Without consulting me?"

"My decision, Major. Not yours. I am in charge here and competition is a good thing in bidding."

"Toler is the best contractor we've ever had work for us."

"Major, you will soon learn it is never a good idea to fall in love with your contractors. I found some new people who I think will do just as good a job. End of subject."

"I want to see the contract, sir."

"Are you questioning the decision of your superior officer, Major? That can be a career ending move, you know."

"You can let me see it or let the Judge Advocate General's Office and CID see it, sir! And for your information, there are a lot of things that can be career ending. My brother's the staff IG with JSOC down at Fort Bragg. I'm sure he can name a few more."

"All right, all right, nothing to get all in a twist about. When you come back…"

"I'm already on the road. I should be there by close of business."

"On the road? It took a lot of time and money to get you in that class, Major. I…"

Adkins ignored him. "Leave it all on my desk."

The line went dead, and Weathers knew Adkins had thrown down the gauntlet. He told that damned Shurepkin this would never work. His only chance had been to slide the new contract in under the radar with no fuss when no one was looking. Now, between that wild man Burke and Charles Adkins, it would never happen. He pulled out his private cellphone and used both thumbs, like a teenage girl, punching in a number he was beginning to know all too well. It rang at least ten times before it finally went to voicemail with a message that Weathers assumed was in Russian, and his panic only got worse. He dialed it again. This time Piotr Shurepkin answered.

"We need to talk," Weathers sputtered. "It's all coming apart here."

"Really? Tell me where I can find this Burke. Where does he live?" Shurepkin asked, his voice hard and angry. "Is he in Chicago at that Toler TeleCom?"

"No, that's where the company office is, but I think he lives down in North Carolina. Why? You aren't thinking of sending those two Goons from McDonald's after him, are you? Burke will chop them up into little pieces."

"Gennady and Zurab? Already happened. They met with your friend Burke this morning. Tried to have 'friendly little business discussion' with him. Gennady is in hospital. Police have Zurab and are questioning him."

"I told you this was a bad idea. Is he going to talk?"

"Zurab? No, he will not talk. Zurab not afraid of police. American police are nothing. Your jails are nothing, not for men used to KGB beatings and jails. Now, you give me this Burke's addresses. Chicago? North Carolina. Him, I will fix myself."

"Look, Piotr, that's an even worse idea. Besides, we have a bigger problem. I got my assistant, Adkins, out of town for a few weeks to a class, but Burke got to him and he's threatening to send your contract to the Judge

Advocate General and to the CID. If that happens, this whole thing's going to blow up in both of our faces."

"Assistant is yours!" Piotr snapped. "I fix Burke. You fix Adkins."

"Me? I don't know how to do things like that; I'm a Finance Corps officer."

"Whose beautiful wife will love her new 'hostess' job in a Baltimore casino. Maybe I will go down and be her first customer. Maybe me and Pavel will go... and Zurab, too. Won't that be fun, Colonel!"

"Leave my family out of this!"

"If you do what I say, my friend. Washington is a bad city. Baltimore worse. Lots of crime. Men get mugged in DC parking lots all over. Enough talk. Do it!"

CHAPTER FOURTEEN

Sherwood Forest

Bob climbed the back stairs to the third floor "Geekdom" two
at a time and strode into the "KGB Spymaster Data Center," as Sasha called
it, just as the Westminster chimes on the grandfather clock in the first floor
hallway struck 12:00. Jimmy and Ronald had been interns at Toler
TeleCom up in the Chicago suburbs, originally hired by Charlie Newcomb,
the company's CFO. The first time Bob saw them, one looked like he was
fifteen and the other looked like his younger brother. He thought they were
summer interns from the local high school until Charlie told him both were
top graduates from Berkeley with advanced degrees in Information
Technology. They didn't even know where the football stadium was. They
spent their free time in massive, international simulation games. Their
wardrobes tended toward superhero T-shirts, and the only way to tell them
apart was Ronald's thick, "Coke bottle bottom" glasses held together with
white first-aid tape.

Sasha had been at Berkeley with them and they pulled him into the
group a year ago with the promise that Linda would buy him a Green Logo
Razor Blade state-of-the-art gaming laptop like they had. And Patsy? She
worked at Toler TeleCom in Chicago. She and Jimmy became a couple
during the Atlantic City trip.

Bob tried not to smile as he saw the three Geeks busily banging away
at their laptops, with Patsy circulating the central console, refilling their
demitasse cups from the $12,000 imported Italian espresso machine Linda
bought for them. Who said you can't hire "good people," Bob thought, then
find ways to motivate them and let them find ways to spend all your
money?

"Okay, what have you come up with, guys?" he asked.

The central work console, a huge desk shaped like a three-leaf clover,
dominated the center of the room. On the edge of each "leaf" was a
semicircular cutout where an operator sat and had 180° access to an array
of machines, keyboards, and consoles. There were three of them, one for
each Geek, with three large monitor screens mounted at eye height around
them. Each screen displayed a flurry of documents and photographs, some
of which were shared to make it easy for them to collaborate. The entire
thing was Jimmy's idea. Each Geek had his own tall, ergonomic "cobra"
chair at his workstation, which was like the command console on the

Battlestar Galactica and almost as complicated. Bob stood next to Jimmy but did not have an unobstructed view across to Sasha, who was on the other side of the desk behind his screens. Still, it was interesting to watch Jimmy's and Ronald's fingers flash across their keyboards, directing the constantly changing show on the screens.

Patsy came back and joined Jimmy, draping herself over his back and whispering in his ear as her talented hands kneaded his neck and shoulders.

"Patsy, time to uncouple, girl," Bob said. "Give the poor boy a break."

"He likes it, Major B. It helps him think."

"Yeah, but about what?" Ronald laughed.

"You guys have any trouble getting into the Army and Pentagon data systems?"

"Major B, really? You should know better." Patsy shook her head, scolding him. "You aren't dealing with garden-variety drudges here."

Ronald said, "No, but you seem to attract an endless supply of lowlifes, don't you?"

"He iz lowlife magnet!" Sasha roared.

"Take this clown, Weathers," Ronald continued as the Lieutenant Colonel's ID photo flashed onto the screen, followed quickly by photos of an attractive woman and three well-scrubbed teenagers in private school blazers.

"I saw their photos on his desk this morning," Bob said. "Nice looking family."

"Preppie money-eating machines," Ronald said. "With his rank and time in, your Colonel makes around $110,000 a year. Lots of money! Then subtract his huge mortgage on a $750,000 Falls Church house, killer real estate taxes of over $9,500, three kids enrolled at the Congressional School, a private academy, at $25,000 a year each, and Virginia taxes. They maxed out nine credit cards, and... well, he's in way over his head."

"Blowing bubbles on the bottom," Patsy chuckled.

Impressive, Bob thought as he looked around from screen to screen. "You figured that all out in an hour and a half?" he asked.

"More like a half hour," Ronald answered with a self-deprecating shrug.

"More like ten minutes," Patsy grinned as she leaned forward, put her arms around Jimmy, and squeezed. "You forget, we were still in bed when you called."

"So Linda tells me," Bob answered. "Now we know what Lieutenant Colonel Steven Weathers has been up to, and it's pretty easy to figure out what his motivation is."

"And what Patsy and Jimmy have been up to, too," Ronald's eyes remained focused on his monitor as his fingers continued attacking his keyboard.

"Ronald, we need to find you a girlfriend," Bob told him.

"Don't let him fool you, he already has one," Patsy quickly countered. "Her name's Debbie. She works in accounting back in the Schaumburg office, and we aren't the only ones who stay up all night. The difference is, they do it FaceTiming on their laptops."

"Not nearly as romantic, I'll bet?" Bob asked, deadpan.

"Or as strenuous," Ronald answered.

"Okay, Ronald, I want you to invite Debbie down for the weekend as my guest," Bob told him. "We're having a big party. Tell her to give the receipt to Maryanne and tell her I said to charge it to my Health and Welfare Account. You got that?"

That got Ronald's attention, as he sat up in his chair and said, "Yes, sir!"

"So? What about poor Sasha's health and welfare, Boss?" The Russian's deeper voice boomed from the other side of the console's computer screens.

"Good point! Sasha deserves some R&R too," Bob quickly agreed. "Patsy, you and Jimmy and Ronald, your next task, after you finish this one, is to get Sasha a date. Aren't there any other girls back in Chicago who would like a road trip down to North Carolina?"

"Don't let Rasputin fool you!" Patsy quickly replied. "There's a girl who works at the River Bottom Inn down at the interstate interchange named Sandy who Sasha's been dancing with. They seem to get along, don't you, Sasha?"

"I teach her drink like Russian; she teaches me clog dance like Tar Heel!"

"Clog dance?" Bob almost lost it. "You?"

"I do Ukrainian 'Hopak' dance, like Cossacks. Put on cowboy hat and boots, nobody know difference."

"Invite her!" Bob told him. "This Saturday night and bring your clog shoes. Now, tell me what you learned about 415 Brighton Beach Boulevard?" he said as he handed him the driver's licenses and Green Cards he took from the two goons in the Pentagon parking lot. Sasha looked them over and handed them back.

"Want me to Xerox them?" Bob asked.

"No need, Boss. Sasha has Xerox machine up here," he tapped his forehead with his index finger. "Steel trap, mind! Sasha forgets nothing."

"Except after he's had a few down at the River Bottom Inn," Jimmy quipped.

"Names are up here," he tapped his forehead again. "Gennady Orlov and Zurab Baratashvili. Sasha never forgets name or face. Russian and Georgian. Bad peoples, Boss, Russian gangster and Georgian gangster, not dumb Italians this time. You got Russian Mafia. They even worse, but I just started. Soon will know more, much more."

"All right, but what's at 415 Brighton Beach Boulevard? What's there? Is it an office building?"

"Oh, no, Boss. Is restaurant: Kalinka's, 'authentic' Russian tearoom. Here," Sasha said as a photo of the front of a gaudy restaurant popped up on the screen in front of Bob. "Bad food, watered drinks, worse people. Brooklyn Russian Mafia."

"Do you think they have any of your pals from the KGB's Moscow Center working there?" Bob asked.

"Who knows? But no, I don't think so," Sasha slowly shook his head. "These are scum, thugs and petty criminals from Gulag. Would not pass KGB intelligence test. This far away from Moscow? Wouldn't play well together. Would kill each other."

"And you did?" Patsy piped up from the other side of the big credenza.

"Hey, woman! I was good boy back then. Very smart. Clean record. Never caught, never in trouble until American goons kidnap poor Sasha in New Jersey, put black bag over his head, and throw him in American helicopter. That is where Sasha fell in with disreputable people."

2.

CHAPTER FIFTEEN

Washington, D.C.

It took Major Charles Adkins longer to drive back to Washington D.C. from Atlanta than he expected. He threw his suitcase in the car and was on the road by 8:30 a.m., but construction in north Georgia on I-85, mid-day congestion around Charlotte and Greensboro, followed by the normally heavy traffic on I-95 from Richmond to DC. It wasn't the first time he had travelled these roads, but no matter the weather or time of year, it was always the same ten hours of busy, boring, hectic, stop-and-go, speeding, and tail-gating every time.

He'd slept poorly the night before, tossing, turning, and thinking of what he would say to Weathers. This isn't my fault, Charles thought. It was all Weathers's. He was the one who should be tossing, turning, and having a terrible night. What he did was unconscionable and probably illegal. It was a wrong that must be put right, and that was exactly what Charles would tell him. Still, the Lieutenant Colonel was Charles's department head and superior officer. Charles knew he should tread softly, but he had enough with that guy and "soft" wasn't likely to last very long. In the car, with nothing but time, he spent most of the drive rehearsing what he would say to Weathers and then to the legal department, the Judge Advocate General people, in the big building across the road.

With stops for gas and twice for coffee and a McLunch, by the time he reached the Beltway it was the height of rush hour. The outbound traffic was nearly at a standstill, but at least the inbound was moving at a nice pace, until he hit I-395, the dreaded Shirley Highway, and took the exit south into the Pentagon City office complex. That was a relief, but it was 6:00 p.m. by the time he pulled in the parking lot for his building. Like the others nearby, it was full of Defense Department, federal civilian agency, TSA, and DEA. Most of their people worked the day shift, and they were now on flex time. That might spread the traffic out, but it didn't reduce it. Still, it petered out around 6 p.m., which meant this was a decent time to find a parking space.

Charles Adkins drove around to the south lot, trying to find a space closest to his entrance. The sun was already going down in the west and the tall buildings were casting shadows across the cars when he saw an open space in the third row back from the side entrance to his building. He smiled. It was a rare day when the Parking Lot Gods cut you any slack at all. When they did, it was never when it was raining, cold outside, or snowing. Coming in this late, however, he saw quite a few spaces open, and that was a minor victory.

Well, he thought, by close of business tomorrow, either he or Lieutenant Colonel Steven Weathers would no longer need a parking space here.

Weathers finally calmed down. It took him all morning, but he finally came up with a rational plan; not that the words rational and murder belonged in the same sentence. He was a numbers guy, a statistician, a finance guy, and a slow, deliberate planner, but here he was with his personal finances in chaos, being pushed and shoved by circumstances beyond his control. But what choice did he have? His wife gave him none. Zero. He had asked her to stop gambling many times, months ago. All that got him was a roll of her eyes and a look of total disdain. Then he ordered her to stop gambling. He even threatened her, but she had been the "alpha dog" in the family since the day they met. As she grew older and learned how to use her body to dominate him, to push all of his buttons, she knew she could completely ignore him. He was powerless to stop her. She had a sickness, a disease, but he was the one who would pay the price. That Russian weasel Shurepkin had him by the throat and there was nothing he could do except give the man what he wanted.

The Army does not tolerate soldiers or their wives who run up gambling debts, big or small, regardless of rank, particularly if they are in the Finance Corps. They'd declare him a security risk and a moral reject, dismiss him from the Army, and toss him out the door as fast as they could scrape the paperwork together. Once that happened, he really would be finished: no job, no savings, no house, and no private schools. No one would ever hire him, none of the vendors or contractors. Still, those were the least of the things that would happen to him and to his wife, Erica, once the casino bosses got their hands on her. No choice. No choice at all. He had to make the deal work with Shurepkin, get the debts in the markers taken care of. Then, he could grab his retirement and get the hell out of the Army. Two years! It would take him two years to get the markers paid off and then retire. He could almost see the possibility of pulling it off until that bastard Charles Adkins stuck in his two cents and threatened to take it up the chain of command.

No matter what else he did, Weathers could not let that happen. Adkins, and maybe that damned Sergeant First Class Goss in the office, were the only ones who might figure out what he was up to, and he had to buy time. That was his only hope now. That meant he must silence Charles

Adkins. He gave Weathers no choice. By threatening to take this new contract with Shurepkin over to the Judge Advocate General, to the Inspector General, or, God forbid, to the Criminal Investigation Division within the Provost Marshall's office, the Major had sealed his own fate. His threats had made him expendable, and that made Weathers's plan perfectly rational, almost mathematical, almost actuarial, which he liked. With Adkins gone, it would break the link. Burke could scream all he wanted. So could Stephanie Goss, but they would have no proof. And if Shurepkin then took care of Burke, Stephanie Goss would not be a problem. As impossibly repugnant as murdering someone seemed to him only a few days ago, he was becoming more and more accustomed to the idea.

Weathers calculated Charlie would hit the road from Atlanta as soon as he got off the phone with him. That was maybe 8:30 a.m. The Lieutenant Colonel was a careful man, very precise. He checked the driving time from Atlanta using three different apps on his computer. They all showed the drive would take Adkins ten hours, give or take a few minutes. He even called the State Departments of Transportation in Georgia, South Carolina, North Carolina, and Virginia to check road construction and to get up-to-the-minute traffic delays. No matter how many times he calculated it, he figured Charlie would drive into the Pentagon City parking lot right around 6 p.m.

One advantage of having your office "off the reservation" was that Weathers could use his connections to get upgraded rental office furniture, at least for his own office, to include a larger faux-wood desk, table, and credenza set. And, since they were at a "remote" location, he convinced the GSA he needed a safe to store contracts and other official documents. The GSA had obliged by adding a 12" x 18" x 18" safe inside the right compartment of the credenza.

Weathers was the only one in the office who had the combination. He quickly opened it, pulled out the Shurepkin contract, and tossed it in his briefcase. Besides contracts, accounting reports, and confidential documents, both he and Charlie Adkins stored their M-9 Beretta 9-millimeter service pistols in the safe. As staff finance officers, they occasionally needed them when they drew escort or payroll duty, and for weapons qualification. Like other staff officers, it was much easier to secure it in your own office safe, if you had one, than to run back and forth to Fort McNair where the Headquarters Company's official arms room was located.

One aspect of the M-9 Beretta that convinced the Army to buy them was its ease of maintenance and interchangeable parts. They replaced parts. They didn't repair them, which made things simple, far less expensive, and life much easier for unit armorers. Six years before, while stationed in the headquarters accounting section in the Green Zone in Baghdad, the top slide on his Beretta kept sticking. The armorer replaced the slide and the barrel. Without giving it much thought back then, Weathers began examining the old barrel, looking through it to study the rifling while the armorer exchanged the parts. For no particular reason, Steven Weathers slipped it into his jacket pocket as a souvenir of sorts. Later, when assigned to the Pentagon, he locked the old barrel in the safe with the rebuilt pistol, without giving it much thought at the time.

Out of sight and out of mind... until that afternoon.

When he pulled the Matryoshka papers from the safe, he saw the two Beretta M-9's lying there in their holsters, his and Charles Adkins's, and the extra barrel underneath them. That was when a plan leapt into his head, fully formed, like a slap in the face. He put his own M-9 Beretta back in the safe, pulled out Adkins's pistol, an empty magazine, and the extra barrel, and returned to his desk. The shooting range had been one of the few things Weathers had found interesting all those years ago in the Finance Officer Basic Course, probably because it was so different from numbers and accounting, his job specialties. It was easy to take apart an M-9. He had Adkins's Beretta disassembled in ten seconds, surprised at how dirty the Major left it. Weathers always thoroughly cleaned his after each firing or trip to the range, but it looked as if the Major hadn't given his side arm a good cleaning and oiling in months.

In the rear of Weathers's bottom desk drawer he kept the usual can of black shoe polish, a shoe brush, Brasso, and spot cleaning fluid, which every officer kept somewhere within handy reach. Weathers also kept a gun-cleaning kit, some rags, a thick hand towel, and a small box of latex gloves: the other parts of a junior officer survival kit from Officer Basic. He put on a pair of latex gloves, placed the parts from Adkins's Beretta on the towel, and carefully cleaned and oiled them. After six years there would be no surviving forensics on his old barrel from Iraq for anyone to check, so he switched out the barrel in Adkins's M-9 with his own spare from the safe. He even used a small computer screwdriver to place an extra nick or two on the firing pin, to eliminate any ID from the primer on a cartridge, and then wiped away any fingerprints from the interior gun parts. Once he had it all back together again, he worked the slide mechanism vigorously several times until it slid smoothly back and forth with no rough spots or catches.

Further back in the drawer he kept several empty magazines and a box of 9x19 9-millimeter Parabellum cartridges for the Beretta. He laid ten of them on the cloth, carefully wiping them off and loading them in a magazine. It held fifteen rounds, but if he needed that many, he'd use the last one on himself as punishment for horrible marksmanship. He seated the magazine in the Beretta, jacked a round in the chamber, and put it in his briefcase along with the towel and a fresh pair of latex gloves. He had a small executive coat closet and pulled out a garment bag he kept there. He changed into gray slacks and a navy polo shirt and hung his uniform in the bag.

At 5:15, Weathers picked up his briefcase, opened his office door, and threw the garment bag over his shoulder. He told Stephanie he was leaving early because he had a PTA meeting at his kids' school that night, and he and his wife were going out to dinner on the way. He wanted no questions or conversation and quickly ducked out the front door, hurrying to the elevator and the parking lot below.

Weathers's car was a beige, nondescript, three-year-old Toyota sedan. Like most of the other cars in the parking lot, it badly needed a wash, helping him to blend in even more. The rush for the exit and the nearby expressways was well underway when he got in the car, so he threw the garment bag in the backseat, placed the briefcase on the seat next to him, and donned a Washington Senators baseball hat. He pulled it low on his forehead before he put the car in gear and drove out of the parking space.

Unlike the other drivers now queuing up for the exit, Weathers did not head that way. Rather, he drove around and parked his car in a space which offered an unobstructed view through the gap between several other cars of the main parking lot entrance from I-395. The space was perfect, he thought. Unlike the Pentagon itself or the higher profile corporate buildings in the area, security services in these multi-tenant office complexes were negotiated in their leases. That usually meant minimum-wage, unarmed, indifferent, rent-a-cops, who occasionally patrolled the lots, but only after dark. So, Weathers scrunched down in the driver's seat, put one of the latex gloves on his right hand, pulled out the M-9, wiped it off one more time with the towel, and waited.

As the minutes slowly passed, he felt the nervous pressure getting to him. Why shouldn't it, and why shouldn't he do it, he thought as he looked at his watch once more and fidgeted with the wristband of the latex glove? It was tight. He was already sweating badly, and the glove had filled with perspiration. He'd love to get rid of it, but by wearing the glove, there would be no trace of gunpowder residue on his hand or fingerprints or DNA on the Beretta.

Finally, just as the clock on his dashboard rolled over to 6:00 p.m., he saw a dark-red four-door Buick sedan come in the entry lane and stop briefly at the security shack. While he didn't have a perfect view of the driver, it was an African American male in uniform behind the wheel and the car fit the description of Adkin's in the department file. Weathers sat up, backed out of the space, and followed Adkins's car down the main aisle heading south, back toward their wing of the building. Perfect, he thought. Freaking perfect, because timing would be everything. He could see his problems fade away and there was no stopping now.

He watched Adkins' car turn off the main aisle and snake his way closer to the building's south entrance, until the Major swung the Buick into an empty space in the third row, between another car and a black SUV. While Adkins appeared to be putting away some maps and papers, Weathers drove slowly around and came back down the same aisle from the other direction, pulling out the Beretta. As Adkins opened the driver side door and put one leg outside on the pavement, he turned and reached back into the passenger seat for his briefcase. Timing, Weathers thought, as he stopped his own car across the gap between Adkins's car and the SUV and quickly got out with the towel-wrapped Beretta hanging at his side.

Adkins heard nothing. In two quick strides, Weathers was at the Major's open car door. Adkins must have seen something then, perhaps his shadow or a reflection, because he turned his head and looked up, surprised to see someone standing beside his car. It wasn't until Weathers reached inside and jammed the Beretta against the center of the Major's chest, that Adkins recognized him.

"You? Colonel, what...?" was all Weathers allowed him to say before he pulled the trigger once, twice, three times. The 9-millimeter rounds slammed into Adkins and drove him backward, sprawling across the passenger seat. He was dead before he stopped moving. Inside the mostly closed car, with the barrel of the Beretta pressed into Adkins like that, the escaping gasses followed the bullets into the body, taking much of the noise with them, further muffling the 9-millimeter automatic as a 'silencer' would. It surprised Weathers that the gunshots didn't make more noise than they did. Even as close as he stood, with his head inside the car, they sounded like a car door slamming shut, nothing more.

Weathers looked around. There were a handful of people in the lot, but they were hurrying off, one way or the other, and he saw no one turning to look back at him. His plan had been to grab Adkins's briefcase and take it with him, but Adkins knocked it off the seat when he fell sideways. Its contents had spilled across the floor on the passenger side. However, Weathers saw the Major's wallet sitting on the console between the two seats, presumably where he set it after he paid some tolls. Weathers picked it up and shoved it in his pocket. No need to worry about the spent brass cartridges. The towel wrapped around his hand caught them all. As he backed out of the car, he raised Adkins's leg, shoved it inside, pushing his body onto the floor before he closed the car door. Unless someone walked by and looked directly down inside the Buick's front seat, they wouldn't see a thing. That would give him plenty of time to put distance between himself and this "random, senseless act of urban violence." That Russian bastard Shurepkin was right. There were dozens of car thefts and armed robberies in these suburban beltway parking lots every day. That's what the cops will call it: an armed robbery gone bad, and then they'll move on to the next one in the stack of unsolved murders in DC.

Too bad, Weathers thought with a thin, cynical smile. He and Charles had worked together for over a year now, and he was almost getting to like the guy. Almost. Now, he'd have to break in a new one. No fun in that.

Weathers drove slowly back around to the north exit of the parking lot, careful to keep to the posted speed. He then maneuvered his way through some complicated loops and turns to exit onto I-395, the Shirley Highway, then up the scenic George Washington Memorial Parkway, which ran up the western bank of the Potomac River between Arlington National Cemetery and the water. The linear park was filled with jogging trails, bicycle paths, picnic areas, and scenic lookouts. In the late afternoon, the picnic grounds were empty, but the jogging trails and bicycle paths hosted a constant stream of active young men and women.

He pulled into one of the mostly empty parking lots along the river where he quickly unwrapped the towel and disassembled Adkins's Beretta, breaking it down to its component parts, which he shoved in his pockets. As casually as he could, he got out of the car, walked over to the bank of the fast-moving river, and began walking up the trail. Every hundred paces, whenever he found the trail empty, he would toss a part into the river, including both barrels, the magazine with the remaining bullets, and the spent brass, before he returned to the car. He stopped two more times to stuff the badly singed towel in one trashcan and the rubber glove in another.

Finally, he stopped to throw the box of bullets, the cleaning kit, and even Adkins's wallet as far out into the water as he could.

Regrets? Of course. It should have never come to this, but the man refused to listen. What choice did he have? Weathers asked himself. Charles did it to himself.

He looked at his watch. It was almost 6:30, just enough time to pick up his wife, grab a quick bite, make sure she had his story straight, and make it to that damned PTA meeting. Afterward, he would have that talk with her about casino gambling and other things, because she was another problem he could no longer put off. The way things were going, Erica might have an accident too, or perhaps he would let Shurepkin and his pals take her up to Baltimore for a long weekend. As the Russian said, "she would not like that." Not all bad, he ruminated. Perhaps they'd return her to him with a long overdue attitude adjustment. Maybe Erica would listen to him for a change. He'd like that.

CHAPTER SIXTEEN

Sherwood Forest

Bob Burke looked at his watch. It was 6:30 p.m., time to check on the Peanut Gallery and see what they had accomplished. He took the stairs two at a time and called out to them from the third-floor landing to give them ample warning, "What've you got for me, guys?"

Ronald started off, "You remember I said Weathers was way over his head in debt? A big, expensive house, expensive private schools, credit cards, yada, yada..."

"Well, guess what? That isn't the worst of it," Patsy added. "Give him the good stuff; Jimmy, give him the good stuff."

"It isn't Weathers!" Jimmy shouted exultantly. "It's his wife, Erica."

"Ah, the root of most problems," Bob ventured.

"Bravely spoken," Pasty answered, "when Linda isn't around."

"I'm only so stupid... but what, pray tell, did the lovely Missus Weathers do?"

"Casino gambling, big time," Jimmy told him.

"By big time, I assume you mean she hasn't been winning."

"Hardly!! She's made a bunch of cash withdrawals against five credit cards at three casinos over in Maryland and maxed them out, which isn't easy to do."

"So what do those fiscally responsible banks and credit card companies do?" Patsy asked. "They send her more cards, raise her credit limits, and her withdrawals immediately increase."

"The biggest withdrawals were at the cash machines at the Horseshoe, up in Baltimore. It's owned by the same cast of characters we bumped into down in Atlantic City: the Genoveses in New York. Remember how we hacked into their data systems last year...?"

"To the tune of $23 million," Sasha crowed, "and counting, Boss!"

"You'd think they'd learn by now, or hire better systems people," Patsy chimed in again.

"Should hire Russians," Sasha said.

"Anyway, after she maxed out the cards, she began with the markers and taking house money."

"Signing markers, losing more, and signing more markers."

"Until they cut her off a week ago," Ronald told him. "She owes them over $70,000, plus $3,000 a week in 'Vig,' which, as you know, compounds..."

"And compounds...," Bob said, truly impressed. "How did you guys learn all that?"

"One more example of our many dark powers," Jimmy shrugged. Bob gave him a look, until Jimmy added, "We left trapdoors in their systems last time. That's how we got in."

"Trapdoors?"

"Some bits of code we put in that let us get back into their software and data files any time we want," Ronald explained. "Little entry points which mere mortals will never find. While we were in there, I did some prowling through the casino's accounting, that's how I found the 'markers' for the gambling debts that the lovely Missus Weathers has run up. Their bean counters properly carry them as receivables, so I added them up – $70,000 plus the Vig. And that doesn't count the credit card balances and maybe a second mortgage she blew in the casinos."

"Looks like well over $150,000," Patsy said.

"A pretty woman with a big Self-Destruct button in the center of her forehead," Bob shook his head. "Okay. Sasha!" Bob shouted over the wall of monitors. "Tell me what else you learned about our friends in Brighton Beach?"

"Iz sandwiched between Coney island and Manhattan Beach on south shore of Brooklyn. Lots of people. Lots of sand and boardwalk, but maybe not good for swim. First came ethnic Jews, then Russian Jews, now just Russians with Jewish names. All immigrants. Lots of criminals: Russians, Georgians, Chechens, Ukrainians, Armenians, Uzbekistanis, Bashkirs, Turks, everybody. All hate each other. All hate KGB worse, but all like vodka, Baltika beer, and Russian food. After fall of Soviet Union, Russia cleaned out jails and gave them all visas."

"Iz dot how you got here? On visa?" Patsy asked Sasha, mimicking him.

"No, dumb girl. Sasha swam here, from Russia, over North Pole," he countered.

"So the 415 Brighton Beach Boulevard address is a front?" Bob asked.

"Da. Iz front of kitschy restaurant. Not house or office, but maybe they live upstairs?"

"Are they connected to the Mafia gangs back in Russia?"

"For sure. Which one? Hard to tell. Russian gangs not like Italians. Lots of little ones all over the place. Every ethnic group. Nobody takes orders from nobody. All branches of gangs back home. All report to council."

"Council? What do you mean council?"

"Vor Council, criminal gangs from prisons and labor camps, council of bosses. Strict rules. The leader of each gang is the 'Vor,' the 'vor v zakone,' or 'thief-in-law' of group. All have eight-pointed star tattoos on shoulder. Like business cards or nametags, star tattoo is for 'made men,' as Italians say. But 'thieves in law' serious people, like holy order, like a holy order of criminals. Can't have wife or children, no legitimate jobs, and no cooperating with police."

"What do you think they're after? Our little contract?"

"Hard to say, Boss. Criminal gangs are criminals. Used to do everything for money. Now? They work with KGB. Secret police and criminals like peas in one pod. Not local criminal police. KGB security police and Mr. Putin's spies. Now, they all one big gang. Only difference is crooks have nicer suits and cars, but KGB has bigger guns. They all work for Putin now."

"But what do they want?" Bob asked. "Let's say they get our contract. PX and commissary logistics? It isn't exactly like they're going to get rich on it. What are they up to?"

"Plenty, Boss, or 'the Czar' wouldn't be having them do it."

"Putin? All right, you got me interested. Keep digging."

"Digging, Boss? If Putin calling shots, we need really big shovel."

CHAPTER SEVENTEEN

Pentagon City, Washington, D.C.

Sergeant First Class Stephanie Goss opened the office door at 6:35 a.m. and stepped inside, surprised to see the interior ceiling lights were already on. More surprisingly, the lights in Lieutenant Colonel Weathers's office were on, and his door was open. She always beat him in by at least ten or fifteen minutes in the morning, but not today. She put her things down on her desk and called out, "Good Morning, Colonel. You're in early. No McDonalds stop this morning?"

"Good morning to you too, Sergeant First Class Goss. No, I wasn't hungry today," he answered. But the truth was he was avoiding the golden arches for a few days, and any possibility of running into Shurepkin and his two weightlifter bodyguards again.

"Did you see the commotion out in the parking lot?" she asked.

"I must have missed that. What's it all about?"

"I don't have a clue," she answered.

"No clue, huh?" he chuckled.

"I don't, but somebody must. Half the Arlington Police Department's out there. There's squad cars and police vans all over the place, and they have most of the south lot roped off with that bright yellow 'Crime Scene' tape of theirs."

"Yeah, I saw the traffic backup and came in the other way."

"You want some coffee?" she asked. "I'll make a pot."

Stephanie took the pot down the hall to the women's restroom to fill it with water. By the time she got back to the office, a baby-faced Army MP private in camouflage ACUs stood blocking the door and asked to see her ID. He looked too young to even be shaving, which made her feel even older. She was still wearing her service uniform coat and started to point to the stripes on her sleeve, the ribbons on her chest, and her name tag, but rather than pull rank and get up in the kid's face, she made nice, pulled out her wallet, handed him her Army ID card, and cut him some slack.

"All right, what's up, Private?" she asked. He appeared to be memorizing the damned thing, front and back, but the kid wasn't talking. Finally, he handed it back, opened the door for her, and allowed her to go inside. The first thing she saw was a tall man in a blue civilian suit talking to Colonel Weathers. The man had a plastic credentials package, or "cred pack," with a gold badge hanging out of his breast pocket, and a Sig-Sauer

M-17 automatic pistol riding on his hip. To her left, a burly MP Sergeant E-5 sat in her desk chair going through her drawers. Another one was in Weathers's office, rifling through his desk, while a third was in Major Adkins's office, apparently doing the same.

Stephanie knew Weathers had a monstrous ego. She had seen him absolutely explode, red-faced, sputtering, and jabbing a pointed finger in someone's chest at far less provocation. To her surprise, he stood there listening intently to the man as he talked, frowning and looking concerned. Admittedly, anyone carrying a badge and a Sig-Sauer could be intimidating, but this proved he had been a closet wuss all along.

As the door closed behind her, Weathers turned and told the guy in the suit, "This is Sergeant First Class Goss, my Administrative Assistant and Office Manager. Steph, remember that commotion you said you saw in the parking lot you came in? This is Mr. Rendell with the CID. He says they found Major Adkins's body in his car early this morning. He'd been shot to death."

The news stunned Stephanie. She set the coffee pot full of water on her desk and turned toward Rendell. "Shot to death?" she asked, confused, as she glanced at Weathers, then at Rendell. "Major Adkins?... Here? In the parking lot?" she stumbled. "But he's in Atlanta... What was he doing here?"

"You know, you're right, Steph," Weathers also sounded confused as he turned back toward Rendell. "I forgot all about that. Major Adkins left two days ago for an IBM training course in Atlanta. He was there yesterday morning. I talked to him about it on the phone."

"I spoke with him yesterday myself," Steph agreed, "I know that's where he was."

"Well," Rendell shrugged and opened his notebook. "At 0430 this morning, a patrol car from the private security service that covers these buildings was on a routine patrol through the parking lots. They had noticed the car there on a previous swing through, and they say it's very unusual for cars to park there overnight. They got out, checked, and found him lying inside, dead, with three bullet holes in his chest. Probably 9-millimeter, maybe a .357 or .45, but they won't know for a while."

"0430?" Weathers asked. "What was he doing here at that hour?"

"That wasn't when he was shot. They think that happened earlier, maybe at 6 or 7 pm," Rendell replied. "We'll build a better timeline when I get the forensics reports later this morning." As he spoke, his eyes moved back and forth from Weathers to Stephanie Goss, watching their reactions. She was in wide-eyed, open-mouthed shock, but the Lieutenant Colonel didn't show much of a reaction at all. His eyes seemed to be going back and forth between the MP sergeants in his office and Adkins's, and the one going through Stephanie's desk. They both looked at Rendell and shook their heads no. Two dry holes there, Stephanie thought.

"What can you tell me about the Major's personal life?" Rendell asked. "Any problems or arguments, maybe some family issues that you're aware of?"

"Sorry, but I make it a point to never get personally involved with my subordinates' private lives," Weathers quickly answered. "Major Adkins was assigned here before I arrived and he did okay work for me, but I knew very little about the man outside the office."

Stephanie bit her tongue and tried not to react as Rendell turned and appeared to study her, waiting for her comment.

"Major Adkins was very easy to work with," she said. "Like the Colonel, I'm not aware of any problems he had outside the office."

Rendell looked around. "I think we're about done here, but what about his family?"

"Well, I know he's from Detroit," Stephanie answered. "And he's single."

"Any romantic interests?" Rendell asked, looking straight at her.

"I wouldn't know. He was a nice guy, but our relationship was strictly professional."

"Why are you asking questions like that, Mr. Rendell? I assumed it was a robbery," Weathers asked, sounding concerned. "From the newspapers, and, frankly, from talk I hear with other tenants in the building, I know it's always a big problem out here."

"Possibly. His wallet was missing, and it took us a few minutes to ID him through the car registration and the DMV photo on file in Richmond," Rendell answered.

"Well, there you go; his wallet was missing," Weathers quickly concluded.

"Maybe, and it's always a problem anywhere near DC, but there are easier places to rob people than one of these parking lots near the Pentagon full of DoD employees. When it happens, the 'vic' usually ends up with a beating, not three rounds in the chest 'up close and personal,' as they say. We already have your fingerprints and DNA on file, but Sergeant Pescotti here needs to take a swab of your hands."

"Gunpowder residue?" Weathers bristled, realizing this investigation was going a lot further and faster than he expected. "You're joking. You don't think..."

"Colonel, I never think. I just follow routine and see where the breadcrumbs take me. By the way, where are your personal weapons? Beretta M-9s, I assume? We need to run ballistics on them and rule them out."

"Mine's in the arms room over at Fort McNair," Stephanie said. "It's been there a couple of months, since the last time I had to qualify."

"Mine's here, in the office safe," Weathers said. "I am a Finance Corps officer. Occasionally, we get tasked to provide escort duty when there's a lot of cash transfers or disbursements involved. I'll get it for you."

"What about Major Adkins's? Is his here too?"

"He keeps it in the safe with yours, doesn't he, Colonel?" Stephanie suggested.

"He used to," Weathers quickly replied. "He took it out some time ago when he went to the range, maybe around the first of the year, but I don't recall exactly. I haven't seen it since, so I guess he never brought it back. He probably left it over at McNair too. But I'll go get mine." Weathers walked back into his office, opened the credenza, punched in the keycode, and opened his safe. As he did, he saw that the lowest drawer in his desk had been left slightly open by the MP sergeant when he searched the desk. Good, he thought. Now they'll have to testify there was nothing here in the office, not a goddamned thing!

Rendell put on a rubber glove and nudged Weathers aside before he pulled the M-9 out of the safe. His sergeant opened a plastic zip lock evidence bag, dropped the pistol inside, and tagged it. "We'll have it back to you in a day or two," he told Weathers.

"No rush, it's not part of my daily job description, thank God," Weathers laughed.

"True, but tell me more about Adkins in his job. I understand you supervise Army contracts. What was he working on? Did he have any problems with other people lately, like vendors or contractors, or any other DoD agencies or people?"

Weathers paused. "Well, the contracts we process are from multi-year bid proposals, usually for supply and distribution software for PX, commissary, and quartermaster applications, things like that. The Quartermaster Corps user groups prepare their specs, and then we supervise the bidding process. PX inventory software is not exactly rocket science. Normally, it's fairly boring work."

"Have you had any lately that weren't boring, Colonel?"

"Well, now that you mention it, we decided to not renew a contract last week with a company called Toler TeleCom. They're located in

Chicago. It was a fairly large contract and Adkins was the project officer. Their owner came in yesterday, first thing. He used to be in the Delta Force, as I understand, and he wasn't very happy with us. Seemed like a loose cannon to me, but you know how those Special Ops guys can get. Maybe one too many trips 'down range.' "

"What's his name?" Rendell asked, suddenly interested.

"Burke. He's a retired Army major. He lives down in Fayetteville near Fort Bragg."

"Did he threaten Major Adkins?"

"Not in so many words, but he didn't take it very well. Burke was pissed about losing the contract, which I can understand. I tried to commiserate with the guy, but I almost had to call Security to get him out of the office."

Stephanie wanted to say something, but she knew it wouldn't be a good idea to contradict Weathers in front of the CID investigator.

"And you say this Burke is from Fort Bragg?"

"Retired," Stephanie finally interjected. "And the Colonel's right. He was Delta, 75th Ranger Regiment and 82nd Airborne."

"Delta? That's interesting," Rendell turned and stared at her for a moment, then looked back at Weathers. "And he lives down at Bragg? The Major's older brother works down there too, Colonel Jefferson Adkins. Did you know that? He's the JSOC IG. Ever meet him?"

"Uh, no, I was unaware he even had a brother. The IG you say?" Weathers said, trying not to sound concerned. "As I said, I try not to get involved in my staff's personal lives. Isn't that right, Steph?" She nodded in agreement but said nothing.

"Colonel Adkins flew up here early this morning, before dawn," Rendell continued. "He was out in the parking lot talking to me and my investigators for a while, but he left and flew back south an hour ago. As you can understand, he's pretty upset."

"I can imagine."

"Oh, and I need to see your cell phones, both of you," he said as he held out his hand. "That's where you always find the good stuff, you know." The request caught Stephanie off balance, but she reached in her hip pocket and handed hers to Rendell. He immediately flipped it open and used his index finger to flip through her recent calls. She was tempted to ask whether he had any legal right to do that, but decided that might not be a good idea, since she had nothing to hide.

"Oh, don't worry, SFC Goss, I'm not interested in your personal business. We found Major Adkins's phone. It was in the car. I'm just verifying connections and timelines, but it looks like you two only talked on the office phone," he said as he tossed it back to her.

"As I said, Mr. Rendell, my relationship with the Major was purely professional."

"And your phone, Colonel?" he asked, holding out his hand. Weathers was less than happy but pulled his out and handed it over.

Rendell flipped through his "Recents" as well and then looked up at him, curious. "You don't use this thing much do you, Colonel? In the past week, the only numbers you called were your home and in Area 917? Where's that?"

"I don't see how that's germane to your investigation, Mr. Rendell..." Weathers bristled until he thought better of it. "Those phone calls are to one of our contractors regarding some terms and conditions." Rendell continued to stare at him, waiting for a better answer. Weathers finally said, "But to answer your question, I think they are in the New York area."

"There's a bunch of area codes up there, Colonel: 212, 332, 718, but I'm not familiar with 917. Where's that?"

"Brooklyn, it's in Brooklyn," Stephanie answered Rendell's question, and then folded her arms across her chest and glared at Weathers.

"Brooklyn, yes, Brooklyn," Weathers quickly agreed. "I think that's correct."

"My people also checked your office phone logs," Rendell went on. "Most of the calls were local, but I noticed Major Adkins called in several times yesterday. Those calls were answered on your extension, Sergeant Goss. I thought you said his class was starting. What did he want?"

"I don't know. The Major asked to talk to the Colonel, but he was busy, so the Major hung up."

"I see he also called in on your direct line, Colonel, but it went to voice mail. What did he want?" Weathers just stood there without answering, so Rendell waited, finally adding, "This is a murder investigation, Colonel... I can get the recording."

"We were having a professional 'disagreement' about a contract, as sometimes happens. I don't want yes-men working for me. It was a project the Major had spent a lot of time on, as did I, but I think healthy dialogue, even an occasional vigorous disagreement, is an excellent way to vet them. So, they aren't at all unusual in my office, and I didn't want you to get the wrong idea."

"Thanks for clarifying that, Colonel. The last thing you want is for me to get the wrong idea," Rendell replied with a thin smile before he turned to Stephanie Goss. "But this call from area code 910 the day before? That's Fort Bragg, isn't it?"

"In the afternoon? Yes, I think that was when Major Burke called..."

"*MISTER* Burke," Weathers was quick to correct her. "I wouldn't want Agent Rendell to get the wrong idea. Burke is a retired officer now, a civilian, just like every other bidder."

"He wanted to talk to the Colonel," Stephanie continued. "I told him the Colonel was out, so *MAJOR* Burke told me he would be here in the office first thing yesterday, which he was. That was all that was in the call."

"Good," Rendell said as he wrote some things in his notebook and then looked at his watch. "I'm afraid we've got to go. We have people canvassing all the buildings in the area, and I need to get back to that. When I have a chance, Colonel, I'll send your M-9 back to you, probably tomorrow. Meanwhile, if either of you think of anything else, please let me know."

As Rendell and his men left, Stephanie turned to Weathers. "Pardon me, Colonel, but I've got to visit the restroom," she said as she grabbed her purse and followed Rendell out the door before Weathers could object. She really didn't need to visit the restroom, but the last place she wanted to be for a while was in a closed office with Weathers. There was something about the way he answered Rendell's questions, particularly the parts about Bob Burke, Charles Adkins, and that Brooklyn contract that had her on edge with a chorus of alarm bells going off in the back of her head. She had no proof, none whatsoever, but she no longer trusted the man; not that there was a damned thing she could do about it at that moment.

Sitting in a stall in the woman's restroom down the hall with the outer door locked behind her, Stephanie pulled out her iPhone and pressed on a number in her Contacts. It didn't take long for the man to answer.

CHAPTER EIGHTEEN

Sherwood Forest

Three hundred miles away, Bob Burke's cell phone rang. He pulled it out of his pants pocket and looked at the screen. To him, that was always the best "call blocker" to eliminate the spam. If he didn't recognize the name or number, he didn't answer. Anybody else could leave a message. However, when he saw the name, "Steph" pop up on the screen, he knew it wasn't spam. Something was up.

"Sergeant First Class Stephanie Goss? How may I help you today?" he asked with a smile in his voice.

He heard no salutation or pleasantries in return. "Charles Adkins is dead," she blurted out. "Somebody shot him to death in our parking lot last night. The CID is all over the place. They even went through our office a little while ago, all the files and everything, an investigator named Rendell."

"What? Charles?" Bob found himself speechless. He had spent a lifetime dealing with the sudden deaths of too many friends and comrades, but that was then, and this is now. Those men were soldiers, battlefield casualties in one godforsaken rat hole or another where an unappreciative country sent them. They weren't unarmed staff officers, desk warriors and bean counters, shot to death in an office parking lot in Arlington, Virginia. It took him a long moment to gather his wits as Stephanie told him more about Rendell's visit. "The CID? What did he say?"

"For one thing, he didn't think it was a robbery. Naturally, that sleaze ball Weathers pointed him in your direction."

"Me?"

"I shouldn't be telling you this since I hardly know you, but I read your file. The way things are going, you're probably the only person involved with this whole thing that I trust. I don't trust that CID Investigator, and I sure as hell don't trust Weathers."

"That makes two of us, Steph, and I appreciate the vote of confidence. Were you able to find out anything more about that company in Brooklyn, Matryoshka Software Alliance?"

"No, whatever Weathers is working on, he's probably got it locked up in his safe, and he was very coy when Rendell asked him about the phone calls he'd been making to that 917 area code."

"Weathers has a safe?"

"Yeah, it is in the credenza in his office. We have plenty of secure file cabinets in the outer office, but I suspect he keeps the stuff he doesn't want me to see in that safe."

"Interesting," Bob told her. "Look, let's stay in touch, Steph. I'm not done with this, or with him. If anything comes up, if you need my help or just someone to talk to, you've got my number."

"Roger that, Major. We Rangers need to stick together."

Half an hour later, Bob's cell phone rang again. It was from the guard in the "Overwatch" office at Sherwood Forest who manned the high-tech cameras around the property and the monitors on the alarm console. It was in Overwatch, the modern security office in the hidden basement of a ramshackle farm building out back. With some help from old friends at Fort Bragg, plus a few others from the "dark side" of the CIA out at Langley, he had installed embassy-level security around the perimeter of Sherwood Forest, with cameras and state-of-the-art motion detectors at the gates and entrances. After the recent "dustup" with "the Professor" and his ISIS pals, he added still more, extending through sensors and cameras through the woods near the outside fencing, out on the highway, and on all the doors and windows of the buildings. As usual, Don Vito put it best, "Women and children can be careless. But not men."

"Major, this is Tim," the guard in Overwatch told him. "I have three vehicles coming in the front drive. The back two are MP patrol cars. The front one looks like one of their unmarked sedans."

Bob pressed an app icon on the phone and immediately got the video feed from the front cameras. "Yep, that looks like the MPs, all right. Call Ace and ask him to meet me at the front door. Thanks."

CHAPTER NINETEEN

Sherwood Forest

Bob walked through the house to the front vestibule and opened the solid-oak front door just as Sharmayne Phillips reached for the doorbell. She was a young, talented, African American Special Agent with the CID, the Criminal Investigation Division of the Army's 10th Military Police Battalion at Fort Bragg, and now one of their top murder and terrorism specialists. Bob worked with her when the bombs began going off over there last year. Too many years in Special Ops had taught him not to get close with the MPs, and too many years in law enforcement had taught her not to get close to out-of-control Special Ops guys either. It took a while, but they soon earned each other's trust. She was instrumental in helping to solve Major General Arnold Stansky's murder. He was Bob's mentor and good friend, and they invited her to become a female member of the Merry Men of Sherwood Forest.

"Sharmayne! Great to see you," Bob said as he noted the two MP sergeants flanking her and two more standing back by the cars. They were all wearing sidearms.

"You too, Major Burke, but I'm afraid this is an 'official' visit."

"Yeah, I see you brought friends, but please come in, all of you," he said with a sweeping bow and led her into the front sitting room of the old house, with Sharmayne in the lead and her two MPs following closely behind. He motioned to some chairs, but they declined, preferring to stand deadpan with their best "serious cop" expressions.

She opened her notebook and using her "official" voice, due no doubt to the audience she brought, said, "I'm here at the request of the CID investigators up in DC. Did you know a Major Charles Adkins?"

"Sure, he was the DoD contracting officer for our software work for the Pentagon. I worked closely with him for the past couple of years. Unfortunately, I had a call from his office this morning. They told me he'd been found shot to death in his car outside his office, but I think you know that. Do they know what happened? Know who did it?"

"No, not that I'm aware, but the Army doesn't like one of their officers being murdered. The CID staff up there is scrambling, interviewing everyone he was in contact with. I understand you were up there yesterday?" she asked as Ace Randall stepped into the room behind Burke, arms folded across his chest, listening, amused at the farce.

"Yes, I went up to DC to see his boss, Colonel Weathers." Burke tried to play it straight, for her benefit. "Major Adkins wasn't there. He and I had spoken several times on the phone, but as far as I know he was in a class down in Atlanta all week."

"What kind of relationship did you have with him?"

"Excellent. He was a great guy to work with. No problems at all."

"I understand they were not renewing your contract."

"Apparently not, but that was his boss, not Charles. In fact, Charles was surprised when he heard it wasn't being renewed. He told me he didn't agree with what Weathers was doing. So, if you're looking for some friction, that's where it is."

"And where were you last night?"

"Ace and I drove up to DC the night before so I could be in Weathers's office when it opened. The meeting didn't last long. He wouldn't talk to me and ordered me out of his office. So Ace and I drove back, getting here about noon yesterday. I stayed on property with family and friends the rest of the day."

"What about weapons? My assumption is you have quite a few rifles and pistols on the property here. Do you have any 9-millimeter handguns?"

"Sure. We have our own indoor target range and do a lot of shooting."

"Would you mind if we took them and ran some ballistics checks on them?"

"Of course I'd mind. If you want to come back with a search warrant, I'll be happy to give you access. Not that I don't trust you, Sharmayne, but I'm not keen on turning that kind of information loose in government channels where it can ping-pong around and end up in places I don't trust at all. I'm sure you understand."

"I do understand, Major Burke. But as you know, I had to ask," she said as she turned and began walking back toward the front door. "By the way, I'm sure you know that Major Charles Adkins was the younger brother of Colonel Jefferson Adkins, whom we both know you have had some... difficulties with from time to time. Did any of that affect your relationship with Major Adkins?"

"Not at all," Bob answered as he opened the front door. "I often joked to him they seemed to be 'brothers from another mother,' and he agreed."

The entourage walked back to the front vestibule. When Bob opened the door for Sharmayne to leave, they saw the very large figure of

Colonel Jefferson Adkins standing outside on the front stoop, his finger extended and about to ring the front doorbell. He was wearing his dress service uniform. Bob was accustomed to seeing him impeccably groomed; but this morning, the Colonel's uniform was badly wrinkled, his jacket unbuttoned and his tie down, unshaven, hunched over, with tired, dark circles under his red eyes. This was not the usual Jefferson Adkins.

Stunned to find him standing outside the front door, both Bob and Sharmayne began to say something at the same time, but it was Adkins who spoke first. "Mind if I come in?" he asked in a voice completely lacking the old, booming bravado.

"Please do, Colonel," Bob said and stepped aside. Sharmayne turned to her MP escort, told them they could return to post. She then followed Bob and Jefferson Adkins into the sitting room. Ace also vanished, leaving the three of them alone, and they all sat down.

"My, my, don't we make one hell of a threesome," Adkins said sadly.

"Jefferson, I can't tell you how terribly sorry I am about Charles," Bob said. "As I told you before, he was a great guy and a lot of fun to work with. And to set the record perfectly straight, you know I had absolutely nothing to do with that."

"Oh, I know that, Burke," Jefferson exhaled painfully, as if the weight of the world had crashed down on his broad shoulders. "You and I have had our tussles over the past couple of years – some really flaming tussles – we're both to blame for them... no, it was mostly me. I know it, and so did Charles. But remember, I have two false-teeth implants and some crooked nose cartilage to prove it. But this is different, way different."

Bob looked at him and nodded. It was hard to disagree and harder not to regret the four years of bad blood between them at a time like this.

"Hell," Jefferson continued. "I even had a few 'misunderstandings' with you, Agent Phillips." She tried to speak, but he waved her aside. "Oh, I knew you were part of his little gang out here ever since that business on post last year. It was all my fault there, too. I was drinking a lot back then, and maybe I was jealous about not being part of it, part of what ya'll were doing. But I had a lot of time to think on my little helicopter rides back and forth to DC last night, and I remembered all the things Charles kept trying to tell me. He said I'd been an ass about all of that. He said I needed to mend some fences instead of continuing our little feud, and I know he was right. I'll take the heat for all that."

"He was right, Jefferson, but we're both to blame," Bob told him.

"I flew back from DC a little while ago. Worst night of my life. I think I spent half of it bouncing around in a helicopter. Hate those things. I drove straight over because I had to."

"Can I get you a drink, Jefferson?" Burke asked.

"God, no, if I start doing that, I won't stop. What you can give me, though, is some straight answers, Burke. I talked to the MPs and that damn CID investigator from the Pentagon for an hour or two. I blistered his ass. All they had were questions with no answers, and most of the questions seemed to center around you. In fact, I'll bet that's why Sharmayne is here, ain't it, girl? 'Cause Rendell told you to come down here and grill Burke."

"Colonel, you know I'm not at liberty..." she began to say.

"Yeah, I know that, too," Adkins said as he leaned forward and let his bloodshot eyes bore into Bob Burke. "But what I mostly know is that Charlie's main job these days was that contract with your company. Besides playing football down there at Indiana, I took a class or two, and not just blocking and tackling, I liked philosophy and logic. Bet you didn't know that. Well, there was this one old professor who taught me about a thing called Occam's Razor. You know what that is, Miz Phillips? It says the simplest answer is usually the right one. The two simple answers I keep comin' up with is that Charlie's death had something to do with Burke's contract; and second, what happened to him in that parking lot was no mugging or stickup. I grew up on the 'mean streets' of Dee-troit, Michigan. Saw a lot of hits, and I know one when I see one. You didn't kill him, Burke, but I think you know who did or at least why it happened. I think CID figured that out too, which is why they're all over your skinny white ass, aren't they?"

Burke stared at Adkins for a moment and finally asked, "What do you want, Jefferson? Answers? The 'truth'? If there is such a thing? Justice for your brother? Or revenge? I want those things too, but I don't want you running off like a bull in a china shop out to kill someone. Nothing good's going to come from that, so what do you want?"

Adkins stared right back and answered, "I want in. I've come to know you a lot better than I did before. I read your 201 File, and I've talked to a lot of people since then. You're like a junkyard dog, Burke. When you get your back up and sink your teeth into something, you don't let go, like when they blew up General Stansky's car that night. When somebody does wrong to you or one of yours, you go after them and you don't quit."

"You think I'm going to go after whoever killed Charles?"

"There's no doubt in my 'military mind' that that's exactly what you're going to do, Major. This whole thing is about you and your DoD contract. Charlie tried to do the right thing and get that termination stopped. That's why he got himself killed. And you and I both know you aren't gonna let that sit. Neither am I. So I want in."

Bob looked at him for a long moment. "I offered you a truce a few days ago, but even that is a long way from us actually working together. Are you sure you can do that? Work with me on my terms? As we both know, my friends and I don't always follow the rules."

"Major, I played big time football. I know how to not follow the rules and not get caught better than you do."

"All right, but there's two other things I'm going to insist on: first, you've got to follow orders, my orders; and second, you forget everything and everyone you see here."

"You have my word on it, Major. I want to be part of it. I'll behave," Adkins said as he stuck out his hand and the two men shook on it, with Jefferson's huge paw engulfing Bob's.

"Sounds good," Bob smiled. "At your size, I'd much rather have you working with me than against me. So, let's go upstairs and I'll show you around. Time to see how the research is going, and I'm waiting for a conference call you should find interesting."

They walked up the broad central staircase to the third floor and through the swinging doors to "The Geekdom," where Ace joined them. Jefferson Adkins may have seen a lot of things in his career, but not a scene like this. At Linda's insistence, the Geeks wore large, over-the-ear, noise-canceling acoustical headsets that covered the sides of their heads. It was a perfect solution. They could each listen to whatever booming hard rock music they liked and not bother anyone else or each other, but it left an eerie silence in the room. Their equipment softly hummed away in the background. Lights blinked, photos and documents flashed silently back and forth across their monitor screens, as the three Geeks clicked away on their keyboards, unaware they had company. They played drum solos with pencils on the edge of their desks and bashed a rainbow-colored beach ball back and forth off the walls and ceilings like high school kids during lunch hour. But you had to listen very hard to hear faint traces of the loud, hard-rock music creeping around the edges of their earphones.

There was a small, red toggle switch on the wall next to the door, which cut off the sound from the music system feeds to their earphones. Linda had it installed when she tired of trying to get their attention over the booming base of Greta Van Fleet, The 69 Eyes, The Dead Daisies, and even the venerable AC/ DC and Led Zeppelin they gravitated to. Bob flipped the switch and the Geeks immediately looked up from their work in unison, turned their heads toward the door, expecting to see Linda standing there, and raised at least one headphone off their ears. She would usually toss them Gummy Bears when they did, like trained seals, but Bob wasn't into operant conditioning or positive reinforcement like she was. Instead, they knew he would "pound on their pointy little heads" if they didn't pay attention, but the result was the same.

"Gang, this is Colonel Adkins and Agent Sharmayne Phillips, who I think you already know."

"What? We getting drafted or arrested?" Sasha asked from the other side of the console. "I already drafted once. Russian Army, not American, but not work for me."

"Your getting arrested didn't help much either," Ronald quipped.

"Hey guys," Bob said. "I have a conference call coming in five minutes from now that I want you to listen in on. The people on the other end may ask you some questions, so jump in if you have anything to offer."

Bob walked Sharmayne and Jefferson around the room to show off the equipment and technical resources. "The conference call was arranged by Ernie Travers, a Chicago Police captain who is Vice Chief of their Organized Crime Task Force with CPD at 35th and South Michigan Avenue. I've worked with Ernie for years. Through him, we'll be tied in with Phil Henderson, the FBI resident agent who has just taken over the FBI office in Trenton, New Jersey. The others are Lieutenant Carmine Bonafacio with the New Jersey State Police Organized Crime Task Force, and Harry Van Zandt, a detective here with the Fayetteville PD. Along with Sharmayne and the Army CID , they are my 'law enforcement' brain trust."

"Got any idea who's behind it?" Adkins asked.

"Oh, that's the simple part, Jefferson. It's the Russian Mafia in Brighton Beach, Brooklyn. They thought they'd muscle in on some federal contracts by blackmailing your brother's boss over his wife's gambling debts. Charles found out, and they killed him. Those are the facts. Now, all we have to do is prove it, figure out a way to stop them, and make sure they never come back again."

"And kick some ass while we're at it?"

"Oh, we'll kick some very serious ass before we're done, or else we wouldn't bother doing it," Bob laughed as his cell phone rang. He looked at the dial, saw the name, and put it on speaker.

"Ernie! Has spring hit the Windy City yet?"

"Ghost! My office is way down in the basement, and they never let me out, so I wouldn't know. But I'm glad you called. Things have been getting way too boring lately, and I needed something to get the juices flowing again. How you been? The wife and kids?"

"Just fine, Ernie. We are having one of our blowout barbecues this Saturday night, we'd love to have you and your wife pop down."

"Actually, that's not a bad idea. We have a new city administration that we're still trying to educate, and I need a freakin' brain break. I have your conference call all lined up, and the others should come online any second now.

"This is Harry Van Zandt from next door in Fayetteville."

"Carmine here from Trenton…"

"And Phil Henderson. Bob, Carm and I are in his office in Trenton. The walls have too many ears over in the Federal Building, but Ernie said you're having problems with the Brighton Beach crowd over in Brooklyn? The Italians weren't enough? Now you went and pissed off the Russians. What the hell have you gotten yourself into this time?"

"Nothing that I started, Phil. It has to do with my software firm in Chicago, Toler TeleCom. There's a company called Matryoshka Software Partners in Brighton Beach that's trying to muscle its way into federal contracting."

"That sounds awfully tame for the Russians," Carmine added. "Most of those guys can't even spell software. They're into strong-arming and breaking things."

"Bob," Ernie jumped in. "With the FBI's long history against the Mafia, particularly in New York, Phil's probably the best judge of what the Russians might be up to."

"I hope somebody is, because they didn't teach us much about them here at Bragg."

"You put some dents in the DiGrigorias in Chicago and the Genoveses in Atlantic City," Phil Henderson answered, "but the Italians are organized top down, with a distinct hierarchy, like the Army. That's not how Russians do it. They really are a 'mob,' a bunch of lowlife crooks in search of a strongman, maybe a loose association of separate little street gangs, if you will; and they aren't the brightest bulbs in the pack. It's survival of the fittest, and they aren't very innovative. They're leg breakers and will always opt for a quick, violent smash-and-grab robbery over taking the time and effort to plan a clever burglary. They prefer protection, murder for hire, arson, loansharking, extortion, hijacking trucks, stealing cargo from the docks and the airports, narcotics, smuggling, prostitution, credit card fraud, identity theft, and gunrunning. And that's just the short list.

"Yeah," Carmine agreed, "one group or boss will get on top and pound down the others for a while, until he ends up in an oil drum out in the Bay. Back in Russia in the long ago old days, they were folk heroes and pretended to be Robin Hoods, robbing from the rich. As time passed, robbing from everyone became easier. And now, they're just vicious thugs and leg breakers."

"Vicious is an understatement," Phil said. "When somebody gets in their way, like a competitor, a journalist, or a cop, they kill him and his family. Over in New York, in Brooklyn, they think they have to be more ruthless than the Colombians or Jamaicans."

"Even the Italians hire them for their 'wet' work now," Carmine laughed.

"Who's in charge, the head guy?" Bob asked.

"Two brothers, Piotr and Evgeni Shurepkin, thirty-ish," Phil told him. "They're the sons of Oleg Shurepkin, a well-known Moscow mob boss. As best we can tell, they took over maybe a year ago. At least that's the last time the previous guy was seen around."

"My guess would be a 55-gallon oil drum at the bottom of Long Island Sound," Carmine agreed.

"Piotr is in charge. He's a typical young smartass, a nasty piece of work. We don't have much of a handle on his little brother, Evgeni. He's maybe eighteen and seems to be 'challenged,' as they now call it, probably autistic, but they say he is something of a savant when it comes to computers and numbers. And they brought a half-dozen muscle guys with them."

"Two less than they had before," Ace quipped.

"They'll remember that. They may not know who you are, not yet anyway. But don't judge them all by the two clowns you put down. Piotr's main muscle is a guy named Pavel Bratsov, another weightlifter on way too many steroids, but smart and particularly vicious. He'll be easy to spot because he's always the one closest to Piotr."

"You aren't thinking of taking them on, are you?" Ernie asked.

"No," Bob answered. "They already took us on."

"Road trip?" Ace asked.

"Road trip," Bob quickly agreed.

"Look, if you're going up there rooting around in their mushroom patch, don't mention my name," Phil Henderson warned.

"Or mine," Carmine quickly agreed. "There's a whole alphabet soup of federal agencies over in Brooklyn who are already watching those guys with phone taps, cameras, the works, so be careful."

"Us?" Bob laughed. "Carmine, haven't you heard? We're the Fayetteville Kiwanis Club on a sightseeing tour of the Big Apple."

"You want, I'll send you over some hats," Harry Van Zandt laughed.

After the other guys got off the call, Jefferson Adkins turned to Bob and Ace and said, "That's an all-day drive up to Brooklyn, maybe eight or ten hours each way. How about I call over the flight section at Pope Field at Bragg. There's always an Apache helicopter pilot who needs some flight hours. We could fly up to Fort Hamilton at the foot of the Verrazano Bridge, borrow an unmarked sedan, and drive down to Brighton Beach. It's maybe four miles down there. What do you think?"

"I knew those eagles on your shoulder would come in handy," Bob said.

"And no TSA, no scanners, and no pat downs," Ace agreed.

"You in too, Sharmayne?" Adkins asked her.

"No, you can make it a boys' day out. I've got reports due out but keep me posted."

"So we're going up there in-cog-ni-to, aren't we?" Ace asked.

CHAPTER TWENTY

Brighton Beach, Brooklyn

None of them had ever been to Brighton Beach, much less anywhere near that part of Brooklyn, except for Jefferson Adkins, who was briefly stationed at Fort Hamilton a few miles east at the foot of the Verrazano Bridge. When they arrived, Jefferson had an unmarked civilian sedan waiting for them. Bob took the wheel and drove east on the Shore Parkway, turned south on Cropsey Avenue to Coney Island, and then east again to Brighton Beach Boulevard. When they reached the main business strip it became a six-lane-wide cave, with an unbroken line of two-story, brick-façade shops and restaurants down each side that dated from the 1920s. Many had second-floor apartments above the shops. Down at street level, the solid line of stores displayed signs in English, Russian and Hebrew in their windows. That wasn't surprising, since fewer than a quarter of the people in the neighborhood were born in the US, and a third didn't even speak English.

Overhead ran an elevated trunk line of the old BMT, the Brooklyn Manhattan Transit, now part of the New York City Subway system. Its multiple tracks and station covered the street below, putting the sidewalks and stores in deep shadow. Whatever each of them had pictured, this was a world none of them was familiar with. Jefferson Adkins grew up in the inner city of Detroit. Maybe he understood the urban immigrant culture better than the rest of them. Bob, however, grew up on Army bases in the south, and Ace Randall was a farm boy from Iowa.

The address Stephanie Goss gave him off the envelope in Weathers's trash can turned out to be Matryoshka Software Alliance, 415 Brighton Beach Boulevard, which was a colorful Russian tearoom, Kalinka's, decorated with rooftop cupolas like Saint Basil's Cathedral in Moscow, as Sasha said. The plan they put together back in North Carolina was to use stealth and guile. Drive by the building and circle the block, get familiar with the target, park a few blocks away, and approach on foot. But this was a much busier place than Bob imagined. He saw pizza parlors, Chinese restaurants, a pharmacy, candy store, McDonalds, shoe stores, a pet store, Sprint phones, Turkish Kabobs, Allstate Insurance, a camera shop, and a Foodland grocery store; and that was merely the stores on the same block.

Traffic was heavy on the congested boulevard, with two lanes trying to move in each direction, plus a parking lane and a lot of delivery trucks, tailgating, and lane changing. Bob drove slowly past #415, which was on the opposite side of the street, continued two blocks further on, and turned around amidst honking cars, shouts, and irritated gestures from other drivers. Driving back on Kalinka's side of the street, he paid closer attention to the building and parked a few doors further down. The plan had been to park the dark-gray Army sedan at least two blocks away and return on foot for a stealthy infiltration until he saw the only parking space within three blocks open up and grabbed it. With all the chaotic activity going on around them, no one would pay any attention if they rode up on a pink elephant.

It was 2 p.m as they approached Kalinka's with Bob in front, the towering figure of Jefferson Adkins behind him, and Ace Randall still further back. They were wearing blue jeans, colorful Reeboks, windbreakers, and the Fayetteville Kiwanis club baseball hats that Harry Van Zandt sent over. They might have been a joke, but they allowed them to spread out and were perfect to spot the others. The lunch crowds on the Boulevard had long since thinned out, but a large goon stood in the restaurant doorway wearing dark sunglasses, a cheap suit, a white shirt unbuttoned halfway down his chest, arms folded across his chest, and gold chains around his neck, blocking the way.

Bob stepped in front of the guy and motioned toward the doors.

"Closed," the goon said with a heavy Russian accent.

"You're kidding," Bob shook his head sadly. "And we came all this way from Rocky Mount just to get some of Kalinka's Chicken Kiev."

"Closed!" the guy repeated without cracking a smile, leaning forward to tower over Bob and make his point.

That was when Jefferson Adkins stepped forward, grabbed the Russian by the crotch with one huge hand, his shirt front by the other, and lifted him off the ground. The guy was big, but Jefferson was much bigger and far more powerful, especially with that look in his eye and his patented nose-to-nose scowl. The Russian's eyes went as wide as pie plates as Jefferson carried him backward through the doors into the restaurant and deposited him in a chair where he slumped over, moaning.

"I like him!" Ace told Bob as he pointed toward Jefferson and took a chair just inside the door next to the goon. "Usually I get stuck taking out the trash. It's nice to have help."

There were still a few patrons scattered about at the tables finishing their lunches, but the main action was in the back-left corner of the room.

A cluster of three men stood around a large corner booth with their backs to the door. It seemed to be the focus of everyone's attention, so Bob began walking in that direction.

When he was halfway there, a waiter swooped in with a tray and some drinks held aloft on the palm of his hand, repeating what the guy outside had said, "Sorry, we are closed."

"Shurepkin?" Bob asked, pointing toward the crowd.

"Uh, yes... but..." the waiter began to say.

"Good enough," Bob said and pushed on past, walked up to the corner table, slipped in around the end guy, and took a seat at the end corner of the booth. There were two bimbos and one guy sitting in the center. Bob nudged one of the bimbos over with his hip. That brought the conversation to a halt.

The guy sitting in the middle was much smaller than the three men standing in front of the table or the doorman, much closer to Bob Burke's size. "You Piotr Shurepkin?" Bob asked.

Apparently, people barging in and rudely demanding to see their boss must not be an everyday occurrence in this neighborhood, Bob thought. The guys standing in front of the table and the two bimbos didn't quite know what to make of it. Finally, the guy nearest Bob reached out and tried to grab Bob's arm to pull him out of the booth, but Bob was much faster. He grabbed the back of the guy's hand, twisted it around, and brought the guys' face down to table level. "Don't be rude," Bob said, looking him in the eyes before he shoved him aside. That was when Jefferson Adkins stepped in, pushed the other two wannabee heroes aside, and assumed the same pose as the doorman outside.

"Yes, I am Shurepkin. Who the hell are you?" the small man in the middle asked, sounding amused.

Bob pointed at his baseball hat. "We're the visiting delegation from Fayetteville. We heard the Brighton Beach Kiwanis Club met here for lunch. Guess we were misinformed."

The two bimbos began chattering in Russian, confused. "Shut up!" Shurepkin snapped as the two men sized each other up. "Kiwanis?... Yes you are... misinformed."

Burke looked up at Jefferson Adkins. "Can you believe that, Kwame? No meeting today," Burke said and then looked back at Shurepkin. "He's an African prince. He doesn't understand a word I say, but he really wanted to meet his Kiwanis brothers. He likes to break things and eat people, and he isn't going to like this one bit when he finally does understand. But, what the heck, if there's no meeting, I guess we'll have to get right down to business."

Burke reached into his shirt pocket, pulled out the driver's licenses he had taken off the two goons he dismantled in the parking lot in DC, and tossed them on the table in front of Shurepkin. "Here, I think these belong to you."

Shurepkin looked down, saw the photographs on the licenses, and his eyes narrowed. "Your big friend from Africa, the one who eats people, he took down my two men, in DC?" the Russian asked.

"No, actually I did those two all by myself."

Shurepkin stared at Burke again, skeptical. "They said it was big man. Very big."

Burke focused his powerful black eyes on the Russian and said, "They lied."

Shurepkin was on uncertain ground here, and he didn't like it. "All right, what do you want, Mr. Kiwanis Club?"

"You're messing with my business. I want you to stop."

"What is this business of yours?"

"Toler TeleCom. You got that dumbass Lieutenant Colonel Weathers to rig a bid and give you a contract that belongs to me. It won't work. You won't get it."

"We shall see," Shurepkin smiled and pointed to his brother in the far booth along the back wall, who was bent over his laptop. "My brother is genius with the computer."

"I don't care how smart he is, Weathers will be in jail before you'll ever see any contract. So, before any more push comes to any more shove, just go away and we'll call it even."

"Even? No, no, I want half. You give me half of gross, then I go away. Otherwise, I'll send work to software shops in Moscow and put you out of business. Trust me, American Defense Department will be happy with our work. Never know the difference."

"But you will. Go away and you won't end up hurt or in jail, or both."

"Jail? One of your American jails? With tennis and volleyball. Well screw you, Mr. Kiwanis Club. You the one going to get hurt," Shurepkin said as he motioned to the two guys left standing at the far end of the table. They reached inside their jackets as Burke pointed across at Shurepkin's chest.

"Tell them not to do that," Burke said. Shurepkin looked down and saw a small red dot of light on the center of his shirt. They saw it too and stopped. Slowly, Shurepkin looked up. His eyes followed the thin beam of light across the room to the laser rangefinder on the automatic pistol Ace Randall held in his lap. His other arm was around the shoulder of the "doorman," who sat there not knowing what to do.

"Tell these two clowns to put their weapons on the table." Shurepkin looked up at them and they immediately complied. Burke nudged the bimbo sitting next to them. "And tell cutie pie here to pull out whatever you've got – just the weapon – and put it on the table too." Shurepkin muttered something to her in Russian. She reached inside his jacket and pulled out a large, chrome .44-caliber Magnum automatic and added it to the pile.

Burke looked at it and shook his head with a wry smile. "Why is it that every annoying little shit like you has to carry a huge 'gangster cannon' like that? You ever fired it? The recoil alone will take your arm off, and you'll never hit a goddamned thing with it. Trust me. I know."

"You know?" Shurepkin glared angrily at him. "I know you will soon regret this day. I will kill you, Mr. Kiwanis."

"I doubt that, Piotr. Oh, you may try, but if you ever mess with my business or come around me or mine again, you'll be the one doing the regrettin'."

Burke got up from the booth, picked up the .44 Magnum and the other two pistols, and walked away. One of Shurepkin's men stepped in to stop Burke, but Jefferson Adkins caught him flush on the nose with his elbow and all 270 pounds behind it. The guy's knees buckled, he went limp as a wet dishrag, and he was out cold before he hit the floor.

"Stick to beating up young women and old men, Piotr. You're way out of your league this time and these Gold's Gym muscle boys won't do you any good."

Burke walked across the room and out the door with Adkins following him. The last one to leave was Ace Randall, who took the doorman's automatic out of his shoulder holster and gave him a love tap on the temple with its butt.

They were in their car, out in traffic, and headed west on Brighton Beach Boulevard before the Russian goon squad piled out the front door onto the sidewalk, looking around, trying to figure out where they went.

"Well, that should stir things up," Jefferson Adkins laughed.

"That's up to him. Sooner or later, he'll decide my piddly little contract isn't worth the trouble. But if he doesn't, I'd rather take him down on my turf than up here on his."

As Bob drove back to the Apache helicopter parked at Fort Hamilton, he still couldn't understand why Shurepkin was making this move. Toler TeleCom in general, and this Army PX and commissary contract in particular, weren't very much, certainly not enough to warrant a big play from organized crime. Perhaps muscling him aside might let the Russians get their foot in the door for bigger DoD work. That could make it a good play on Piotr Shurepkin's part, but hardly big money. So, why? Sasha said they wouldn't do anything without Putin's approval. What the hell is he up to?

There was a small apartment on the second floor across the street from Kalinka's, above a woman's hair and nail salon. Inside, a group of four men and a young blonde woman were busy operating cameras on tripods with big telephoto lenses, videotape cameras, parabolic microphones, and several digital audio recorders. Fortunately, the room faced north, so they didn't have the direct afternoon sun shining in the windows, but there was no air conditioning up there. The temperature was almost 100° in the room. They had their suit jackets off, but with all the equipment running, the temperature was unbearable. The men were down to shirtsleeves and all had large, growing sweat stains on their shirts, particularly underneath the harnesses of their shoulder holsters.

When the three men in the baseball caps came back out the front door of Kalinka's in what appeared to be a big hurry, all hell broke loose in the apartment. The Agent-in-Charge shouted, "What's going on over there? What was that all about?"

"Who are those guys?" another agent asked.

"Did anybody get their faces?"

"Is the audio working inside?"

"I want to know what they were doing in there! Now!" the AIC demanded.

The guy on the camera with the big telephoto lens said, "That was Viktor Svetkov guarding the front door. He's gotta run 230 to 240. That big black guy picked him up and carried him inside like he was a rag doll. Jesus!"

When the three men came out the door, the agents noticed they were carrying a handful of guns in their arms. They turned south on the boulevard, and walked away at a fast pace, disappearing into the crowd. Several Russian thugs they were well familiar with by now poured out Kalinka's front door, frantically trying to see where the other men went, but the thick, steel support beams, traffic on the Boulevard, and the random pattern of blinding sunshine and dark shadows under the elevated railroad made that impossible.

"With those goddamn baseball hats on, I couldn't get any kind of a shot of their faces," the cameraman said excitedly as he continued to snap off photographs.

"Look down there, I think they got in a car. Anybody see it?" another guy asked.

"No luck," the cameraman replied, camera clicking. "It might've been a dark sedan, but I couldn't get any kind of decent shot of the car or the license plate."

While all the men scrambled around trying to get a side view of the street, the blonde woman sitting in front of the recording devices appeared amused. She put on a set of headphones, rewound the last few minutes of the recorded audio, and played it back, squinting as she tried to understand the words that had been said inside. Finally, she took off the headset. "It was Burke," she calmly told the others.

One of the men groaned, while the other two just looked at each other puzzled. "Who the hell is Burke?" the Agent-in-Charge demanded to know.

"Are you sure, Sylvia?" the other one asked her.

"Will somebody tell me who the hell this Burke is!" the AIC shouted, frustrated.

When they reached Fort Hamilton, they sat for a few minutes in the Flight Section's lounge, waiting for the pilot to get his maps and clearances. That was when Bob's cell phone rang. He looked at the screen and saw it was Sasha. The Russian Bear had never phoned him before, so Bob answered the call.

"Comrade Kandarski, what can I do for you this afternoon?" he asked.

"Not Comrade no more, Boss, but got solution!" Sasha sounded almost giggly.

"Make it quick, we've got a helicopter to catch."

"You got black bag over head?"

"No, does it help?"

"No, Boss, but you know Al Capone…"

"Not really, he's been dead for a few years."

"Oh, I know that, Boss! But you know what got Big Al? What put them in jail?"

"Taxes, the IRS."

"Yeah, sure, but what really got him were details, stupid little details. Bad guys always forget details. Like dumb Russians up in Brooklyn."

"Okay, what did they forget?"

"Silly little things, Boss, like County Business License, one that matches names on proposal and contract, right? In Moscow, who cares? You pay everybody off anyhow, so nobody sweat details. In New York, maybe you pay off people sometimes, but you still gotta have New York City Business Registration, Health Insurance Certificate, Unemployment and Worker's Comp Certificates, State Registration of Corporation, and Federal TIN, right?"

"Yep, same in Illinois or North Carolina."

"Right! All executed and up to date. Lots of papers, right? Way too many to payoff and you always miss somebody. And then there're the Federals, right Boss? First, you gotta get every pain in ass state and city certificates before you file with Feds, right?"

"Right again, Sasha, and you're telling me they got lazy and missed a few?"

"No, Boss, not lazy. They missed them all! Sasha been through all Brooklyn, New York State, and Federal Databases. No Matryoshka Software Alliance, not nowhere, and no DBA at 415 Brighton Beach Boulevard. So, Federal Request for Proposal and weasel Colonel Weathers's contract not valid, Boss. Like Big Al, all those little details bite them on the butt. Maybe your new big friend, Colonel Adkins, can call Pentagon and have them pull their plug."

Bob handed the phone to Jefferson Adkins with a big smile. "It's my Russian Geek, Sasha, wait till you hear this one..."

CHAPTER TWENTY-ONE

Washington, D.C.

It was only 10:00 a.m., and Sergeant First Class Stephanie Goss had already heard all she could stand. Lieutenant Colonel Weathers's cell phone had rung one too many times on the other side of his closed office door. It had been happening almost nonstop since CID Agent Rendell and his three sergeants finally left them alone after their second visit around midmorning. She didn't know what was going on for sure, but Weathers wasn't a stockbroker, a real estate agent, or a bookie, nor did he have a girlfriend. Those being the case, no officer in *her* army, much less a Field Grade one, should keep secrets and conduct official business on his private goddamn cell phone! He should ask Hillary Clinton where that led. Well, at least she hoped the dumb bastard had it plugged in, otherwise he wouldn't have any battery left.

In the past, Weathers invariably used his office landline for his official calls. As far as she knew, he never even turned on his cell phone. Probably too cheap. And when he used the landline, she could tell how long he was talking by how long the white light on her master console remained lit. She also knew how the office phone hub worked and knew where to find the ingoing and outgoing phone log. She doubted he knew she could do that, but maybe he did. Maybe that was why he was using his cell phone now.

Well, whoever he was talking to, the conversations didn't sound very pleasant. Now and then she would even hear him shout and argue. Those were two things Weathers never did. The loud talking was always muffled, but loud anything was most unlike him. Lieutenant Colonel Steven Weathers might be an arrogant, pompous paper pusher, but he had always been quiet, professional, and boring to a fault. She had never heard him raise his voice, even over the phone. The rest of the time, when he wasn't arguing, he must have been trying to keep his voice down, because she couldn't hear anything. She had been running Army offices long enough to know that those were really bad signs. Nothing good ever came from secret phone calls in the Army.

Finally, she had had enough. She was willing to throw the whole thing into the lap of the CID, but after what she had seen and heard over the past three days, it was time to have it out with the Colonel. In fairness, she'd give him a chance to explain. But if that didn't get her anywhere, she was going to "take it up the line," to his superiors, the IG, and maybe even

Agent Rendell over at the CID. Stephanie was seventeen years old when she enlisted in the Army and she was Infantry, Airborne and Ranger trained, now an E-7 with fifteen years in and three tours "downrange" in Iraq and Afghanistan. Her tours weren't spent in a cushy, air-conditioned trailer in the Green Zone. She had earned a Silver Star and a Purple Heart in line units out in the desert and the mountains, and there weren't many women in the Army with her record. In fact, she'd match it with Weathers's any day of the week if it ever came to that, which it wouldn't. She trusted the Army, and she trusted they would clean this up. Besides, this had been her office long before Weathers showed up, and she took pride in running a good ship. It was time he learned that was how it was going to work.

She heard his voice grow loud and angry again on the other side of the door. Enough was enough. She got up from her desk chair, stormed across the room, and headed for his office door. Her hand was on the knob when the door suddenly opened, almost pulling her into the office as Weathers was coming out. They collided in the middle of the doorway and he angrily shoved her aside.

"Get out of my way!" was all he said, red-faced, cell phone still in hand, as he pulled on his coat.

"Colonel Weathers, we need to talk!"

"You'll stay out of this, if you know what's good for you, Sergeant!" he told her as he brushed past, knocking her against the door frame as he headed for the office door.

"This won't do, Colonel!" She tried to follow, but he almost ran out the door and never looked back. Fists clenched, she stood there, feeling her own anger build. Finally, she grabbed her jacket and keys and also headed for the door. There were questions that he needed answer, and she'd be damned if she would let him get away with it before he did. But by the time she got out in the hallway and turned toward the bank of elevators, he was already gone.

Their office was on the fourth floor. She hurried down the hall to the elevator and slapped the down button. There were four elevators, two per side, but three were going up or were stopped on upper floors. The fourth was already on the second floor and headed down. That was probably the one Weathers took. She jabbed the down button with an angry finger and did it again and again, even though she knew it didn't care how many times you did. Futile as she knew that was, at least she felt like she was doing something.

Finally, an elevator arrived, and the door opened. She jumped inside and pressed the first-floor button. When she got there, she rushed out into the lobby; but by then, Weathers was gone. There were tall revolving doors on both sides of the building which led to the front and rear parking lots. First, she ran out the front door, paused, and looked around. Weathers was nowhere to be seen, just an unbroken field of automobile rooftops; so she ran back inside and out the back door, scanning that side of the lot. Finally, she saw him, or at least his head and shoulders, standing with two other men between several cars three or four rows back and to the left. Even from that distance, she could hear them arguing. Clearly, Weathers was having a bad day. Whatever was behind all that, Stephanie Goss decided she would get to the bottom of it.

She had forgotten to change into her black, low-heel pumps and was still wearing the pair of bright-pink Nike cross trainers she wore around the office. They didn't exactly go with her dark green dress uniform, but they were more comfortable and a lot easier on her bad knee. Keeping them in sight, she quickly zigzagged her way from row to aisle to row until she got near where Weathers was standing. The closer she got, the more she could see that the argument was growing serious. One of the two men was big, broad shouldered, and stood at least a head taller than Weathers. The other man was much smaller, but he was right up in Weathers's face, red-faced, shouting, and finger-pointing.

As she got closer still, she heard Weathers shout back at the little man, "It wasn't me! It must have been that bastard Burke, and there's nothing I can do about it now. The IG froze the contract."

As she got parallel to them, two rows over, she saw that Weathers's wife, Erica, was there too; and she couldn't remember the last time she saw Erica over here at the office. Stephanie couldn't get an unobstructed view of her, only the back of her head. The big guy screened the rest of Erica from her view. As Stephanie got closer, she realized that guy was a lot bigger than he first looked back at the building. Fortunately, the two strangers faced away from her, but then she saw the big guy held a fistful of Erica's hair in his left hand. As the argument got even worse, the little guy shoved Weathers back against a car. The big gorilla pulled Erica hard against him by her hair; and, for the first time, Stephanie saw he had a large, gunmetal gray automatic pistol pressed against the side of her head.

Weathers faced in Stephanie's direction, but he was too absorbed in his argument with the little guy to see her approaching. As soon as she got within striking distance behind the big guy, she shouted, "Hey, meatball, let her go!" He turned and tried to look back over his shoulder to see where this sudden threat was coming from. As he did, all he saw was a blonde woman in an American Army uniform with an angry look on her face standing behind him. He was more than twice her size and appeared to dismiss her threat with an angry snort, like a bull in a Spanish bullring. Rather than turn and put Erica between them, he only turned his shoulders, swung the pistol away from the side of her head, and began turning it around toward Stephanie. Big mistake.

Being a woman who spent most of her fifteen-year career serving in male combat units had toughened her up. It forced her to hold her own, to become better than them with weapons and in hand-to-hand combat. Over the years, she had taken every form of self-defense and street fighting the Army offered, picking and choosing the particular disciplines and moves that suited her best. But she was no petite debutante to begin with. She worked out every day and had exceptional muscle tone and strength, but she didn't look it. At 5'10" tall and 140 pounds, the net result was a surprisingly well-honed female fighting machine. That was why the handful of actual fights she had ever gotten into were over before they started.

Over the years, as she grew older and less agile, she adapted her skills to keep up with her own changing reality. She particularly liked Savate, French kickboxing, and Muay Thai, another discipline from Thailand with a unique mix of kicks, knees, elbows, and punches. Both disciplines use fast moves, a lot of kicking, and caused less damage to her hands. As an office manager instead of an infantry squad and platoon sergeant now, that was important. Broken fingers really hurt when you had to bang away on a keyboard the next morning.

As the big gunman turned toward her with his pistol, he twisted his torso and shifted even more of his heavyweight onto his right leg. She waited until he was completely off balance, and then snapped a quick Gastrizein kick which sent 2,000 pounds of force onto his right knee, blowing out all the surrounding tendons. The gunman's eyes went wide, and he went down on the pavement like a sack of potatoes. As he did, it was a simple matter for her to grab the barrel of the automatic pistol in his hand, twist it, and take it away from him almost effortlessly. As he fell down to her level, she gave him a hard elbow to the left temple, and he was out before he hit the ground.

That set of moves did not take much over three or four seconds. The other two men were still arguing, and her little sideshow didn't register with them until Erica began screaming. The big guy still had a handful of her hair and he pulled her down on top of him as he fell the rest of the way. Stephanie ignored her in favor of more pressing matters. The big gunman's pistol she now held in her hand was a large, heavy automatic, a cheap Russian or Czech brand she was fairly sure. Since neither Weathers nor the little guy had a weapon, Stephanie immediately took control of the situation by pulling the slide back and jacking a fresh round into the chamber. The automatic had probably not been cleaned or oiled in a long time and the parts were not well-made to begin with, because they made a very loud "Snick! Snick!" that got their attention. She then raised the pistol and pointed it at them.

"Shut up, both of you!" she ordered in her most commanding drill instructor voice. "Down on the ground! Now!"

Weathers turned his head toward her, and his mouth dropped open. He didn't know what to do. The other man turned and glared angrily at her and muttered something which sounded a lot like Russian. His eyes darted around, and she realized the last thing he intended was to give himself up, especially not to an American woman, gun or not. He was quick, Stephanie had to give him that. He shoved Weathers into her, jumped behind him, and using him as a screen he took off running, bent low, zigzagging between parked cars.

Weathers, on the other hand, was useless. He began screaming at Stephanie, "Kill him, kill him!" As far as she knew, the little man was unarmed. Unless her life or someone else's was in danger, she wasn't about to do that; so she let him go. That was a mistake, she soon realized. The guy must have been carrying a gun after all, because when he got two or three rows away from her, he suddenly rose up, turned, and fired three quick shots in her direction.

Stephanie had qualified Expert with almost all of the individual weapons in the Army inventory. She had always preferred rifles to handguns, especially to a cheap foreign brand pistol which she had never fired before. Nonetheless, a handgun was a handgun, and nothing focuses the mind faster than the sound of bullets whizzing by your head. She turned, extended her arm in a solid offhand firing position, exactly as they taught her in training, and lined up the heavy automatic on the man. He turned and took off running again, so she took a slow deep breath and squeezed off three rounds at him.

Her first shot missed the little weasel, but it blew out the side window of an Audi parked next to him. Close, but no cigar. The second shot, however, clipped him high and outside on the back of his shoulder. She knew he went down because she didn't see him anymore. That was good luck for the Russian. If he hadn't dropped down, the third shot would have taken his head off. And it was good for her, because there were no more gunshots and bullets coming in her direction.

At that point, her attention returned to the three people on the ground at her feet. Erica had completely lost it and screamed uncontrollably. Understandable, because she had been thoroughly terrorized, and that was her release. Weathers was also screaming, but at Erica, to get her to shut up, and at Stephanie, who was not about to obey his orders anymore. The hulking gunman on the ground was now coming out of it too, which was when the pain hit him. He grabbed his knee, moaning, and began rolling back and forth at her feet.

Prioritize, prioritize, Stephanie kept telling herself. The little weasel was now out of sight. She had the automatic pointed at Weathers, which took him off the board. With the situation now stable, she bent down, reached inside the big gunman's jacket, and pulled out his wallet. Other than cash, it contained a New York State Driver's License in the name of Leonid Korsunsky. Figures, she thought, another goddamned Russian!

By that time, she'd really had enough of Weathers. She took a deep breath and pulled out her cell phone. When Weathers saw she was about to make a call, probably to the cops or the MPs, he really went nuts. "No! No! Don't do that!" he screamed even louder at her.

"Sit! I'm not gonna tell you again!" she said as she pointed the big automatic at his nose. As one of her drill sergeants had told her many years before, "Nothing gets a man's attention faster than staring down the barrel of a loaded gun." Amen, she thought as she pressed Favorites in her Contacts and found the new phone number she had added just the day before.

"Mr. Rendell?" she said when he answered, trying to remain calm. "This is Stephanie Goss over at Pentagon City. You better get over here and bring the cavalry. I'm in the rear parking lot, and I've got two down and one in custody... Weathers? No, he's the one in custody, but you'd better get here quick before I decide to put a bullet in him too."

She lowered the phone and paused before she pressed a second number in her speed dial. This one was in Area Code 910, Fayetteville, North Carolina. She let it ring, but no one answered, and it went to voice mail. "Bob," she said, "call me as soon as you get this. It's important."

CHAPTER TWENTY-TWO

Fayetteville, North Carolina

Bob would have returned Stephanie's phone call, but he was tied up at the moment. So were Jefferson Adkins and Ace Randall. Well, they weren't actually tied up, more correctly they were locked inside the interrogation rooms of the FBI office at 4200 Morgantown Road in Fayetteville, North Carolina. It was located just off The All-American Highway, midway between the city and Fort Bragg, which seemed like the "800-pound gorilla" perched on the small city's shoulder to the northwest of town. The Fayetteville FBI office was not one of those massive, secure federal buildings like you see in the TV shows. Why? Fayetteville only had 200,000 people, so the FBI was in leased space on the top floor of a two-story, red-brick bank building that offered lots of glass and no character. It made Bob smile every time he thought about it. The door to the interrogation room was locked, but if they pissed him off, he'd simply punch through the cheap plasterboard on either side of the doorframe and be out in the hallway before the agents could turn around in their chairs. What a joke!

Bob and his two fellow Kiwanians had returned from Brooklyn around 6:00 p.m. the night before, after which he spent some long-overdue family time with Linda and the kids. At 9:30 a.m. the next morning he was going over some bills with Linda when the FBI came knocking on his front door, complete with dark shoes and sunglasses, looking eerily like the main characters in *Men in Black,* who hauled Bob and Ace back across the river to their office in the back seats of two government sedans in handcuffs, of course. Bob was fairly sure he'd find Jefferson Adkins when they got there, but he doubted they had handcuffs big enough to fit the big African American colonel. It didn't matter. The three men had worked out their stories long before their helicopter landed back at Fort Bragg.

After being questioned for two hours and sitting there for another, the door finally opened, and the two suits walked back in. One of them removed the handcuff from Bob's left wrist and intended to re-fasten it to the table leg, when Bob looked up at him and laughed, "Seriously, Agent Parvenuti?" He looked surprised that Bob had used his name until he glanced down and realized that both he and agent Kaczynski had "Cred packs" hanging from their shirt pockets. At that point, embarrassed,

Parvenuti glanced over to the other agent and unfastened the handcuff from Bob's other wrist, as well.

"Mr. Burke," the other agent began, trying to sound baritone-official. "What were you doing up in Brighton Beach yesterday afternoon?"

"Strictly 'need to know,' Agent Kaczynski, 'need to know,'" Burke stared at him for a moment and then asked, "I've examined Agent Parvenuti's ID, would you mind if I see yours too?"

"Mr. Burke, we are the FBI," he answered in his most official voice, tying to dismiss the challenge and regain control of the interrogation, but Burke was having none of it.

"Maybe, but this is a freakin' bank building. For all I know, you two are scamming me for a home equity loan. And I saw the Baskin-Robbins regional office down the hall. Maybe you're pushing ice cream, because neither of you looks like J. Edgar Hoover," Bob calmly replied as he held out his hand. "As you should know by now, I don't scare easily and I'm sure as hell not intimidated by badges."

Realizing they'd lost Round One, the other FBI guy sighed, pulled out his ID and pushed it across the table. Burke picked it up and began studying it. Impatient and now off balance, the FBI guy drummed his fingers on the table, deciding to switch gears to a more reasonable tone. "Mr. Burke, as you see on my ID card, I'm Special Agent Brian Kaczynski. Sal and I work in the..."

But Burke held up his hand and stopped him while he slowly read both sides of the man's ID card. "Okay, Agent Kaczynski. What were you saying?"

"I'm part of the Brooklyn Organized Crime Task Force. Would you mind telling me what you and your two associates were doing in Kalinka's in Brighton Beach yesterday afternoon?"

"Trying the borscht and Chicken Kiev. We heard it was dynamite."

Kaczynski stared at him. "Don't push your luck, Major. You were in there for ten minutes, max; and you didn't eat a damned thing."

"That was Ace's fault. We got there too late, and they weren't serving lunch anymore."

Kaczynski grew exasperated. "The guy in the back booth with the two bimbos who was running things was Piotr Shurepkin, as I'm sure you know. He runs the Russian Mafia up in Brighton Beach."

"Aren't you supposed to say 'reportedly'? 'Reportedly runs the reported Russian Mafia rumored to be in Brooklyn,' that bastion of law and order? Well, I'm shocked. The Russians have a Mafia? Do the Italians know that? Why don't you arrest them?"

"We're working on it, Mr. Burke," Kaczynski said as he opened a large brown envelope, pulled out a stack of 5"x 8" black-and-white photographs and spread them on the table in front of Burke. They were shots of the interior of Kalinka's, poorly lit, but showing him sitting in the booth with the Russians and Jefferson Adkins standing next to him. "We have audio too, but the sound quality in a large room like that isn't the best."

"The photos aren't bad. But if you have the audio, what do you expect me to add?

"What did you talk to Shurepkin about?"

"I would say none of your goddamned business, but it really is your business, isn't it? Shurepkin fraudulently obtained a US government contract that was supposed to go to my company, and I want it back. It's as simple as that. The contract means a lot to my employees, like their jobs."

"Mr. Burke, you're meddling in a federal investigation."

"Because they're meddling in my business."

"We have Shurepkin and his associates under close observation…"

"Then you know what they're doing. Shut them down."

"We can't, not yet."

"When, then?"

"We don't know, but we want you to back off and leave them alone until we can move."

"When will that be?"

"I'm afraid I can't say."

"You gonna get me my contract back while you're waiting?"

"There's nothing I can do about that. It's up to the Army, not me, Mr. Burke."

Bob Burke leaned back in the chair and smiled at him. "Agent Kaczynski, I assume you reviewed my records before you dragged me in here."

"With a microscope, Mr. Burke."

"Good! Then you know handcuffs, the backseat of a government car, and a grimy little interrogation room isn't likely to intimidate me. In a nutshell, agent Kaczynski, I want my contract. So you can 'lead, follow, or get out of my way.' " That said, Bob stood up.

"I didn't say you could leave," Kaczynski told him.

"Yes you did, when you let him take my handcuffs off. I'm obviously not under arrest, and I'm leaving. When you get my contract back, you'll have all the help I can give you."

"If you get in our way again, we will shut you down."

"No, you won't. I know the US Attorney better than you do, and you won't even try. If you do, I'll be the one shutting you down. I'm not trying to be a prick about this… then again, I guess I am. But those are the facts. So sit back, shut up, relax, and watch."

The FBI released all three of them at the same time, just before noon. When the "Feeb's clerk handed them their personal effects in brown paper envelopes, including his cell phone, Bob smiled. No doubt they tried to mine it for useful information, but he had better tech people than they did. His used a ten letter and numeric code the Geeks installed, one Alexander Graham Bell couldn't get past. With the phone live again, he called an Uber rather than take another ride in "public transportation" in the back seat of an FBI sedan.

While they were waiting, Bob opened his cell phone and quickly thumbed through the morning's e-mail and voicemail. That was when he saw the call from Stephanie Goss and immediately pressed on the number. Her phone rang six or seven times and finally went to voicemail too, but he didn't leave a message. He figured he'd call her back every five minutes until she answered. He didn't have to. The phone rang ten seconds later, and it wasn't Stephanie Goss.

"Major Burke?" a man asked. "Your name came up on the screen. This is Agent Rendell, CID."

"Where's Stephanie?" he asked.

"There's been an incident up here, and…"

"Is she okay?"

"Oh, she's fine," he laughed, "although she's about the only one in the office who is. It's been some day up here. It appears she 'intervened' in a confrontation in the parking lot between Colonel Weathers and two Russians, both of whom were armed, one of whom was holding a pistol to Weathers's wife's head."

"Jeez! But Steph's all right?"

"She disarmed one of them, a big lout over 300 pounds, the one who had the pistol up against Erica Weathers's head."

"That's my girl! It goes with the Ranger tab on her shoulder. The big guy wasn't my friend Evsei Baratashvili, the Georgian weightlifter from the last time I was up there, was it?" Bob asked.

"No, but from your description it could be his twin brother. This one's name is Leonid Korsunsky, like a fireplug on legs. Sergeant First Class Goss broke his knee, knocked him out cold, took his pistol away, an old Russian Tokarev semi-automatic, took Weathers in custody, and traded shots with the other Russian, who we think was Piotr Shurepkin himself. That all happened in maybe thirty seconds."

"Did she get Shurepkin?"

"No, he got away, but we think she clipped him, based on a blood trail we found."

"Too bad she didn't put him down for keeps."

"Agreed. We're still looking for him, but we think he had a car stashed somewhere, and it looks like he got away."

"And Steph isn't in any trouble?" Bob asked.

"No, not with us, although the locals are now talking to her. I thought it best to keep her off the street until we're sure Shurepkin and his pals are long gone. Since you're involved in this mess too, I thought you should know."

"Thanks, I appreciate the heads up. The FBI's after Shurepkin, too. That's where I've been for the past few hours: handcuffs, thumbscrews, the dungeon, you get the picture."

"That office building they are in down in Fayetteville? The one off the All-American Highway? What a joke," Rendell laughed. "From what we hear in Moscow, Shurepkin isn't. He's a nasty little shit, and I doubt we've heard the last of him."

"You might do me a favor and phone FBI Agents Kaczynski or Parvenuti. They're out of the Brooklyn office but they're down here in Fayetteville scratching their heads after grilling us. You might bring them up to date. Did Weathers have much to say?"

"He's still in complete denial, like, 'Who, me? I didn't do anything.' "

"Well, my tech guys did a deep dive into the paperwork and found some major flaws in that proposal Shurepkin had Weathers trying to push through DoD purchasing."

"No surprise there. I'll be turning that package over to our forensic accounting people," Rendell said.

"There are obvious things missing that even a trainee should have known regarding local and state licenses and permits, bonds, insurance, and federal tax ID numbers. The fact Weathers ignored all that means he set himself up for a prima facie charge of fraud."

"Oh, he's headed to Leavenworth, but until we get the rest of his pals up in Brooklyn locked up too, watch your 'Six,' Major."

"Roger that, Agent Rendell. I always do."

CHAPTER TWENTY-THREE

DC and Baltimore

CID Agent Rendell was right, Piotr Shurepkin had a rental car hidden in one of the outside rows of the parking lot. He stayed low, darting from row to row and finally found it. By then, however, his shoulder was throbbing with pain and blood was running down his back. The car was a silver Mercedes sedan with Delaware license plates he rented at the airport using a phony ID and credit card. The bleeding was slowing down, but he needed to get the shoulder attended to, which meant he would have to drive back north, not fly. The police had no license plate or car to look for, so he headed east and north, moving with the speed of the other traffic, trying to blend in.

It was all that damned Korsunsky's fault, Shurepkin swore. How could the big ape let himself get taken down by a woman! Piotr told his father a half-dozen times he needed better help, at least one or two good men to do what his father wanted him to do. So what does he send? Musclebound weightlifters and clowns!

Piotr's Makarov automatic was on the seat next to him. He pulled out his cell phone and thumbed through his Favorites until he found Alexander Volkov, his personal doctor in Brooklyn. He was his father's age and still had family in Moscow.

After five rings, Volkov finally answered. "Piotr? I am sorry, but I am with patients."

"It is an emergency."

"Then how I can help? What do you need from me?"

"A doctor. I have been shot, but not seriously. The bullet clipped the back of my shoulder. I am bleeding, not as much as before, but I need stitches."

"Where are you?"

"In my car, driving, heading north out of Washington DC."

"Am I to assume a hospital is out of the question, and you cannot make it home?"

"Da, yes."

Volkov paused for a moment, thinking, then said, "I know a man in Baltimore, a doctor. He is Pakistani, but he can handle this with… discretion. I will call him and text you his address."

"And you say he can be trusted."

"I believe so… but it would be well to pay him generously."

"I will meet him, only him. Tell him no one else."

The driving time from DC to Baltimore was just short of an hour, straight up I-95, and Piotr Shurepkin was in pain the entire way. The doctor's office was on West Lombard, on the first floor of an old white Victorian house which was not far north of I-95, west of the university, and easy to find. In the front yard was a small, tastefully made sign on a white post that said, "D. M. Patel, Internal Medicine."

The lights were on inside and the shades were drawn as Piotr pulled into the driveway and parked. He sat there for a moment, studying the house. Finally, he opened the car door and swung his legs out. By that time, the blood on his back had partially dried and stuck to the car seat. Leaning forward, he ripped the shirt and jacket loose and a firebolt of pain shot through his back and down his arm.

That was when his cell phone rang. He considered not answering it or even tossing the damned thing into the street, but he didn't. The call was from Russia, from Moscow.

"Yes?" Piotr answered tentatively, "Who is this?"

"It is your father! They tell me your big plans for the Washington software operation blew up in your face… and in mine!"

"Father, I…"

"I am tired of your excuses, you stupid boy. You let this cowboy – what is his name, Burke? You let him enter your restaurant, disarm your men, and threaten you in front of them? With your whores hanging all over you, and the white powder on the tables, you will kill us both, you fool. You have acted like an out-of-control child and you lost whatever respect anyone had for you back here."

"Who is telling you these things?"

"Who? People who work for you; and, more importantly, who work for me. And now you let a woman chase you out of Washington? First you lose Orlov and then Baratashvili…"

"They were idiots, both of them. You send me morons, Papa!"

"And now you lose Korsunsky…"

"Another weightlifter, and an idiot."

"… to a woman! Why didn't you take Bratsov with you instead of them? If you had, there would be no problem."

"I left Pavel in Brooklyn to run things, and to protect Evgeni. You told me…"

"That was then. Now is now. Paretsky and Kuryakin have already gone to see Putin. I warned you while I was over there, the vultures are circling, waiting for me to make a mistake, waiting for YOU to make a mistake. So what did you do? You made a bushel basket full of them. Our heads are on the block now, Piotr. You must solve this. Kill this Burke and get those contracts before they come for both of us."

Piotr wanted to keep arguing, but he saw that the line had gone dead. His father hung up on him. That only made him angrier. Kill Burke? Oh, is that all you want Father?

Cradling his left arm to his chest, Piotr walked across the weeds and hard-packed dirt that passed for the front yard of the doctor's office and knocked on his door. An old, shriveled-up, dark-skinned, Pakistani opened it and stared at Piotr for a moment before he stepped aside and motioned for him to enter.

"Are you the doctor?" Piotr asked the old man.

"No, that is my father," a much younger man said as he stepped into the front vestibule. "Come, please," the young man led him to the back of the building and into a small medical treatment room.

Shurepkin glared at him. "You were told just you, no one else."

"My father helps me around the office with my patients. He is a nurse, but he speaks neither English nor Russian," the doctor answered as he helped Shurepkin up onto an operating table and helped him peel off his jacket and shirt so he could get a closer look. "Yes, it appears to be a bullet wound, which cut across your upper back and shoulder. It is deep, but it does not appear to have nicked any bones, only soft tissue, and passed on through. That said, you still should go to hospital to get proper treatment."

"That is impossible. Clean it up, stitch it up, and give me painkillers and antibiotics. And while you do that, tell your father to clean up the front seat of my car."

Doctor Patel pointed at the 9-millimeter automatic tucked in Piotr's belt and said, "You won't need that in here."

"We shall see," Shurepkin answered.

"As you wish," the Doctor shrugged and set to work, numbing the area with several shots, and then cleaning and stitching Shurepkin.

Thirty minutes later, the doctor finished with the last stitch and applied a thick gauze pad and tape across the wound. His father came in and the two Pakistanis helped Shurepkin sit up. Doctor Patel quickly checked Piotr's eyes and said, "The painkillers and antibiotics I gave you are powerful, but it took seventeen stitches to close that gash. You may experience some nausea and dizziness. I suggest you find a motel here in town and stay in bed for a few days."

"Not possible," Shurepkin dismissed the thought, pointing to his own bloody shirt and jacket on the floor. "Put those in a trash bag. Also all gloves, scissors, scalpel, bandages, anything else with my blood on them. Do you understand?"

Turning to Dr. Patel's father, Piotr asked, "The car seat is clean? Down between cushions? On floor?" He saw a flash of arrogant anger in the son's eyes, but he translated and the old man quickly nodded and answered him.

While Patel's father gathered up everything in the surgical room and stuffed it in the bag, Shurepkin looked at his clothes, all bloody and torn. He turned to the doctor and said, "Help me into one of your surgical gowns." It was far too long, almost coming down to his knees, but Piotr used a pair of the Doctor's surgical scissors to cut off the rest and tucked them inside his pants. The Russian saw a windbreaker hanging on a coat rack and put it on. It didn't fit, but it would do. "So, what do I owe you, Doctor?" he asked.

Patel shrugged and looked around the examining room. "I believe $2,000 would be adequate to cover the services and ensure our complete discretion in the matter."

"Yes, I'm sure that would be adequate," Shurepkin said as he reached into his waistband and fired two 9-millimeter rounds into the doctor's chest, turned, and fired two more into his father's. He got up off the table, went around the other side, and fired one round into each of their heads. "Adequate, but this is a better guarantee."

CHAPTER TWENTY-FOUR

Baltimore, Maryland

Piotr opened the front door of Patel's office and looked up and down the street. Nothing. It was midafternoon. His car was still sitting in the driveway, and if anyone on the street or in the neighboring buildings heard the gunshots, they weren't acting like they had. Then again, this was not a neighborhood where people paid any attention to such things. Carrying the plastic bag containing his bloody coat, shirt, and the surgical instruments, he walked calmly to the car and threw it in the trunk.

He drove back south and east through the city until he saw the signs to the entrance ramp to I-95 and looked at his watch. It was 3:30 p.m. It would take at least four hours, maybe five, to drive back to Brooklyn through the thickening rush-hour traffic.

He picked up his cell phone and dialed Pavel Bratsov's number.

"Da," his burly enforcer answered.

"I am headed back. Send that fat slob Bogdan Schlimovitz out to New Jersey. I want him to drive my car and meet me at 8 p.m. at that little airport west of I-95, where your friend works. If he so much as puts a scratch on my car, I'll kill him. And I want you to arrange for one of those big private jets out of Newark to pick us up there. At 8:00 and not a minute later!"

"Where to?"

"I'll tell the pilot when he gets there. And I want you go into my office. I have a clean shirt in my bottom drawer and there is a blue windbreaker behind the door. Have that weasel Bogdan bring those. And on the floor in the closet there is a small box. He's to bring that too."

"Yes Boss, anything else you want? You don't want me to come?"

Piotr paused, silently fuming. "No, my father phoned an hour ago. He let slip that he has a spy in my organization, someone who is telling him everything It isn't you, is it, Pavel?"

"No, Piotr, I swear! He's the Boss, but you are my boss. You know I'm not stupid enough to cross you like that."

"Perhaps not, Pavel, so if I am looking for someone who *is* 'stupid enough;' perhaps that is why I am having Bogdan is meet me at the airport, not you... not yet, anyway."

Piotr stared at the phone and hung up.

The small private airfield in Linden, New Jersey, is located off I-95, on a straight line through Staten Island from Brooklyn. Pavel Bratsov arranged for a very discreet charter service based at the much larger Teterboro Airport to fly one of their Gulfstream G-5s down and pick them up. Linden had no tower, no records, and was deserted in the evening, making it even more "private" at night than its big cousin twenty miles to the north.

A G-5 is plush. It sits up to sixteen, is fast, and has a range of 7,000 miles at 585 miles per hour. With the distinctive upward flip of its wingtips and its sleek, pointed nose, it is the undisputed king of civil aviation. Chartering a G-5 was expensive, but since Piotr would not tell him where they were going, choosing a big G-5 was the safe way to avoid another snit with the little shit. He also ordered a full crew of four: the pilot, co-pilot, and two bimbos in back, with enough food and booze to make it to Miami, LA, or even London. He also sent a duffle bag with four pistols, two short-barrel, folding-stock AK-47 automatic rifles with Bogdan, and enough magazines and boxes of shells to start a small war. He also had the dumb kitchen manager bring that small box that Piotr wanted from his office in Kalinka's.

Bratsov had ordered the G-5 for 7:00 p.m., and Bogdan had been standing there on the tarmac since 7:45, waiting nervously until Piotr finally drove in and parked in the grass near the side of the hangar. But as Shurepkin slowly got out of his car, Bogdan saw something wasn't right. The younger man was always expensively dressed, trendy and even trashy, but tonight he wore what looked like a pull-on white peasant shirt and a baseball jacket.

"You okay, Boss?" Bogdan asked, sounding concerned as he walked over.

"Yeah, tell them to go, now," Shurepkin growled as he stretched his arm and shoulder. "You brought the box and the other things?"

"Like you told Pavel, Boss. What do I tell the pilot? Where are we going?"

"Chicago. A small airport northwest, a place called Schaumburg. Tell him that is where we are going. It is unmanned. I want to slip in and slip out."

They climbed the narrow fold-down stairs and got aboard, with Piotr collapsing onto one of the plush leather seats in back while Bogdan stuck his head into the cockpit. When he came back, he said, "The pilot says it is 800 miles. We should be there in an hour and fifteen minutes once he gets his clearances and we get airborne."

Shurepkin nodded and stood up. "Give me a hand," he asked as he gently pulled off the white shirt which Bogdan could now see was a cut-off hospital gown.

With it off, the big Bulgarian saw a thick, 12" x 4" bandage on the backside of Piotr's shoulder. "Geez, Boss, what happened to you?"

"A bad shot," Piotr grimaced. "Now, help me put on the shirt and the windbreaker."

Getting Piotr changed and seated comfortably in one of those chairs was a major undertaking. Shurepkin popped two pills from a bottle in his pants pocket, turned to Bogdan, and said, "I heard you have friends on north side of Chicago."

"Not friends, Albanians."

"I do not trust Albanians."

"Who does? But I trust them more than I trust any 'Russians' in Chicago. They are all Ukrainians and Georgians... and Chechens."

"All right, all right, they will do," Shurepkin said, frustrated. "We need car... No, we need two cars."

"Two? What do you...?"

"Do what I tell you! Two cars, one they get back, one they will not. Nothing flashy. Old cars. And not too hot. Have them swap out the plates, but we only need the cars for a few hours. One I want at the airport when we land, that means in an hour. That one they will not get back. Second car I want left at..." he paused and looked at a piece of paper he pulled from his pants pocket. "Restaurant is named 'Wild Berry Pancake House' on Meacham Road."

"Where are we..."

Piotr's eyes narrowed as he fixed his anger on the much bigger man. "I am not in a good mood, Bogdan. Do as I say or take next flight back to Moscow. I am Boss here, not my father!"

"Yes, yes, of course you are Boss, Piotr, it sounded odd, that is all."

Piotr continued to stare at him, and then added, "Tell them to park the car away from pancake house building, on highway side. They should text you license plate number and leave keys under the mat. That one they will come and pick up at airport at 11:00 p.m. You have all that, Bogdan? Pay what they want. I want no alarm bells, you hear?"

The Bulgarian picked up the console phone at his seat, sat back, and began dialing.

The Schaumburg Regional Airport was on the backside of the huge Motorola factory and office complex on the opposite side of the sprawling suburb, about five miles southwest of the equally huge Woodfield Mall complex.

"Tell the pilot we will be back in an hour. He should keep engines running."

"That will burn up a lot of gas, Boss."

Shurepkin glared at him. "Do not question me again, do you hear!"

It was 9:00 p.m. Chicago time when they got in the car. The airport was small, but it had maintenance hangars, a building, and dozens of corporate jets, prop planes, and helicopters parked on the sides of the taxiways. All in all, it looked considerably more prosperous than the tiny airstrip at Linden they took off from. Shurepkin looked out the window on final approach and saw it was well past rush hour on the busy northwest expressways and main roads around them. That was all that mattered, and there was still a nice flow of traffic to get lost in, which was even better.

The sleek jet landed as soft as a feather and then taxied over to its assigned space, where a gray, three-year-old Ford Taurus was parked. Looking out the window, Shurepkin saw it had enough dust, dirt, and dents to pose as a commuter.

Piece 'a crap!" the Bulgarian grunted when he saw it.

"Yes, is exactly what I wanted," Shurepkin corrected him. "Looks like every other 'piece 'a crap' on the road and we won't get noticed."

As soon as the copilot lowered the stairs, Shurepkin picked up the cardboard box and left the heavy duffel bag for Bogdan. They walked over to the car, but before they touched anything, Shurepkin put the cardboard box on the ground and pulled out two pairs of latex surgical gloves. He then placed the box on the passenger side floor and told Bogdan to put the duffel bag in the rear seat.

"You drive," Shurepkin told him as he sat gingerly in the passenger seat, careful to protect his back. He pulled out his own cell phone, opened "Maps," and punched in an address as the bigger man squeezed behind the wheel and started the car and headed for the entrance.

The main road was West Irving Park. Bogdan stopped at the traffic light and asked, "Okay, where to, Boss?"

"Turn right," the female robot voice on the phone told him, and then began giving them directions. "In twelve hundred feet, turn left on Roselle Road and continue north..."Bogdan

"Be a good boy for a change and do what the lady says, Bogdan. You ask where we going? To put a pain in the ass out of business," Shurepkin answered as he reached into the box again and pulled out two blocks of Semtex plastic explosive, a detonator, and a cell phone.

Toler TeleCom's offices ran more to the dumpy and practical than to any architectural-design-magazine modern. They were located in a boring, two-story, thirty-year-old brick office-warehouse a half-mile west of the big Motorola plant in corporate offices on the northern edge of Schaumburg in the middle of a dozen other office and light industrial business parks. There was nothing fancy about them.

The building had an ample buffer with trees on each side of the parking lot, separating it from its neighbors. In front was a large lot with several hundred spaces, broken up by landscaped islands that held trees and parking lot lights. Because the building and business park were now over fifteen years old, the trees had grown tall and leafy and the streetlights were old tech, leaving little more than yellow pools of light between the shadows. That made the front façade and front parking lot very pretty, particularly during the day, but were not the best for security at night. The rear of the building was much more functional, with bright overhead lights over a set of truck doors and no trees to diminish the harsh lighting over the hard stand and outside equipment storage.

In addition to the Semtex, the box also held several burner phones, small spools of plastic-coated wire, electrical tape, and wire cutters. While Schlimovitz drove the car north, Piotr Shurepkin was busily at work, bent over the cardboard box, taping two blocks of Semtex together with the duct tape, wiring and attaching a burner phone to it with more duct tape, then carefully entering its phone number into his favorites.

"Need any help with that, Boss?" Bogdan asked nervously.

Shurepkin smiled. "You don't think I know how to do this?"

"Oh, no, I'm sure you know how, I was just…"

"…Afraid I'll blow you to pieces?" Shurepkin looked over at him with a mischievous grin. "Well, truth is, I have not wired one of these in a long time. So, you never can tell," he said as he tossed the Semtex up and down his hand. "I might, but you and I will never know, will we?" he asked pleased to be the one intimidating the bigger man for once.

The streets in the business park were deserted. They passed a few cars headed out toward the exit and continued around until Shurepkin found the address he was looking for.

"There, there, that is it," he said as he stared at the building through the trees. "Keep going, once more around. We see if there are police or private security around." And Shurepkin was right. They passed one white and blue Schaumburg Police Department patrol car parked in a bank parking lot near the entrance. It appeared as if the two cops inside were doing little more than chatting and drinking their coffee while they finished their doughnuts. That was fine, Shurepkin thought. Too bad he was about to disturb their evening. He turned around in the seat, wincing from the pain in his shoulder, reached inside the duffel bag, and pulled out one of the cut-down AK-47s. After checking the thirty-round magazine before jacking one into the chamber, he told Bogdan to continue around the circle, and they made two more turns until they reached the entrance to the Toler TeleCom lot and turned in.

There were eight cars scattered through the parking lot, obviously from the skeleton crew that worked the 4-12 shift. From Piotr's own experience, that would be the night bookkeepers and janitors, maybe a few others in back handling receiving. They should pose no problem.

"Pull up to the front door," Shurepkin told him as he shoved the AK-47 into the Bulgarian's chest and switched off the domed ceiling light inside the car. "If you see that police car coming, let them get close, then hit them with this."

"Police, Boss? Shouldn't we just wait and..." he tried to say, but Shurepkin wasn't listening to him anymore.

The front entrance to the building was at the left front corner. It had a semicircular, recessed entry with a revolving door and three imitation-concrete columns holding up the roof. Behind the doors sat a small atrium lobby with a large reception desk, a seating area, and potted plants. Behind the lobby was a two-story wall with the company's name in raised, decorative lettering. The administrative and sales offices were on the other side of the wall. They took up the front half of the building, while the warehouse, shipping, receiving, equipment storage, bench repair operations and truck doors occupied the rear half. The facilities gave the impression of a solid, old-fashioned, conservative business, which was exactly what its former and present owners wanted for their company. Too bad the image wouldn't last very much longer, Piotr Shurepkin thought as a cynical smile crossed his face.

He did not wait for the Ford Taurus to come to a stop in front of the lobby. He got out of the car and walked over to the revolving doors. As he expected, they were locked, so he placed the bomb directly behind one of the concrete columns, facing the lobby. From the rudimentary explosives training they gave him, Piotr knew that the explosion would take the column out, but the concrete column would also serve to reflect the explosive power of the Semtex back into the open lobby, and two blocks of Semtex should be more than enough to blow it all to hell.

As he turned and walked back to the car, he saw that damned white and blue Schaumburg police car had turned in the entrance to the parking lot. For some reason, those two doughnut-eating cops had followed them, and began driving slowly in their direction.

"Stop next to them," Piotr said as he grabbed the AK-47 out of Bogdan's lap.

"Boss, you aren't thinking of..."

"Roll down your window and smile."

The two cars stopped only two feet apart, side-by-side, pointed in opposite directions. Shurepkin didn't wait for the driver of the police car to roll down his window before he shoved the AK-47 in front of Bogdan Schlimovitz, holding it with one hand as he pulled the trigger. The AK-47 was a muscular assault rifle that fired a moderately heavy 7.62-millimeter bullet. On full automatic, it could fire 600 rounds per minute, which was a moot point since it held a 30-round magazine. It was also moot because in a few seconds those 30 rounds blasted through the side window of the police car, which completely ripped it apart as well as the two policemen in the front seat.

In his last few seconds of life after he saw the submachine gun, the policeman behind the wheel must have pressed his foot down on the accelerator, because the cruiser suddenly sped forward and crashed into the side of the office building. It smashed through the floor-to-ceiling lobby windows and on into the lobby, hitting a couch, a coffee table and chair, and a desk until it slammed into the far interior wall. The car's engine died, and a cloud of steam came rolling out of its broken radiator.

The effect on Bogdan was equally dramatic. Thirty rounds of automatic rifle fire had gone off right under his chin, with the spent brass shells flying out of the AK's ejector port into his face and neck. The ear-shattering noise, the smell, the concussions, and the shock effect of thirty rounds going off inside the enclosed car stunned him.

"Go, go!" Shurepkin screamed in his face, grinning, riding a huge high.

It took a second or two, but the fat Bulgarian finally stepped on the accelerator and tore out of the parking lot, wide-eyed, careening onto the access road and speeding away.

"Slow down you fool! No one is after us... not yet."

Bogdan pulled his foot away and quickly complied but sweat was pouring off him and his hands were shaking.

"Too much violence for you?" Shurepkin laughed at him and pulled out his cell phone. "Well, if you did not like that one, you really will not like this one," and pressed the Call button on the cell phone. There was a delay of about two seconds until the there was a horrific explosion a quarter mile behind them that lit up the tree line with an orange fireball. "Bye-bye competition, Bogdan."

"What was that?"

"Toler TeleCom, they called themselves. Now, they are a pile of bricks. So drive east to Meacham Road. We pick up second car and go home."

"But why two cars, Piotr?"

"We'll burn this car in the parking lot of the shopping center. Then, there will be no evidence of anything. All burned up, while we drive away in the other car. Now go!"

It took only ten minutes to reach the parking lot of the pancake house and pull up behind the second car. Bogdan began to get out, but Shurepkin stopped him. "No, I drive that one. You drive this one... the mirrors are all set, and I don't want to sit in your sweat," he laughed.

"But I'm not sure of the way, Piotr."

"Follow me, I studied map. But do not get close. We do not want to raise suspicions. We will be at airport in fifteen minutes and on way back to Kalinka's. Then we crack open that special bottle of my favorite, pepper vodka, eh?"

"Sure boss, pepper vodka, that would be great," the fat Bulgarian grinned.

The second car was a Chevrolet, older and in worse condition than the first car, but the engine turned over and it started up. Shurepkin backed out of the parking space, drove back to Meacham Road, and headed south with Bogdan following a few hundred feet behind. Traffic was light. They passed under Golf Road and up ahead he saw Woodfield Road, the entrance to the shopping center. That light ahead was red, so Shurepkin slowed until it turned green. He accelerated, pulled out his cell phone again, and pressed the number of a second burner phone. That call detonated the two remaining blocks of Semtex sitting in the bottom of the box on the floor of the Bulgarian's car. It triggered a second massive orange fireball, like the one at Toler TeleCom, that blew the small sedan apart and lifted its flaming chassis ten feet in the air.

"Bogdan, there are bosses, and then again there are Bosses," Piotr laughed to himself as he looked at his watch. It was only 10:45. Pepper vodka sounded even better, and maybe a few girls.

CHAPTER TWENTY-FIVE

Sherwood Forest, North Carolina

It was 11:30 p.m. when his cell phone on the nightstand next to his bed vibrated. That was most unusual. First, only a small and very select group of people had that number. Second, being an 'early to bed and early to rise' kind of guy, he'd been sound asleep for an hour and a half, and the people who had that number knew that. Still, after all those years in the infantry out in the field in places where you really didn't want to be, there were certain sounds that made the brain snap wide awake in a split second: rifle fire, explosions, a tactical radio call, and now, the faint vibration of a cell phone.

He picked up the phone and looked at the small screen. It was Maryanne Simpson, the president and former office manager of the Toler TeleCom office near Chicago, and he knew in a heartbeat that any time she called, particularly in the middle of the night, it was bad news.

"Maryanne, what's up?" he said, and as soon as he did, Linda also snapped wide awake and sat up in bed next to him.

Maryanne wasn't sugarcoating anything. With Bob, she knew to get right to the point. "A bomb went off at the office about an hour ago, a big one..."

"A bomb? You gotta be kidding!

"I wish I were. It went off near the front entrance. It killed two of the night auditors working in accounting right above there and injured a private security guard and a janitor. The security guard will be okay, but the janitor's still in surgery."

"Names?" he asked.

"Shirley Johnson and Tammy Adduci. They worked nights, but knowing you, you probably remember them anyway, from way back. The janitor is Clarence. Same for him, but the security guard was a private rent-a-cop we brought in. I doubt you've met him. Needless to say, we have cops and bomb squads all over the place – Schaumburg, county, state, and the FBI and ATF are on the way. Maybe the South Dakota National Guard and the Mounties too, I don't know. They called me and I got here thirty minutes ago, but they've had me cornered answering questions and this was the first break I got to call you."

"Understood."

"Thanks. The bomb was bad enough, but there's a Schaumburg city police car with two dead police officers sitting right in the middle of our lobby. Apparently, it crashed through the plate-glass windows and was inside when the bomb went off just outside, a few feet away. They're still trying to figure that out."

"Christ!" Bob kept thinking. "Have you called Grierson?"

"George! I completely forgot. We should have the company attorney out here, shouldn't we?"

"It's time he earned that retainer we've been paying him. Don't worry, you're busy. I'll call him and then grab Ace. We'll be out there as soon as we can."

Bob ended the call, hit Ace Randall's number in his Favorites, and quickly brought him up to speed on the bomb in Chicago. Ace had been his senior Delta force NCO, not part of his Chicago Toler TeleCom staff, but Ace learned fast.

"We need to get up there, quick," Bob told him. "I doubt we'll be there very long but grab your emergency bag. While I make some other calls, try that charter air service we've used down at Gray's Creek Aviation south of town. Tell them it's an emergency and get us a jet, tonight if possible, ASAP, to Chicago. Also, you know a couple of the senior NCOs in Explosive Ordnance on post, don't you? See if they'd like a road trip."

"They're the best in the business, Ghost. They run special classes for the FBI and ATF on IEDs and terrorist bombs. I think they trained most of FBI and ATF people, so they might like a trip and see what their students have been up to."

"Good, I want to have our own eyes and ears up there. Tell them there'll be a retirement bonus in it for them and I know a good 24-hour steak house up there."

"Good, those guys can always use a new bass boat, and we can all use   a   steak."

Bob's next call was to another confidential cell phone number. This one rang on Chicago Police Department Captain Ernie Travers's bedside table in his condo just off North Lake Shore Drive.

"You again?" the big man answered. "It's almost midnight. What'd you get yourself into now?"

"Somebody blew up my Schaumburg office a couple of hours ago. Two dead, two wounded, and two dead Schaumburg police officers too."

"Holy crap! You figure it's those damned Russians we talked about a few days ago with Phil and Carmine?"

"Hard not to think that. I haven't kicked any other hornets' nests lately."

"Anything I can do?"

"Yeah, I'm afraid so. I'm flying up as fast as I can get there. I know the Schaumburg Police Chief and some of his lieutenants, but you know all the state and county cops who might show up, probably most of the Feds too. I could use somebody to help run interference for me. They'll talk to you, but they sure as hell won't talk to me."

"I'm on my way. Whistle when you get there, and I'll call if anything comes up before then."

"My Office Manager Maryanne Simpson is already there."

"I remember Maryanne. I'll find her."

"Great. I'm bringing Ace and two of our top EOD people from Special Ops."

"The Feds aren't gonna like that. They're 'turf monsters.' "

"I'm told these guys probably trained most of them at Quantico."

"That'll help open a few doors."

Gray's Creek Aviation was a small, private airstrip five miles south of Fayetteville on the other side of I-95. By the time he and Ace got down there 45 minutes later, there was a Cessna Citation X+ from Executive Charter Services inbound from Raleigh on final approach. Bob thought that was amazingly quick service until the pilot told him the small, sleek Citation X+ with twin Rolls-Royce turbofan engines could reach speeds of over 700 miles an hour and cruise at over 600, which it didn't even have time to reach on the quick hop from Raleigh.

Ace's two pals from Fort Bragg, Master Sergeants Tim Enders and George Themopolis, arrived at the same time as the jet. The four men threw their "go" bags inside and jumped on board as soon as the stairs came down. The cabin attendant had them buckled in, the small jet turned around, and was back in the air in minutes.

To say the interior of a Citation is plush, is putting it mildly. The cabin attendant/purser looked at his watch and said, "Let me know what you guys want to drink, and we have some snacks and sandwiches I can bring out. I understand we're heading to Schaumburg Muni outside Chicago and you asked for 'quick.' That's about 800 miles. It's 12:15 now. We gain an hour, so we should be on the ground by 12:30 or so, Chicago time."

Bob told him to bring out four beers and a tray of sandwiches. He and Ace took one and the two sergeants each took two for starters. Being Deltas meant never knowing when the next meal might come, so you ate when there was food, particularly if it was free.

Ace made the introductions all around. George Themopolis spoke up first and said, "We remember the Major. I think Tim and I were in Kandahar and then Bagram during your last couple of tours. You were mostly out in the field and we were mostly on the roads and in the villages working IEDs, but we passed in the dust from time to time."

"I remember your names, but now that I've seen you two guys I recognize the faces too. Unfortunately, it's been a few years."

"Yeah," Themopolis agreed. "Maybe I'm just getting old, but all those tours have blurred into one big sandbox with big pieces of scrap metal."

"You got that right!" Tim Enders agreed. "Ace said you have a 'situation' at your office up in Chicago." While Bob told them what he knew, Themopolis opened what looked like a high-security briefcase, exposing a GETAC high-performance, rugged-environment state-of-the-art tactical laptop computer and began working the keyboard.

"That must be the new model," Bob laughed. "I have three super techies back at the farm who would die for one of those."

"They'd have to," Thermopolis answered, "because it isn't exactly off-the-shelf. EOD and special ops have an exclusive contract for them. But I saw this jet has secure Wi-Fi in addition to the cold beer, and we can access the ATF and FBI databases right from here. We might be too early, but I thought I would see what the chatter was about your explosion and see who's handling the investigation." He continued typing and then said, "Here we go. It must've caught somebody's attention... substantial damage to the building, they think it's Semtex, and Al Peterson from ATF is now on the scene."

"That's good," Enders nodded. "He knows us."

"We'll slip him the secret EOD handshake and see what we can learn." Thermopolis said. "He's a good man and knows his business."

"What's the secret handshake?" Ace asked. "Four fingers and half a thumb?"

"And it looks like there was a second explosion several miles away. A car got blown all to hell. One crispy critter, they think, and it looks like the explosives match."

"Maybe that's the bomber?" Ace asked. "Maybe he blew himself up."

"Maybe," Bob replied.

As advertised, it was 12:45 **a.m.** when they went wheels down at Schaumburg Regional Airport. Maryanne had arranged for a stretched black Chevy suburban to be waiting for them in the parking lot. As soon as Bob saw it, he figured it was a great choice, hopefully letting them blend in with the Feds. At that dead, dark time of the night, there was very little traffic on any of the roads. Bob got in the driver's seat, as he always did, with Ace riding shotgun and the two Fort Bragg EOD guys in the back on their computers.

As they approached the office building, they hit three roadblocks: one was at the business park entrance on the main road, one at the head of the street his office was on, and one was at the entrance to his parking lot. They had to show ID each time. Finally, having proved he owned the company and the building, they allowed Bob to go as far as the yellow crime scene tape, which was where personal connections took over. In short order, Master Sergeants Tim Enders and George Themopolis saw one of the EOD guys walking by in a white protective suit. They waved him over and after a few handshakes and backslaps, the white-clad guy raised the tape and led them inside to where Al Peterson of ATF was working at a table under a white tent and powerful lights.

At about the same time, Ernie Travers waved and walked over with Maryanne and George Grierson in tow. At 6'4" tall and 240 pounds, the Chicago Police Department captain was a hard man to miss. "Man, you got here quick," Ernie said.

Bob Burke heard Ernie's words, but his mind went with his eyes and his heart to the front façade of the Toler TeleCom building. It had always been a physical manifestation of the company and Ed Toler: simple and solid. He saw the left front corner of the building, where the lobby was located, had been ripped apart. In the glare of emergency pole lights, it had been replaced by a gaping black hole. Dozens of forensic techs clad in bright-yellow jumpsuits and booties sifted through the rubble for clues.

Bob did a good job running Toler TeleCom, as had Maryanne, but this would always be Ed Toler's company. He started it; he built it; and he passed it to Bob on his deathbed. A company was more than bricks, glass, desks, and computers. It was other people's jobs and livelihoods. To an old military guy, that was a heavy responsibility, fiduciary, bordering on the sacred. To now be standing there seeing how Ed's building and his company had been assaulted like this on Bob's watch ate at his guts. He had been careless. He wasn't sure exactly how or why yet, but he should have been more careful.

He didn't need to wait for the forensic reports on the tiny bits of wire they found, the trace amounts of chemicals, or the fragments of a cell phone. They would all point to the Russians and Shurepkin. There was no doubt in his mind about that and it got him as ice-cold angry as he may have ever been in his life. His eyes flashed. Shurepkin may not know it yet, but it was never a good idea to get an old Delta angry. Wherever this was going, Burke knew he would kill the little bastard, sooner or later. Unlike the Corleones or Virgil Sollozzo, to Bob Burke, it wasn't business; it was personal... very personal.

CHAPTER TWENTY-SIX

Toler TeleCom Building, Schaumburg

"Bob, are you okay?" Ernie Travers stepped into his line of sight and asked.

"Yeah, kinda. But it's like a gut punch," he said as he finally turned away from the shattered building and focused on Ernie and four men he brought with him.

"You already know Detective Larry Pomerantz from the Schaumburg PD, from when you used to live up here, and these are Special Agent Barfield and Special Agent Donner from the regional FBI office downtown," Ernie said as he stepped aside and made introductions.

"Mind if I look at the building?" Bob asked the two Feds.

"No problem," Barfield answered. "In fact, we'd like to get your take on this." Bob ducked under the tape and joined them as they walked through the parking lot toward the building. "You have a long list of interesting friends, Mr. Burke," the FBI Agent went on.

"And some even more interesting enemies," Bob answered.

"It would appear so, but Ernie here and our agent in charge in Trenton, New Jersey, Phil Henderson, both of whom I've known for years, think you walk on water. Your name also came up regarding an investigation being conducted by our organized crime task force in Brooklyn. I talked to Agent Parvenuti a little while ago. His view wasn't so much that you walked on water as it was his wanting to see you tossed into the deep end."

"Guess you can't please everyone, Agent Barfield."

They soon reached another taped off area around the building's front entrance, and Barfield said, "Agent Parvenuti claimed you were interfering with their investigation of a Russian mob operation in Brooklyn, Mr. Burke."

"Then shame on him. He should have arrested me, shouldn't he?"

"You think they're the ones behind this?" Barfield asked. "I worked in the Newark office for a few years. When I described what happened here to Parvenuti, he thought it was a strong possibility. Something about a contract the Russians screwed you out of?"

"Then Parvenuti should've arrested them too, shouldn't he? Maybe this wouldn't have happened." Bob gave him what was left of a friendly smile, but the rest disappeared when they reached what was left of the lobby. The windows were gone, the police cruiser had smashed into the far wall, and the explosion had brought the acoustical ceiling and pink batts of insulation down on top of the car and everything else. Barfield turned toward Detective Pomerantz and asked, "Larry, you guys got any idea yet how the hell your cruiser ended up in there?"

"Yeah, kind of. We've spent the past hour trying to reconstruct it. The car was on patrol and stopped out in the lot when someone machine-gunned it and the two officers inside at close range. From the places the bullets hit inside the car, the gunman pointed the weapon and sprayed it. He wasn't even aiming, firing somewhere between twenty and thirty rounds of 7.62 ball ammunition, the .30-caliber Soviet Short, as it's called."

"Sounds like an AK-47," Bob offered. "Unfortunately, you can get that kind of ammo at most gun shops, even Walmart."

"We found brass casings out in the lot, at least a dozen of them, some twenty-five feet away from here. We figure the two police officers were sitting in their car, window down, and the gunman was maybe three or four feet away, standing next to them or more likely sitting in another car. We are missing a lot of brass. So, unless he stopped and policed the rest of it up, which we doubt, we figure the rest must have stayed inside his car.

"Twenty to thirty rounds? That's an entire magazine," Bob said. "Hard to miss at that range."

"Yeah," Barfield agreed. "The gunman was trying to make a point. If we find the weapon, we can probably match it; but ATF says source is almost untraceable."

"Neither officer appears to have drawn his sidearm," Pomerantz said. "They never stood a chance. The driver must've jammed his foot down on the accelerator because the cruiser leapt forward, crashed through the window, and went on into the lobby until the wall stopped it. It was sometime after that, maybe a minute, that the bomb detonated."

"You don't see this kind of nasty overkill very often," Agent Donner added.

"No," Bob agreed. "Like you said, whoever did it was trying to make a point, or he's just crazy."

"Add to that, we have that car that blew up a couple of miles away on Meacham Road. ATF and another FBI crew are still sifting through what's left of it. Everything is black and burned, but everybody's sure we'll get chemical matches to this batch. They also found a cache of weapons in the backseat, and we found some brass casings in the front seat. They are mostly burned and scorched, but when the analysis is done, maybe we'll get a match to the ones he left over here."

"You mind if we go around to the fire entrance and look upstairs? I'd like to see how much damage we've had on the second floor."

They walked around to the side entrance and went up the interior fire stairs. Even using flashlights, it was still very dark inside. "Your accounting office was directly above the lobby and took the brunt of the explosion, Bob," Pomerantz said. "That was where the two female fatalities were. The two men, the janitor and the security guard, were on the first floor down the hallway. They got hit by flying glass and other material."

From the door Bob could see the wreckage of the accounting office. He turned away and walked down the corridor, briefly looking in the other offices until he came to his own. Most managers put their own offices in the far corner of the space, usually at the end of the longest hallway, around a few corners, well out of sight from everyone, with big outside windows. That "boss cave" was exactly what Ed Toler refused to have. His hallways had glass walls and none of the offices had doors. Ed then placed his office in the middle with no windows but where the hallways intersected. That way he could see, hear, and feel everything that was going on.

"I want to see what my people are doing. More importantly, I want them to see what *I'm* doing," Ed once told Bob. "I can't imagine running a company any other way." Neither could Bob.

Pomerantz and the two Feds followed him inside his old office. Maryanne was now the president, but she stayed in her old space and wanted him to keep his for his occasional trips up from North Carolina. Looking around, he saw several ceiling tiles had fallen and most of the "rogues' gallery" of photographs and plaques, which used to cover one of the side walls, were now lying on the floor in a field of broken glass. Most were standard company PR stuff that Ed left behind: plaques and awards that the company received over the years, shots of a few of their big customers, of Ed shaking hands with people, and of key company staff. But there were two photos of Bob that dated back to Angie, his late first wife. She hung them on the wall, not him; and she used those big drywall butterfly screws, so he couldn't take them down without tearing the wall apart. Even the bomb didn't bring those two down.

Agent Donner immediately zeroed in on them, walked over, and turned on his flashlight for a closer look. Compared to the brightly colored corporate shots, they looked beige on dusty, dull beige. The top one dated from the first Iraq war — the good one. Donner saw a young, smiling

Lieutenant Robert Burke kneeling in the center of two or three dozen laughing, grinning American soldiers in full battle dress. Behind them sat two large, battered M-113 Armored Personnel Carriers, an Abrams tank, and an empty, rock-strewn desert that stretched to the horizon.

It was an interesting shot, but it was the other photo that drew his attention even more. It was of a smaller group of eight heavily armed men — American Special Ops soldiers — set against a craggy, snowcapped mountain range. They had beards, baggy pants, shawls, and the flat "pakol" hats that the native Afghans wore. To a man, they looked older and more battle-weary than the other group, with forced smiles. Their smiles were forced; but the eager young men in the first photo had won their war. In Iraq, they had kicked ass in a matter of days and were soon on their way home from their first and only tour. The men in the second photo, however, were on their second, third, or even fourth tours, trapped in a war that ground on and on, kicking everyone's ass.

But there was that guy in the center. Donner leaned closer with his flashlight and studied him. He was by far the smallest in the group, leaning on a long-barreled Barrett M-82A1 .50-caliber sniper rifle. Above his thick beard and mustache, Donner recognized the hard, black eyes of Bob Burke. Next to him stood a taller, more muscular man who Donner knew was one of the three men who accompanied him here tonight, and who was outside with the ATF guys.

Detective Pomerantz walked over, and Donner pointed at the photograph. "You know, Bob, there's an old Polish proverb that says, 'You can tell a lot about a man's character by the quality of his friends.' "

That was when they heard an unfamiliar voice speak to them from the doorway in crisp, accented English. "Actually, it is an old Polish misquote of older Russian proverb: 'You can tell much about a man's character by the quality of his *ENEMIES.*' "

CHAPTER TWENTY-SEVEN

Second Floor, Toler TeleCom Building

The four men inside the office turned and saw a short, barrel-chested man standing in the doorway dressed in an unusual, forest-green dress uniform with wheat sheaves on its collars, pale-gold shoulder boards with two thin red stripes and three gold stars. He had five narrow rows of colorful ribbons, a name tag written in Cyrillic, and a pale blue beret on his head. His eyes locked on Bob's and he said, "Major Burke, I have long looked forward to meeting you. My name is Colonel Vladimir Rostov, currently with the Russian Embassy in Washington," he said as he stepped forward and extended his hand toward Burke.

Trying not to look too puzzled, Bob met him halfway. Bob was a small man. Rostov was an inch or two taller, but at least sixty or seventy pounds heavier, with broad shoulders, and a thick torso and neck. They shook, and Bob could feel the muscle and power behind it, thinking to himself, "You can also tell a lot about a man by his handshake." Back home in Tar Heel land, folks would say the Colonel was built like "a brick shit house." Bob always prided himself at being a good judge of character. He couldn't put his finger on why, but soldier to soldier, there was something about this stocky Russian he liked.

As they shook hands, Bob scoped out the man's uniform. He was no expert on the Russian military. They changed their insignia and regalia more often than even the US did, but he had attended enough officer-to-officer exchanges at Fort Bragg to recognize the colors and insignia of the Russian Army GRU, their military intelligence branch, his rank of colonel, and many decorations for bravery in combat. He was probably too young to have served during the Russian occupation of Afghanistan, so the decorations probably dated from Chechnya, the Ukraine, Syria, and several other minor wars where Putin had sent Russian troops in the last twenty years.

Bob also recognized Rostov's unit insignia. "The 45th Guards Independent Recon Brigade," Bob said with a nod. "My compliments, sir."

"Ah, you have heard of us, then?" the Russian smiled.

"The elite of the elite," Bob answered with a second polite nod.

"Much like your own 75th Ranger Regiment and Delta Force, eh?" Rostov replied, to Bob's mild surprise. Membership in Delta was supposed to be a closely guarded secret, but the truth was we knew most of the

Russians' stuff and there was no reason to think they didn't know most of ours.

"We sound like two junk yard dogs circling each other," Rostov laughed. "Later, when you have a moment, we must compare notes, Major."

"Uh, I hate to ruin detente, Colonel, but this is a crime scene," Detective Pomeranz finally spoke up. "And how did you get in here?"

Rostov looked around, feigning surprise. "Perhaps there's more than one 'Ghost' here, eh, Major Burke?"

"Why don't we just say he's with me, Larry," Bob interceded. "He's a consultant I asked to help us ID any Russian equipment or explosives. I'll vouch for him."

Pomerantz shrugged, "It's your building, Bob, so I guess it doesn't matter anymore; but let's not have any more 'ghosting,' Colonel. We ought to take it back outside, anyway. ATF and our EOD people have some stuff to show us."

They went back down the rear stairs, out the fire door, and walked over to the ATF forensic table where Master Sergeants Enders and Themopolis were in a deep discussion with Al Peterson and two of his bomb techs. Enders looked up at Burke and the others and said to Peterson, "Show them what you have on the wires and detonators."

They all gathered around the table, even Rostov, who stood behind Peterson and watched as he pushed some small shards and pieces of wire around two large, white sheets of paper. "The items on the left are from here, and the ones on the right are from the car. Same wire. We also made preliminary matches on the 7.62-caliber brass. Same for the phones. Further tests will show the same make and model – cheap burner throwaways. More importantly, Semtex has built-in markers called detection taggants. The trace vapor residue from the two bombs indicate both were Semtex 10 and the batches match."

"Manufactured in Czech Republic?" Rostov asked.

Peterson answered without looking at the questioner. "That's the only known manufacturing source, but they export enough of it all over the place to render any further tracing problematical."

Further back on the table lay what was left of a canvas bag and some badly burned and melted pieces of metal. Rostov extended his arm around Peterson and asked, "May I?"

Peterson finally turned and looked over his shoulder at the speaker. He did a double take when he saw a Russian colonel in full uniform standing behind him. Unsure, he glanced over at the FBI agents who nodded their assent, and handed the longer, burned hunk of metal to Rostov who looked it over from one end to the other. "It is an old Kalashnikov."

Peterson looked skeptical. "It's all burnt. Without tests, how can you tell?"

Rostov shrugged. "I have seen more than my share of burnt ones over the years. And those bullets," he said, pointing to a pile at the back of the table. "They are 7.62 by 39, standard Russian issue for that weapon. And those others, the burnt semiautomatic pistols, I would say they are a PL-15 and a Makarov. "

"Correct," Peterson said, glancing at the two FBI agents again. "And you are?"

"A visiting Fire Chief from Minsk, nothing more," Rostov answered straight-faced as he walked away from the table. "Seen enough, Major Burke? The weapons and plastic explosives are all from our mutual 'friends' in Brooklyn."

It was obvious to Bob that Rostov wasn't there by accident and had things to say, so Bob joined him as they walked back toward the office building's front entrance. A work crew from one of the local construction companies Maryanne called in was installing wooden bracing and jacks under the steel beams and masonry façade around the front entrance, while a large tow truck was attempting to pull the police cruiser out of the lobby.

"Colonel," Bob slowed his pace. "What did you mean when you said, 'from our mutual friends' in Brooklyn?"

"Brooklyn and Moscow, actually... the Shurepkins, of course."

"You're certain about that?"

"Positive, aren't you? You lost two of your female employees here tonight and nearly lost two more. Piotr Shurepkin is responsible for those. Even if he did not pull the trigger, and I personally believe he did, because his monstrous ego would not have allowed anyone else to do it. I also believe he is responsible for the death of your friend Major Charles Adkins. Perhaps his finger was not on the trigger, because he was likely up in New York at that time, but you know he caused it to happen every bit as much as I do."

"All right," Bob stopped walking and the two men turned and faced each other. "Why are you here, Colonel?"

Rostov appeared surprised by the question. "Why? To kill them, of course, to kill them all – that little shit Piotr, his brother, Evgeni, especially their father Oleg in Moscow, and as many of their gunmen as I can. Given our mutual interests and backgrounds, I believe you want to kill them all as much as I do."

Bob stared at Rostov for a long moment, thinking. Russians were known to be blunt and say what they thought, but he had never met one like this. "And you think that's what I'm going to do? You think I'm going to help you kill them."

"Of course you are. I have read your personnel file, Major Burke. I know it as well as I know my own: all those tours in Iraq and Afghanistan. Your recent adventures in Chicago, Atlantic City, and Fort Bragg, even that very commendable long-rifle shot you made to take out that self-appointed Caliph in Syria last year. I know it all," he said with cold, hard eyes as he tapped his forehead. "And yes, I believe that is exactly what you intend to do... what WE intend to do."

"All right, I know why I want to kill them, but why are you after them, Colonel?"

"Because they killed my eldest son, Alexei. He was a decorated police officer, a senior investigator with the Ministry of Internal Affairs in Moscow. In my country, that can be a very political business in the best of times. Two years ago, Alexei found himself in the middle of a major corruption case. It involved Oleg Shurepkin. He ordered one of his underlings, his lead bodyguard named Dema Kropotkin, to kill my son."

"Unless I'm mistaken, isn't that a Master Sniper Badge on your uniform?" Bob asked.

Rostov glanced down at his jacket front. "Yes, mastery of the long gun. It is a skill you and I share, is it not?"

"Couldn't you have taken Shurepkin out with one of those new Chukavin sniper rifles you guys are bragging about? I've fired one. If you're good with a long gun, you can't miss with one of those."

"At the time, Oleg Shurepkin had too many highly placed friends, but his fortunes and his friends are quickly disappearing now. Besides, that was not how I wanted to do it. A long-range rifle shot to an unexpectant target? No, I want Oleg Shurepkin to know exactly which sins have caught up with him. Power constantly shifts in Moscow. Today, Vladimir Putin no longer cares what happens to Shurepkin or his cronies. If Putin did, I would not be here talking to you, Major, I would be in a basement cell in the Lubyanka. But now, I believe you and I have the complementary skills and motivation to roll up his organization and take him out."

Burke looked into Rostov's eyes and saw the man was deadly serious.

"Understand, Major, I am Russian," Rostov went on. "We prefer to take our revenge in small, painful bites. First, I want to bring his organization down, then I want to kill his sons, as he killed mine. Finally, when he is a gutted, broken man, I will kill him, too."

"You'll go that far? To Brooklyn? Even back to Moscow to get them?" Bob asked, seeing in the man's eyes that he was deadly serious. "You have big plans, Colonel. Assuming we can trust each other, how do you think you can pull something like that off?"

"I shall rely on Shurepkin to do it to himself before I finish him off. You see, Vladimir Putin is a hungry beast that must be constantly fed. Oleg Shurepkin's fortunes and power are now in decline. He can no longer give Putin what he wants, so he has lost favor. His rivals sense that and circle like vultures, ready to swoop in and tear off a piece of him. When he sent his two sons to New York, it was a desperate gamble on his part. He needed a big score. His younger son, Evgeni, the autistic one, designs, if that is the proper word, whole computer programs in his head. He can barely write fast enough to put them down on paper."

"Like Mozart composing music."

"Yes, in a perverse way, perhaps. Their goal was to steal your business, but that was only the beginning. Like camel sticking his nose under the Pentagon, the plan is to start in an innocent area and expand in every direction like a thousand snakes that will let them get into the more important Pentagon things. Oleg Shurepkin and his underworld friends may be after the money, but Putin is after more. He wants to hack the entire Pentagon system, all of it. Steal your secrets and then crash it. But, as Oleg Shurepkin is learning, the higher you fly the more painful the crash when you fall. So, when I saw who owned this business he was targeting, I knew I found the ally I need."

"You've been watching me, Colonel?"

The Russian laughed. "Actually, Robert – if I may call you that, and please call me Volodya – yes, I've been watching you for many years, I believe even in Afghanistan."

"In Afghanistan?" Bob asked, surprised by the comment.

"My assignment for six months was to create a sniper school for several of the more hardline Taliban hill tribes."

"Those guys? I didn't think they needed to be taught how to shoot."

"You are correct, of course. My job was to put better weapons into the right hands and give them the right training. One night, I was out with a small Taliban team. I believe we spotted you and your squad of Deltas set up on a trail in the hills near Kunduz, across a small valley where we were," Rostov smiled. "We moved when you moved, and I tracked you in my scope for quite some time, until you stopped above a small cluster of mud huts before sunrise. In mid-morning, a short, sharp battle ensued, which you ended with airpower."

"But you didn't take a shot?"

Rostov looked at him. "No, it was not part of 'my brief,' as the British would say. Besides, I would not have found that 'sporting,' since you were not *MY* enemy. Now, if one of my Afghans took the shot, not my problem, but I would not take it myself. I must confess, it would have been a difficult shot, even for me. You were dug in and beyond my reasonably maximum range."

"Still, you could have taken it," Bob commented.

"To what end? Miss and warn you? Change the dynamics in the valley? I believe another group of Taliban had an ambush in progress, so it would have given up our positions and warned you at the same time. No, tactically not wise."

"But if one of your men chose to take the shot?"

"Well, that would have been a 'horse of a different color,' as you say. But they weren't nearly good enough, not then, anyway. Even still, I figure you owe me one."

"It is odd, but I remember having the odd feeling that morning that someone was watching me. I even said something to Ace about it."

"An infantryman's sixth sense, we call it. I have had it myself from time to time in the field," Rostov chuckled, and then paused and looked at him again. "Now, you know my reasons for going after the Shurepkins. But why are *YOU* doing this, Robert? This contract they steal from you is 'small potatoes.' You could have let them have it and gone to work on others. Even your lovely office building here, you can rebuild it, no? I understand your reputation and your past; but Russian Mafia is not to be trifled with, as I hope you understand, or you soon will."

"My friends are not to be trifled with either. Charles Adkins and my two bookkeepers on the second floor did not deserve what happened to them. Neither did your son. So I think it falls to those of us who *CAN* do something to act. And you are right, Volodya, they are in serious need of killing, all of them. Like you, I want to take down his organization first, take his money, and put all of his people in jail or in the ground, so the next bunch of clowns, wherever they are from, will think twice before they try to bother us."

Rostov extended his hand again, rock solid, and looked Burke right in the eye as he said, "Agreed. And that is what we will do. You have my word, Robert."

"And you have mine, Volodya," Bob nodded, and they shook on it. "But to pull this off, we need a 'can opener,' something which will help us get inside."

As they turned and walked away, they walked over to where Ace, Maryanne, and George Grierson were standing and looking at the building. "George, assuming the police finish their work and give us our building back, we need to get some structural engineers and a top contractor in here to determine the damage, maybe a good 'clerk of the works' to coordinate it all for us. You and Maryanne need to find one for us up here. So, I will leave that, the insurance, and all the rest of it in your capable hands and Maryanne's. Keep the staff on full salary. I'd like to be up and running in the other areas of the building and maybe in some temporary space ASAP."

"And here I was giving some thought to retiring," George looked at the building and moaned.

"Instead, you have a full-time job for a while," Bob laughed. "Then you can retire. You and Maryanne plan on a daily conference call. Meanwhile, Ace and I are headed back to North Carolina. We have a couple of other problems to work on. Right, Ace?" He turned to the big Master Sergeant and said, "Let's head back to the barn."

He turned toward the Russian Colonel and asked, "How did you get here?"

"By private jet, from Washington. I used some influence and got myself assigned to the Embassy last month as Assistant Military Attaché. When I heard what happened here, I had our transportation people hire one to fly me down to Fayetteville hoping to catch you there. Unfortunately, you had just left. So we followed and landed just behind you."

"Too bad the Embassy doesn't give you frequent flyer miles."

"Very true, but the service on the private jets is much better, as are the seats. With my build and the older I get, the more important that becomes," Rostov laughed.

"Fly back with me then. You can spend a few days at my farm. It will give us time to recon and make some plans. Meanwhile, I'm gonna call my computer staff and put them to work on a few ideas."

Rostov looked at his watch. "At this time of night your people are working, Robert? You must have some very dedicated people."

Bob smiled. "I'm not sure if that's the word I would use."

CHAPTER TWENTY-EIGHT

Sherwood Forest

During the flight back to North Carolina, the drive up from Gray's Aviation and a big breakfast at Bob's favorite country diner just off I-75, Bob and Ace had plenty of time to get debriefed by Master Sergeants Tim Enders and George Themopolis on what they had gleaned from the site and the ATF guys. Mostly it confirmed what they already learned standing around the table with Agent Al Peterson. When the more detailed lab reports came back from the FBI lab at Quantico, except for learning more about the origin of the Semtex, the reports weren't likely to change the basic conclusions.

After he introduced Colonel Rostov to Linda and the security staff, Bob gave him a quick tour of the property and got him checked into one of the guest rooms in the conference wing outback. Finally, it was time to show him the third floor. At the top of the stairs, Bob watched Rostov's reaction when he saw the sign over the double doors to the Geekdom that said, "KGB Spymaster Data Center." It was impossible to miss.

"Your people have strange sense of humor," the Russian said with an amused smile.

"You haven't seen the half of it," Bob laughed. "One of my tech support guys, Sasha Kandarsky, is Russian. He has a very advanced degree from Berkeley, like the other two, but from time to time he lets it slip that he started out working in the KGB's data center outside Moscow."

"And you trust him enough to hire him?" Rostov asked, sounding surprised. "I am not certain I would."

They walked inside. After more introductions, while Jimmy Barker showed the Colonel around the equipment, Sasha eyed his uniform up and down, took Bob's arm, and walked him around to the other side of the central work desk. "Boss, you know Sasha is careful, very careful person," he whispered. "This Russian colonel you brought in is KGB."

"He says he's GRU, Sasha, military intelligence and special ops."

"Tomatoes, potatoes, Boss."

"You mean to-may-toes, to-mah-toes, Sasha?"

"That's what I said, Boss – KGB and GRU, potatoes and Putin. All the same."

"Except I think this guy's on our side."

"If you say so, Boss, but KGB is only on KGB's side… and Putin's. Still, you wanted me to check him out. Here's report," Sasha said as he stuck a sheaf of papers into Bob's pocket.

Bob then took Sasha by the arm and walked him around to the other side, where he and Rostov eyed each other suspiciously for a moment. Both men were thick, barrel-chested, about the same height, with dark eyes. Rostov was much older. Sasha had a big, bushy beard, while Rostov was clean shaven with a short buzz cut. Other than that, the two men could be father and son.

"The KGB Spymaster Data Center?" Rostov commented dryly. "They say 'once KGB, always KGB.' "

"I know! See, Boss, I tell you same thing," Sasha looked back at Bob and grinned.

"I am GRU, a soldier," Rostov corrected him.

"I tell Boss, tomatoes, potatoes."

Rostov paused, thinking that over. "I see. But anyone with that much confusion must be KGB."

When Jimmy, Ronald, and Patsy heard that one, they began laughing hysterically.

Bob realized it was time for him to intervene. "Sasha, the Colonel and I have an idea. You tried to hack into that restaurant, Kalinka's, into their accounting, payroll, and the phony corporations they registered up there, but you couldn't get in, right?"

Sasha shrugged. "I got in, but too many tripwires. You said for Sasha to be careful, so I tiptoed through their payroll and personnel files and stayed away from financial files."

"Can you tell who does their systems and software work? Recognize any names?"

"Maybe one, a stiff named Kirschman. Vyacheslav 'Slava' Kirschman his name. He took class with me long time ago in Moscow. Was not good with software. Never made it into school's advanced program. Was what you call 'bottom feeder.' Gopher. Future high school teacher, Sasha figured. I see his fingerprints all over Kalinka software. Even left his initials. Stupid fellow! You want, I break him like a twig."

"Not yet. You did the right thing backing away. I didn't want to set off any alarm bells back then. On the airplane, I explained to the Colonel how we recruited you."

"Recruited!" Sasha began muttering to himself in Russian. "That was not funny, Boss – a black-bag kidnapping of poor Sasha, throwing me in helicopter and having that general interrogate me. Not funny!"

"But effective…"

"Well, yes! Effective, but Sasha not like it."

Vyacheslav "Slava" Kirschman lived in a small, two-room apartment with seven other young Russian men one block north of Kalinka's. They all worked for the Shurepkins bussing tables at the restaurant, helping the wait staff, cleaning dishes, and working with the computers between meals. The apartment was a smelly, filthy, firetrap on the rear side of the second floor of a converted house. The furniture was threadbare, and the beds were sway-back, jammed in the bedrooms. The kitchen had a tiny refrigerator and stove, but they had no money to buy anything to put in it or to cook. They were fed in the restaurant in a room off the kitchen and would spend ten to twelve hours a day working there.

Between meals, Slava did bookkeeping, inputting bills and receipts into the computer, and doing the tedious scut-work on various software Evgeni Shurepkin was developing. For his "break," they would let him spend two hours after lunch and three hours in the evening every day working upstairs in the restaurant's big kitchen washing dishes. No money, no passports, just work, seven days a week. It wasn't what he bargained for when they talked him into this great opportunity back in Moscow. As soon as he arrived, they told him he had to "pay off" the airplane ticket, pay rent for the room, and pay for meals. They said they were sending the rest of the money home to his mother, but he didn't believe them. Time off? Holidays? Even Sunday? That was just another workday to them.

"What do you expect?" Piotr would snap at him. "Get Sunday off? You must think we are Catholics!"

The best part of Vyacheslav's miserable day was the time he spent writing computer programs with Evgeni for different business applications they were developing in New York and back home. He actually felt like he was doing something. Vyacheslav had taken programming classes in Moscow. But while some in the class went on to the advanced courses and got good government jobs, he was passed over and was lucky to get what was left over: freelance work for crooks. That was why he jumped at the job in New York. He thought it would be a new start, until he got here. Instead of Madison Avenue and Broadway, he got Brighton Beach.

Slava still believed he was reasonably competent with a computer, until they told him to help Evgeni. After that, he spent every afternoon from 2 p.m. to 6 p.m. sitting next to Evgeni in the rear booth at the back of Kalinka's, mouth hanging open, mesmerized as he watched the young savant type codes at lightning-fast speed into his laptop. At first,

Vyacheslav understood little of what Evgeni was doing. Between Evgeni's grunts and giggles as he pointed at the screen, Vyacheslav slowly understood and learned how to communicate with him. Evgeni was eight years younger than Vyacheslav and the other guys in the apartment called him an "idiot" and a "half-wit," but he was a genius when it came to computer coding.

The small apartment they shared was a block north of Kalinka's in the "low-rent district" further away from the beach. The street was a broken line of small, cheap, two-story houses with brick facades on the first floors, aluminum siding above, and chain-link fences around their front and back yards. They used to belong to working-class families where the husband and wife worked in the local businesses. Now, they were crammed with young Russian immigrants.

Slava would usually get out of bed around 10:00 a.m. for his fifteen reserved minutes in the bathroom and leave for the restaurant around 10:45. It was a five-minute walk door-to-door, less when the light on the Boulevard was green. If he could, he'd stretch it to ten minutes, because it was the only sun or fresh air he would see all day.

That morning, the sky was a bright blue, the air was a perfect seventy degrees, and the flowers in the window boxes of the other houses along the street showed bright reds and blues. Vyacheslav slowed his pace, happy to take it all in, when a dark blue van with tinted windows swung in next to him. The driver leaned out the window with a map and called him over, "Pardon me, but can you show me where Ocean Beach Avenue is?"

The young Russian was happy to find still another diversion, walked over to the curb, and began looking at the map as the van's side door slid open. In the blink of an eye, two men came up behind him, pulled a pillowcase over his head, and threw him inside the van. The next thing he knew, he was lying on the floor with his hands tied behind his back. He felt something hard press against the back of his neck and a gruff voice said to him in Russian, "Make noise, and you die!"

Vyacheslav was terrified and lost all track of time and direction as the van drove away and made a quick series of left and right turns. If they meant to confuse him, it didn't matter. Once he got a block or two away from Kalinka's he had no idea where he was, anyway. Eventually, the van stopped, the door slid open, two big men picked him up by his arms, and carried him a few feet into a small motel room. They shoved him into a chair, and he heard the door behind him slam. They pulled the pillowcase off his head, and he found himself staring into two bright lights on a table in front of him that were shining directly in his face.

"Vyacheslav!" a deep voice spoke to him from beyond the lights, in Russian again. "How long have you been a traitor to the Rodina, to the Motherland?"

"But I'm not, I'm not a traitor," he pleaded. "I'm only a simple computer programmer, a bookkeeper... and a miserable dishwasher."

"Who is working for criminals, for mobsters, who are trying to bring down the government," another man right behind him spoke up, hissing in his ear.

"No, no, I know nothing about that. They brought me here under false pretenses. I am slave. I have no money and I have no papers. I have no idea what they are doing."

"Your mother says different," the first man said.

"She says you wanted to come here and work for them, the Shurepkins," a third man whispered in his ear in English.

"My mother... Why...?"

"She has been very helpful to us," the man next to him said in his ear in Russian.

"Are you FSB, the security police?" Slava dared ask. "If you are, you should arrest them, not me."

"We arrest traitors, and if you want to save yourself and your mother, you will tell us everything you know about the Shurepkins and what they are doing here."

"Yes, yes! I tell you everything! But please, the lights, they hurt...!"

"Tell us about the laptop computer Evgeni uses, what brand, what model, what size and speed..." the man behind him demanded to know in a rapid staccato of questions.

"Is nothing, an old, off-the-shelf Toshiba he brought from Moscow, same model they let me use when I help him."

"Where they keep second Toshiba?"

"In the office in back, I go get it before I sit in booth with Evgeni. But Toshiba is nothing. Computer is nothing. It is Evgeni, not machine."

"You work with him, with Evgeni?"

"Yes, yes, some days. Now, I go in and work in kitchen until lunch is over, cleaning, washing dishes, getting supplies from the basement, whatever kitchen manager tells me to do."

"When do you work with Evgeni?" a voice behind him asked.

"Maybe 2 p.m., until 5:30, then they sent me back to the kitchen. At 8 p.m., when the rush is over, they send me to the back office. I post bills and receipts for day on the office computer in Piotr's office. Sometimes I stock shelves."

"What about Internet?" the English-speaking man behind him asked.

"Wi-Fi for laptops. Wire connection for computer. It depends on what we do and who we send things to. Router is in back, in Piotr's office."

There was silence for a few minutes as the three men stepped into the bathroom and closed the door. Vyacheslav could hear them talking but could not understand the words. Finally, they came out and resumed the interrogation.

"All right, Vyacheslav, there may be a way for you to save yourself and your mother."

"Anything, anything," the young Russian pleaded.

"We will take you back and drop you off around the corner from the restaurant…"

"No! No, I don't want to go back there. Never. You must help me!"

"Only if you do what we say."

"All right, all right," Slava slumped in the chair. "Tell me what you want."

"You are late for shift now. That is okay. Tell them you got stomach problems, but you okay now. You work with Evgeni at 2 p.m.?" the man across from him asked. "My friend Sasha here – show him your face, Sasha." The big bear stepped out of the shadows, bent over, and put his thickly bearded face into the light right in front of Slava.

Startled, Slava leaned away, then frowned and said, "I know you. You are Sasha Kandarsky. We were in class together, in Moscow!"

"That's right," the man across the table continued. "Sasha will go in the restaurant at 3 p.m. to get something to eat. You will see each other and act like long-lost friends. You will then introduce him to Piotr and Evgeni. Tell them you studied together at Moscow Coding School on Tverskaya Street…"

"Yes, yes, that's right. We did."

"They'll check, and that's what they'll find out, too. Sasha will tell them he's broke and looking for a job. You will tell them he is much smarter than you, and he went on to Moscow State University. They'll check that too. Sasha will say if they let him use your laptop, he'll show them. Then he'll put on a little demonstration."

"And Sasha will come to work and help me?"

"That's the plan," the man behind him answered and then placed a computer flash drive on the table in front of Vyacheslav, under the bright circles of light. "Does Evgeni ever leave his laptop on the table in the restaurant?"

"No, not much, almost never. It is his pet. He even takes it to toilet."

"All right," the man paused, thinking. "First, this afternoon, when you go to the office to get your laptop, slip this into it, into the data port. Do you understand?"

"There's nothing to be worried about," the man across the table tried to reassure him. "It will take less than a minute to upload some tracking software and quickly download some files we want. It is quite easy, and it leaves no trace. Tonight, when they send you to the office to enter all the day's receipts, you do the same thing on the office machine. And we want it uploaded into Evgeni's too."

"They will kill me if they catch me."

"Then you must be careful not to get caught! But if you don't do what we say, we will be the ones who kill you," the Russian across the table said.

"Tonight, when you go home, one of us will wait for you around the corner when you walk home," the third man said in English. "You will give us back the flash drive, continue on to your apartment. Hopefully, Sasha will start working today or tomorrow and that will be it. Is that clear?"

"No! I don't want to go back to the apartment, or to the restaurant. I want out of here. I want to go home!"

The Russian behind the table who seemed in charge, paused for a moment. "We will arrange that, Vyacheslav, but it takes a few days. Three days, most likely. So, you must do what we say until then. For now, you go to Kalinka's and work like nothing happened. In three days, we pull you out."

"What about my passport? They have my passport. I have no money, no nothing."

"I'll get you a new passport."

Vyacheslav frowned, suddenly suspicious. "You get me new Russian passport?"

"I can do that."

The young man frowned. "You must be KGB, FSB. Show me?"

A loud irritated sigh came out of Colonel Rostov, but he finally slid an open wallet with a badge and ID card into the light under the lamps, and just as quickly withdrew it. "I am with GRU, the Ministry of Internal Affairs, not the FSB. We don't trust them either. And if you ever breathe a word of this and don't do exactly what we tell you, you will spend the next ten years in a very cold place chipping coal from the permafrost with a pickax. You believe I can do that, Vyacheslav?"

"Yes, yes, not a word, I won't say a word, then you leave my mother alone?"

"We will even get you your back pay," the English-speaking man behind him said.

"Deal!" The young Russian grinned. "But no bag over my head and no handcuffs. Please. I close my eyes. I don't look. Three days, I do whatever you want."

CHAPTER TWENTY-NINE

Brighton Beach, Brooklyn

They dropped the young Russian around the corner from Kalinka's, and watched him scamper across Brighton Beach Boulevard and into the restaurant, grinning. Bob had Ace drive around to one of the side streets and park behind the building that faced the Russian tearoom. He asked Sasha and Rostov to wait in the van, while he and Ace went in the rear door and climbed the steep back staircase to the second floor. Bob knocked on the door of the narrow apartment that faced Brighton Beach Boulevard. It didn't take long for FBI Agent Parvenuti to open the door, frowning, with a 9-millimeter Glock automatic in his hand. "Burke! Why doesn't it surprise me to see you out there?"

They brushed past him and walked into the small apartment, through the kitchen into the front living room, and looked around at the array of electronic equipment, videotape cameras, audio recorders, and tripod-mounted directional microphones scattered about.

"What do you think, Ace?"

"I bet they didn't buy this stuff wholesale at Larry's Gidgets and Gadgets down the street."

"Or the pawnshop next door, but all of their stuff is hot."

Finally, Parvenuti had heard enough. "Tryin' out for the Comedy Club? What do you two want?"

"Oh, we came up here to get a better view of where that bomb came from," Bob answered. "I'll bet it came from across the street, wouldn't you, Agent Kaczynski?"

"We heard something went boom in the night back in Chicago. Unfortunately, Shurepkin and his pals come and go so fast it would be hard to pin a timeline on them."

"Then you're no further along than you were before?" Bob asked, waiting for an answer that didn't come. "That's what I thought. Look, Phil Henderson over in Trenton is an old friend of mine. We've been known to scratch each other's backs. You can call him if you want a recommendation."

"We already have, Bob, otherwise we'd have locked your ass up back in DC."

"Oh, you can try, but Phil probably told you that doesn't work too well. Anyway, I'm just giving you guys a heads up that we are around. But don't get excited. If it leads to anything, we share. You'll get it all: all the credit and all the good stuff we find. So, do everyone a favor and just let it play itself out."

"Yeah," Parvenuti answered. "Phil told us you'd say that too."

"If you look at what desk he's now sitting at in Trenton, we didn't do his career any harm, either."

"Anything beats the crap out of Brooklyn, Burke," Kaczynski shrugged.

"Except New Jersey," Parvenuti countered.

"There is that. Kind of a lateral, I guess." Kaczynski agreed.

At 3:15 p.m., Sasha Kandarski walked through the front door of Kalinka's and looked around. The restaurant-bar-nightclub was nearly empty at that hour, but it was still in its daytime tearoom mode. The lights were on, the drapes were open on the front windows, and sun was filtering in between the elevated subway tracks over the street. The tables had colorful calico-red tablecloths with kitschy Russian dessert plates and ceramic Russian ballerina salt-and-pepper shakers. Cute, he thought. Not.

In the left front corner of the restaurant was a small gift shop. They stacked it to the ceiling with brightly colored Russian peasant dresses, balalaikas, nesting dolls, gilt icon paintings, tea sets, bottle openers, coasters, and lacquer boxes. Just like the ones in the gift shops on Nevsky Prospekt in St. Petersburg and the Izmailovsky Flea Market in Moscow, everything had authentic looking Russian tags, but if a customer was rude enough to look in the cabinets underneath the counters, the shipping boxes were all from China.

Along the right-hand wall ran a long, brightly polished bar, where a surly, unshaven bartender, a cigarette dangling from his lips, washed the last glasses from lunch. On the shelves behind the bar stood dozens of cheap brands of vodka from Bakon and Belvedere, to Burnett's and Johnkovic's, mostly undrinkable swill from Poland.

Sasha sat down at a table in the middle of the room and picked up a menu. After a few minutes, an overweight, late-middle-aged waitress with heavy makeup, and what was supposed to pass for a Russian peasant's blouse and white-and-red skirt, sauntered over with an order pad and a Bic pen. She looked down at Sasha and cocked her head. "What I get you, honey?"

"Baltika beer and golubtsy."

"The stuffed cabbage? No soup?" she asked.

"Is it good?" he asked. She rolled her eyes, which was answer enough, so he said, "Just beer and cabbage, please."

While he waited, Sasha glanced around the nearly empty room. The large circular booth in the left back corner, where Bob Burke and Ace Randall said Piotr Shurepkin held court, was empty. However, in the identically shaped booth in the opposite corner, Vyacheslav Kirschman sat side by side with another young man, hunched over a pair of laptop computers. Sasha waited until the waitress came back with his Baltika beer and golubtsy before he made any move. He drank half the beer at one swallow, then coughed and seriously regretted the choice. He had been in the States drinking Budweiser with the rest of the Sherwood Forest crew for too long, and quickly realized how bad his favorite Russian beer Baltika truly was. To kill the horrible aftertaste, he dug into the stuffed cabbage leaves. They were quite good, he conceded as he looked up again at the back booth. Then again, Sasha was hungry.

That was when Vyacheslav looked up and pretended to be surprised to see him. He slid around the side of the booth, threw his arms in the air, and ran over to Sasha's table. "My God, it is hairy Russian bear!" he shouted, loud enough for everyone in the building to hear. Sasha immediately stood up and the two men met in the middle of the floor and feigned a friendly Russian hug. Sasha was six inches taller and at least seventy pounds heavier, with a round face, long hair, and a full beard and dwarfed the younger man.

"Sasha! What are you doing in Brooklyn?" the smaller man asked.

"Anything I can, Slava," Sasha in a voice loud enough to be heard in the back of the room. "Mostly looking for job."

"Are you legal?"

"Of course not!" Sasha roared. "Went to Canada for bus tour and snuck across. You?"

"Boss got me in."

"He need anyone else? I do anything," Sasha quickly replied as the back door opened and three men came walking out of the rear office. One of them continued on toward the front door, but the best-dressed of the group paused and gave Sasha a long, hard look. Sasha guessed it must be Piotr Shurepkin, from the description Bob Burke gave him. Piotr glanced over at Evgeni, who was clattering away on his keyboard, oblivious to everything going on in the room, so Piotr turned, looked at Sasha and Vyacheslav, and walked over. The third man, stocky and powerfully built, stayed close to Piotr, and followed close behind. He must be Piotr's bodyguard, Sasha figured.

"Mr. Shurepkin... Boss," Vyacheslav said as he turned toward Piotr, not waiting for Piotr to tear into him. "This my old friend Sasha from Russia. He classmate at Moscow Coding School and is looking for job. Sasha, smart guy, smarter than me. He go on to Moscow State University, then worked for agency we can't talk about, can we Sasha?"

Piotr chucked. "You mean the old 'insurance company' building on Dzerzhinsky Square?" he asked, "the one with the parquet floors and pale blue walls inside?" referring to the notorious KGB headquarters that had been an insurance company before the Revolution.

"No," Sasha corrected him. "My insurance company building had *green* walls and basements under basements, the kind you didn't want to go visit."

"Green! Of course, Sasha, you are right. I meant to say green walls."

"Not matter. In cubicles where I worked, walls hadn't been painted since Beria left."

Piotr laughed. "And you went to computer school with Slava before that? Interesting. So tell me, what brings you here to our little restaurant? Not for the stuffed cabbage and bad beer, I assume."

"No, no," Sasha laughed sadly. "I rode here on subway from New Jersey. I hear lots of Russians live here, lots of Russian businesses. I need job."

Piotr stared at him. "Let me see your papers?" he asked as he held out his hand.

Sasha dug into his pants pocket and pulled out a dogeared Russian passport. Piotr quickly thumbed through it and handed it to the big man behind him, who thumbed through some more pages and then walked back to the office. Sasha frowned and looked concerned. "Like I told Slava, I have no visa, so..."

Piotr smiled, "Relax. I am Piotr Shurepkin, from Moscow. That is my brother Evgeni back in the booth. We own this place. You don't need visa. I was just checking you out."

"Shurepkin... from Moscow?" Sasha blinked, sounding concerned.

Piotr laughed. "Relax, I said. That's our father. You are in no danger from us, Sasha. We are the last people who would call the immigration police on you. Slava said you looking for a job. What can you do?

"Anything, Boss. Computers, bookkeeping, programming, and I wait on tables, wash dishes, scrub floors, or clean toilets. I am down to last $10. I work hard. You'll see."

The bodyguard came back, handed Sasha's passport to Piotr, and nodded. "Okay..." Piotr opened the passport again and said, "Sasha Kandarski. Finish your stuffed cabbages, then go back to New Jersey. Come back here at 10:30 tomorrow morning with all your stuff and I give you a job. Slava will meet you here and take you to the apartment where our people stay. He'll find you a bed."

"Boss, I think all beds are taken," Slava said apologetically.

Piotr's lips formed a thin smile. "No, Slava, two beds will be empty tonight. Sergei and Avram leave us. Someone should have told them it's a long swim home. So your friend can have his choice of beds."

Piotr reached into his pocket and pulled out a thick, gold money clip, peeled off a $100 bill and handed it to Sasha. "An advance. I don't want my people hungry. When you get here tomorrow, you shadow Slava. Help them out in the kitchen, then you will work with Evgeni and show him what you can do with computer. After that it's the kitchen again, and then you can finish up helping Slava post all the accounts," he said as he handed Sasha's passport back to the big guy again. "For safekeeping, Sasha... so it doesn't get lost, you understand."

Bob Burke and Ace Randall waited outside Kalinka's for Sasha to reappear. Bob was up on the elevated subway train platform, with a clear view of the front door. Ace was three doors down on the other side of the street in a cigar shop. He had been inside too long and both men were getting nervous until Sasha reappeared just before 4 p.m..

As Bob pounded into Sasha's pointy little head over and over again on the drive over, he was to walk down Brighton Beach Boulevard, take the stairs up to the elevated subway platform, and take the first local train headed west for Manhattan. Bob would be across the street standing inside the small neighborhood market watching the street, while Ace would be up on the subway platform. Ace would get on the train behind Sasha. They would ride three stops, get off, and wait there for Bob, making note of anyone else who got off. When Bob arrived, Ace and Sasha would exit the station and come back up on the other side where the eastbound trains came in, with Bob following. Spread out down the platform, they would wait for the first eastbound local and return to Brighton Beach and the van.

"Looks like you're clean, Sasha," Bob told him.

"I always clean, Boss."

"Next step is to see what Slava accomplished inside. If he could upload the Trojan Horse and get the financial data files we need, then we will not mess around. Neither of you will go to work. There's no reason to take any more risks. Just like Atlantic City, we'll hit their computers around noon tomorrow, and then get the hell out of Dodge."

CHAPTER THIRTY

Brighton Beach, Brooklyn

Inside Kalinka's, Vyacheslav "Slava" Kirschman was a nervous wreck. When the Americans had him in that motel room, they gave him a thumb drive and three simple things to do before they set him free. First, he was to put it in his own laptop for practice and hopefully to get over his nervousness. Second, the next time he was working with Evgeni, he was to slip it into the young man's Toshiba laptop if the young savant ever left him alone with it in the booth. The two laptops were identical, the same model, but Slava would need to be quick and decisive to get it done before Evgeni got back. And third, and most importantly, he was to slip it into the desktop computer in the restaurant office later that afternoon when everyone was out, or in the evening when he was posting the bills and receipts, doing the daily accounting. Three things! That was all those men in the shadows behind him and the one in the bright lights across the table asked him to do. Simple enough, it probably sounded to them, but if Piotr Shurepkin caught him, he would have Pavel Bratsov kill him for sure, maybe snap his neck like a chicken or tear his head off, as Bratsov had threatened to do to him a dozen times before.

When the Americans finished questioning him, they dropped him off around the corner from the restaurant. By the time he reported for work in the kitchen, it was almost noon, which made him forty-five minutes late. For some reason, Bogdan Schlimovitz wasn't there, and Pavel Bratsov was running the kitchen. Pavel grabbed Sasha by the throat and reamed him out good before he turned him over to the cooks to run meals to the tables. Then, at 12:20 p.m., he got an order badly messed up in the kitchen and delivered the wrong lunches to the wrong people at the wrong table, one of whom began eating the wrong meal and had to send it all back to the kitchen. Next, at 12:45, he was helping a waitress bring drinks to a large party and spilled a glass of water in front of the bar, splashing water all over a female customer's foot. She and the bartender got up in his face and snarled at him for that mistake. Then at 1:15, after being banished to the kitchen to wash dishes for the rest of his shift, he dropped a heavy stack of seventeen dinner plates on the concrete floor, watching helplessly as they smashed into a bazillion pieces. That really set Bratsov off. He yelled and screamed at Slava for at least ten minutes, threatening to rip off his ears and use his head for a bowling ball if he ever dropped anything in his kitchen again.

It had been some day, he thought. His nerves were completely shot, and things were about to get a lot worse.

It was 2:45 p.m. by the time he had the mess in the kitchen cleaned up, the rest of the dishes washed, and the kitchen floor scrubbed twice with a bucket and an old, rat-tailed mop. Finally, Pavel finished with him in the kitchen, so Sasha went out into the now empty restaurant and tried to find Evgeni. At least the younger Shurepkin brother never picked on him. Slava wasn't certain Evgeni even knew he was there half the time, but that was perfectly fine for Slava. Cowering next to Evgeni, he felt safe for the first time since he arrived for work, and he didn't want to leave that rear booth. Apparently neither did Evgeni. He sat banging away on his laptop's keyboard until 5 p.m., when it was time for Slava to report back to the kitchen. He groaned, realizing he had not accomplished the first two things on the Americans' list.

Fortunately, dinner traffic in the restaurant was light that evening. They didn't need his help in the front with the tables, delivering orders, or cleaning up, so he spent the entire shift in the kitchen washing pots, pans, and dishes under the cook's watchful glare. Slava made it through his shift in the kitchen without dropping anything, breaking anything, or messing up any meals. At 8 o'clock they served the kitchen staff the leftovers, gave them a beer, and left them alone.

It was 8:20 p.m., before he could finally hang up his apron and head for the restaurant office to do the day's bookkeeping. That sounded like a small enough task for a little business the size of Kalinka's, but he had to keep three different sets of books: one in English for the state and federal tax collectors, one set in Russian with the same numbers to show to their mob bosses in Moscow, and another set with the real numbers on the computer, so Piotr could tell what was true and what was not. All of them had the same expenses, but the first two only showed half the receipts that went through the front cash register.

Before Slava arrived in the office, Piotr would have already taken the books out of the safe and put them on the desk. The safe was an old, boxy floor model that sat in the corner. Slava would post the day's expenses and receipts in both of the physical ledgers and the computer. When he finished, he would put the books back inside the safe and lock it. There was a lot of cash in there too, but not much else; and Slava knew not to touch a dime of it. Piotr knew exactly how much was in there. If so much as a dollar was missing, Piotr said he would have Pavel Bratsov tear him to pieces, literally.

When Slava was finished that night, he still had that flash drive in the bottom of his pants pocket. It was his last chance, and he was determined not to screw up that one last job the Americans gave him. All he had to do was pull it out, insert it in the desktop, and let it run. It would download the books and upload their Trojan horse. Then, he could go back to the apartment to meet the Americans.

Unfortunately, nothing went right that day.

As Slava turned the corner and walked down the hallway toward the office, he saw Bratsov standing outside the office door, his powerful arms crossed over his chest, blocking his way. "No bookkeeping tonight," Bratsov told him. "Piotr has meeting in office. You go mop restaurant floor. Go," he said, dismissing him with a flick of his fingers.

Slava opened his mouth and wanted to argue, but he realized it would be a waste of time. Bratsov didn't care what he thought and wasn't about to let him in the office. It was almost 8:30 p.m., and he had accomplished none of the things the Americans wanted. He turned and slowly walked back into the restaurant. How did the Americans say it in those baseball games they played? He tried to remember. "Strike one, strike two, strike three, you're out." That was it. He had struck out three times today. He was a failure, and he would never make it back home to Russia again. Never.

So, at 10:45, when he finished mopping the floor, it was a thoroughly discouraged and disappointed Slava Kirschman who put his mop and bucket away in the broom closet and walked out Kalinka's front door into the night, knowing it would be an unpleasant meeting with the Americans.

Ten minutes later, in the rear of the van, Slava's prophecy came true.

"The flash drive?" Bob Burke held out his hand and asked before Slava could even get settled. "Did you get it all done?" When Slava's shoulders slumped and he broke eye contact, Bob knew he had his answer. "Okay, what happened?"

"Everything!" The Russian began to sob. After dinner, there was big meeting in office. Pavel Bratsov, Piotr's bodyguard, blocked the door and wouldn't let me in to do bookkeeping and couldn't get to desktop computer. They told me to go mop the floor instead."

"What about Evgeni's laptop?" Sasha broke in.

178

"He sat in booth all afternoon, typing on it, drinking can after can of that damn Red Bull. Three hours. He typed and he drank; he drank and he typed. He never even went to toilet. He must be a camel."

"Looks like we go to Plan 'B,' "Jefferson Adkins spoke up.

"We have a Plan B?" Ace asked.

"Sure, we walk in tomorrow and kill them all," Adkins answered.

"Perhaps we should think of something a little stealthier," Bob added, "considering that the FBI is recording and videotaping everything that goes on in there. Even they have their limits."

He turned back to Sasha and said, "Looks like you'll be the one who goes in there tomorrow and does it. Show up at 11 a.m. with Slava, just like you told them you would do. Then, the two of you do the normal kitchen work. When the time is right, say at 1:15, when no one is in the office, Slava, you see if you can hit one or both of the laptops. Sasha, you go into the office and use the flash drive on the desktop. We also need to grab those books out of the safe somehow. I want to break them, take their money, turn their books over to the Feds, to Parvenuti and Kaczynski across the street, and watch Piotr and Evgeni Shurepkin and their pals do the 'perp walk' in handcuffs on the 6 p.m. news. If they look stupid on TV, Moscow will take care of the rest. But before any of that happens, we'll get you guys out of there, out the back door into the parking lot."

"But... but office is locked, so is safe," Slava stammered. "And back door is steel, with bars and locks. How are you going to...?"

"Don't worry, I know just the guy to handle those locks for us," Bob turned to Sasha. "Do you remember Dimitri Karides from the Atlantic City casino?"

Sasha scratched his beard. "Yeah, sure, Boss, the little guy with the fancy clothes?"

"That's him. I'll see if I can get him down to take care of the two doors and the safe. But when we send you back in and send Dimitri in, we have a problem. They know Ace and me from our last visit, so we can't go in with you. They might recognize Jefferson too, but we need someone inside. Try a New York Giants hat, grab a table, order some food, and keep your head down. He'll be our eyes and ears in case there's any trouble. Got that?" Bob asked as he looked around from face to face.

"Meanwhile, Jimmy and Ronald are back at Sherwood Forest with our big equipment, right, Sasha? Do you think they can hack into the FBI servers and turn off those cameras and microphones? You've gotten into the Fed's systems before. All they have to do is black them out for maybe ten or twelve minutes tomorrow afternoon."

"I don't know Boss. My two junior associates are not quite up to my higher level of competence, but I believe I can coach them through it."

"I'd tell them you said that, but I don't want to set off another of your thermonuclear war electronic battles like last time, with the lines of dancing pink rabbits bouncing across their computer screens singing obscene songs in Russian. No, maybe I'll just tell Patsy."

"No, no, Boss, most unnecessary," Sasha shook his head. Those two I can handle. Her, not so much."

"Okay, you get that set up and tell them I'll phone them when I want them to cut the FBI's feed. Meanwhile, I'll make some other phone calls. At 11 a.m. tomorrow, you and Slava are going in. We'll be right behind you if anything goes wrong, but we need those flash drives uploaded and we need the books from the safe. So everyone get some sleep tonight. You will need it tomorrow."

As soon as the two young Russians got out of the van three doors down from their apartment, the van drove away, Bob pulled out his cell phone and pressed the speed dial number for Ernie Travers, his Chicago Police Department captain friend.

"Ernie, I didn't wake you up, did I?"

"Do you really care if you did?"

"No, I was just trying to sound contrite and sympathetic. Where is my favorite pickpocket and sneak thief Dimitri Karides these days? Still in Cook County jail?"

"Dimitri? This doesn't sound good, but no. Based on his past usefulness to this Department, and to certain other unnamed friends of law enforcement, they gave him an early release a few months ago."

"Can you call him and tell him I need a favor? I need him in Brooklyn tomorrow afternoon for a 'little job.' Tell him to bring his tools for a door and an old floor safe. As usual, he will be well compensated."

"He'll love that. He wouldn't do it for me, but I'm sure he would for you. And the timing shouldn't be a problem. He's in Boston for a family wedding. It's three and a half hours by bullet train."

"And no TSA. Anyway, give him my cell phone number. Tell him we'll coordinate in the morning. Thanks, Ernie."

CHAPTER THIRTY-ONE

Moscow on a Rainy Spring Morning

It was the middle of the night in New York City, but midmorning in Moscow. Still, despite the spectacular views and the interior furnishings in the top-floor conference room of the Four Seasons Hotel in Moscow, the impressive view across Red Square to the Kremlin, and the lovely, green wooded countryside on the horizon beyond, it was all depressing in the rain.

A cold, driving rain had blown in overnight from the northeast, and spring had vanished. This was, after all, only April, and glimpses of spring in Moscow remained precious and fleeting. The freshly greened trees around the city had disappeared in the mist and driving rain. The normally busy square was empty, and heavy clouds sat on top of Saint Basil's a mile to the south, dropping a dull shroud over its brightly colored onion domes.

With nothing outside to distract him, Oleg Shurepkin was forced to sit on his "throne" at the end of the Council table, listening to the mounting criticism being heaped upon him by the other Vors. There was no subtlety this morning. His enemies no longer felt the need to use surrogates to lead the attacks at him. This time, Yuri Paretsky, his old nemesis from Kazan, began the Inquisition. He then passed the banner to Isok Kuryakin to continue the charge, then to Leonid Makarov, Viktor Lutarski from Volgograd, the boss of the Crimea, Avram Abramov from Vladimir, Aleksandr Zinovyev, and then back to Paretsky for the final slicing and dicing. Paretsky had his sharp knives out and was going in for the kill, something he had patiently waited to do for many years. He intended to savor every moment.

The others were little men, petty thugs, if the truth be known. Not even Paretsky had the nerve to take Oleg Shurepkin on in the past, but Shurepkin had given him the golden opportunity. His plans to rapidly expand his criminal operations in America and penetrate the Pentagon had stalled and produced nothing so far. That was all the fault of his two idiot sons. He knew it, and each of the sharks sitting around that table knew it. His sons may have been the ones responsible, but it was his plans, which made them his mistakes in the end. Now, he would pay for it. Paretsky wanted the chair at the end of the table, he wanted Putin's ear, and he wanted Shurepkin's head on a pike over the Kremlin's Borovitsky gate if he could get it.

The drumming pressure on him had all begun with Putin, the only place it could have begun. The "Czar" sensed failure, and blood was in the water. Putin's position had steadily become more powerful over recent years and he took the opportunity to hit them with a new levy. Last month he wanted an additional 10% of their gross. This month it was 20%. Next month it would be either 30% or Shurepkin's head, depending upon his mood at the time. After that, it would be the heads of the others as he either had them replaced or decided he did not need them at all.

The entire Council showed up today, which was understandable, since it was their futures that were being decided every bit as much as his. By the Council's standing rules, each Vor could bring one man with him into the room, an assistant or a bodyguard, which was usually the case, but no cell phones, and no weapons. Their men stood evenly spaced around the walls of the large room, staring nervously at each other and at their principals sitting around the table. Shurepkin's man, Dema Kropotkin, the one the others uniformly feared, stood with his back to the exit door like the Colossus of Rhodes, his broad shoulders and muscular frame filling the doorway and preventing anyone from going in or out until the meeting was over.

After each of the others had his chance to speak, Paretsky leaned forward and pointed a long, bony, accusatory finger down the table at Shurepkin. "Where is the money, Oleg? That is what Putin wants to know, and that is what we want to know. You made promises to him and you failed. Now, he is coming for us."

From the murmuring around the table it was obvious the others agreed with that conclusion, but they were all wrong. At that dramatic moment, the exit door from the conference room, the one behind Dema Kropotkin, opened from the outside. That was an unheard of violation of council rules. It even surprised Kropotkin. He turned his head and looked back over his shoulder. Behind him he saw a man in a dark, well-tailored business suit every bit as large as himself. It was Boris Orsunov, #2 in command of Vladimir Putin's personal bodyguards, often his errand boy and enforcer, accompanied by a half-dozen similarly dressed men carrying small, compact, PP-2000 submachine guns slung around their necks.

Dema Kropotkin would not have moved out of the doorway for almost anyone, but as soon as he saw the closely cropped hair and rugged visage of Orsunov, and knowing whom he represented, Kropotkin stepped aside. Orsunov stepped in, followed closely by his well-drilled squad, who took up positions in a semicircle behind him with their submachine guns covering everyone else in the room. The weapons weren't necessary though, not with the absolute power Orsunov and his small squad commanded.

He stepped forward and gave Oleg Shurepkin a cold hard stare, raised his hand, and used a single, dismissive, crooked finger to indicate the head of the Council should follow him. $7,000 Savile Road suit or not, Shurepkin's shoulders slumped. He seemed to deflate as he rose from the chair and followed Orsunov out of the room.

Down the hall an elevator stood open, waiting. It whisked them down to the first-floor lobby. Every eye down there watched the show, but pretended not to watch, as a pathway suddenly opened through the crowd. Like Moses parting the Red Sea, Orsunov led Shurepkin, flanked by pairs of armed guards, and marched him across the plush carpeting and out the hotel's front entrance. At the curb, a line of three large, 590 hp Russian-made Aurus Senat Rolls Royce lookalike armored limousines waited. There was no need for flags on the fenders or medallions on their bumpers. Everyone in Moscow knew who those big beasts belonged to. Big and powerful, each car could carry seven in the back.

As Shurepkin arrived, a guard standing next to the middle car promptly opened its rear door and roughly pushed Shurepkin inside. As quickly as it had opened, the door closed behind him. Awkwardly regaining his balance, Oleg found the rear-facing bench seat, managed to turn around, and fell down on it. As he straightened his jacket and pushed himself upright, he looked back and saw that the only other person in the passenger compartment besides himself was Vladimir Vladimirovich Putin, President of Russia, who sat in the center of the rear bench seat staring at him, stone-faced as always, as if he was observing a bug under a microscope. He appeared to enjoy putting others in awkward situations to see how they reacted to the awkward situations he put them in. Stalin did the same thing to test people. Perhaps it came with the office.

The car did not move. None of them did. They sat at the curb idling, which likely meant that this would not be a long conversation. For days, Shurepkin had expected that they would summon him to the Kremlin, perhaps even escort him into Putin's office for a personal dressing down. But a meeting like this, alone, in the backseat of an idling car? It came as a complete shock.

"Mr. President... I...," Shurepkin stumbled. "To what do I owe this honor?"

"This honor?" Putin asked as he cocked his head slightly to one side and smirked at him. "What honor can there be when you have repeatedly lied to me about what you can accomplish and failed to deliver on any of your promises, not only to that band of criminals up on the fourth floor, but to me, to your country, and to its people."

"Yes, yes, Mr. President, I know that we have not yet been able to accomplish the plan I laid out before you, but we are on the cusp of getting inside the Pentagon's computer system as we speak. I am certain that given a bit more time, perhaps another month, or even a few weeks..."

"You bore me with your excuses, Shurepkin. I thought you were more intelligent than the rest of them or I would have never let it drag on this long."

"I know we have failed you. I know I have failed you, and..."

"Enough of your lies, Shurepkin. I know exactly what is going on in New York and Washington. You and your people have failed. You are an embarrassment. My reason for even talking to you today is to tell you that your trial begins in three days."

"My... trial, Mr. President? For what, I...?"

"For treason, of course! Today is Monday, and the trial starts at noon on Thursday in the Central Courtroom in the Ministry of Internal Affairs building. You and your two sons will be charged with conspiracy to commit treason. You know what the punishment is."

"Mr. President, what can I do to set this right?" Shurepkin pleaded, hoping that Putin would come up with a number.

"Set it right?" Putin scoffed. "I suppose if you were actually able to deliver your vaunted entry into the Pentagon computers I might reopen the case, even though it is extremely late for it to mean very much, you might gain some sympathy... in return for a substantial fine, of course."

"Yes, yes Mr. President, a fine. How much do you think that would likely be?"

"Nothing less than twenty million would seem appropriate, given the magnitude of your crimes."

Shurepkin's mouth dropped open. "Twenty million?... Rubles?" He stammered.

"Rubles?" Putin scoffed. "Dollars, of course."

Twenty million dollars? Shurepkin's head was spinning. He would have to liquidate everything he owned to even come close to a number like that.

"Yes, twenty million... dollars," Putin seemed to think it over and then answer himself with a thin smile. "That seems a most appropriate amount to me. Now get out of my car. They just polished the leather and you are sweating all over my car seat."

There were several large tour groups visiting Brooklyn's "Little Odessa" along Brighton Beach Boulevard that morning, and the lunch traffic was brisk at Kalinka's. As soon as they arrived, Sasha and Slava found themselves hopping back and forth between putting orders together in the kitchen, helping the waitresses, and bussing the tables out in the dining room. Table turnover was continuous.

Sasha was not worried. After Atlantic City and some of his previous escapades back in Russia, he had done things far more dangerous than this. So he calmly went about his work, thinking the best, not the worst. Slava, on the other hand, was a nervous wreck, even worse than the day before. But the younger man was right about one thing. Evgeni remained in that back booth since Slava and Sasha arrived, beating on his keyboard, laughing, and giggling to himself as usual while he wolfed down several orders of French fries and washed them down with more cans of Red Bull.

Sasha remembered Dimitri Karides from Atlantic City. He was a sneaky little bastard, but opening the office door and the safe, much less the restaurant's back door, would be difficult. Karides wasn't arriving until after Sasha and Slava left for work, but he would be hard to miss, even in a restaurant like this. Short and fat with thick glasses and a big warm smile, Dimitri resembled a dapper, middle-aged lawyer in his trademark camel-colored wool overcoat and fashionable grey fedora. As Bob told them in Atlantic City, Dimitri was not a pickpocket or a thief. He was a freak of nature, a "hand magician," as he called himself. If you had something anywhere on your person, in a pocket, any pocket, or hanging around your neck, or fastened to your wrist under your clothes that Dimitri Karides decided he wanted, it will be gone in a matter of seconds. But he was really a nice guy who referred to himself as a "financial liberationist."

"I only 'acquire' things from people who will never miss them and really don't need them," he said with a stern wag of his finger, "and I never, ever steal from the poor."

Sasha had the two thumb drives in his pocket. He kept glancing at the front door and at the lunchtime crowd, hoping to see the friendly face of Dimitri Karides, because the timing was perfect. The restaurant office appeared to be empty. No one had gone in or come out of the office since he had arrived. As far as he could tell the office was empty.

It was 1:15, tail end of the busiest hour of the day. Sasha walked out of the kitchen double-time carrying two plates on each arm, when a short, heavy man in a beige overcoat and gray hat brushed past him like a gentle breeze. "Is that my friend Sasha beneath the big, bushy beard?" Karides leaned in and said, then walked over to the bar. After Sasha delivered the plates to the table, he circled back to where the man was now standing. "Tell me, Sasha, who would have the keys on him?" Dimitri asked.

Sasha looked around. Piotr was not there. Neither was Bogdan Schlimovitz, the big, ugly, and usually half-drunk kitchen manager who was always there. As best he knew, Evgeni never carried any keys. That left Viktor Svetkov, one of the bouncers and sometime bartender as the only choice. At that moment, he was standing at the far end of the bar studying a tear sheet in Russian for the day's horse races at Aqueduct Racetrack in nearby Queens. "Him," Sasha said. "But be most careful."

Dimitri smiled and shook his head as one would to a "challenged" second grader. "Meet me at the door to the office in three minutes," he said. "After we clean out the safe, I plan to quickly depart. Kindly let the other fellow, Slava, know of my plan, if you will," he added, as he slowly drifted off into the crowd, magically reappearing a few moments later at Svetkov's side. Dimitri leaned in next to him, extending his hand and pointing to a section of the racing schedule. The two men then began to laugh and talk for a moment until they shook hands like best friends and Dimitri finally walked away. The entire encounter took less than a minute, but as he turned away, Dimitri caught Sasha's eyes and he headed toward the hallway to the restrooms and the restaurant office.

At the same time, Sasha noticed that Colonel Jefferson Adkins, the huge black man whom Major Burke had introduced to them to a few days before, was standing near the entrance to the gift shop also watching Dimitri. As soon as the pickpocket walked away from Svetkov, Adkins pulled out a cell phone and made a quick call.

Sasha also pulled out his cell and sent a prearranged signal to Jimmy in the 3rd Floor KGB Spymaster Data Center in Fayetteville to throw his stone into Goliath's eye, temporarily taking down the FBI's audio and video streams from Kalinka's. Within seconds there would be three or four FBI Agents in the nest across the street yelling, screaming, pointing, and blaming each other for blowing a fuse or tripping on a cord.

That done, Sasha walked into the kitchen where Slava was putting some salads together and whispered, "Go to restroom in three minutes. We meet you at the office door."

Sasha then walked back out into the restaurant without breaking stride and turned the corner into the service hallway. To his surprise, Karides was nowhere to be seen, but as Sasha kept walking and passed the restrooms, he noticed the office door was slightly ajar. He blinked and wondered, "How did he do that?" But behind him, out of the corner of his eye, across the room he saw Svetkov drop the horse racing sheet and hurry toward the restaurant's front door. Well, Sasha thought, at least he isn't coming after me.

Sasha slipped into the office and closed the door behind him. The safe was a big old-fashioned floor model, and Dimitri was kneeling down next to it with a doctor's stethoscope in his ears, ever-so-gently turning the dial. Sasha wasted no time either. He sat in the desk chair, inserted the flash drive in its port, turned on the computer, and waited for the computer to power up. As it did, the progression of startup commands diverted to the flash drive, the financial files downloaded, after which Sasha's Trojan Horse uploaded into the computer. One or two minutes would be all it would take. Then, they would have all they needed to clean out the Shurepkins.

Sasha heard a soft knocking on the door and quickly got up to let Slava in.

CHAPTER THIRTY-TWO

Moscow, Sheremetyevo International Airport

Sheremetyevo is 24 kilometers and 50 minutes northwest of the Kremlin, longer in the city's molasses-like rush-hour traffic, but much shorter if you are in a hurry, have a lot of money, and have access to a private helicopter. Oleg Shurepkin possessed all of those, plus a burning anger recently added to the list.

As Putin dismissed him from the back of his limousine, the sky outside had gotten even darker. The days were long at this time of year in Moscow, almost the longest of the year, and it should be daylight bright, but not today. Oleg needed to clear his mind, so he took a brisk one-and-a-half-mile walk around the perimeter of Red Square. He once heard that one of the country's Grand Master chess players did this to plan the myriad of moves and countermoves he would need in an upcoming chess match. Dema Kropotkin followed ten paces behind to give him "breathing" room; or, perhaps, to avoid being splattered if Oleg's head exploded from spontaneous combustion from having spent too many long minutes in the backseat of Vladimir Putin's limousine alone with The Czar. Whichever, Dema knew to keep his distance.

Oleg passed the State History Museum, Lenin's Mausoleum, the long red brick wall of the Kremlin, the onion domes of Saint Basil's Cathedral at the far end, and then the long façade of GUM Department Store coming up the other side. Oleg never had the patience for chess, but he was a Grand Master plotter. This time he found himself in the match of his life, and having a clear head was imperative.

When he reached the front steps of the State History Museum at the end of the loop, he paused and pulled out his cell phone. He dialed the personal cell phone of his secretary, Tatiana. She would be at home by now, but that was irrelevant. "Call Sergei Tarasov at Aeroflot," he began with no introduction or pleasantries. "I want two seats, first class, on the overnight nonstop flight to New York, for Dema and me. I think it leaves around midnight. As usual, he will be armed," Oleg added as he hung up and began a second lap around Red Square.

He had just passed the front entrance to Saint Basil's Cathedral when he received the return call from Tatiana. "I… I do not understand it, Mr. Shurepkin. There are apparently no first-class seats available… only coach… and they are on a flight that has two stops and leaves at 11 p.m..

He says the midnight flight is completely booked. He also says I should tell you they can no longer guarantee your weapons will be allowed through either Sheremetyevo or Kennedy."

"You spoke with Tarasov himself?" Oleg asked, quietly seething.

"No, sir, I tried... I even insisted... but I could not get past his assistant. Do you want me to book those seats for you anyway?"

"That is all right, Tatiana, it is not your fault. Yes, go ahead and book them," he told her. He stopped walking and stared across the nearly empty square at the tall red-brick walls of the Kremlin. He understood exactly what was happening to him. In this place, at this time, if The Czar throws a rock in the pond, even in the darkest night, everyone sees the ripples. One cannot hide when power was such a fleeting thing, subject to the whim of one man. And Shurepkin was already walking on thin ice.

"Dema," he looked over his shoulder at his hulking bodyguard. "I assume you heard? We have time to pick up some things... and arrange for the helicopter. This will be a miserable enough trip without subjecting ourselves to still more indignities."

Oleg waited until they were beginning their descent into Kennedy airport before he picked up the telephone handset in the headrest in front of him. He had not flown coach in over twenty years and was unaware they even had phones back here in the cattle car. He slipped his credit card into the slot and dialed the number, pleased to learn that at least they hadn't interfered with his bank accounts and credit cards, not yet anyway.

As he expected, it took time for someone to answer, and it wasn't his son, not that he expected Piotr to be up this early. It was only noon! Finally, a man answered, speaking Russian. It was Pavel Bratsov. That was good, Oleg thought. At least he wouldn't need to identify himself or explain. "Tell my sons I shall land at Kennedy in forty-five minutes. I will meet them at the restaurant as soon as I can get there. And Pavel, bring a gun, a clean Glock, a 9-millimeter," he said and hung up.

Piotr Shurepkin had never been an easy riser, especially not on four hours of sleep, badly hung over from a caustic combination of vodka shots, Don Perignon champagne, various little white powders, and three bimbos, all of whom were intertwined over and under him in his round, twelve-foot diameter bed in the second-floor bedroom of his large house in Lindenhurst, Long Island, overlooking the bay. It took Bratsov a full minute to get Piotr awake enough to understand the meaning of his father's phone call and the dire message it contained.

"My father?" Piotr shoved the bimbos aside, forgetting about the stitches and gash in his shoulder until the pain fought its way through his drug haze. "Ah, ah, ah!" he screamed and jumped out of the bed, dancing around until the pain subsided and he could think.

"Look at the bright side," Bratsov said.

"There is no bright side, you dumb ass!"

"At least he called. Imagine what would have happened if he had simply shown up?" Bratsov dared to say as he glanced at the three naked bimbos on the bed. "I will start the shower, put the coffee on downstairs, and bring the car around... Oh, and your father wants a gun."

"A gun?"

"Relax. He only wants one gun, which means it is not for him. It is for Kropotkin."

Piotr nodded. "Yes, and the way this is going, if my father decides to kill me, he will use his bare hands."

As soon as Pavel went downstairs, Piotr stumbled out of bed trying to gather his wits, then walked over to his dresser where there were several open vials of cocaine. He quickly drew out a line on the glass top and snorted it, knowing that it would take a lot more than a scalding shower and a cup of hot coffee to get his brain working today.

This time, it was Bob Burke and Vladimir Rostov who stood inside the pet shop across the street from Kalinka's, while Ace Randall provided the high watch from the subway station directly above the restaurant's entrance. Dimitri Karides took the high-speed Acela bullet train down from Boston, and Jefferson Adkins left to pick him up at Penn Station in Manhattan and would bring him over as soon as he arrived. The three men, and soon Dimitri and Jefferson, wore small earbuds. They were part of a small, state-of-the-art low frequency, PRC 154A Rifleman tactical radio network Bob had on loan from some CIA friends he had met in Kandahar several years before and invited down to the Merry Men parties at Sherwood. The network had proven to be an invaluable piece of tactical equipment for the Merry Men on several past operations, and the CIA had so many toys cluttering up their supply rooms they would never notice it was missing.

They took up their positions around Kalinka's at 11 a.m., before Sasha and Slava reported in for work. Things inside had been quiet ever since. At 1:15, Dimitri Karides, short, round, and unmistakable in his perfectly tailored beige topcoat and gray fedora, came sauntering down the street. Fifty feet behind him walked a tall, powerfully built black man in a

Yankees baseball hat, neither of which were seen very often in this part of Brooklyn.

Jefferson followed Dimitri inside to be their eyes and ears. While he was waiting, he was forced to kill time by eating his way through a large order of Chicken Kiev and pelmeni at one of the tables. That left Bob and Ace outside at their posts, watching and waiting like the cavalry on the other side of the hill.

Ten minutes later a short, elevated train came into the elevated train station where Ace stood, stopped briefly, and departed just as quickly. That was when Bob heard Ace say, "Ghost, I think we have a problem."

Bob quickly looked out the store window at the front of the restaurant. Nothing caught his attention, so he asked, "Why? What do you see?"

"Coming down the far stairs from the elevated platform. Isn't that Stephanie Goss?"

Not used to seeing her in civilian clothes, it took a moment for Bob to get a clear view of her face. "Damn, can you stop her?"

"No, she got off the train at the opposite end of the platform, and with all the noise up here she'll never hear me."

Bob slipped out the front door of the pet shop with Vladimir Rostov close on his heels. He saw Stephanie, but she was 100 yards away. She stopped two doors short of Kalinka's to look around, but she didn't see Bob through all the cars and deep shadows under the elevated tracks. He tried to call out to her, but with the passing cars, it was like an echo chamber down at street level. There was no chance she would hear him as she turned back and continued toward the restaurant's front door.

As Bob reached the curb between two parked cars on the opposite side of the street from Kalinka's, a black Lexus LS 500 made a quick stop in front of the restaurant. When the passenger-side rear door flew open, Rostov grabbed Burke's arm and pulled him down the sidewalk away from Kalinka's. Piotr Shurepkin popped out of the Lexus wearing a dark-blue pinstripe suit, open-collared white shirt unbuttoned to the middle of his chest, and dark sunglasses. His left arm was in a black sling as he slammed the car door behind him and headed for the front door of the tearoom.

Rostov was right to grab him, Bob realized, and he continued walking away with him. With the rest of his guys inside and no plan, this wasn't the time or place to take on Piotr Shurepkin. Unfortunately, Stephanie didn't have that option. She was almost at the door before she saw Piotr right in front of her and heading her way. He looked up at almost the same moment and saw her too. There was a split second in which

Shurepkin seemed to pause in mid-stride. His eyes flared and his right hand went inside his jacket, coming back out holding a small Makarov PM 9-millimeter pocket gun. Piotr didn't stop. He stepped right up to her and jammed the compact pistol into her side.

"What have we here? My blonde leg-breaking friend from the parking lot!" Shurepkin hissed. "Perhaps you like Russian food? I show you Russian food. Get inside," he said and shoved her toward the door of the restaurant.

At the same time, his black Lexus continued forward, pulled over to the curb, and parked between two large "No Parking" signs. No doubt it was his "reserved space," because the driver's side door immediately opened, Pavel Bratsov got out, and also headed for the restaurant. The driver's side rear door also opened, and Evgeni Shurepkin got out, clutching his computer bag to his chest and followed the other two inside, as if an afterthought.

"Heads up in there," Bob said over the radio net. "The Shurepkins and Bratsov are coming in, and they've got Stephanie Goss with them, at gunpoint."

"I've got 'eyes on,' Bob. They just came in," Jefferson Adkins quickly reported. "Crap, it looks like they're headed for the office. Wake up in there, Dimitri. You're about to have company, and one of them has an automatic in his hand."

Bob then pulled out his cell phone and pressed the direct dial number to Patsy's desk on the third floor of Sherwood Forest. "Patsy, it's time. Have Jimmy take his hands off you long enough to turn off the FBI's eyes and ears in Brighton Beach, Sweet Pea."

"Must I?" she sighed. "The things we do for love."

"Life can be a bitch sometimes," he said, hung up, and headed for the front door.

Dimitri already had the safe open. On the top shelf lay a stack of three accounting ledger books. He pulled them out and saw they had been carefully labeled 2020, 2019, and 2018. He slipped them into the rear, inside pockets of his topcoat which hung behind his knees. He looked inside the safe again and saw stacks of bound paper money, US and Russian, on the second shelf, and a half-dozen automatic pistols lying on the bottom shelf. He wasn't sure what else to take, but the thick stacks of US $100 bills were entirely too tempting to leave behind. He slipped several handfuls of them into other inside pockets as he heard Bob Burke's voice speaking in his earbud on the tactical radio net they had set up.

Puzzled, Dimitri turned to the other two and asked, "Who is Piotr?"
Slava suddenly looked terrified, "Piotr?"

That was all the answer Dimitri needed. "Not to worry, my young friend, the Major is on his way with help, but he thinks we should leave here. Now would be an excellent time."

CHAPTER THIRTY-THREE

Inside Kalinka's

In the office, Dimitri had just stuffed the last ledger book and several stacks of hundred-dollar bills into the inside rear pockets of the stylish topcoat, specially tailored for him by the wife of an old cellmate in Cook County jail. It was a thief's delight. It hung perfectly from his shoulders, but with enough "storage room" in the middle of his back and along his lower legs to allow him to walk out of a Safeway store with a full Thanksgiving dinner for twelve; or, in this case, the financial books for Piotr Shurepkin's Russian Mafia operations for the past three years plus a nice nest egg of cash.

Sasha did not have one of the radio earphones, but he could tell something was going on when Dimitri ceased stuffing stacks of $100 bills from the safe into his pockets and pressed his hand to his ear. "Too late, gentlemen" Dimitri told them as he hurried to the door and flipped the deadbolts closed. "Well, that should keep them out."

Sasha frowned. "You realize we are now locked in here."

"I prefer to think of it as they are locked out there. But not to worry, I am told John Wayne and the cavalry are on their way."

Sasha turned back to the computer screen and waited impatiently for the colorful green Windows file manager "download" bar on the computer screen to plod its way from left to right and transfer the last of Piotr Shurepkin's hard drives to Dimitri's USB 3.0 1 TB Extreme Pro flash drive. Sasha was accustomed to working with extremely high-speed gaming computers and had no patience for slow machines like this. Finally, the bar showed "Done." With a series of quick keystrokes, he opened his little surprise package on the flash drive and watched as it quickly uploaded into the desktop's operating system. Ten seconds later he turned to Dimitri and said, "All done. So what we do now?"

Piotr Shurepkin wanted to shoot the blonde American woman in the head out on the street the moment he saw her, because she was the one responsible for the grazing bullet wound in his back. He almost did, but even in the drugged, hungover state of mind he was in, he had enough sense to know Brighton Beach Boulevard in broad daylight was not the time or place. She was the Army bitch who took down Leonid Korsunsky in that Alexandria parking lot.

Leonid was a big, dumb hunk of beef, but reportedly one of the top gun hands in Moscow. Still, this woman kicked his ass like you might smack down a misbehaving teenager. Piotr managed to run away and fired two or three shots back in her general direction, figuring she'd wet her pants when he did that. Instead, she shot back and hit him from at least one hundred and fifty feet away. Some shot. He suspected she would have hit him in the head with her next shot if he hadn't stumbled just as she pulled the trigger. Good luck for him, then. Bad luck for her now, he thought as he shoved her through the still busy restaurant toward the hallway back to the office.

By the time they reached the office door, Pavel Bratsov had caught up and Piotr saw one of his muscle-bound bouncers, Viktor Svetkov look over from where he was sitting at the bar. As soon as he saw them, Svetkov dropped his Racing Form and pried himself off of his barstool. Even Evgeni caught up, still clutching his laptop computer to his chest.

"Open that door!" he ordered Svetkov, motioning toward the office and poked Stephanie in the ribs again with the automatic.

She looked back over her shoulder and glared at him. "Do that again and you're gonna eat that thing!" she snarled as she tried to turn the knob. He backed off, but the knob wouldn't turn and the door wouldn't open. "Guess what, smart guy," she told him. "It's locked. What next?"

Piotr glared at the door and was about to shove the pistol into her again, but stopped, sensing that this crazy woman might do what she said she would do. With one arm in a sling and the other holding the Makarov, he couldn't reach his keys, so he looked at Svetkov and shouted, "Open the goddamned door, you fat moron!"

Flustered, the big bouncer stuck his hands in his pockets and patted down his other pockets, but his keys were nowhere to be found. "I... I... I had them in my pocket just..."

That sent Piotr into another rage. "Pavel, where are your keys?"

The hallway was narrow. Bratsov pulled out his keys, shoved Svetkov aside, and stepped around Piotr and the woman. He put his key into the lock, turned it, and tried to push the heavy oak door open, but the deadbolt locks on the inside stopped him. So did the nudge of a pistol barrel pressing into the back of his neck.

Shurepkin grew angrier. "Open the damn door!" he snapped, turning his head to see what the problem was. At the same time, a huge black fist closed around his gun hand, pushing it away from Stephanie Goss and squeezing like a steel vice. Shurepkin's eyes went wide as a bolt of intense pain shot up his arm right to his brain. One finger was caught in the trigger guard and his others were awkwardly wrapped around the handgrip. He screamed and tried to pull his hand away, to release the pistol, but that black hand didn't seem to care. It kept squeezing, harder and harder. Shurepkin felt bones begin to break in the back of his hand and in his fingers. He looked back over his shoulder in a panic and found himself eyeball-to-eyeball with a very black and very angry face.

Bob tried the doorknob. Like Bratsov, he found the door still locked from the inside. He knocked on the door. From the sound, it was made of solid oak, maybe steel reinforced, and it would take a battering ram to get through it. So, he tried the earphone mic and said, "Open the door, Sasha, it's us."

The door swung open and the crowd in the hallway shoved, fell, and pushed its way into the office. As Bob took his pistol away from Pavel Bratsov's neck, the powerful Russian took a swing at him. It was a nicely compact right hook aimed at the side of Burke's head. Given the difference in their height and weight, and Bratsov's "Gold's Gym" upper body muscles, had he connected, Bob would have been out cold, or even dead, but that didn't happen. What he did not have in muscle, Bob more than made up for in quickness, agility, and defensive skills. He slipped the punch, delivered a quick kick into Bratsov's solar plexus, pivoted, and sent a rock-hard fist into the Russian's kidneys, dropping him on the floor with a second shot to the back of his head behind the ear.

Afraid to face Piotr's wrath for doing nothing, Viktor the bouncer made a mad rush for Burke like an overweight landslide. Like Bratsov, he never got that far either. In a heartbeat, Vladimir Rostov cut him off and dropped him to the floor on top of the other thug with a series of unique SYSTEMA martial arts moves now favored in the Russian Speznaz hand-to-hand combat training schools.

Bob's eyes met Vladimir's, and he gave him a quick nod of appreciation. He had heard of SYSTEMA. It was actually an old Russian martial art with its roots in a medieval fighting style favored by the Cossacks in the Ukraine, but Bob had never seen it on display. Like the dozen or two other fighting styles out there, they all work if you are quick, practiced, and confident. Colonel Rostov appeared to have each of those in abundance.

Also having those three in abundance was Stephanie Goss. Not wanting to be left out of the fun, she turned and gave Piotr Shurepkin a straight right, from the shoulder, feet set, weight moving forward, with a slight twist that caught him flush on the nose, bounced him off the wall and dropped him to the floor in a heap, out cold. The punch no doubt broke his nose. Added to his crushed hand and the bullet wound in the shoulder, this has not been a good few days for the young Russian to mess with Americans, she thought.

The truth was none of them had been in much danger from the beginning. Ace Randall stood behind them in the doorway with his Glock 19 loosely covering the crowd.

Bob turned to Sasha and Dimitri Karides, who stood on the other side of the room. "You guys all done?" he asked.

"Yes, and a most impressive display of martial arts, Major," Karides answered with a bow and a sweep of his hat.

"All done, Boss," Sasha seconded.

Bob then looked at Slava Kirschman, who was hiding behind them, and said, "Get their cell phones, Slava. And get me Piotr Shurepkin's, too. Then, let's get the hell out of here."

He slipped Shurepkin's Galaxy cell phone in his pocket, noting that all of his people were still standing, and all of Shurepkin's were on the floor, except for Evgeni. He stood against the wall clutching his backpack computer bag to his chest. Bob pointed at him and told Sasha, "And grab that laptop. Something tells me it's the Keys to the Kingdom."

Bob looked at the safe. The door was still hanging open. He saw several handguns on the bottom and more stacks of cash on the middle shelf. "Sasha, you take the laptop and give Slava his backpack. Slava, fill it with that hardware in the safe and the rest of the wrapped stacks of cash. And Dimitri," he said as he turned to Karides, "Time to do your magic on the back door."

"That should be no problem, Major," Dimitri smiled. "If you will follow me please," he said as he headed toward the rear door to the alley.

While the others followed Dimitri into the hall, Sasha stepped over to Evgeni and tried to take the laptop away, but the younger man began to scream and struggle, refusing to let go of it. Sasha was a powerful, muscular bear, but Evgeni was like an octopus with all eight arms alternately wrapped around his laptop or shoving Sasha away.

Exasperated, Sasha looked at him, hands on hips, and said, "It is cheap, off-the-shelf Toshiba, Evgeni. Get a life!" Tired of chicken fighting with the younger man, Sasha nailed him with a fist right in the center of his forehead. Evgeni's eyes rolled up, and he soon joined the others on the floor as Sasha took the laptop from his hands.

True to his word, by the time Bob reached the hallway, he saw that Dimitri Karides already had the multiple locks on the back door open. "Excellent job!" he told him.

Almost embarrassed, Dimitri held up the set of keys he had liberated from Viktor Svetkov. "I cheated," he admitted.

With all of his guys now on the outside, filing out the back door, and all the bad guys in the office on the floor, Bob noticed that Bratsov's key was still in the office door lock. He pulled the heavy oak office door closed, turned the key twice to double lock it and struck the key with the butt of his own pistol, snapping it off in the lock. That won't stop a roomful of angry men for long, but it will slow them down just enough, he concluded.

CHAPTER THIRTY-FOUR

Brooklyn

They piled into the dark-blue van with the tinted windows parked in the alley behind Kalinka's in no particular order, except for Ace at the wheel and Bob riding shotgun in the front passenger seat.

"I think I saw this bit on *YouTube*," Jefferson Adkins commented, "but they used a Volkswagen and had a bunch of clowns inside."

"An easy mistake to make," Stephanie quickly added. "And whoever's hand that is had better rethink." Sasha grinned, but she got no replies.

While it was a tight fit, they got everyone inside and drove away down the alley. At the end of the block stood two large rusty dumpsters. Bob had Ace stop. He opened the backpack, pulled out the cash, left ledger books and the Russian pistols inside, and tossed the backpack into the second dumpster. As soon as they turned north toward the Belt Parkway and headed towards to I-278, he opened one of the stolen phones and dialed 911. That connected to the dispatchers for the NYPDs 60th Precinct, which covered the coastal beach communities in southern Brooklyn.

As soon as the dispatcher answered, he said, "You gotta send some cars over to that Russian tearoom on the Boulevard, Kalinka's they call it. Some guys grabbed a girl and took her in back and there's a big fight going on in the office... No, I don't want to get involved with those people. They have guns, man; they all have guns," he added and hung up.

"That should stir things up, should it not, Major?" Rostov said with a smile.

Bob pulled out his own cell phone and called FBI agent Sal Parvenuti's private cell phone number, which the Geeks had found for him.

"Who is this?" Parvenuti answered suspiciously from their nest across the street from Kalinka's.

"Christmas is coming early for you this year, Agent Parvenuti," Bob said without identifying himself.

"Burke? Is that you, Burke?"

"No, it isn't. But drop what you're doing and go look in the dumpster in the head of the alley behind Kalinka's. If you hurry, you might beat the winos and the homeless to it. Oh, and check your email in a couple minutes."

"Burke, what the hell...?"

Bob didn't listen to the rest of what he figured Parvenuti would say. He ended the call and turned toward Sasha, who had cleared out a spot around him big enough to open the hard case on his own laptop and was already online through a high tech Defense Department satellite connection Ronald had hacked into a few months ago and was basking in the lime-green glow of his Razer Blade 15's keyboard screen. Slava leaned over, mesmerized at the state-of-the-art machine. It was the latest present from Linda. It was one of the fastest beasts on the planet, at least until the next Blade model came out. He inserted the thumb drive with the Shurepkin data files and books, the real ones, showing their income and disbursements, and bank accounts across the Tri-State area. As they reached the top of the tall Verrazano Bridge on I-95 and looked down on Staten Island, he made his connections, pressed Enter, and uploaded the data.

"We have liftoff, Boss!"

"Outstanding, Sasha, now are you ready to take their money?"

"Operation Sticky Fingers II almost ready, Boss. Still going through last files and accounts from their computer… There! All set. Want Sasha to push button again?"

"No," Bob said as he turned in his seat and looked back at Jefferson Adkins. "This time, the privilege should be yours, Jefferson. For Charles."

Sasha handed him the computer and pointed to the Enter button on the keyboard. "For Charles!" Jefferson repeated as he pressed it and then stared at the computer. "Almost anticlimactic, isn't it? Not a sound, not a ripple."

"Oh, there will be!" Bob laughed. "Trust me, we just hit them right where it will hurt the most."

Sasha took the Razer back and began uploading Piotr's accounting files to the computers of FBI Agents Sal Parvenuti and Brian Kaczynski on the stakeout in Brighton Beach, with a duplicate set to Phil Henderson in the FBI's regional office in Trenton and another to Carmine Bonafacio with the New Jersey State Police Organized Crime Task Force, who would pass it on to Interpol in Lyon, France. It might take a while, a day or two at the most, but the boys in Brighton Beach, Brooklyn, and New York City were about to be papered with countless search warrants, wiretaps, and subpoenas. Shurepkin's bank accounts would be frozen, but prove surprisingly empty, but his restaurant, houses, boats, cars, and other assets could be seized now that the Feds knew where to look. That might take weeks and even months, but the Shurepkins would be slowly bled to death by lawyers, audits, grand juries, indictments, and more lawyers. Their entire empire would soon crash down, with reverberations felt all the way back to Moscow.

After they crossed into New Jersey and turned north on I-95, Bob looked into the backseat where Stephanie Goss was doing her best to hide behind Slava Kirschman, without succeeding. "Sergeant First Class Goss, would you mind telling me what in THE hell you were doing walking down Brighton Beach Boulevard toward Kalinka's this afternoon? You almost screwed this whole thing up big time," Bob asked.

"I figured you'd get around to me eventually," she said, chagrined. "See, I had some free time and wrote myself a three-day pass so I could check out that 'Matryoshka Software Alliance' at 415 Brighton Beach Boulevard. You know, the ones who submitted the bid on your contract."

"Yeah, I think we know," Bob answered straight-faced.

"Well, and I thought I'd walk past and check it out... maybe talk myself inside and see what their offices looked like."

"Ah! And what did they look like?"

"Like a crummy Russian tearoom."

"Which you could've figured out if you'd looked it up on Google maps."

"Well, yeah, but I didn't think of that... and then that bastard shoved a gun in my ribs."

"You're lucky that's all he did."

"Maybe, but I was about to put them down when you guys came charging in and saved them."

"You were going to put all three of them down?" Bob smiled. "I'll give you Shurepkin, and maybe the fat Bulgarian, but Bratsov too? Even Superwoman would have her hands full with all three of them."

"I guess we'll never know... but where are you taking us?" she looked out the window and asked.

"As far away from there as we can get for a little while, down to Sherwood Forest where we can regroup and make a few plans until things settle down."

Ace continued twenty miles north on I-95 and took exit 16 west to the large private airport in Teterboro, where a Challenger 350 charter commuter jet was waiting. With a plush, well-appointed interior, it sat twelve comfortably, leaving plenty of room to spread out for their fairly quick hop south to Fayetteville, North Carolina.

Once everyone settled in and the jet was in the air, Bob said, "Good job, guys, you have all done the Merry Men proud, and you're all invited into the club. Some of you have been Merry Men since the beginning, like Ace and me. Some came on board more recently, like Dimitri Karides here, and Sasha the Mad Russian, as his third-floor associates Jimmy, Ronald, and Patsy call him. They are already members, as are Ernie Travers, Phil Henderson, Sharmayne Phillips..."

"I knew it, I knew it, you bastard!" Jefferson Adkins roared.

"Oh, don't fret, Colonel, now you're a member too, so we're even. And so is Stephanie, Colonel Volodya Rostov, and even Slava."

"What do you do to become Merry?" Slava asked.

"All it takes is to be a part of one of our operations, and you just did. I'm the membership committee, and I'll explain it all when we get there, and I can show you around. But I've got to tell you," he added, looking around at them. "We've put together some odd groups for our brief adventures from time to time, but this group..."

"I think I'd prefer to be called 'asymmetrical'," Rostov interjected.

"You got that right," Ace quickly agreed. "Asymmetrical."

"Speaking of asymmetrical," Bob said as he looked directly at Dimitri Karides, "Dimi, you appear to have added some unusual bulges since the last time we saw you."

"Unfortunately, yes, Major, you know how difficult it is to eat sensibly out on the road... Oh! I completely forgot," Karides said as he slapped his forehead and pulled bundle after bundle of wrapped stacks of hundred-dollar bills from his various inside pockets. "The cash from the safe."

"Yes, the cash from the safe," Bob smiled, "and it should go a long way to pay for the next Merry monthly get together."

At that point, Colonel Vladimir Rostov leaned in closer and said, "Major Burke, I am not sure I would do too much celebrating just now. Not yet, anyway. You may have wounded them and put a serious dent in their operations, but Oleg Shurepkin is an old Zek, a prison camp survivor from the Gulags under Stalin. He is a very hard man, much harder than his sons. But they didn't fall far from the tree. Piotr came after you once. Now, he has a much stronger motivation and may well do so again."

"I'm afraid you're right, Volodya. We'll set some tactical plans in motion as soon as we get there. Got that, Ace?"

"Roger that, Ghost, I've already been going over some options in my head."

CHAPTER THIRTY-FIVE

Brooklyn

When Oleg Shurepkin and Dimi Kropotkin landed at Kennedy, instead of his usual Aeroflot VIP line and diplomatic credentials, they had to work their way through TSA security, customs, and immigration with the rest of the "great unwashed." Next came the paperwork at the rental car counter, followed by the usual midafternoon New York traffic. The sprawling JFK airplane terminal was only 15 miles from Kalinka's but navigating that distance could take an eternity, even for veterans of Moscow traffic.

His secretary had reserved a top-of-the-line, midnight-blue Mercedes S Class sedan. Old habits die hard. While Dema Kropotkin drove, Oleg sat alone on the passenger side of the backseat, where one burst of bullets was less likely to get them both. A rental car like this came stocked with international newspapers and a full minibar, but Oleg Shurepkin was interested in neither.

They drove in from the west on the Belt Parkway, crossing out of Queens into Brooklyn and then turning south onto Coney Island Avenue. The sky, which had been a pleasant bright blue when they landed, turned to a gloomy gray the further west they went. What that might presage, Oleg Shurepkin wasn't certain. However, as soon as they turned again onto Brighton Beach Boulevard, both he and Dema saw the bright staccato of flashing red emergency lights several blocks ahead. He saw no smoke rising into the sky, and to an old crook who had spent his entire life on the other side of the law, that meant flashing lights were on police cars, not fire trucks or ambulances, and there were a lot of them.

At 2:30 p.m. traffic on Brighton Beach Boulevard ground to a halt, and the next four blocks took them thirty minutes. Still, Oleg Shurepkin was in no hurry. He needed answers much more than he needed time. Up ahead, they saw the police had the street blocked off and were diverting the traffic onto a cross street. Through some clever maneuvering and fortunate timing, Kropotkin saw a delivery truck pulling out, and he pulled in and parked. They got out of the Mercedes, crossed the street, and walked west. With both of them still wearing their best business suits from the morning meeting in Moscow, they were now considerably overdressed for a late afternoon walk in Brighton Beach, Brooklyn. Being in a precarious position now with both the Russian government and the Russian organized crime families, standing out wasn't something Oleg Shurepkin intended when he flew in today. He had hoped to stay well under the radar until he could corner his two sons.

At the end of the next block, they came to the police barricade, which had all traffic stopped before the 400 block. Beyond the barricade, police cars jammed both sides of the road, at least a dozen of them, parked on every sort of odd angle, with their red and blue light bars flashing away. Down here under the elevated train tracks, the effect of the red strobing lights was even more harsh and dramatic.

The police let them walk around the barricade on the south side of the street. When they were directly across from Kalinka's they stopped and looked. Obviously, the tearoom was the center of the NYPD's attention this afternoon. What had happened, Oleg could only wonder. What had his two moronic sons done now? Oleg pulled out his cell phone and dialed Piotr's number.

The phone rang a half-dozen times until someone finally answered. "Piotr...!" Oleg began in Russian, trying to keep his anger in check as he continued. "What in blazes are..."

"Oh, I'm sorry," a man interrupted in overly pleasant voice, speaking English. "I'll bet you were calling Piotr Shurepkin, weren't you? Sadly, Piotr isn't available at the moment."

"What? Who the hell are you?" Oleg growled in English.

"Me? I'm Bob Burke, the guy who took his phone, took his lunch money, cleaned out his safe, and kicked his ass. Who the hell are you?"

"I am his father," the grim, Russian accented voice answered.

"Oh, Oleg? Great! Hey, congratulations. That's some kid you have here. I'll bet you took him to Council meetings when it was 'father and son day,' or did he get that stupid on his own? You know, I expected you to call from Moscow, but from the screen on his phone, I see this is a New York local call, isn't it? That means you're here in the Big Apple. Down near Brighton Beach, I'll bet," Bob waited, but he didn't get a response. "Well, you know what you ought to do next?"

"No, Mr. Burke, you tell me what I should do next?" Oleg asked, his voice now cold as stone.

"I would grab those two nitwit mutts of yours, get on the first Aeroflot flight I can find, and get my butt back to Moscow."

"Why should I do that, Mr. Burke? We like it here in America; we are just getting our new business started."

"You might have been, but along with his phone and lunch money, I took his ledger books, your ledger books, and all your computer files, and turned it all over to the FBI. I figure you have until noon tomorrow at the most to get out of the country before the Feds grab all three of you. Comrade Putin won't like that, especially when it ends up all over the Russian newspapers; will he? Anyway, you have a pleasant night, Oleg," Burke said, and then hung up on him.

Oleg went into a rage, but all he could do was stand there staring through the red flashing lights at Kalinka's, wondering what the hell had gone wrong and what the hell was going on in there. There were two lower-ranking uniformed policemen standing on guard at the front door checking the credentials of everyone who went inside who wasn't in uniform.

Finally, Dema Kropotkin asked him, "Want me to see what I can find out? Maybe try the back door?"

As much as Shurepkin wanted to know more, he knew that wasn't a good idea. "No, this is not a good time to attract any attention. We shall wait."

A uniformed policeman with sergeant stripes slowly walked down their side of the street inside the yellow tape. As he got even with them, Shurepkin asked in a friendly voice, "Sergeant, what is going on over there?"

"There was a kidnapping and a big fight inside. They told me the detectives are sorting it all out," he said as he continued his rounds inside the tape.

Shurepkin stood there another five minutes when the double glass front doors opened and at least a dozen uniformed and plainclothes policemen came out. In the center walked an angry, badly ruffled Pavel Bratsov, his arms handcuffed behind him, struggling with four policemen, all the while yelling and screaming at them in Russian. Behind him walked Viktor Schlimovitz, Evsei Baratashvili, and three other of the lesser street soldiers he had sent over from Moscow when he sent his two sons six months before. They were handcuffed in a long daisy chain, but at least they realized the uselessness of struggling when so greatly outnumbered by police. Behind them came Evgeni, also handcuffed, with a large, fresh bruise on his forehead. He appeared very animated, as if he were talking to someone, perhaps himself. Last in line came Piotr, one arm in a sling, his other hand wrapped in bandages, and a piece of tape across his nose.

The police immediately separated them, shoving each of them into the caged rear seats of separate police cruisers. With that task completed, the police cars drove away, picking up speed as they headed north towards the NYPD 60th Precinct Station in Brooklyn.

If this could get any worse, Oleg Shurepkin didn't know how. "Call that lawyer we have down here," he ordered Kropotkin. "Tell him to get his ass to the police station now! I want my sons bailed out before this gets any worse."

"What about the others?"

"He can bail out Bratsov too, and the cooks, but the rest of them can sit in jail for all I care."

Ten minutes later the last of the police came out. They pulled down the bright yellow crime scene tape and the line of police cars drove away. He and Kropotkin quickly crossed the street and walked up to the doors of Kalinka's. They were locked, so Dema pounded on them twice with his fist. "Open the door," he snarled.

"Can't you see we are closed," an older woman yelled back at him.

"Open the door or I'll rip your head off and crap down your neck!"

They heard the deadbolts open on the other side and an overly made-up dishwater-blonde waitress looked out through the gap between the doors. Oleg leaned forward and when she saw who it was, she immediately opened the door and stepped aside. "Sorry, Mr. Shurepkin, I…"

Shurepkin blew inside, followed by Kropotkin. The ceiling lights were on, but the place was now a mess. Small groups of waiters, waitresses, and cooks had been standing around squawking at each other; but when they saw him, the room fell silent. Oleg fixed each of them with the cold icy stare of a mortician and then shouted at them in Russian, "Get this place cleaned up and ready to open! Now! This is a restaurant, make it look like one."

He turned away and walked across the room to the corridor leading back to the office. He immediately saw that the thick oak door had a huge dent in the center and had been knocked off its hinges, presumably from a police battering ram. Inside, tables and chairs were overturned, and the drawers of Piotr's desk were lying upside down on the floor. Worse, the thick door of the steel floor safe stood wide open and there was nothing inside.

Oleg was in shock. If half of what that bastard on the telephone told him was true, he was finished and did indeed need to get out of this country as fast as they could. However, Oleg Shurepkin did not get where he was by backing down from a fight, by not striking back, blow for blow. Someone would pay for this with blood, he swore.

CHAPTER THIRTY-SIX

Brooklyn New York

At its west end, Brighton Beach Boulevard terminates at 5th Street. By turning south to Surf Avenue, west again, and then north on 8th Street, you soon reach the NYPD's large 60th Precinct Station, which is responsible for the southwest sector of Brooklyn and the beaches. The building itself is a two-and three-story red brick and gray concrete monstrosity, half of which is occupied by two New York Fire Department truck companies and half by the NYPD. Sandwiched between Luna Park, the Aquarium, the DMV, the Metro Station, the Coney Island Boardwalk, and a sea of asphalt parking lots, there is never a dull moment around there, and never a pretty one, either.

At 7:50 a.m., Oleg Shurepkin sat in the rear seat of the midnight-blue Mercedes, showered, shaven, and unmoving, wearing a freshly pressed double-breasted, deep blue suit, a starched white shirt, and a maroon silk tie. He and Dema had been there for almost an hour with the engine and air conditioning running, double-parked across the street from the entrance to the police station, waiting for them to release Piotr and Evgeni, either outright, or on bond. Dema stood outside, arms folded across his chest, leaning against the car, ever vigilant, his eyes sweeping back and forth across the buildings and the parking lots. That was one trait the two men shared. Like big-game hunters, they had endless patience. Oleg's came from those years in the work camps. Dema's came from his years waiting on Oleg.

Dema spoke to their lawyer four times during the night. He was an ex-pat Russian named Andrei Shermayev, who assured Oleg that his sons would soon be released. He cost enough money that he had better know what he was talking about, Oleg thought. Piotr and Evgeni had committed no crimes, not this time. Even if they had, the police had no evidence tying them to anything. There were no guns in the tearoom, no drugs, no unexplained large caches of money, no papers, notebooks, and no victim of any "kidnapping." All of that had disappeared, compliments of whoever had beaten the crap out of Piotr and his people. The lawyer kept pressing that they were victims, not criminals, but the police arrested them anyway, on the paper-thin claims of resisting arrest and assaulting a police officer. Everyone knew those charges wouldn't pass the sniff test in court, even here in Brooklyn. The detectives were hassling them because they were mouthy, arrogant Russians and well-known mobsters. Guilty as charged, and everyone knew that too. They arrested every male in the place, including the cooks and the bartender, trying to get one of them to make a mistake and talk. However, despite the grilling and excessive questioning of all nine of them, the police still had nothing.

They scheduled the transport to King's County Criminal Court in northern Brooklyn for arraignment at 8:00 a.m., where they would be officially charged, if they were to be officially charged. Shermayev was betting they wouldn't, and they'd be released prior to then. Shermayev was right. Just before 8:00, the front door of the precinct station swung open, and a battered and bruised Piotr Shurepkin walked out, followed closely by his younger brother Evgeni, Pavel Bratsov, and the other members of his crew. The restaurant workers trailed slowly behind them. Dema Kropotkin remained standing where he was next to the Mercedes. The sun was well up in the sky by then and he wore very dark sunglasses. He was a hard man to miss under the best of circumstances, but from his expression when Piotr locked eyes on him, it was obvious this was not one of them.

When Piotr and Evgeni reached the Mercedes, Dema opened the rear door and stepped aside to let them in, but he held out his hand and blocked Pavel Bratsov from joining the others. "No," was all he said as he closed the rear door and opened the driver's door. "Return to the restaurant with the others."

"But… we don't have a car. You want me to go with them?" Bratsov whined as he looked over his shoulder at his underlings and the cooks.

"Try Uber," Dema shrugged as he glanced back at Svetkov and the rest of the cast of misfits. "Or walk."

The Mercedes was spacious in back. Oleg sat silently in the center of the rear seat with his knees crossed and hands folded in his lap. Piotr knew to take the rearward-facing bench opposite him, and Evgeni joined him there. Piotr's suit coat was torn and soiled. His white shirt was smudged and wrinkled. The police never gave him back his tie. His hair was a mess. He had a large Band-Aid across the bridge of his nose, and the beginnings of two black eyes. Evgeni wasn't quite as messed up, but even he had a large, dark bruise in the center of his forehead. All in all, this was not the image Piotr knew would impress his father, who, for the moment at least, was content to sit and glare at them, his face devoid of any emotion, but his eyes on fire.

Piotr chose to remain silent too, rather than volunteer anything which he knew from experience his father would chew into tiny pieces and spit back at him. Evgeni didn't know any better.

"Poppa, Poppa, they took my computer. They took my computer," he babbled.

"Your computer? The one you use for the programming?" Oleg asked, straining to remain calm.

"Yes, yes! And Sasha hit me. Here!" Evgeni pointed to the bruise on his forehead.

Oleg's eyes narrowed as he focused them on Piotr, who had by then slumped down the seat, sullen, and angry. "Sit up! Who is this Sasha who you let hit your brother? Is he the same one who broke your nose?"

"No, that was a girl, that was a girl!" Evgeni giggled.

Oleg was speechless. Finally, he said, "I assume both of those people work for this man Burke, the one who said he 'took your lunch money'...?"

Piotr's head shot up. "How do you...?"

"How do I know about this man Burke?" Oleg asked, his eyes burning into Piotr like two laser beams. "We spoke on the phone yesterday. I called your cell number, and he answered. You were perhaps lying unconscious on your office floor or already in the hands of the police at that time, but we had a nice chat. He told me he had our books, he had Evgeni's computers, and he had cleaned out the safe, taking the pistols and all the cash, and he was turning it all over to FBI. What else he may have taken I do not know, but my guess is it could have been anything he wanted, since you and your people apparently put up no fight. Worse, you let them beat up your brother. You let a woman break your nose. And you let them walk out with anything they could carry. What kind of man are you?"

Piotr slumped down in the car seat, feeling even worse this time.

"I understand you bombed this man Burke's office?"

"Yes, I... I thought that would..."

"That was the one right thing you did, Piotr," Oleg cut him off. "You acted! Unfortunately, this fellow Burke is a better Russian than you. He took your punch, swung back, and hit you twice as hard. He put you on the floor, as a real man would do, as a Zek would do. Now, tell me what *YOU are* going to do?"

Piotr looked up and stared at him. "Strike back," he offered tentatively.

"Yesterday I had the pleasure of being pulled out of a Council meeting by Putin's enforcer, one of his bodyguards, just before the Council was to vote to depose me," Oleg's voice sliced through him. "That was bad enough, but I soon found myself in a car, much as you are now, being grilled by Vladimir Vladimirovich Putin himself, that smug, smileless, balding bastard, who told me we would be put on trial for treason the day after tomorrow, in Moscow. Me, you, and Evgeni. I falsely assumed Putin would not bother with you two, that he would put you up against some convenient wall in the courtyard of the Lubyanka and rid himself of you both, like yesterday's garbage, but I was wrong. All three of us will be on trial for treason."

Piotr sat up, as the enormity of their situation finally sunk home to him. "Poppa, I had no idea it was…"

"Stop your incessant whining!" Oleg silenced him. "You had no idea? I told you there would be consequences on my last trip. Did you listen? No! It appears you can blow things up, and blow people up, but you are utterly useless when confronted by a real man… or a real woman, I would add. Now, where does this fellow Burke live? Where does his family live? And all the others who came here with him?"

"North Carolina… in North Carolina."

"You will gather all your men and you will go down to this North Carolina and you will kill them, you kill them all, do you hear me? No one does this to us and lives. If you can do nothing else, you can at least get your self-respect back."

"Yes, Poppa," Piotr mumbled, shoulders slumped down, his chin on his chest.

"Or you can die there, do you hear me, Piotr? Kill them all, or don't come back."

With the resident crew of Bob, Ace, and Sasha safely ensconced back at Sherwood Forest, they gave their temporary guests rooms in the guest building: Colonel Vladimir Rostov, Jefferson Adkins, Demetri Karides, Stephanie Goss, and even Slava Kirschman. Bob tried to get back to a normal schedule as soon as possible. He was up at his usual 5:30 a.m. for a fast but extreme workout in the gym and then back in the breakfast nook and online as the sun came up. He had a call scheduled with Maryanne for 8 a.m. and a conference call with her, George Grierson, their attorney, and their insurance agent, architect, and a structural engineer, back in Schaumburg. Toler TeleCom needed to be rebuilt, reopened, and working at full speed with all hands on deck as quickly as possible; if for no other reason, than to demonstrate it would take more than a few ounces of Semtex to shut them down.

What Bob didn't expect, as he finished a couple of quick, full-speed laps around the track after his workout, was that he'd be met out there by Colonel Rostov and Stephanie Goss, dressed in the Sherwood Forest sweatshirt, sweatpants, and muddy running shoes they provided all the guests. They were both red-faced and sweaty, and Rostov had leaves and dirt on his knees.

"Tell me you two didn't do the obstacle course in the dark?" Bob asked.

They exchanged guilty looks. "Call it morning madness," Rostov admitted.

"We were both working out in the gym and one thing led to another, you know? US Army Ranger versus Speznaz," she admitted.

"I keep telling this woman that I am GRU, 45th Guards Independent Reconnaissance Brigade, not people to be trifled with, but she would not listen."

"So the only way to settle it was the obstacle course... in the dark?" Bob laughed. "It's difficult enough to run through those woods in broad daylight."

"So we learned," Rostov said as he brushed some leaves off his sweatpants.

"And I kicked his butt!" Stephanie crowed. "Bad knee and all."

"Only because I fell."

"It sounds to me like you two need to try the course again but wait until the sun comes up next time," Bob told them. "Meanwhile, I wanted to let you both know that we'll arrange a plane to take you back to DC when you need to go. Dimitri Karides has to go on to Boston, although it usually takes dynamite to get him out of here. But you're welcome to stay as long as you want. Membership has its privileges."

"Speaking of privileges, Major, we passed your shooting range while we were out there. Perhaps you and I could do a little shooting at your convenience."

Bob smiled. "Looking to get your butt kicked again, Colonel?"

"I heard a rumor that you were a fair shot," Volodya smiled back. "As you may not be *FULLY* aware, I am a fair shot as well, and we Russians take marksmanship seriously. So it should be an interesting competition."

"Any specific weapon you have in mind?"

"Not really. I have fired almost everything in the American inventory."

"We have all of those and most of yours in our arms room, even one of your new Chukavin sniper rifles. I'll have Ace bring out a nice cross-section, perhaps after lunch?"

"Excellent! And you have a Barrett? One of my favorites. It would behoove both of us to get our eyes back on target, because I think we shall need it. As I told you, Oleg Shurepkin will not let this rest. He is under far too much pressure back home, and yesterday will be an enormous embarrassment to him. Piotr struck you and you now struck Piotr. Unfortunately, they are honor bound to come after you again. That is the thieves' code, my friend."

"Agreed. Before we hit the rifle range, you, me, and Ace will sit down and review our security plan and show you our security control room. I think you'll be surprised and pleased to see all the remote-sensing equipment we already have in place."

"Very good, because one way or the other, Oleg Shurepkin will not let that be the end of it."

"That suits me fine, Colonel, same for Jefferson Adkins and for you. I'd love to get them here on my turf. We'll be ready. Now, allow me to buy you a cup of coffee."

"I am a tea drinker, Major, but we Russians also enjoy strong black coffee in the morning, a preference we may have learned from our Turkish neighbors to the south."

"My wife is a tea drinker too, Colonel."

• Rostov smiled. "I do not mean one of those little bags of Lipton tea that you Americans drink. I mean real Russian *zavarka*, a strong black tea with lemon, sugar, cinnamon, and cloves, mixed fresh with boiling water from a well-broken-in samovar, served in a *podstakannik*, a metal and glass goblet with a *sushkie,* a special ring-shaped cookie that is dipped into the tea. It is a cultural treat, and when you allow me to host you at my house outside Moscow, it will be my duty to educate you on what a proper cup of Russian tea tastes like. I assure you; you shall enjoy it."

"Sounds like great fun. Until then, we'll have to content ourselves with a big, fresh pot of Maxwell House and a box of Dunkin' Donuts.

CHAPTER THIRTY-SEVEN

The Rifle Range

At 1:30 p.m a crowd of Merry Men and Women and friends, most of whom came across the river from Fort Bragg to watch the show, gathered at the modern Sherwood Forest rifle range in the thick woods behind the main house. It was an engineered, eight-foot-wide, four-foot-deep trough, with French drains and six inches of sand and gravel that took rainwater to the river. Dug below grade, the dirt had been piled up on each bank for an extra margin of safety and to muffle most of the sound of gunfire.

At the far end, just beyond the targets, was an upward bank of soft dirt covered by a downward section of concrete set at a 45° angle, ensuring any inaccurate rounds ended in the dirt, not on adjoining property or down river. It featured twin shooting stations set at 100, 500, 1,000, and 1,200 meters, which was just under three-quarters of a mile, the distance Bob liked to practice at. Snipers had made shots longer than that, but if you can make tight shot groups at 1,200 meters, with a good spotter you can hit anything. There were also the latest pop-up and random moving targets for variety

"All right," Ace Randall announced over a bullhorn, "here's the rules of today's shoot-off between Major Robert Burke, the Reigning Champion of the 75th Rangers, and Colonel Vladimir Rostov, the Challenger, representing the 45th Guards Independent Reconnaissance Brigade of the Russian Armed Forces, for the Long Gun Championship of Sherwood Forest! Officiating will be myself, since I am usually regarded as the most impartial guy around..." After the laughter and guffaws died down, he went on. "I will be assisted in my duties by Sergeant First Class Kozlowski, Staff Sergeant Blackledge, Master Sergeant Spagnolo, and Sergeant Washington, and Sergeant First Class Stephanie Goss, a visiting Ranger from DC. By mutual agreement, 'Koz' will officiate today, no doubt as even-handedly as I would. 'Chester' Blackledge will spot for the Major and to even things up, I shall spot for the Colonel."

"Traitor, traitor!" came more cries from the crowd.

"No doubt! But an exceptionally fair one. Sergeants Henry and Washington, and SFC Goss will be the lane graders and score the targets in the shack downrange. SFC Goss said that she, 'wants to take on the winner,' but since none of us knows what that means, we are choosing to ignore it."

"To make things interesting and kill some time before we all hit the bar and the barbecue up at the house," there were loud cheers from the crowd this time, "each contestant will shoot forty, '4-zero' rounds, ten each from four different weapons, two weapons of their choice at 500 followed by two others at 1,200 meters. The rifles are the new US M2010 bolt action Enhanced Sniper Rifle firing the .300 Winchester Magnum round, and the vintage 'old school' Vietnam era bolt action M-40 A-3 .308 with a Redfield scope. The two Russian rifles are the new Chukavin SVC, adapted to the .338 Lapua Magnum round, and the classic, old-school Dragunov 7.62 SVD. Again, each shooter shoots all four weapons in the prone position. They can use sandbags and bipods, but no shooting tables or other funky stuff. The rifles have already been zeroed and test fired by Koz and me, and each shooter can have three rounds to further adjust the settings and acclimate to the weapon. There will be ten-point scoring per round. Total shooting time is thirty minutes for each shooter from first shot until last. We will announce scores at the end of each ten-round set, and the decision of two out of three judges is final. Fair, eh?"

"Complicated!" someone screamed from the back of the crowd.

"Like your wife," Ace shot back, "but exceedingly fair."

Burke looked at Rostov and they both nodded.

The choice of weapons was straightforward. For the 500-yard shots, the range they were designed for, they each chose the Dragunov SVD, the mainstay Soviet sniper rifle from the 1960s, and the bolt-action US M-40 A-3, the sniper's choice in Vietnam. They reserved the newer US M2010 ESR Remington .300 Winchester Magnum, which replaced the more robust .50-caliber M-107 Barrett, and the Soviet Chukavin SVC for the longer and more precise 1,200 meter shots. Each started with his own country's rifles, with which they were most familiar.

"Gentlemen, now that we have all that crap done with, let's begin," Koz said as he took over the bullhorn from Ace and announced, "Ya'll have one minute to build your positions and three more minutes to zero, then the clock starts." Bob let Rostov choose first. He picked the Dragunov, as Bob expected, and Bob took the M-40, and both quickly built firing positions about three feet apart with sandbags. While Bob dropped into a prone position on the mat, 'Chester' Blackledge, his spotter set up his tripod and scope to his left. When Koz announced the firing line was clear, Bob took his three test rounds and discovered Ace was right. It had been well-zeroed. He made a slight adjustment to the scope, but the M40 had always been a dream to fire and the rifle was already on target.

Bob took a deep breath, settled in, cleared his mind, and commenced firing at the 500-meter target. After each round struck, Chester gave him immediate feedback: 10, 10, 9, 10…, and so on, for a total of 96 points. He rolled onto his side, opened the bolt, checked the breech, and looked over at Rostov. The Dragunov was semi-automatic, making the transition from shot to shot sometimes less accurate for multiple shots than the bolt-action M40. That proved to be the case when Ace announced the Russian's score of 98.

"Game on!" Bob laughed as they exchanged weapons and both men settled back into their firing positions. He took the three test rounds because he could, but Rostov already had it right on the money. Loading the 10-round magazine, he took his time and was pleased to hear Chester read off a series of 10s and only one 9 for a score of 99, giving him a cumulative total of 195. As he suspected, Rostov had spent less time firing a bolt-action rifle in recent years as Burke had, and Ace announced a 96, giving him a total score of 194, now one point back.

When the graders at the far end of the lane confirmed those scores, he and Rostov gave each other a respectful back slap and began the long hike back to the 1,200-meter positions to the accompaniment of light applause and encouragement from the growing gallery flanking the narrow range. Given their skill levels, both men expected high scores from 500 meters and knew the real test would be from 1,200 meters, requiring not only elite skills, but luck.

Rostov had the honors this time, but he insisted Bob have first choice on the weapon. Bob picked the new Russian Chukavin SVD, the superb new sniper rifle from Kalashnikov, now going into mass production. Bob had fired it before, and it was equal to any standard. Rostov would start with the American Remington M2010. They had finished the 500-meter shooting far ahead of schedule, knowing they'd want to more carefully zero the long rifles and take more time between shots at the greater distance.

Bob and Chester settled in, knowing the scores would not be nearly as high at this distance. After the test shots, he heard Rostov commence firing while Bob made a slight adjustment to his scope. After each shot, he waited for Chester to give not only the score, but the location. "That's a 7 low and left… 8 low and left… 9 right…" Chester relayed, and Bob made another slight modification. "6 high… 8 left… 7… high… 8 low left again… 9 right… 6 low… and 9 high… I have that as 77, and a total of… 272."

Bob was too busy to pay any attention to Rostov's shooting, but he soon heard Ace announce that Vladimir had fired a 79, giving him a 273 which put him back into a one-point lead.

"Game on, indeed, Bob!" the Russian smiled as the two men switched rifles again.

Bob looked at his watch. They had twelve minutes left. With that amount of time and the growing pressure to make each shot count, this last set would be more deliberative. Fortunately, he knew he could rely on his favorite rifle, the new US M2010, much as Rostov would rely on his Chukavin. After three more test rounds, both men were ready.

Bob was still settling into a comfortable, stable position when he heard Rostov fire his first rounds. Putting his eye to the sight and easing his finger onto the trigger, he took three deep breaths to settle his heart rate and slowly eased into the first shot. "10, dead center," he heard Chester say, and relaxed even more, feeling himself ease into the rhythm of the shots. "8 left... 7 left," he continued, "7 low left... 3 low left," following which Bob stopped and stared at the target. That was the worst shot of the day, but he blocked it out, tried to relax, and became one with the sandbags. He felt his whole upper body grow calm as he squeezed off the next shot. "10!" Chester said, followed by 9 right... and 10 again!" Bob paused for one more easy breath, let it out and fired the last two shots "9 low... and, I think, a 10! Great shooting, Major! That's... probably 83 and a 355! Fantastic shooting, Ghost!" Chester crowed.

Then they turned and saw Rostov was still shooting, Ace hunched over behind him, scoping every shot, and quietly providing the Colonel with feedback. When Rostov made his last shot, he paused for a moment staring through the scope before he released the magazine, cleared and checked the breech, and set the rifle aside. Ace patted him on the shoulder and said, "An 82 or 83. The fifth shot is marginal, right on the line. At this distance, I can't tell."

"Then we shall wait, Master Sergeant Randall, but if I do not prevail, the fault lies with my shooting, not your spotting. You did a fine job, and now we shall wait for the scores."

Obviously, the graders downrange in the shack had a problem. Bob turned and looked at Koz, who was on the field telephone arguing and laughing with the crew in the shack. Finally, he put the phone down, shook his head, and walked over to the two shooters.

"Problem, Koz?" Bob asked as Ace and Chester crowded in

"As they say in Vegas in the Friday Night Fights... We are going to the cards!"

"You best use the bullhorn," Ace told him as he pointed to the crowd on the banks. "The natives are getting restless."

"They just want the beer and brats," Chester said.

"Cynical bastard," Koz answered as he raised the bullhorn, doing his best Michael Buffer impersonation. "Ladies and Gentlemen. We have a split decision..." followed by a crescendo of Boos! from the crowd. "Bullets do tear holes in paper targets, guys. But Judge 'Spaghettios' Spagnolo scores it 355 to 353 for the Ghost, while Judge 'Prez' Washington scores it 354 to 353 for the Colonel... 'Going to the cards,' Sergeant First Class Goss scores it 354 to 354, so the match is officially declared great shooting and a draw... The bar is open!"

Vladimir Rostov turned to Bob, grinning. "I could not ask for a more appropriate conclusion to this outstanding match, Major!"

"Bob, Ghost, verrückter Amerikaner, anything you like, but not Major, Volodya."

"You are right, Bob. And after seeing you shoot, and the spirit of your men, I cannot wait for the Shurepkins to arrive."

"You still think they are coming, don't you?"

"Oh, yes."

"Why?"

"Because it is what I would do. They are Russian, and we keep grudges."

CHAPTER THIRTY-EIGHT

Brighton Beach

Twenty-four hours later and five hundred and fifty miles to the north, there was a much less happy gathering in Kalinka's Russian Tea Room in Brighton Beach. The restaurant had been closed since the police raid, and both Oleg Shurepkin and Dema Kropotkin had flown back to Moscow. Nonetheless, small groups of men had been arriving through the front and back doors of Kalinka's for the last half hour, summoned by Pavel Bratsov. At Piotr's direction, he had scraped together every member of the half-dozen Bratva street crews who could fire a gun that he could find. There were now twenty-two Russian men in their twenties and thirties sitting around the bare tables more or less by crew, smoking, and drinking beer and vodka. Bored, impatient, and unhappy about being there in the first place, they whispered among each other and gave hard stares across the room at their old enemies in the other crews. Sporting dark sunglasses, open-collared shirts, gold chains, and medallions hanging around their necks, it was easy to differentiate them from the normal midday tourist traffic on Brighton Beach Boulevard.

Finally, Piotr, battered and bruised, stepped out of his office, followed by Pavel Bratsov. He paused and looked around the room at the faces. He was not happy either. "Is this the best you can do?" he turned and glared at Bratsov. "I do not even know who half of them are."

"Our men, their friends, and friends of friends. Some of our people are still in jail, and I didn't think you wanted me to call up to the Bronx or over to Newark to get some of theirs. That would be dangerous. And asking the Italians was out of the question."

"How many?"

"Twenty-two, plus you and me. A few have military training of one sort or another. We'll put them in charge of small groups. The others are more accustomed to using their fists and large-caliber pistols, so I don't know how good they will be with rifles. But with twenty-three of them, that should not matter."

"Is Gennady Kremoy one of them? Is he here?"

"Yes, although what you want with that skinny old weasel I do not understand. He will to be useless down there."

"He owes me money. If he cannot perform up here, then he can die down there. Is that clear, Pavel? And you have enough guns and ammunition and the other stuff?"

"Plenty. And I scraped up two RPGs and a block of Semtex."

"Good. I want to leave nothing but kindling wood down there."

As satisfied as he would likely ever be, Piotr strode to the middle of the room and banged the butt of his Makarov pistol on a table. "Shut up and listen!" he said as he glared around the room, making eye contact with as many of them as he could. "We're taking a road trip, all of us. We are flying somewhere and flying right back, tonight. You'll all be back here by 2 a.m., maybe earlier. It is one night's work, and there's $10,000 cash in it for each of you. Got that?"

"Who we gotta kill?" a fat guy in the back of the room laughed.

"Come on, Piotr I got a big family dinner tonight for my cousin," one of them whined.

"No!" Piotr shook his head. "Everyone's in. No excuses if you're not, I never want to see your sorry ass around here again. Ever! Where's my best friend, Gennady Kremoy?" Piotr asked as he scanned the room, waiting.

"Here, I am here, Piotr," the skinny, older man in a leather jacket with gold chains around his neck, a bad hair dye job, and two black eyes raised his hand and tried to smile.

"Good, Gennady, I was afraid you might not make it. But if you do well tonight, I'll forgive your Vig this week. So I'm expecting big things from you. That goes for the rest of you. But no cell phones. They stay here. All of them. Pull them out now and leave them on the table. Same for all those stupid gold chains you're wearing. You ain't gonna want them around your neck where we're going. Everybody got that?"

He looked around the room, but nobody got up and left. "We're going down to North Carolina. We're gonna blow the hell out of a house down there and kill everybody inside. Understand? Then we're flying right back here."

"You givin' us freakin' frequent flyer miles, Piotr?" the fat smartass in the back of the room asked.

That got some smiles from the crowd and broke the tension. "No, we got automatic rifles instead: AK's, AR-15s, and some hand grenades. I want you to use all of it. We're gonna make a 'statement,' as they like to say on TV." He looked around at the faces in the room and saw they were all listening now. "Pavel will organize you into smaller groups. A few of you were in the Army. You're gonna be the squad leaders. I don't care what crew you're from, I expect you to shut up and do what you're told. Everybody got that? Pavel?" he turned the rest over to Bratsov.

"We got five big vans parked out back, one for each squad, and as Piotr said, I'm putting a former Army guy in charge of each one. The guns and stuff are in the big canvas bags. We'll hand those out when we get to the other end. Now let's get going."

Across the street in the FBI safe house in a small apartment on the second floor, Agents Sal Parvenuti and Brian Kaczynski had been disconnecting and packing up their electronic gear since 9 a.m. that morning. With the NYPD raid on Kalinka's, the arrest of ten gang members and the restaurant staff, and the treasure trove of accounting information that some "concerned citizen" had left for them in a dumpster, both the 60th Precinct and the FBI Field Office had more than enough to keep themselves busy. Parvenuti and Kaczynski didn't agree, but with the tearoom shut down and their restaurant and liquor licenses suspended, the Brooklyn office shut them down. They decided there was no sense wasting staff time and equipment monitoring the place any longer.

The audio equipment had already been disconnected and packed, and they had started on the cameras and video equipment, when they both noticed the parade of two dozen very recognizable Russian gang members going inside through the front and the back doors.

Kaczynski exploded. "What the hell's going on down there, Sal?"

"They're sure as hell up to something again, goddamn it! And right after we shut off the audio. Most of them came in the front. What are you seeing on the back camera?"

"Looks like they're piling into some vans back there. There's at least twenty guys, and some heavy bags."

"Don't look like it's for softball practice, either," Parvenuti agreed.

"Goddamnit, we don't even have any backup to put a tail on them."

"Call it in. Maybe they can check the cameras on the Parkway and the bridges."

Kaczynski continued looking at the monitor. "You don't suppose they're going after Burke, do you?"

"What makes you think that?"

"Twenty guys? After what he did to them? Where else would they be going? Should we call him?"

"He's a big kid; he can take care of himself. And they don't want to admit we were ever here, so they'd crap all over us downtown if they ever found out we did."

CHAPTER THIRTY-NINE

Sherwood Forest

This wasn't the first time someone attacked or threatened Sherwood Forest. Bob put Ace in charge of defense right after they moved in, and he developed tactical plans for any contingency, with a rotating roster of Merry Men Deltas from Fort Bragg and a small permanent contingent of top-end private security guards, each of whom was a skilled, disciplined former Ranger. When you added in integrated electronic "tripwires" and motion sensors around the property, strategically placed coiled razor wire, and optical, thermal, and infrared cameras, short of the White House, CIA headquarters, or Fort Knox, few sites in the world had better systems in place.

As soon as they returned from Brooklyn, Ace phoned the operators of the half-dozen private airports within 50 miles of Fayetteville, asking them to let him know if any unusual-looking group of ten men or more arrived by private plane, from anywhere, particularly from the New York area. Since they knew a case of steaks or a case of bourbon was riding on their cooperation and those old Army guys down at Sherwood Forest always paid off, they had been more than willing to help.

"What exactly are you looking for?" one of them asked.

"You'll know it when you see it," was the best answer Ace could give them. "A group of guys who look out of place, like they don't belong down here and ain't goin' duck hunting or to a NASCAR race."

It was just after 7 p.m. that afternoon when Ace's cell phone rang. It was George Trombley who ran the maintenance shop and gas truck for Piedmont Aviation, a small, private airstrip adjacent to Fayetteville Regional Airport on the other side of town.

"Ace, you said to call you if I saw some group arrive that looked a little out of the ordinary, and how I'd know 'em when I saw 'em. Well, I think I just saw 'em. Ah didn't see a single NASCAR jacket among the lot of 'em, and they didn't look like no duck hunters, neither. 'Sides, the season don't even open for another three months."

That call triggered an immediate series of alerts. The first very succinct report went to Bob. "Twenty plus men arrived at Piedmont Aviation in two private jets out of Newark at 6:30 p.m.. The field says the two airplanes are still there, but the rest piled into five white rental vans. No suitcases. Just some heavy canvas duffel bags."

"Looks like Volodya was right," Bob said, looking at the Russian who was sitting next to them. "Initiate the plan. If they've just left the airport, they're probably twenty or thirty minutes out."

A second call immediately went to Linda Burke. She, their kids, and Ace's wife Dorothy were to stop what they were doing and head for Cross Creek Mall on the north side of Fayetteville for dinner and a Disney movie. If things weren't safe by then, they were to find a motel for the night. Linda was no novice at this stuff, this being at least the fourth dustup they had involved her in over the past few years, and the second attack on Sherwood Forest. She didn't like it, but she knew that this wasn't the time to argue with Ace or Bob.

Before she left, she grabbed Bob by the ear and let him know in no uncertain terms, "I know I need to get the kids out of here, but I just got this place fixed up from the last time you got in one of your little pissing contests. I know it's not your fault, blah blah blah; but if you tear up my house again, it will be your butt, Burke!"

Ace went to the command center bunker under an outbuilding where the monitoring equipment was located. The on-site crew immediately went on alert, standby personnel went to their defensive positions, and a call went out to any other available men up at Fort Bragg to go to their designated off-site and reserve positions. They activated the door, window, and perimeter monitors. The nonmilitary personnel, like the Geeks, and any nonmilitary guests on property went with Ace and were put in the small underground support bunker next to the command bunker.

Also, per the farm's defense plan, Bob went to the attic of the main house, below the roof peak. It was crude, with exposed wooden rafters and bracing running in various directions. He had added a plywood floor covered with a thick outdoor carpeting that made it a little more comfortable to sit, kneel, or lie on for longer periods of time. During the thorough security review which Bob had conducted three years before with friends from both Fort Bragg and the CIA headquarters at Langley, they suggested the attic be converted into a "Nest": a defensive fighting position with lightweight composite armor plating in place around a series of nearly invisible 6" shooting slits through the roof. They had hinged, "push aside" shingle covers, which made them invisible from outside and provided 360° visibility around the house and into the woods. In the center, they stored a small arsenal of various weapons and ammunition in a securely locked steel cabinet. It contained a bit of everything, from automatic rifles to sniper rifles, LAWS, which were light antitank rockets, and several prototype versions of a compact, new Israeli anti-aircraft missile.

Ace, being the best tactician and quickest thinker in the organization, next to Bob, coordinated the defense from the command bunker, where all the electronics and perimeter security systems fed. Bob, being the best shot and strategist, operated from "the Nest" under the roof where he had fields of fire that could easily cover the entire battlefield or allow him to shift to other parts of the building or the property as needed. Making matters even more interesting tonight, Colonel Vladimir Rostov, now of certified equal ability with the long guns, went with him up to the Nest.

It was pitch black up there with no lights, to allow their eyes to adjust to the darkness. Even with night vision goggles and night vision telescopic scopes on the rifles, that was still the best approach to take for a night operation. They sat together in the nest up under the roof peak, arranging their rifles and magazines to be within easy reach.

Sherwood Forest was a substantial piece of property. Its 600 acres lay in a rectangle on the east side of the Cape Fear River, fronting on River Road to the east and running back to the river on the west. Two hundred and fifty years before, the colonial owners had cleared the land at the center to plant tobacco, but the front, rear, and sides remained densely wooded. Bob strategically thinned some of that woodland to the rear for trails, the rifle range, and the obstacle course, but he left most of the land along the road and down the sides as impenetrable thickets. In addition to the sensors and cameras, Bob installed nearly invisible remote cameras up and down the riverbank and a quarter mile up and down River Road beyond the Sherwood Forest property lines, which neither the state nor county highway departments knew anything about.

After they got off the airplanes at Piedmont Aviation, Bratsov had his men form a circle around him. With a malevolent glare and a pointed finger, he looked each one of them in the eyes and said, "You will follow your team leader and do what he says. I don't care if you are from his crew or not, because he is telling you to do what I'm telling him to do. And if any of you get out of line or don't do exactly what you're told, your return trip to New Jersey will be from 3,000 feet out the side door of the airplane without a parachute, if I let you live that long! Is there anyone here who doesn't think I will do that?" Bratsov asked, hands on his hips, as he spun around in a quick circle, fixing each of them again with his hard, dark eyes.

Piotr Shurepkin then stepped into the center of the group. "Where is my friend Gennady Kremoy?" he looked around the circle, taunting the older man.

Kremoy slowly stepped forward and raised a tentative hand. "Here, here I am, Piotr."

Piotr turned and walked over to him. Kremoy still wore his black leather jacket, but the gold chains were gone from around his neck. Piotr looked down and saw the older man's polished black-leather dress shoes and said, "Those cardboard soles will not do you much good in the woods, will they? Well, let's hope it's not too muddy out there tonight. It would be terrible if you got them all scuffed and had to buy a new pair at the outlet mall so you can take your wife to church next week, wouldn't it?"

"Now get in the vans, all of you! And Gennady," Piotr said as he handed him a loaded AK-47. "I will be watching you every minute."

While his "street soldiers" got in the vans, Bratsov called his team leaders over. "Piotr and I are going in the lead van. After we all pass the entrance to this farm, I'll wave so you can look. Then, about a hundred yards past it, pull over, turn around, stop on the other side of the road, and wait. We will drive back to the other side of the entrance and enter the property from that side on foot. When everyone's set, I'll flash my lights, then we're going in. You guys wait five minutes. Make sure all your men are ready. Five minutes! Then you start the vans, turn in that entrance and drive like bats out of hell down that driveway. The house will be straight in front of you. When you get there, everybody jumps out and hits the place. Kill anything that moves: men, women, kids, dogs, everything. Got that?" he asked as he looked around at their faces. They were all nodding and saying they were ready, but Bratsov had heard that one before. Squad leaders were never ready for an operation until after the fighting was over.

Piotr drove the lead van from the airport south to I-95, with the other four vans loosely following him. It didn't help that all he could get were matching white Ford Transit twelve-passenger vans left over from a cancelled fleet sale. Bratsov figured that killed any hope of stealth. He rode shotgun in the front passenger seat with six of his better men and a large equipment bag filled with automatic rifles and ammunition. I-95, which ran southwest to northeast, took them the short distance across the Cape Fear River to River Road, where they turned north. From the County tax maps, he knew that Burke's Sherwood Forest farm was about four miles up ahead on the left. It wouldn't be long now, and revenge would be ever so sweet.

The first warning came twenty minutes later. The sun had set, and the moon was just coming up over the trees.

"Ghost, Ace here," Bob heard in his earpiece. "Traffic out on River Road. I've switched to infrared. Five vehicles went past, all white vans. One of them came back and stopped around the bend to the north of our entrance. The others are parked to the south with their lights out, but I see brake lights. So far, they're just sitting there. If they move, I'll let you know. Nothing on the river, though."

"Roger that," he said to Ace and then turned to Rostov. "What? You Russians don't like water? Can't swim?"

"Of course not. Russians talk of the Motherland, 'the Rodina,' but you've never heard one talk of 'Mother water' have you? But I don't know what Piotr Shurepkin thinks he's doing. It will be dark out there, even darker in the woods. If those were Speznaz or my Recon troops, we would think nothing of infiltrating quietly through the woods to attack this house. Better still, come in from the river. But those are street thugs and petty gangsters. They will get lost out there in the woods and end up shooting each other."

"I've wondered about that myself. But unless he is completely stupid...?"

"That is not what he will do."

"A frontal assault right down the road?" Bob asked. "You think that's what he'll do?"

"Russian boys grow up watching those old patriotic World War II movies with tanks charging at each other across the Steppes. That's what they think war is all about. It's what got us in trouble in Afghanistan and Chechnya. But if he doesn't care how many men he loses..."

"He'll come right down the road at us."

"Correct. Like the German panzers at the Kursk."

"While the Russians held their fortified positions and picked them off."

"Like we are about to do."

Bob got Ace on the radio. "Be advised, Volodya thinks they'll try to haul ass and come right down the driveway at us."

"Like the freaking Marines!" Ace commented. "And you guys get all the fun."

"Yup, let me know if you see anything like that happening."

"I'm moving two men forward to the corners of the house to better protect the driveway and the flanks – Prez to the left and Spaghettios to the right."

"Excellent move. You guys online?"

"Roger that... Roger," he heard them say. "If they charge on in, we'll hit them with LAWS from here, and you guys can take out any who are stupid enough to continue on foot."

"Copy... Copy."

"I'm leaving the other riflemen in position on the other sides and in reserve," Ace said.

"Agreed. We need to have options. Ghost out."

"Volodya," he said, turning toward Rostov. "Let's get some toys," and led him to the weapons locker in the center of the attic. He picked out two M-72 LAWS, the Army's Light Anti-Armor Weapon, a short, highly effective, one-shot, shoulder-fired rocket that replaced the old rifle-fired grenade and the bazooka before that. He handed one to Rostov. "You seem to like all of our stuff, so I assume you're familiar with these guys, too."

"Somewhat," Rostov answered, "although I've never fired one. Ours are much larger, but these appear easier to handle."

"And fairly accurate. Just pull it open, point it, and squeeze the trigger on top. If they're coming at us in civilian vans with no armor, wait until they get halfway down the road before you fire. It won't be pretty."

"Excellent! But don't expect Shurepkin or Bratsov to be in the lead vehicles. I know men like that. Bratsov briefly served in the Speznaz, but he wasn't particularly good at it and they tossed him out. As for the Shurepkins, Oleg is a tough old bird, as tough as they come, but his two sons are worthless. Piotr isn't the type to lead by example from the front. He'll be yelling at his men from the rear if he comes in at all."

That was when they heard footsteps climbing the ladder from the third floor. Soon, Stephanie Goss's head appeared wearing a set of night-vision goggles and carrying a M2010 ESR slung over her shoulder equipped with the new 10-inch AAC Titan QD noise suppressor. Whisper soft, with one of those on the barrel, the bad guys literally "never heard what hit them."

"I can't let you guys have all the fun," she said as she joined them. "Remember, I owe Piotr a few shots myself, and it looks like you have an empty shooting slit or two I could use."

"You're always welcome, Steph. Take your choice. Volodya and I have two LAWS laid out, but why don't you take the middle with the long gun as backup."

"Sounds good to me," she said as she took up a prone position behind a slit opening onto the driveway, put the standard five-round magazine into the breech of the rifle, and laid an extra one next to it on the floor.

"Two magazines? That only gives you ten rounds," Bob said. "I think we have some extra boxes of .300-caliber magnums in the cabinet."

Stephanie smiled. "Ten rounds should do. I don't want to be a hog. This afternoon, I would have offered to take on the winner, but everyone was already headed for the bar by the time I got back from the range shack and I didn't want to burst anyone's bubble." That said, she jacked a round into the chamber, eased the barrel out of the roof firing slit, and took aim up the road.

CHAPTER FORTY

Sherwood Forest

Piotr flashed his headlights and turned to his men waiting impatiently in the rear seat of his van with loaded rifles. "All right, let's go, let's go!" he said as Bratsov jumped out, and he motioned for them to get out the side door. "And keep the damned safeties on until we get closer. I don't want you morons shooting each other in the woods. And I sure as hell don't want you shooting me or Piotr, either!"

Bratsov handpicked his group from the others to include several of his more intelligent street soldiers. They were the best men in Piotr's organization. Before they left Brooklyn, he looked online and printed a small county map of this area, so he at least knew where the roads and the river went. From the wide spot in the road shoulder where he parked, the woods ran right up to the highway right-of-way next to the van. There was no fence barbed wire to worry about. That was fortunate, he thought. The trees were thick, but with no fence they should be able to move through them quickly.

It didn't take long for Piotr Shurepkin's plan to unfold and just as quickly collapse. Ten minutes had passed since the vans stopped on the side of the road, and Ace's voice on the tactical radio net broke the silence.

"Ghost, I have vans approaching the entrance out on the highway. They have their headlights off, but I've got them on infrared. They're coming fast," Ace said.

"Copy. All five?" Bob asked.

"No, I only see four. One's missing. I think it's still parked on the road north of the entrance."

"They're probably coming in through the woods, trying to flank us."

"If they do, they'll likely get lost in all the brambles," Rostov laughed.

"The vans are turning in the drive," Ace said. "Four of them, picking up speed."

"We have eyes on, Ace," Bob said as he picked up a LAW, opened it, pushed the cover off the firing slit, and knelt in front of it. Rostov did the same. They were looking straight down the driveway as the four white vans appeared, coming toward them in a column.

"Straight on, like the French at Trafalgar and Waterloo, eh? Amateurs!" Rostov said.

"Volodya, you take the lead van. I'll go for the one in the rear, but not yet. Wait until they get into the open, halfway here. And Steph, you're free to take on targets of opportunity."

"An excellent plan, Major, we'll have the two in the middle trapped in a cauldron."

"On my mark, then… three, two, one, Fire!"

Seconds apart, two bright orange streaks flashed down from the roof at slightly different angles to the ground. A LAW flies line-of-sight and fast. Aim straight, squeeze the pressure bar on top, and Whoosh! What you see is what you hit.

Firing down at a 30° angle, Rostov aimed for the van's front grill, but his shot was late by a split second. It went high, punching through the front windshield and exploding inside, lifting the van six feet off the ground, and blowing it to pieces.

"Ah-deen!" One! he said in Russian. "And I like this thing!" Rostov crowed and picked up a second LAW.

The second van veered out of the way as the first van exploded directly in front of it and flew into the air, end over end. The driver of the second van tried to brake, but he was too close and couldn't avoid the flaming debris. The driver of the third van hit his brakes and swerved out of the way to miss them too. He ran into the grass, leaving the fourth van exposed. That was when Bob fired, seconds after Rostov. When the rear driver also hit the brakes, it caused Bob's rocket to land short, strike the asphalt driveway, and bounce up into the van's front grill and engine block. It exploded, blowing the vehicle off the ground.

"Dva!" Two, Bob answered.

"Cleanup in aisle one!" Stephanie quipped.

Bratsov ducked between two trees, and double timed into the woods. That was when he heard the first explosions and bright flashes of light just to the south, where the driveway would be.

"What was that?" Piotr demanded to know, his voice already in a panic.

"I would say that is trouble," Bratsov answered, wishing he could find a boss with half a brain in his head for a change. "Keep moving, keep moving!" he shouted to the others, turned, and moved quickly between two large pines, which was where he hit the razor wire. Those bastards! Coils of fairly new, loosely anchored five-wire razor wire with razor-sharp blades and barbs meandered between the trees, well back from the road. They were intended to ensnare and cut an intruder to pieces, not to keep them out. Painted a dull, dark gray, they were well hidden and virtually invisible, especially at night. Once you got in it, tripped, and went down, it was nearly impossible to get back out without a lot of time-consuming help.

Two of his men had also found the wire, and a third quickly got entangled in it as well. Fortunately, he had brought a pair of wire cutters from the toolbox in the maintenance room at Kalinka's in the event they ran into wire, so he set to work clipping the wires in front of him, and then the wire his men had gotten into. It only took a few minutes to get them back on track and heading toward the house, but that time was lost forever, never to return. That was the problem with time. Waste it and you are screwed. It was gone and so was the plan.

To his left, he now saw flashes and flames more clearly – big orange-black things, roiling above the trees, and he heard gunshots and more explosions. Late. They were too damned late, too damned late to make a difference.

"Ghost, I'm also picking up movement at the fence line in the woods at 11 o'clock," Ace reported. "Probably supposed to be their flanking element."

"Steph, you have the night vision sight. While Volodya and I focus on the driveway, slide over to the left corner and see what's happening over there," he asked her.

"Roger that," she said as she got to her feet and carried her rifle and remaining magazine to the left, where one of the roof slits was wider and afforded a better angle toward that corner of the property. Clipping the AN/PVS-30 Sniper Night Sight attachment onto the rail in front of the day vision scope, she reported on the radio, "I have a half dozen tangos coming out of the woods. They appear to be armed with automatic rifles, so I doubt they're a Boy Scout troop on a star hike. Four of them are out front, carrying what look like AKs. The other two are further back in the trees, but I can't tell what they are carrying. Maybe they're the rear guard or something."

"That is not a rear guard," Rostov reassured her. "That is probably Bratsov and that little weasel Piotr Shurepkin hiding behind the others. We need to stop those two cowards."

"Copy that, Colonel," Stephanie said as she went into a prone position, extended her rifle out the firing slit on its tripod, and took careful aim. The M2010 ESR came equipped with the new TrackingPoint "smart" computerized telescopic sight, laser equipped to determine distances precisely, with or without the night vision site attached. Together, they were amazing inventions that automatically compensated for angles and elevation. They didn't substitute for good marksmanship, but they made it better and easier to accurately engage a target during daytime or the dead of night.

As his small contingent finally cleared the wood line and stepped out into the open field beyond one corner of the house, Bratsov slowed his pace. He may have been many things, but he was no fool. He decided the vans should attack straight down the driveway for shock effect. They should've already been at the house and be attacking it with the rifles and hand grenades before he even cleared the tree line. Worst case, if they came under fire and slowed down, they would be a diversion for his flanking attack out of the trees. But when he saw two of the vans on fire and exploding from direct hits from antitank rockets, Bratsov immediately realized that they had bumbled into an ambush.

The two gunmen in the center of the line coming out of the woods were slightly in front of the other two. Never a good idea, Stephanie knew. If you want to make a bunch of amateurs turn and run, take out the leader or the center target, making sure that all the others see him go down. If you hit him, nine times out of ten, the rest will turn and run. However, if you want to put them all down, not chase them away, then pick them off one at a time from the edges and from the rear until no one is left except that leader. The odds are that the guys in front are too busy and too excited to even notice until it is too late. Even if they do, and become aware of what's going on around them, they'll soon degenerate into a disorganized mob.

The distance was 250 yards at a downward angle of 27°. That was an embarrassingly easy shot for a marksman of Stephanie's skill level. She placed the crosshairs of her telescopic sight on the man to the far left, seen clear as a bell in the bright green light of the scope, and gently squeezed the trigger. The rifle fired. The 10-inch Titan noise suppressor at the end of the barrel absorbed most of the noise and all the muzzle flash, and the rifle's shock-absorbing frame absorbed most of the recoil. The .300-caliber Magnum bullet hit the gunman in the center of his chest, right where Stephanie was aiming. Her right hand calmly pulled the bolt up and back to eject the spent round and then pushed it forward to seat the next round in the breech from the magazine below. The rifle was ready to fire as she pivoted slightly to the right and took aim on the man at the far end of the line.

She was about to pull the trigger when the Russian went down from a well-placed headshot. From the way the body fell, she could tell the bullet was on the same angle that she was, but had come from lower down, from the base of the foundation of the house below.

"Do we have men down below us?" she quickly asked Bob.

"Yeah, I forgot to tell you. Ace moved Prez Washington into a concealed firing position in the bushes at this corner of the house. Spaghettios is on the ground on at the other corner."

"Just checkin,' " she laughed, 'cause somebody down there just took one of them out and it wasn't me. Nice shot, Prez."

"You're more than welcome, ma'am," they heard Prez's deep baritone reply.

" 'Ma'am?' You call me 'ma'am?' Staff Sergeant. Don't you know I work for a living? But back to the matter at hand," she answered as she leaned forward into the telescopic sight again. "I see two tangos advancing into the open. I'll take the one on the left. Prez, you've got the one on the right. He's all yours."

"Roger that, and thank you kindly," they heard him laugh. They both fired at almost the same moment, and the two Russians went down, sprawled on the ground. That only left the two dim figures who had remained back at the wood line. "I think that's your pal Piotr Shurepkin and what looks like Pavel Bratsov," she told the others. "I'm taking Piotr. He's all mine... if there are no objections!"

Lying down at ground level, Prez tried to hit Bratsov. The air was growing cooler and the evening mist from the river rose into the meadows as it did every evening after the sun went down, making long rifle shots from ground level difficult.

CHAPTER FORTY-ONE

Sherwood Forest

The front and rear vans had been destroyed, but it didn't take long for the handful of survivors inside to crawl out of the wreckage and begin running, some toward the house and some back toward the road. It was chaos, as one would expect from the street punks and disorganized rabble Piotr brought with him. With the driveway blocked by the burning hulks of the front and rear vans, the third van had no choice but to skid to a stop in the mud. The men inside poured out. The last place they wanted to be was inside the next target of whoever was shooting those rockets. Halfway between the road and the house, they were trapped. Some of the men began shooting wildly at the house with AKs, ARs, even pistols, while others turned and ran. However, the second van didn't stop.

Stephanie had already identified her targets by the time Bob picked up his own M2010 and took up a solid sitting position with his elbows on his knees and began scanning the front yard through his telescopic sight.

"Steph, if they're running away, back to the road, let them go; but if they're coming this way or holding guns and shooting, take them out."

"Wouldn't we be doing the NYPD a big favor by taking them all out now?" She said.

"Probably, but these guys are amateurs. Putting them down while they are running away just doesn't seem sporting, like shooting ducks on a pond. Although I must admit, it's a close decision."

"Roger that... Ghost," she replied.

"Volodya, that second van isn't stopping," Bob said. "Take it out with that last LAW." It had run off the driveway into the grass and was fishtailing and tearing up the lawn as it came, but continuing on toward the house. It had only gone fifty feet further when the third LAW streaked down from the firing slit in the roof. It missed the vehicle and landed a few feet to the left, but the explosion was enough to blow the van over onto its side.

Who were these people! Bratsov yelled for the others to stop and pull back into the trees, but he was already too late. As he watched, his men in front dropped one by one like green-headed teal ducks and Eurasian wigeons on the first day of hunting season in the lakes and farm fields north of

Moscow. That was when he knew the attack had already failed and it was time to get out of there.

"Piotr, back into the trees!" he screamed, but the younger man didn't need to be told. He was already down on all fours, scrambling back into the cover behind the trees. Because of Bratsov's concern for his boss, he was slow getting to the ground, and a bullet grazed his head, ripping off a chunk of his right ear. Someone at that house was a deadly shot, Bratsov realized, and that put a quick damper on whatever remained of any further interest he had in this one-sided gun battle.

By crawling and rolling across the ground, the two men got further back into the deep shadows behind several large pine trees. He assumed the bastard with the sniper rifle had night vision, so the shadows provided little safety, but the thick trunks of the pine trees did. They also gave them a ringside seat to the one-sided battle now taking place on the driveway to their left.

The men ahead of Piotr had already gone down, and he realized that standing in the open in the clearing in the trees was not such a good idea. Taking cover might be a better one. Someone fired a shot at him just as he dropped to his knees, and a heavy Magnum bullet smacked into the thick pine tree exactly where his head had been a moment before. He bent even lower, got down on his hands and knees, and crab-walked back into the trees, zigzagging from one tree trunk to another. Someone took two more shots at him, but other than smacking him with painful splinters and pieces of wood, he got away.

Hiding behind the trunk of a thick pine, Piotr had his cell phone out and began punching telephone number after telephone number of the guys in the other group who had driven down the driveway. One of them finally answered, but he was babbling incoherently and drowned out by the screaming of another man nearby. Piotr hung up and tried calling his brother, who had insisted on going with the others when they attacked the house.

Evgeni Shurepkin rode in the third van, on the middle bench seat next to Genady Kremoy, who was trying his best to hide in the corner on the floor, wide-eyed, shivering in fear as the first van suddenly blew up, right in front of them. Their driver tried to avoid the flying, burning wreckage and turned the wheels hard right, after which their van was not only hit by the debris but by well-aimed bullets that began punching through the windows and slamming into the van's body panels.

Someone then pulled back on the handle of the sliding side door. It rolled open and three of the men inside jumped out with rifles in hand and began shooting at the house.

Evgeni jumped out too, then turned back to reach inside and grab Kremoy's arm. "Come! Come!" Evgeni laughed and giggled. "Come!" and pulled the skinny, older man out of the van and onto the ground. "The house! The house!" Evgeni screamed as he grabbed one of the AK-47s from the floor of the van, jumping up and down and pointing at Sherwood Forest.

The two vans in front of them were on fire, as was the one to the rear. Dazed and wounded men were crawling out of them, confused, some attacking the house, others trying to run away. The explosions, the gunshots, the screaming, the flames, and the smoke put Kremoy in sensory overload and pushed him over the edge. He grabbed the AK-47 out of Evgeni's hand and began screaming, "Yes, yes!"

Evgeni felt his cell phone vibrating in his pants pocket, but he ignored it and didn't answer. He knew it was Piotr and he was trying to stop him. "No, no," Evgeni screamed at no one, "Papa wants us to get them, Piotr. Papa wants us to get them. Not stopping, not stopping!"

He reached back inside the van and saw one of the RPGs lying on the floor. He grabbed it and turned back to face Kremoy. "We go now, Genady! We go." He turned and ran toward the house.

Kremoy suddenly found himself caught up in it, too, despite himself. It was infectious, and he became as out of control as Evgeni as he ran after him. They were soon side by side, running across the front lawn toward the house, both men open-mouthed and screaming. Genady fired the AK-47 at the house, spraying the first- and second-floor windows with bullets. It was a "high" he had never felt in his life. That was when Evgeni raised the RPG, still running, feet pounding and nearly out of breath. Then he stopped and pointed it at the front of the house, at the center, at that tall set of wooden front doors.

It had all seemed so easy back in Brooklyn, so very easy, Piotr thought as he watched helplessly, letting the cell phone ring. "Evgeni," he screamed. "Stop, get out of there!"

In the driveway to his left, seven men stumbled from the burning wreckage and huddled together behind the carcass of a van. Two of them had AK-47s, two of them carried pistols, one of them had nothing, and one carried an RPG, a rocket-propelled grenade. Two of the men, armed with only a pistol and one with an AR-14, looked at each other, dropped their weapons, and took off running away up the driveway. The one who had the AR threw it down and ran even faster, passing the other one. However, the other five behind the van did not appear to be ready to give up, perhaps they were more worried about Piotr than they were about whoever was in the house. They looked at each other for a burst of courage, and when one got up, they all got up and began running toward the house, firing their AK-47s. Bad idea. With precise single shots, Bob and Volodya began putting them down.

Soon, there were only two attackers left.

The front lawn of the house was bathed in a roiling, bright-orange and dull-black glow from the flames of the burning vans, the gasoline, and burning tires. Bob swung the barrel of his M-2010 sniper rifle around and pointed it down at the vans, taking aim through his telescopic sight. As Bob looked for a new target, he saw two men running toward the house and he shifted the ball of his finger onto the trigger. The distance could not have been much over 100 yards. Bob was firing at a steep angle, 45° or 50°, but it was still a routine shot, all things considered. That was when the sudden realization hit him that his crosshairs were on Evgeni Shurepkin, Piotr's autistic younger brother.

The young man wasn't carrying a rifle like the others. Instead, he was carrying a deadly RPG, a rocket-propelled grenade antitank weapon, which he raised to his shoulder, mouth wide open, screaming as he ran straight up the remaining driveway toward the front door of Sherwood Forest.

CHAPTER FORTY-TWO

Sherwood Forest

Vladimir Rostov was lying on the floor next to Bob at the next shooting port. "Take the shot, Major," he told him in a firm, calm voice. Rostov waited, then repeated, "Major, you must take the shot… now! If you will not shoot the Shurepkin boy, then shoot the other one, the madman with the Kalashnikov, but do something!"

But Bob couldn't. He couldn't shoot the other one either, because his mind was fixed on Evgeni. The young man held an RPG raised to his shoulder as he ran. An RPG, for God's sake, but he was young and autistic. There was something about shooting a kid like that, even if he was a savant and maybe the brightest guy in Shurepkin's entire Brooklyn operation, that prevented Bob's trigger finger from working. He had shot and killed dozens of men in his day, dozens upon dozens. But they were enemy soldiers, uniformed or not, in one rotten war or another. He was doing his job, and they were doing theirs, but this was different.

Maybe Evgeni Shurepkin was one too many, or one too wrong, but Bob couldn't do it. Shoot his arrogant brother Piotr? Any day of the week! Or his father. Or the white horse they all rode in on. But he just couldn't kill that kid.

Rostov didn't have that problem. As Evgeni stopped and pointed the RPG at the front of the house, the Colonel took the shot with his Chukavin SVC. He hit Evgeni in the forehead. A .300 caliber Magnum bullet is a powerful thing when it hits the human body, especially the head. It blew him backwards, head over heels, killing him instantly, but not before Evgeni squeezed the trigger on the RPG. There was a flash of light, a burst of smoke out the back of the rocket tube, and a streak of white as the warhead flew across the grass and struck the big white Victorian house in the center of the first floor, right in its double-wide, steel-reinforced oak front doors. There was a loud "Thunk!" that echoed through the house like hitting a bass drum, but there was no explosion. Nothing. All three riflemen in the attic – Volodya, Stephanie, and Bob – two floors directly above the point of impact, held their breaths, expecting to hear, see, and feel a terrific explosion. They held their collective breaths, but as the echo died away, nothing happened.

Rostov had no problem shooting, and neither did Stephanie Goss. As the loud reverberations of the RPG striking the wooden door died away, she took aim at the second man, who was still screaming and spraying the front of the house with bullets, and put a round in the center of his chest with her M-2010. That shut him up, permanently.

"It was a dud; the goddamned RPG was a dud!" Bob whispered as his forehead dropped to the floor. "Can you believe it? A goddamned dud!"

"Chinese!" Volodya laughed. "Out-of-code Chinese Army surplus, no doubt."

"Or some of the bootleg counterfeit versions of almost everything else they make and sell out the back door of their factories," Stephanie laughed too.

"We must consider ourselves lucky they did not pay full price for good Russian equipment."

"Lucky us," Stephanie agreed.

"Yes, very lucky," Rostov agreed as he looked over at Bob. "Major, do not be embarrassed by your inability to fire on that young man. I did not like doing it either, but we could not expect that RPG to fail. If it had exploded, you would've had a very large hole in the front of your house, and I believe we would've had a major problem up here above it."

Bob slowly nodded in agreement. "I don't know. For a second, I just froze. That's never happened to me, but that kid was just a dumb civilian. I couldn't do it."

"The blame lies with the Shurepkins, with both Piotr and Oleg. They were the ones who placed the boy there with an RPG in his hands, not you. When his gunman in Moscow shot my son, ruthlessly, out on the street, with no regard that he was a policeman or whether there were innocent bystanders around, I swore I would return the favor someday. I will admit it was Piotr I had in mind, and still do, not poor Evgeni, but such are the fortunes of war. It was the game they chose to play. I have no regrets. You should have none either."

While they were talking, Stephanie turned the telescopic sight on her rifle back to the wood line to the left, where the last two men who had come in on foot appeared to have disappeared. She fired off three more rounds where she had last seen them, and said, "That was to make sure they kept moving, but I think they're long gone."

Bob got on the radio and called Ace. "You got anything?" he asked.

"No, there are a few lying out front that are seriously wounded, but that's about it. The stragglers took off running to the road. What do you want to do about them?"

"Let them go. It's not worth risking any of our people to go after them. They're either headed back to the airport where their planes came in, or they'll try to hitch a ride and make it back north up I-95. We can let the cops and the FBI pick them up."

"Copy," Ace agreed.

"Call around to the crew and see if we've had any casualties or other damage, while I call the Fayetteville Police, EMS, and the FBI."

"I'm surprised our phones aren't already ringing off the hook."

"Roger that, but I think this show is about over..."

"Ace, Ghost, Prez here. We have a major problem. That RPG that didn't go off. It's stuck in your front door. I'd suggest nobody go near it until we get it checked out and defused."

"Stuck in the front door?" he heard Ace chuckling. "Oh, Linda's gonna love that."

"She's gonna love me a whole lot less if it goes off," Bob conceded. "What about those two Master Sergeant EOD instructor pals of yours over at Bragg?"

"Enders and George Themopolis?"

"Yeah, they might have more experience with one of those than the local police bomb squad. Give 'em a call. Tell them we have a little job for them over here, a 'teaching moment,' if they want to bring some of their students and their equipment over here... the whole van, I would think."

Ace broke up laughing. "You are so lucky that thing didn't go off. Linda just redid the wallpaper in the entry, didn't she? She would've killed you if the RPG didn't."

"Copy that."

Pavel Bratsov pulled on Piotr's arm again, trying to get him up on his feet, but he wouldn't budge. "Come on! We've got to get out of here," he told him. "There will be cops all over the place in a few minutes, and there's nothing we can do for those guys now."

Bratsov had been shot before, but he never had a bullet graze his head and rip off a piece of his ear before. His head was throbbing, his ear hurt like hell, and it was bleeding badly, with blood running down the side of his face. He kept pressing his hand against the ear to stop the bleeding, but all that accomplished was to smear blood all over his hands and get it running down his arms. The head still hurt, and the ear was screaming in pain. Piotr lay against the base of the pine tree and he kept pushing Bratsov's bloody hands away, refusing to get up. Even when Bratsov got his fingers around one of Piotr's skinny arms, his hands were so slippery from the blood that he couldn't get a firm grip.

Piotr finally moved and peeked out around the tree, looking toward the flaming wreckage on the driveway. "That was Evgeni who went down. I know it was!" he said. "He had an RPG, and they shot him. He is dead, isn't he?"

"Piotr, there is nothing you can do for him now. Get a hold of yourself! If your brother is dead, he died bravely, and we must get out of here."

Piotr wasn't listening. "My father will kill me; he will kill me."

"No, because those men down there will kill you first and your father will never know what happened here if we do not get out of here, now. Otherwise, they will kill us both!"

"He told me I was to take care of Evgeni, nothing else matters. My father told me to take care of him, and now he is dead."

Having completely run out of patience, Bratsov reached down with both hands, took a firm grip on Piotr's forearm. He tried to yank him off the ground and back into the present, but Piotr continued to struggle. Finally, Bratsov slapped him across the face. "Enough! We are going if I must drag you back to the van."

Perhaps Bratsov finally wore him out, but he was successful in pulling the younger man away from the tree and half dragging him through the woods without getting shot again. He found the hole he cut in the razor wire and made it back to the van out on the road. Pavel looked at his own hands and saw they were still slippery and covered with blood. He didn't know how he could drive, but Piotr was an emotional wreck. Giving him the wheel would be an even worse idea. Bratsov wiped his hands on the back of Piotr's shirt under the guise of helping them up into the passenger seat. It would have to do. He started the van, made a U-turn in the road, and sped off into the night, ignoring stop signs and speed limits.

Once he was a mile away, he pulled out his cell phone and called the lead pilot at the airport. "Get the airplanes ready to take off. Get your clearances. We'll be there in ten minutes, maybe more, both planes."

CHAPTER FORTY-THREE

Sherwood Forest

Bob was the last one down the stairs, because he was dialing Harry Van Zandt's cell phone number. Harry and George Greenfield were the "new school" and "old school" detectives with the Fayetteville Police Department and recent inductees into the Merry Men after the little dustup with ISIS terrorists almost a year before.

"Harry…" Bob began with as friendly a tone of voice as he could muster.

"Dammit, there goes $20! George and I were sitting here in the office cleaning up some paperwork and we saw flashes and heard some muffled explosions down southeast, but didn't think much of it. We figured that was probably a storm front coming. You know, thunder and lightning, weather kind of stuff…?"

"Yeah, well, that's what I'm calling about."

"You hear that, George? Burke says that's what he's callin' about!" Harry Van Zandt laughed. " 'Cause when the hot line started getting a bunch of 911 calls from down there across the river, George said, 'I'll bet you twenty bucks it's Burke blowing the crap out of something again,' but I said 'No, no, it can't be him, not him again.' "

Bob laughed along with him. "I think you lost the bet, Harry, but it wasn't our fault."

"It's never your fault, Bob, or at least that's what you keep telling us. Somehow, though, things keep blowing up around you, and people keep getting shot. Admittedly, it's usually the bad guys. Okay, we'll drive on down."

"Yeah, well, I think you might also get hold of the fire department… maybe the whole fire department."

"The whole fire department?"

"Yeah, and I guess as many rescue squad units as you got… and cops, yours and the County. The State guys, too. You're gonna need them."

"You took on the Arabs again? I didn't think there were any of them left."

"No, no Arabs, Harry. This time it's the Russian mob from Brooklyn. Fortunately, they aren't nearly as well led or good at blowing things up as the Arabs were."

"Geez, that's really great to hear, Bob. You had me worried there for a minute. How about a few details I can pass on to the EMS guys?"

"Well, for starters, there's four large vans on fire in my front yard..."

"I don't suppose you have any idea what hit them, do you?"

"We were wondering the same thing, Harry. Spontaneous combustion was the best answer any of us could come up with. And there's a dozen or more heavily armed men killed or wounded lying in and around them."

"Same thing with them, I assume? More spontaneous combustion?"

"No, those were self-defense, and we have the bullet holes in the house to prove it. In fact, I have a Chinese RPG stuck in my front door at this very moment, if you can believe that. But the EOD guys over at Bragg will take care of it."

"Nice to know you're spreading the work around."

"We try."

"The Russian mob from Brooklyn, huh?"

"Well, the Brighton Beach part of it, anyway."

"Can't wait to see this, Bob. We should be there in twenty minutes."

"Just head for the orange glow, Harry, you can't miss it."

Pavel Bratsov drove the van through the gate of Piedmont Aviation and parked next to their hangar on the corporate side of Fayetteville Regional Airport. It was on the southwest side of town, where their two private jets from New Jersey were waiting. When they flew in, just before sunset, they told the airport office and the pilots that they would be back in an hour. Bratsov looked at his watch and saw that they still had fifteen minutes to spare.

The pilots were expecting to see twenty-two men in five vans, not two badly battered men in one van. The plane crews were waiting, but when they saw him holding the side of his face with one hand, his shirt and left arm covered with blood, half-carrying Piotr Shurepkin with the other arm, they looked at each other, but no one said anything.

Bratsov shoved Piotr up the stairs, turned to the pilot, and said, "Ready? Let's go."

The pilot looked back toward the gate and asked, "The others?"

"They are driving back. Do not worry about them. Fly us back to New Jersey, both planes. The other one will go empty. Now!"

The copilot pulled up the stairs and closed the door. He looked at the two men and their blood-soaked clothes, reached into a cabinet, and put a large first-aid kit on the table in front of Bratsov. "Here," he said disgustedly. "It appears you might need this." Then he turned, went up to the cockpit, and left Piotr and Bratsov alone in the back.

"What are we going to do now?" Piotr asked as he slumped forward in his seat, his head in his hands.

"We cannot stay here," Bratsov quickly answered.

"I know we cannot stay *HERE,* Pavel!" Piotr snapped at him, frustrated.

"I mean we cannot stay *here, IN AMERICA!*" Bratsov glared at him, his patience running paper-thin. Piotr might be his boss's son, but he sorely wanted to give him a thorough beating. "The police will be all over us by tomorrow. We have to get out of the country, back to Russia, and we have to do it quick, tonight."

Piotr's eyes went wide. "To Russia? But our operations in Brooklyn...?"

"What operations? The restaurant is closed, you got nowhere with the government contracting, and most of our men are now dead or in jail. It won't be long before they are all talking their heads off."

"But go back? Evgeni is dead. How can I face my father?"

"He will forgive you."

"You don't know him. My father loves me, but not like he loved Evgeni."

"You are the prodigal son coming home, and now you are the only son he has. Of course he will forgive you. But that American Burke will not. We must get out of here."

As they felt the airplane take off, Bratsov looked at his hands and at his shirt, then at Piotr. "There's a late night flight to Moscow out of Kennedy, the one your father took. We need to change clothes and get our passports, and some money, but we can make that."

Avoiding the foyer and the front door, Bob followed Volodya Rostov and Stephanie Goss out the back door and up one of the gravel paths to the front of the house where he took in the scene. It looked bad from the attic, but it looked even worse down at ground level, like the seventh of Dante's *Nine Circles of Hell,* the one reserved for thugs and murderers and filled with blood and fire.

The fires in and around the four shattered vans were dying down, but not out. They bathed the front yard in an eerie orange glow and black smoke. As they walked out into the yard, there were a half a dozen wounded or badly shaken men sitting or lying in and around the blackened sections of the vans, and at least that many more who were dead. All the Deltas on duty that night were experts in first aid, and they had already gone to work trying to help the ones that might have a future, as did Stephanie. One thing for sure, he thought, it would take some flatbed wreckers, a lot of new sod, and a growing season or two to get this part of the property looking decent again.

In the distance, Bob heard the sirens on a half-dozen police cars, fire trucks, and rescue squad units approaching. With all of that work underway, Bob pulled out his cell phone and took two quick pictures of the flaming wreckage.

His next call went to Sal Parvenuti in the FBI office up in Brooklyn.

"Sal! Hey, this is Bob Burke. You guys still sitting on that tearoom in Brighton Beach?"

"Don't you ever sleep? Do you know what time it is?"

"Crime fighters never sleep. Wasn't that something J Edgar Hoover said?"

"No, probably Batman. I'm in a sleeping bag in that stinking second-floor apartment and was almost asleep when you called. After thirty-six hours straight beating my head against the wall up here, I think I'm entitled."

"So the answer is you're still sitting on it, then?"

"You didn't let me finish. The answer's yes and no. After the police raid, the city and county pulled Kalinka's permits and shut it down. With nobody coming or going, our regional office decided to shut us down too. Way too much overtime, they said. Anyway, we had about half of our gear taken apart and put back in the boxes when things got weird late this afternoon. A bunch of guys, Piotr's guys by the looks of them, suddenly showed up and went inside. As best we can tell, they all left a little while later out the back in some vans."

"I can probably give you their names in a little while," Bob told him. "Most of them are lying in my front yard right now along with what used to be four vans they rented at our local airport. Take a look in your email. I just sent you some photographs of the yard and some facial photos of the attackers. Half of them are dead, the other half pretty well shot up, but maybe you can run them through your Bureau facial recognition software."

"You're kidding! What about the two Shurepkins and Bratsov?"

"Evgeni Shurepkin is dead. He charged my house like a maniac and fired an RPG at my front door before someone put him down."

"And the other two?"

"We're still looking, but we think they got away."

"We'll keep an eye out for them up here. And I'll let our guys in Fayetteville know. They need to get out to your place."

"It will be hard to miss. All they have to do is follow the flashing red lights."

"Brian and I will be down in a couple of hours, as soon as we can get one of the Bureau jets up here to pick us up."

"If your boss didn't like the overtime in Brighton Beach, he's really not going to like this one."

CHAPTER FORTY-FOUR

Sherwood Forest

It took the rest of that night and well into the next day to get things under control at Sherwood Forest. The fire department extinguished the remaining fires in fairly short order. They took fourteen of the attackers to the Cape Fear Valley Medical Center across the river in Fayetteville. Some went to the emergency room, and some went to the morgue. They captured four others before daybreak attempting to hitchhike their way back north. Every available Fayetteville police officer, North Carolina Highway Patrol trooper and sheriff's deputy in a three-county area was at the jail or the hospital questioning the survivors or out on the road looking for more. It wasn't a good night to be wandering the back roads with a thick Eastern European accent, wearing muddy big-city shoes, and carrying a New York driver's license bearing a name Barney Fife would have a tough time pronouncing.

By 2 a.m., FBI forensics teams from Raleigh and Quantico were on site combing through the grass and the wreckage of the vans. Bob walked the site with Ace, Sal Parvenuti from the FBI, and Harry Van Zandt watching the Feds work the site, gathering up every brass shell casing and all the arms and explosive materials. The Feds had taken jurisdiction and the Russian Brighton Beach crowd were all in custody, whether they could walk or were under guard in the hospital. They were all being charged with a litany of federal terrorist and racketeering charges. And while the opera may not be over until "the fat lady sings," most of those guys already were.

In TV police dramas, there's frequent friction between the locals and the Feds on cases, but not this time. "You can have the lot of them," Harry Van Zandt told Sal, and the County Sheriff quickly agreed. "You FBI guys and the US Attorneys have the big budgets. By the time our little county gets finished with all the extra police work these cases will entail, and then pays for all the extra lawyers, the translators, and the retired judges we'll have to bring in, the experts, and put on a bunch of high-profile trials… We'll need to float a bond issue to pay for it all. No thanks, guys, you can keep the Comrades," the Sheriff said.

"Oh, come on, think of all the hotel rooms and restaurant meals you'd sell all those snarky reporters," Sal laughed. "Your Chamber of Commerce will love it."

"In the first place, those damned New York and Washington reporters skip out on more meals than they pay for, and the networks do it all by satellite now, so our police chief will be quite happy if you bus them all up to Raleigh and get them out of here."

Sal told them an armload of Federal arrest warrants and search warrants were being issued for a bunch more "wise guys" up in Brooklyn. Unfortunately, the two Russians they wanted most, Piotr Shurepkin and Pavel Bratsov, were nowhere to be found.

That was when Sal's cell phone buzzed. The conversation was brief, and then he turned to Bob. "There's two women with a couple of kids out at our roadblock on the highway who claim they live here. It's their third time back, and our guys are beginning to fear for their lives from the one who claims to be your wife. She says she wants in so she can wring your neck before you run away and hide. Given our dedication to law and order, my first inclination was not to let her through, but I think we could all use some comic relief before the EOD guys get that RPG round out of your front door. I figure you've got about a five minutes head start on her if you get moving."

"Not nearly enough time, Bob. You might as well let her through and face the music," Ace shook his head sadly. "That woman is fast, especially when she's highly motivated, like I suspect she is tonight."

"I believe I've met her," Harry interjected. "Ace is right. You can run, but you can't hide."

It took almost an hour for Linda to track him down. It helped to have snitches around the property who would keep him advised by texts of her position. As she went down one side, he would circle up the other, always keeping the house between them. Nice to know they'd do that, given that the entire staff liked her a hell of a lot more than they liked him. But that wasn't why. If she caught up and killed him, which he probably deserved, they'd all end up having to testify for her Justifiable Homicide defense, so it was easier to keep them apart until she cooled off.

Good plan. Might have worked, if Bob hadn't stopped to watch Tim Enders and George Themopolis, the EOD guys from Bragg, finally finish defusing the badly dented RPG warhead stuck in his front door, remove the charge, and slowly wiggle it free from the thick oak door panel.

"Does that mean it won't blow up the front of my house?" she asked Enders. He nodded, but it didn't matter. "That would have been the second time someone blew it up, and I like this house," she said as she turned and looked at the ruined, badly burned front yard. "I used to like my front yard, too. Now look at it!"

"Linda, it wasn't my fault."

"Possession's nine-tenths of the law, Bob."

"Come on, honey, what's that supposed to mean?" he asked, confused.

"They're your cases and your enemies, but it's my house. Remember all those itty-bitty legal words in the Merry Men documents? You wanted to keep your name out of the deeds, so we used mine with my maiden name. Sooo… stop blowing up my house!"

"Yes, ma'am," he finally answered. "Now can we go to bed?"

"You should be so lucky. Call Sasha. Maybe he'll take you in."

CHAPTER FORTY-FIVE

Sherwood Forest

Instead of a bed in one of the guest rooms out back, Bob opted for the living room couch, figuring that was the last place Linda would look for him. At 6:15 the next morning he was in his usual spot in the breakfast nook off the kitchen at the back of the house, watching dawn break gently over the undamaged part of the farm and catching up on e-mail and online news, before the non-stop racket of hammers and saws out front made thinking all but impossible. He was working on his second cup of coffee when Volodya Rostov walked in, grabbed a cup of his own, and sat down.

Rostov looked across at him and said, "My friend, thank you most kindly for your gracious hospitality, the shooting contest, and all the amazing fun we had until last night. You are a wonderful host. However, I am afraid it is time I must leave."

"Too much noise? I'd complain to the hotel manager."

"No, no, I have imposed long enough on your fine hospitality and that of your wife."

"Back to the embassy in DC? You never did tell me what you do there."

"Nothing, actually. I am the Deputy Military Attaché, a largely ceremonial post. I attend many pleasant parties, get to travel around your country, and visit many military bases, some of which I am invited to, others not; but your people don't seem to care. Neither do ours. Between satellites, commercial Aeroflot flights with high-tech cameras, paid spies, embedded ones, bloggers, Facebook, and everything else available on the internet, we already know most of what there is to know. Your people know that we know it. We know that they know. Same at our end. And since both sides know everything, there are no secrets any longer and nothing to fear from the other guy. If you think about it, it is a perfect solution for peace."

"Except for the Chinese and the Arabs."

"Well, yes, except for the Chinese and the Arabs. There is always someone who decides to crap in the well and ruin a good thing, isn't there?" Rostov said, and they both laughed.

"So you're returning to DC?"

"Why are you so interested in my travels, my friend?"

Burke shrugged. "Somehow, I thought we might meander back to Brooklyn – you, me, and probably Jefferson Adkins – I think he'll insist –

and pay another visit to the surviving Shurepkin brother. We have unfinished business with him. I thought that's what you wanted to do, too, Volodya."

"That is what I wanted to do," Rostov agreed. "But you will note I used your past tense. Running to Brooklyn will do us no good now because Piotr Shurepkin is not there. He and his pit bull, Pavel Bratsov, found two seats on the late-night Aeroflot flight from JFK to Moscow. They are long gone."

"Yeah, Sal Parvenuti forwarded an e-mail to me a little while ago that the FBI couldn't find them up in Brooklyn either. The tearoom is shut down and empty, as we already knew, but so is Piotr's big house on Long Island. I don't think it's far from JFK. He said by the time they finally got the search warrant and could get inside, all they found was a bunch of dirty, torn clothes, some with a lot of blood on them, but no bad guys."

"As one would have expected. Piotr is not stupid," Rostov said sadly. "In truth, he was never my target. He might be yours and Jefferson's, and for good reason, but he was never mine. To me, both he and Evgeni are, or were, only my means to an end."

"That end being Oleg Shurepkin?"

"Him, and his pit bull, Dema Kropotkin. He is the one who actually killed my son, on Oleg's orders, of course."

"Then why the hell are you going back to DC?"

"DC? I never said I was returning to DC. You are the one who said that," Rostov corrected him. "I am going to Moscow."

"Moscow? I thought you said Oleg had too many powerful friends and too many connections, even in the Kremlin, for you to take him on."

"It is funny how friendships can blow with the wind, isn't it?" Rostov answered with a thin smile. "Vladimir Putin controls absolutely everything. With all the state intelligence assets he has whispering in his ear – the FSB, the old KGB; the SVR, who deal with foreign intelligence; as well as my own GRU, for military intelligence, there isn't much the man doesn't hear in 'real time,' as you say."

"You figure he already knows about Piotr's screw ups in New York and down here?"

"Perhaps not this attack, not yet anyway, but he soon will. But I am certain he already knows about all the rest of it, and what happened up in Brooklyn. Oleg Shurepkin was of value to Putin when he was the head of the Vor Council, the group that coordinates the Russian Mafia, or at least that part of it around Moscow, because Putin got a large piece of everything

– big business, the oligarchs, big arms deals and other exports, and organized crime."

Bob chuckled. "He gets to 'wet his beak?' "

"Ah, you like the Godfather! Wonderful! I assure you, Vladimir Putin does a lot more than merely wetting it. Like the vulture, he usually tears off the largest piece for himself. That is why he is very forgiving of 'collateral damage' as you Americans call it, provided he gets his piece."

"Like the murder of your son?"

"Yes, but my son was a high-ranking local police official. That caused many eyebrows to raise and many more questions to be asked, I assure you."

"But not enough?"

"Back then, Oleg Shurepkin was untouchable so long as the money continued to roll in. In recent months, however, he lost his Midas touch. Many of his friends and allies have backed away and abandoned him now, as his string of failures mounted. Make no mistake, he remains a powerful, protective, and vicious man. But in recent days it is obvious he lost Putin's support. The Council has dethroned him, his big schemes for America have failed, and his fortunes are in freefall."

"So it is time to strike?"

"Yes, it is time to strike, that is why I am returning to Moscow."

"Let me help you," Bob said. "You can't out-gun them or out-bomb them. The way you destroy them is to pull their pants down in the middle of Red Square and spank them."

Rostov stared at him across the table. "I am listening," he asked, curious.

"You take away their money and all their toys."

"Like you did with New York and Chicago mobs?" Rostov asked. "Interesting, but Russia is different, I think. The Russian Mafia is different. They do not trust banks, at least not banks in Russia or America."

"You saw what my three computer guys can do, especially Sasha. He's been working on Evgeni's laptop ever since we got back. If there's money to be found anywhere, in bank accounts or anywhere else, he'll find it. And money is the key, Putin's money. That is the best way to undermine his support and destroy him. I figure if we can't kill him, let's leave him sitting in Red Square with a tin cup, begging for his next meal. Let me turn Sasha loose."

Rostov looked at him. "No harm in trying, Robert. Perhaps you are right. Taking his money may be the best way to push Oleg over the edge."

"But if you go back to Moscow, I want to go too. That's his turf, Volodya, and you can't take him on alone back there."

"Oh, I will not be alone. My younger son, Ivan, is a recently commissioned infantry lieutenant. He is with me, as is my old Sergeant Major, Nikolai Volek, and several of my oldest son's friends from the police. They want Shurepkin's blood as badly as I do, and I trust those men completely."

"I'm sure you do, but Ace, Jefferson Adkins, and myself would help you even the odds."

"You cannot bring your Merry Men. They are still Deltas on active duty. That could trigger an international incident, and I cannot allow that."

"Actually, I had someone else in mind, a former lieutenant in the Dutch Royal Marines, the 'Black Devils,' their special forces, named Theo Van Gries. He has done some private 'contracting' for me and been a big help in putting together specialized teams all around the world.

"Theo Van Gries?" Rostov frowned. "I have heard of this fellow. A 'merc' I believe you call them: very competent, very efficient, very much outside the law, and very expensive."

"As you and Sasha discussed a few days ago, 'potatoes, tomatoes.' Let me worry about the cost. Shurepkin will be paying anyway. You said Oleg has worn out his welcome with Putin and the other mob bosses, but politics is always a fragile balance of power. Perhaps they'd like someone else to solve their problem for them and take him off their hands?"

"Perhaps," Rostov finally answered, "but this is still Russia. It might not be 1951 when the police state was monolithic and all-powerful, but foreigners, especially ones with a background like yours, do not wander in uninvited and expect to survive the experience. You do however make an excellent point about taking the problem off Putin's hands and giving him some deniability. That might be of value to him. I shall make a few phone calls."

"If we fly into Helsinki, or maybe Tallinn or Riga in the Baltic countries instead of Moscow or St. Petersburg? Could you get us across the border from one of those?"

"Possibly, but the Russian FSB and SVR watch those points of entry even more than they watch our own. After all, what kind of maniacs would fly straight into Moscow, right into the lion's mouth, eh? But allow me to find out about that. If Putin is interested enough in the outcome, he may not care about the form."

"Meanwhile, I'll track down Theo Van Gries, and talk to Sasha to see how far he's gotten."

"Excellent," Volodya said. "Let's have lunch together later. We can compare notes and see what makes sense."

It was 7:15 a.m., still far too early in the morning to visit the third floor "Geekdom," so Bob pulled out his cell phone and placed an international call to a very unlisted number in Switzerland. No one answered and there was no recorded greeting to listen to, not that he expected either of those, only silence. Nor was there any indication of how many other servers around the world the call bounced through before it finally found a home. That was how Theo Van Gries operated: discreetly.

By prior arrangement, Bob knew to leave nothing, not a name or even a phone number. Theo's system automatically recorded the incoming number. That told him everything he needed to know. If Theo was available, which was always a big "if," and if he was alive and interested, two other big "ifs," he might eventually call back. With Theo Van Gries, any of those things were possible.

CHAPTER FORTY-SIX

Sherwood Forest

Bob looked at his watch again. It was 7:30 a.m., still too early to go visit the Geekdom, so he put in a quick phone call to Maryanne in Chicago and got an update on the cleanup and repair work for the Toler TeleCom office building in Schaumburg. Cleanup, getting a good structural analysis, and getting the correct material on order always took a lot of time, but things were moving along. The business was functioning in the back half of the building and up and running in some nearby rental space. One thing that bound his people together up there was the fact that they were not about to let a bunch of terrorists stop their work and take their jobs.

That phone call out of the way, he decided the time had come to climb the staircase to the third floor and see if there was any sign of life this early in the "KGB Spymaster Data Center." Being nocturnal creatures one and all, he figured they were all in bed, sound asleep. This morning, however, he was wrong. As soon as he reached the landing between the second and third floors, while they had turned off the fluorescent ceiling lights in the data center, he could see a thin ribbon of light coming under the double doors. Someone was awake in there, he decided. When he pushed the door open and stepped inside, he was surprised to see the light was coming from the shaded desk lamp and the 'under-counter' LED lights at Sasha's workstation on the far side of the console.

"*Privyet*, Sasha!" Hello, Sasha, Bob called out to him.

"*Privyet*, Comrade General! Tell me, is it now safe for serfs like poor Sasha to come out of our bunkers? Are the *Bratva*, the Mafia gangsters, all dead or in shackles now?"

"Some, not all, but the rest have fled the scene and you may safely crawl out of your burrow." Bob pulled a chair around and surprised Sasha by sitting next to the "Mad Russian," as the other geeks called him. It was obvious from the clutter on his desk and from his personal appearance that Sasha had been here all night, perhaps for several days or more. How long? Hard to tell since time has no meaning in the Geek-iverse. In Sasha's case, it was especially hard to tell. Once he got his head into a project, he tended not to stop until he finished or fell out of the chair in total exhaustion.

Sasha's hair stuck out from the top and sides of his head in clumps, spikes, and uncombed tufts. His beard was even more scraggly than usual and could be hiding a family of squirrels, as Patsy often accused him of doing. He wore one of his favorite stained, torn Berkeley football T-shirts, and his trashcan was overflowing with empty Red Bull cans and Hostess Twinkie and Ding-Dong wrappers. Not a good look. However, his fingers continued to pound away on the keyboard with a manic intensity and the disk drive and router lights on his computer were flashing. All three video monitors above his cubicle were alive with changing documents and spreadsheets. More importantly, he had what appeared to be Evgeni Shurepkin's Toshiba laptop open on the desk in front of him and plugged into his own.

"How's the data mining coming?" Bob asked.

"Almost to bottom of shaft, Boss. I think I see upside-down basement lights in China."

"Find anything on Evgeni's laptop yet, or was he a complete phony?"

"Oh, no phony! Only seventeen years old? Boy is genius with computer. Within a hair of being up to my standard."

"Was. He made the mistake of trying to charge the house with an RPG last night."

Sasha winced. "Not end well, Boss?"

"Not end well. What about their bank accounts and financial transactions?"

"Boy was also genius finding ways to move and hide money."

"How close are you to figuring it all out?"

"Boss, Boss..." Sasha slowly shook his head and looked disappointed, like you would to a young child who had just wet his pants. "This Sasha you talking to. Evgeni was good, I better. Like loose threads on Chinese sweater you buy at Walmart. Pick one and pull. Then you find next thread and pull, and next. Pretty soon, no sweater. Is complicated, yes; but I follow each transaction to end. Every three-four days, maybe once a week, somebody, probably somebody big and carrying a gun, deposits big bag of cash at Israeli bank branch in Brighton Beach. Deposit then wired to French bank in Caymans. All French are sleaze balls, trust me. French banks are worse. Then 'Poof!' money rerouted to private bank in Switzerland. They say 'Pree-vat,' " he grinned. Swiss are French with nicer clothes. Still sleaze balls. Finally, it goes to Russian Sberbank branch in Lagos, Nigeria. Sberbank make French look honest. Is owned by Russian government, which means owned by Putin and cronies. Very crooked. Piggy bank for pigs is what my mother call it back home."

"You have a mother? This is the first time you've ever mentioned her. The rest of us thought you popped up in the spring with the mushrooms."

"No, Boss, Sasha have mother, not come from mushroom patch. She live in Bryansk, very old city southeast of Moscow. She used to drive truck. Very tough lady."

"Why don't you invite her over to visit?"

"No Green Card, Boss. Sasha been hiding out here. How can he invite mother without Green Card? You try to get me one?"

"Tell you what, Sasha, I'll do better than that. I'll turn Linda loose on it."

Sasha grinned, wide-eyed. "Linda? You turn Mizzus Boss loose? Then is in bag! Thank you, Boss. Now we see how much money we can squeeze from those Moscow sleaze balls," he said as he turned back to the screens. "Sberbank money gets sent on to Turkey, sometimes to Lichtenstein, then back to different accounts in different names in three different Swiss banks in Berne. Complicated. Almost untraceable… Almost!"

"But not to a mad Russian riding high on Red Bull. Tell me about the accounts."

"You know Swiss, very meticulous, very tedious, very secret. One account is Shurepkin's. Evgeni put money in, Evgeni take money back out again. Sometimes it sits. Other accounts not like that. Evgeni put money in those, but other people take out; so, first account is Shurepkin's."

"That could be where they're laundering it, splitting it with the others."

"Good, Boss, you learning how Russian mob operates. There is Shurepkin account, but there is second group of seven accounts. Not Shurepkin's, but same size. Money goes in in equal amounts. Most stays there. More piggy banks. Then there is eighth account. Same size as other seven put together. Maybe owned by one Russian. Evgeni put money in, but money doesn't stay long there. The bank moves it to other accounts, sometimes in other banks, always Swiss banks."

"Got any idea who the accounts belong to?"

Sasha sat back and glanced over at Bob. "Boss, Sasha iz not stupid. Sasha reads underground press. Sasha Googles. Seven accounts? Seven old Zeks plus Shurepkin on Mafia Vor Council. Everybody in Moscow knows that. So Sasha picks out three and digs deeper, because I knew you would tell me to. Like peeling the onion. One belongs to Yuri Paretsky, one to Avram Avramov, and one to Sergei Demitrov. Like Shurepkin, old Zeks on Mafia Council. Big names back there. Like hockey player trading cards we collect as kids. We get cards for Ovechkin, Fetisov, Fedorov, Malkin, Igor Kravchuk, Andre Kovalenko, and now Panarin. They play on CSKA, Dynamo, Spartak, or NHL. Everyone knows names and teams. Same for Mafia heads. We not have trading cards yet, but everyone knows names."

"So who owns the big account?"

Sasha looked at him again. "Boss, only one 'big' account in Russia. Everyone in Moscow knows that too. Belongs to 'Czar.' He loves to play hockey too. Plays with the pros and his bodyguards. Putin shoots puck, goalie steps aside."

"Like a matador in a Spanish bullring, huh?'

"Same deal, Boss. Worst thing that can happen to goalie is if Putin shoot puck too hard. Maybe goalie fall down or can't get out of the way, puck hits him, and not go in goal. Not good."

"How much money are we talking about?"

"Lots, Boss. Shurepkin maybe $8 million in Swiss accounts. Used to be much more. Chump change now. Must be going broke. Other seven have $16 to $18 million each. Total is $100 million, a little less."

"And your 'Czar?' "

"Not my Czar, Boss. Maybe another $100 million, split into four accounts."

"How hard would it be to grab it?"

"Easy to grab Shurepkin's. Accounts linked. We have laptop. We know routing codes. Other seven Vor accounts, some easy, some not so much, depends on bank. 'Doable,' as Patsy says. But Czar's money? Not recommended. Like stealing virginity from old, grumpy spinster. Can get it but not be much fun. Afterward, she turn dogs on you."

"Understood. Go get some sleep and then keep digging. We'll focus on Shurepkin and the other Vors."

"Good idea, Boss. Life iz too long for serfs to mess with Czar."

"You mean life's too short?"

"No, Boss, life's too long. He never stop until he make you pay, big time."

Three and one-half hours later, Bob's cell phone rang. Looking at the screen, he saw that the identity of the caller and his number were blocked, but he answered anyway.

"Ghost! What are you up to, my friend?" he heard a friendly male voice at the other end with a crisp, distinctive Dutch accent. It was Theo Van Gries. The two men faced off against each other in Atlantic City when a mob casino owner brought him and his foreign mercenaries in to eliminate Bob's team of Merry Men. Head to head, it didn't go so well for Theo's mercs. In the end, Bob allowed the Dutchman to walk away. He was a professional doing a job, nothing more. They stayed in touch and had become friends of sorts. Van Gries returned the favor when Bob and Ace needed a helicopter and another gun in the rocky Syrian desert when Bob took a half-mile shot at night with his Barrett to take out "the Sheikh."

As Theo later joked to him over drinks under the potted palms of the rooftop bar of the Sheraton in Amman, Jordan, "Ghost, if you're ever throwing a firefight in some other godforsaken place at the ass end of the world and don't think to invite me, I will be very disappointed."

"Theo," Bob began, "are you familiar with Oleg Shurepkin?"

"Most assuredly," the Dutchman answered. "A nasty piece of work if there ever was one. Are you thinking of mounting an operation against him? On his turf?"

"Yes, on both counts."

"That will not be easy, my friend. Send me a plan and your requirements to my drop box, and I'll be back to you."

"Things are moving fairly quickly."

"I heard some rumors on the jungle drums."

"They are pretty much true. How much do you need up front?"

"Nothing. We can settle up on my out-of-pocket expenses afterward, if any of us make it back out alive. Me, you get for free, because that old bastard Shurepkin is in serious need of killing."

"You aren't alone in that sentiment."

"No doubt about it, but you seem to make a habit of getting on the wrong side of people like that, people who the world is better off without."

"My wife says I seem to attract them," Bob laughed.

"Then you should take up a new hobby in your retirement. But you realize that his turf will not be the easiest place in the world to operate, my friend. And he will prove to be a hard target to hit."

"We have some inside connections."

"Good. They had better be incredibly good ones, otherwise it could become a suicide mission, and neither you nor I are into those."

CHAPTER FORTY-SEVEN

Sherwood Forest

At noon, they held a "war council" in the small conference room at the far end of the Geekdom on the third floor. Bob figured it would be out of sight from almost everyone, including the snoopy Feds; but most importantly, from Linda. He knew what her reaction would be, so the less she knew for the time being, the better. The Geeks rarely left their custom-made ergonomic chairs around the big computer console, so the meeting room had devolved into a sometime lunchroom and nap couch. Since the janitors had rebelled and refused to clean it up anymore without hazmat suits, the job fell to Patsy. This time, however, because they were bringing in outsiders, Bob told all four of them to clean it up under penalty of having their computers unplugged. That got the job done in short order.

The attendees comprised Bob, Ace, Jefferson Adkins, Stephanie Goss, Volodya Rostov, and the three Geeks. Bob had no intention of inviting Jefferson or Stephanie to come along on an op inside Russia, but they insisted on being kept up to date on the planning. If he didn't invite them in, Bob knew Jefferson and Stephanie would show up, anyway.

"Look," he told Jefferson and Stephanie. "There's no way you two can come. You're both on active duty, and that would be a no-no if you got caught. It could create an international incident and a big problem for the US government and for the rest of us. We are civilians, but you two aren't, and you'd end up in a big show trial in Moscow. We're trying to slip in under the radar. Stephanie's blonde and could probably pass for a local, but there's no way to disguise a 6'7" 270-pound black guy over there with all those Slavs and Nordic types."

Surprisingly, Jefferson didn't get pissed, jump out of his chair, or try to pound lumps on him. Instead, he reached into a paper grocery bag at his feet, pulled out a brightly colored red, green, and gold African agbada, an ankle-length cover-up with a matching kufi cap, stood up, and put them on, with a pair of black-framed, horn-rimmed dark sunglasses. "You are mistaken, sir," he said in a thick West African accent with British overtones. "I am Usman Ayodele, a Nigerian architecture student on his way to a seminar at the University of Moscow."

"You are Eddie Murphy, from movie!" Sasha roared. "*Coming to America.*"

Jefferson looked at him and tossed a Nigerian passport on the table in front of Bob.

Bob looked at it and then picked it up and flipped through the pages. "Is this legit? Or will it get you in the basement of the Lubyanka the first time we run into an FSB checkpoint?"

"It's completely legit. The last time I worked at the Pentagon, one of my neighbors in Silver Spring was the Nigerian military attaché. He was more than happy to oblige for a case of bourbon from the Class Six store at Fort McNair."

"Dark sunglasses, smiley white teeth, and a big laugh," Ace agreed. "Hopefully, the Russians will be so busy looking at him that they won't even notice us. In fact, maybe the rest of us can hide underneath that dashiki and walk right through."

Rostov rolled his eyes. "Are you certain those papers are still good?"

"I checked with him this morning."

Bob turned his attention to Stephanie. "This is no joke. What kind of papers do you have?"

"I have a US civilian passport, same as you guys had when you were on active duty," she answered. "We all travel through countries and airports where they didn't want us to use our military ID cards. It's good."

"What about weapons," Bob turned and asked Rostov. "I doubt we can take anything in with us."

"No need," Rostov answered. "My son will provide us with whatever we need. Give me a list of your preferences. I spoke with him this morning. He informs me that Oleg Shurepkin has left the city. He is now holed up in his dacha in the Odintsovsky District west of Moscow, not far from Putin's dacha, actually."

"Do we know who else is out there with him?" Bob asked.

"They are trying to find out. Piotr and Dema Kropotkin, for sure. Probably Pavel Bratsov, and some of his Moscow gunmen and thugs, no doubt. How many? Hard to say. His fortunes are falling fast, particularly after the fiascos in Brooklyn and down here. How many of them would die for him now? We won't know until we get there."

"What's this dacha of his look like?" Adkins asked. "You mean like a cabin, or a vacation home on a lake, or something?"

Rostov smiled. "It is a lot more than that. Dachas are Russian institutions. Everyone wants one. Many have one. Most are very modest cottages and even shacks out in the country where people keep gardens. However, they are much more than that in the Odintsovsky area, where

Putin and many of his business and government cronies have them. They may have started out as rustic hunting lodges a hundred years ago, but most have been expanded and upgraded, and are far more palatial, with large houses and lots. My son thinks Shurepkin has probably hunkered down there."

"Gone 'to mattresses,' like in *Godfather*, eh?" Sasha asked.

Rostov rolled his eyes. "Actually, not far from the truth, and he isn't likely to leave there anytime soon, especially now that his son Piotr has arrived. He is hiding, sulking, and licking his wounds, probably in fear of being arrested if he leaves."

"A good assumption," Bob said.

"We shall find out soon. His dacha is our target."

"Was your son able to have any discussions with Putin's people about us taking care of that problem for them?" Bob asked.

"Yes, he was. There is a man named Boris Orsunov who is in Putin's bodyguards. That is a job you do not get unless he trusts you, unless you're a total loyalist, and unless you have the man's ear. He is former Speznaz and a classmate of my older son at Frunze, the very prestigious joint arms military academy in Moscow. They spoke twice this morning and agreed that Putin will have his people "turn their backs," allow us to go in, take care of business, and most importantly, to get back out. They expect there to be bloodshed, a lot of it, so better ours than theirs."

"That sounds simple enough," Jefferson Adkins said. "What does the bastard want?"

Rostov smiled. "Money, of course. It is what you call a love-hate relationship between Putin and the Bratva: a mutually beneficial marriage of convenience, useful to control criminal elements in the country. But like Cossacks a century ago, they have become too independent for their own good. Putin wants to knock them down a few notches and replace them with his own people."

"Bullshit. What he wants is their Swiss bank accounts," Bob smiled knowingly.

"Equally true. The deal we have tentatively agreed upon is that if we take Shurepkin out, the Czar will graciously allow us to keep Shurepkin's money to cover our expenses, but Putin gets the accounts of the seven Vors."

"Piggy banks. Like I tell you, Boss, piggy banks for chief pig."

"Eight million dollars in exchange for one hundred million?" Ace asked. "How generous of him. And we get rid of his problem for him, all eight of his problems, actually."

"He is not a shy man. He holds most of the cards and knows it. So I also told him we would split the Vor accounts 50/50 after we are safely back in Germany."

"And they'll buy that?" Ace asked.

"No. He wanted 80/20, and we settled on 75/25. I never thought he'd let us have that much, so I agreed. No one trusts no one anymore, and we both need an incentive. It is what they would expect."

"Wow, that's another $25 million, if we live that long. But how are we getting in there?" Bob asked. "Through Finland? Lithuania, maybe?"

"That is what I had been thinking, until I spoke with my son before I came up here," Rostov answered. "Putin's people want us to go in and out of Moscow."

"That'll make it easier to keep an eye on us," Ace said.

"Which they will, anyway," Rostov conceded. "So why sneak in? They know who we are and where we are going. Why waste time? We will fly into Moscow, into Sheremetyevo, or Pushkin, as they call it now. It is north-north-west of the city. Shurepkin's dacha is an hour or two away to the west. We can be in and out before they have time to screw with us."

"Good. When do we go?" Bob asked.

"Quickly. Russians love a good conspiracy, and secrets do not remain secret for long. Perhaps tonight," Rostov answered as he turned and looked at Sasha. "If they decide to double cross us…"

"*WHEN* they decide to double cross us."

"More likely," Rostov conceded. "What can you do to ensure they don't?"

Sasha frowned and then ran his fingers through his thick beard, violently yanking on it as he thought the question over for a minute or two. Finally, he smiled. "Tell them you have genius software engineer called 'Mad Russian.' Tell them he trained at Moscow Coding School, Lomonosov Moscow University, and worked at KGB, before graduating from Berkeley. If they ask at MCS or Lomonosov, people remember him."

"Is that true?" Rostov looked at Sasha and asked. Even the Mad Russian knew it was easy for people not to believe him.

"Iz true, Comrade Colonel. I am smarter than everyone they have put together."

"He really is," Bob smiled. "And as they say, it ain't braggin' if you can do it."

"Tell Orsunov if you not come back out and smile at security cameras in Frankfurt, money disappears – all money: Shurepkin's, Seven Dwarf's, and Czar's too – all of it, forever. Tell him 6:00 p.m. tonight, watch their computer screens. I give demonstration. Money in accounts of the big man with no name will disappear from his Swiss accounts for one minute – only one minute – all money, all his accounts, all to zero, one minute, long enough to prove I can do. Then I put it all back. Tell them they should have all their computer people and bean counters watch their monitors. Won't matter. Still won't figure out what I did."

"That should get their attention," Ace laughed."

"Tell them to leave all money where it is until then. If they try to move it or double cross, I take it again. This time, Sasha will not put back. When you arrive in Moscow airport, you text me, I move half of Czar's 75% of Vor accounts into Czar's accounts. Once everyone leave Moscow and back on ground in Germany looking at security cameras, smiling, I move second half of Vor money into Czar's accounts. Then Sasha not bother them again, ever."

"And you can do that, Sasha?" Bob asked.

"I can do. Money is Russian life insurance," Sasha laughed. "The only life insurance."

"What if they figure out who you are, Sasha?" Patsy asked. "Your mother's still over there."

Sasha frowned. "Who is kidding who, woman? When they hear Moscow Coding School, Lomonosov, and Berkeley, they figure out who Sasha is. Probably already know."

"Your mother's in Russia?" Ronald asked.

Bob turned to Rostov. "Volodya, can your son get papers and a passport for her, so she can fly back out with us?"

Rostov shrugged. "I don't see why not. I shall have Ivan tell Boris Orsunov it is one of our conditions. Orsunov can make it happen."

"No tickie, no washy," Ronald added.

"She in Moscow, idiot, not Beijing!" Sasha smacked him on the back of his head.

Bob ignored their usual Geek-chaos as he thought it over for a moment. "Tell Orsunov we will transfer $2 million of our share of Shurepkin's money into Orsunov's bank account when Sasha's mother lands in Frankfurt with the rest of us. Like you said, nothing like a little incentive."

Sasha's mouth fell open. "Boss!" he sputtered and threw his arms around Bob.

Bob managed to pry himself loose from the hairy Russian and turned to Rostov. "Enough! And I assume you and your son are coming out with us?"

"No, we are staying in Moscow. It is our country. But do not worry about us. We will be in no danger from them once this is over."

CHAPTER FORTY-EIGHT

Frankfurt International Airport

They flew into Frankfurt – Bob, Ace, Volodya Rostov, Stephanie Goss, and Jefferson Adkins, or Usman Ayodele, the Nigerian architecture student he was still hopelessly pretending to be – and landed at 11:00 a.m. At the gate, they rendezvoused with Theo Van Gries and the two men he brought with him.

"Hope I didn't interrupt your vacation," Bob asked as he and Theo smiled and shook hands warmly. Neither man was the type to give out respect or friendship lightly, but they did with each other. "More volunteers?" Bob asked as he looked at the two men behind Theo: rugged and fit, each of them faced slightly outward, alert, his eyes continuously scanning the concourse like radar. Professionals, former soldiers, Bob immediately guessed.

"Volunteers? No, but two of my best men. Let me introduce you," Theo turned and motioned them forward. "Paul here was with the GCP…"

"The French Foreign Legion parachute commandos," Bob extended a hand.

"… and Franz was with the German Bundeswehr KSK. Gentlemen, this is The Ghost." Both men took their eyes off the crowd and returned the handshake with a very respectful nod, after which Bob introduced his group.

When they were finished, Franz leaned in and whispered to Theo, "Herr Leutnant, there is a man on the upper level above the bookstore with a camera and a large telephoto lens taking our photographs. Should we relieve him of his film?"

Rostov shrugged and said, "Do not bother. He is not the only one. They were waiting when we landed. FSB or SVR, no doubt, but there will be many more in Moscow. I shall discuss that with them after we land."

Forty-five minutes later they boarded a Lufthansa flight to Moscow. Volodya had booked seats on the German carrier to stay away from Russian state-owned enterprises like Aeroflot, because everyone knew where their orders came from.

The name Sheremetyevo Alexander S. Pushkin International Airport is far too long to put on a T-shirt or a baseball hat, much less road signs, particularly if you don't read words written in the rather difficult Cyrillic alphabet. The airport itself had grown and prospered under Putin's administrations. He likes contemporary design to show the modern Russia. Besides, the old terminals needed to be renovated. Putin wants to put a new, glitzy façade on what was still a backward country when you get off the major highways into the countryside, or away from Nevsky Prospekt in St Petersburg or Tverskaya Ulitsa in Moscow. And you didn't need to go far into the country to find backward, like a hundred years ago backward.

Terminal E, where international flights arrive and depart, is smaller, but as open and modern as the best airports in the west – Heathrow, Charles De Gaulle, or Frankfurt. What they share is robust security from the entry roads, into the parking lots, and right into the terminals. There were security cameras on all the levels inside, at ticketing, at security, at the departure and arrival gates, the luggage carousels, the shops, and in all the restaurants. Security? Second only to Ben Gurion in Tel Aviv, in Sheremetyevo there were CCTV cameras, x-ray machines and scanners, dogs, and armed guards everywhere. The apologists say it is to keep the Russian people safe from Chechen separatists, ISIS terrorists, Ukrainians, Georgians, drug smugglers, American spies, and about everyone else. Others say Putin's one and only aim is to avoid embarrassment and bad international press.

The flight from Frankfurt to Moscow took five hours, plus the one-hour time difference, which put them at the gate of Terminal E at 4 p.m. Daytime and nighttime were always relative this far north, in Russia. At this time of the year, in the late spring, there are over eighteen hours of "daylight" in Moscow. Even then, the evening and morning twilight adds at least another hour or two of half-light and anything even close to darkness lasts but a few hours, dictating tactical planning.

The flight was uneventful. Bob wondered how many FSB agents were on the plane, probably enough to outnumber them. The landing was smooth, and it didn't take long after they walked from the jetway into the concourse to realize they weren't being treated like ordinary passengers. A polite young man in a blue business suit stood at the gate with a professionally labeled sign that read "Rostov Party."

"Colonel, gentlemen, my name is Mikhail. Please follow me," he said in almost perfect English and set off down the concourse. All he needed was an umbrella or a small flag to be a proper Intourist tour guide.

Ace leaned in and said, "In Vegas there would be a stretch limo waiting for us outside with bimbos and a bucket of iced champagne. Think they'll give us any of those?"

To a casual observer, the security in the concourse appeared normal, but Bob, Ace, Theo, and Volodya weren't casual observers. They immediately spotted additional men trailing them from the upper concourse, some with cameras like the one they saw in Frankfurt, and some observing and talking into their lapel and wrist microphones. When they reached the snaking line that led to the security checkpoint for Russian Immigration and Customs, they saw six uniformed members of the FSB border guards, two with dogs and the rest with short-barreled AK-74s hanging across their chests standing around the checkpoint. Normally, that would be intimidating, but Mikhail motioned back over his shoulder to ensure they were following him as he led the seven men and one woman around the lines, past the guards and interview officers, around security, and around the scanners and the document checkers into the center of the cavernous main airport concourse, where three other men were waiting for them.

At that point, Volodya Rostov took over and said to the young man, "My son and associates will take us from here."

"Perfect," Mikhail smiled, staying in character. "And you have no luggage? You need no ground transportation?" he asked politely.

"No, but I assume your superiors are nearby? And I assume you are wired," Volodya asked. The young man continued to smile but said nothing, like a well-scripted robot. At that point, Volodya reached into Mikhail's pocket and pulled out his cell phone. "Pardon my rudeness, but it is important that I speak to him, so I will call him myself."

Mikhail's eyes turned toward a nearby gift shop, where a tall, middle-aged man in an expensive civilian suit emerged and walked across the concourse to where they were standing. Rostov smiled when he recognized him. "Ah, Simyon!" Rostov said as he and the other man shook hands. They made an interesting pair. Rostov was short and bulky like a pit bull, while the other man was tall and thin. "I was not sure it would be you they would send, but I am honored. I shall not bother introducing you to our small group, since you already know everything about them."

Rostov turned to Bob Burke and said, "Major, I'd like to introduce you to General Simyon Kuznetsov of the FSB, a dear friend of mine going back many years." Bob reached out and shook Kuznetsov's hand, trying to take a cue from Volodya's expression, but the old fox kept his cards close to his chest and it was hard to tell whether he was serious or not.

"Major Burke, welcome to Russia. Your reputation precedes you."

"Here is the thing, Simyon," Rostov stepped closer. "I know the 'appropriate party' briefed you and you have your detailed orders. So, if there are no objections, I shall now phone our people and have the first phase of the money transferred, as promised." With that, Rostov turned away, pulled out his own cell phone and sent a prearranged text. When Volodya turned back, he looked at Kuznetsov and said, "Simyon, with that accomplished, I must insist that all of your surveillance stop. No minders, no more cameras, or drones, or trail cars. They will only interfere and create problems. Is that agreeable?"

"Volodya, my dear friend," Kuznetsov pleaded as if the Colonel was ripping his heart out. "You must know you are putting me in an impossible position. 'Certain parties' will never agree to that."

"I understand, I understand, truly, but I also know his top priority is seeing a successful operation and see we deliver as promised. Not everyone is as loyal to him as you and I are, and 'the walls have ears,' as they say, often the wrong kind. We cannot accomplish our mission if we are 'pulling a long tail.' So please remind him of that."

"I shall try, Volodya," the general sighed.

"Good. When we have accomplished our mission later tonight, we shall return to this very spot," Rostov said, jokingly making an X on the floor with the toe of his shoe, "in time for the 6 a.m. Lufthansa flight back to Frankfurt. If we think we need more time, we will take one of the later flights tomorrow morning or perhaps tomorrow afternoon."

"And you need nothing from us?"

"Nothing, Simyon." Rostov glanced at his watch. "I assume you are aware of the 6 p.m. test my systems people will run on 'certain' bank accounts, so I must make a phone call." Kuznetsov nodded painfully. "Please do what I'm asking you to do. No surveillance, no interference, and everyone will end up happy, I assure you. Well, everyone except the Shurepkins and the Vor Council. So kindly leave now and take your people with you. We shall do our best to avoid any 'collateral damage,' so there should be no reason for us to see each other again."

Kuznetsov turned and walked away, motioning for his people to follow. As Bob and the others watched, at least a dozen men and women in the concourse, in various shops and stores, and up on the balcony, disengaged and followed him.

"Think he'll do that?" Bob asked Volodya.

"Of course not, but they will be much more discreet now."

CHAPTER FORTY-NINE

Pushkin International Airport, Moscow

Vladimir Rostov turned toward the younger of three men who were now approaching them. He had a broad grin on his face and appeared leaner and less stocky, but the eyes and smile were unmistakably Volodya's.

"Bob, this is my son, Ivan, my old Sergeant Major Nikolai Volek, and this is Anton Kravchuk, one of my older son's former associates with the Moscow police."

Ivan was lean and nimble. The Sergeant Major was a scarred, barrel-chested, and crudely chiseled hunk of granite similar to the Colonel, and Anton fit somewhere in the middle.

"Anton's partner, Sergei, is out in the parking lot keeping an eye on our vehicles. They also drove their Moscow police cruisers, which should give us some official presence."

"Do you get many car thefts out here at the airport?" Adkins asked the policeman.

"We are not so much worried about people taking things, Jefferson, as we are about people leaving 'bugs' and trackers behind," Anton laughed and corrected him. "One learns to be careful."

Ivan looked around and saw that Kuznetsov's FSB security people had miraculously disappeared. "It appears you have not lost your old 'magic' touch, Father," Ivan said. "I suggest we continue our discussion in the parking lot out by the cars before the General has time to reorganize his men."

Ivan turned and headed for the side exit, wending his way through the parking lot until he came to three older, beat up Land Rovers sitting between two Moscow police cruisers. While Ace and the two policemen kept an eye on the surrounding lot, Ivan spread a large, detailed map out on the hood and began orienting them to the roads and the plan he had put together. He then passed around a series of photographs of the house and the nearby countryside, which appeared mostly wooded with scattered large houses.

"As you will soon see, the major problem we have tonight is too much daylight until very late, and then the sun comes up very early again," Ivan began.

"That gives all the advantage to the defense," Bob quickly agreed.

"Given the narrow time window of darkness, we would like to strike at 2 a.m., be out of there, and long gone by 3 a.m. If we can't do it in an hour or so, it can't be done, but that would give us plenty of time to be back here to meet the 6 a.m. flight to Frankfurt." He paused and looked Jefferson Adkins up and down. "Who is the African Prince? Eddie Murphy?"

Adkins's face opened in an embarrassed smile. "I guess this is bullshit,   isn't   it?"
"The FSB and Putin's people probably watch more HBO and Showtime than you do."

"Yeah, and all this cloth will only get in my way," he finally admitted as he pulled the colorful robe over his head and tossed it and the red and gold skull cap into the backseat.

Bob looked at the photographs of Shurepkin's dacha. They took some from the air, but most were from the ground, from the surrounding roads and woods. They built the 'dacha' in the middle of a large plot of land, several acres at least, which appeared densely wooded except for the center, like Sherwood Forest, where the dacha was located. There were similar buildings on each side and up and down the narrow road it fronted on. It appeared to be substantial, made of block or concrete covered with stucco that had been painted a now badly faded pink.

They call them the 'old flamingoes,' Ivan said.

Bob guessed the rambling, one-story house contained three or four thousand square feet, with wings, additions, and roofs extending out in several directions. Still, it was a clapboard summer cottage where the city dwellers went to raise a few tomatoes and pick mushrooms.

A tall masonry wall ran around the entire perimeter, perhaps with rolls of razor wire on top. There was a single, tall, wrought-iron gate in the center of the wall along the road frontage, electronically controlled. A long gravel driveway extended back from it to a turnaround in front of the house. In the photos, there were always from two to four vehicles parked there. This would not be an easy target, especially if it was well-defended by people who knew what they were doing.

"Does he have any electronic surveillance, motion detectors, or cameras around the perimeter of the property," Bob asked, "or on the doors and windows."

"On those, perhaps," Ivan answered, "but this is Russia, my friend. People don't understand electronics, so they don't trust it. Besides, guards are cheaper and don't break down as often when the power goes out. But I believe the only people who would dare break into Oleg Shurepkin's house are people who would face no consequences if caught."

"What if we cut the electricity?" Bob asked.

"That would take any alarms or cameras offline. If he has an emergency generator, they would come back up, but we would know that very quickly."

"Do you have any idea how many men Shurepkin has in there?" Bob asked.

"Not a precise head count, but given the faces we've seen and the different cars parked around the house, it appears he's brought quite a few of his 'associates' over from Moscow, probably the ones he thinks he can count on. How long that will last is arguable, but with Piotr, Pavel Bratsov, and Dema Kropotkin, it could be close to twenty men."

"Training and weapons?"

"Kropotkin and Bratsov were Speznaz, but Bratsov was at the lowest rank and skill level," Ivan answered. "We know that four of his men served in the Army; again, without any distinction. The others are worse, little more than street thugs. Weapons? They have had access to most toys in the Army Christmas catalog if they want them, but given their skill levels I doubt they have effective use of much more than pistols and automatic rifles, perhaps an RPG or a hand grenade, but not any of the more advanced weapon systems."

"Night vision scopes or infrared?"

"Possibly, but would they have them on and ready to use, much less know how to use them when the power goes out? Unlikely."

His father looked at his watch. "It is almost 5 p.m.. I suggest we get out of here and work our way southwest. We will find a good country restaurant in one of the villages. We have had a long day. We shall eat and relax. Real food! It is hard to say when we might get another chance. We can check out our own weapons, finish our tactical plan, head toward the house around 11 p.m., and get in position. Is that an acceptable plan, Major?"

"Very sound, Colonel, but you wouldn't expect me to disagree with a skilled Recon Brigade commander on his own turf, would you?" Bob smiled.

"Excellent. It appears the American Army trains their officers as well in diplomacy as they do in tactics. And I think I know the perfect place for us to stop and eat in Zhukovka, a little family restaurant where I can introduce you to the finer points of a good Russian meal."

"That sounds fantastic," Bob agreed. "But let us declare a moratorium on vodka. I know what Russian meals are like. I've enjoyed some before, but if this bunch starts drinking, we'll still be there when the sun comes up, half of us lying on the floor."

They piled into the three Range Rovers and set out from the airport on a twisting set of back roads through the woods and fields of central Russia, no doubt meant to confuse anyone attempting to follow them. An hour later, they parked the three vehicles behind a large house that had been converted into a town restaurant. Before they went in, Bob gathered everyone behind the vehicles where Ivan disbursed a wide range of pistols and rifles, including three Chukavin SVC sniper rifles, a half-dozen AK-12 assault rifles, a stack of Makarov and Yarov semi-automatic pistols, and night vision goggles.

Volodya Rostov took one of the Chukavin Russian sniper rifles, and Bob took the other two. He gave one to Ace Randall and handed the other to Stephanie Goss, choosing one of the AK-12s for himself.

"What?" Ace asked in feigned shock. "You're giving me the long gun, Ghost? Me?"

"You're almost as good of a shot as I am. So is Stephanie, I am forced to admit. So I think that's the best way to utilize your skills once we get there."

"Almost as good? Is that what you said?"

Bob looked at him and shook his head. "I guess we'll have to have another range competition when we get back to Sherwood, won't we?" Bob quickly replied.

"A three-way this time," Stephanie insisted. "Because I shall teach both of you a lesson you won't forget."

"Ah, another challenger heard from. Okay, sometimes you need to teach a lesson more than once to prove a point. But I may go inside, so the Chukavin would be wasted on me." That said, he opened the briefcase he had been carrying since North Carolina. It contained a battery-powered squad tactical radio net, with a dozen earpiece microphones. "Before we leave here, everybody takes one and we'll test the system. Since we'll be spread out around the perimeter, it's important that we communicate to avoid any friendly fire situations... But these are still on loan from the CIA, so take care of them. Some day they might want them back, so don't keep them as souvenirs."

Alternating guard duty on the trucks out back, they all had plenty of time to eat. At 11 p.m., they were all thoroughly sated after a huge meal of black bread, borscht, pelmeni, Olivier salad, herring, pirozhki, beets, plov, shashlik, salmon, stroganoff, and kotleti, finished off with homemade ice cream, berries, honey cake, and Russian tea served with hot water from a huge samovar in the middle of the room.

After Bob had time to savor the hot tea, he said, "Now I see what you meant by the real thing, Volodya, with zavarka, served in a podstakannik," and raised his ornate, silver-covered glass in salute.

"Many thanks, Robert," Volodya said as he twisted around and looked out the restaurant's side window. "The twilight is finally creeping in. I believe it is time we go out and slay the dragon, my friend."

"Copy that!" Bob answered. In the half-light in the parking lot out back, the team changed from their civilian traveling clothes and shoes into a wide variety of camouflage utilities and combat boots, depending on their home army, and prepped their weapons and ammunition.

"Time for kickoff," Theo looked around and got serious.

CHAPTER FIFTY

Odintsovsky District West of Moscow

The Ring Road around Moscow is ten lanes wide, almost 70 miles long, and effectively the border between the city and the vast rural hinterland of forests and rolling fields which surround it in all directions. Scattered through those woodlands outside the Ring, particularly to the west, are tens of thousands of dachas. They are small, one-story structures on tiny plots of land, a cultural phenomenon that goes back hundreds of years, even as far back as Peter the Great. Russians, regardless of their wealth or status, view their dachas much as Americans view their summer vacations; a sacred and inviolable right, something they live and work for and an essential part of their lives. Even if the dacha was nothing more than a cottage or even a falling-down tool shed, it was where they go to get away from the hassle of the city, grow vegetables, hunt mushrooms, breathe fresh air, and read their Pushkin, Turgenev, and Gogol.

In the Odintsovsky District, five to ten miles west of the Ring, there are dozens and dozens of far more palatial dachas dating to the Stalin years and earlier, when they belonged to the party and government elite, who were ministers, Politburo members, party secretaries, generals, and ambassadors. They were the professional and politically connected ruling class of the Soviet Union until the mid-1990s, when it all fell apart. Their jobs, money, power, and influence quickly vanished and the newly rich and powerful gobbled up their dachas. They were the start-up millionaires, oligarchs, corrupt police officials, present and former KGB, and the underworld bosses who could now operate in the open and flaunt their wealth.

Oleg Shurepkin was one of those. He had bought his dacha eighteen years before, when men with cash could have their pick. Or, more accurately, he sent Dema Kropotkin to convince its former owner to sell it to Shurepkin for next to nothing. That was 2002 during the "good" years, as some would call them. It was the time of Gorbachev, Perestroika, Yeltsin, and Glasnost. They drove the Soviet Union to its knees while one hundred little minorities tore it apart from the inside. Putin, a KGB hand from the good old days who had run East Germany, had risen to Chief of the FSB, and would soon become the Prime Minister of Russia. In 2002, however, he was still consolidating his power. Like Chicago in the 1920s, it was often hard to tell the criminals and the police apart. Life was good for those who had power and knew how to use it, which included men like Oleg Shurepkin.

He wanted this big dacha because he was an old Zek who had finally made it, and he wanted the status it conveyed. But once he had the property, he rarely used it. At heart, he was a city boy who preferred the fast pace of the nation's capital. For several years, he rarely went there, and it showed. The building needed painting. The lot and woods were overgrown with trees and thick underbrush. The furniture was old. The appliances and plumbing were almost antique. Now, it was where he went because it was the only place he had left to go.

As "The Czar" became more powerful and more popular by standing up against the West, and the Americans in particular, he curbed the power of both the KGB and the Army, bringing them to heel. Next came the oligarchs, the billionaires who were allowed to buy the country's industries. That happened in the dark days when Gorbachev and Yeltsin were in charge, and they sold them off for ten Kopeks on the Ruble. Eventually, the billionaires were squeezed and run out of the country, joining the lengthy list of Russian crooks in Miami Beach and Los Angeles. Those who thought they could defy him and wait him out in Russia were arrested and put on trial, where the only questions were the length and degrees of punishment. Those who fled soon realized there was nowhere they could go to escape his long reach. Soon, after he dealt with the other groups he used to climb the tall ladder to power, it was the Mafia's turn. Like the others, Putin had allowed them to operate freely for a few years. But like the others, he would take them down and become the last man standing.

Despite Oleg Shurepkin's tenuous position, he knew two things The Czar did not know. First, he had been down before, lower than any man could fall and hope to survive; not just low, but underground, breaking rock in the gold mines near the Arctic Circle. Second, he had been knocked to the ground more times than even he could count. But Oleg Shurepkin always got back up, stronger than before, and killed the men who put him down. Putin had only been a freshly commissioned KGB officer, but he had seen the Gulag as it was being dismantled. More than anyone, he should have realized if you want to kill an old Zek like Oleg Shurepkin, you must put a bullet in his head and rip out his heart. Even then, the old Zek would never quit or surrender.

Putin had become a major problem for Oleg Shurepkin, perhaps the biggest; but he was not the only one. Like a man caught in a flash flood, what was dragging Oleg down were the idiots around him, the largest of whom was his own son, his heir, Piotr.

There wasn't much that happened in Moscow or in Brooklyn that Oleg wasn't quickly told about. When Piotr and Pavel Bratsov returned from New York with their tails between their legs, they flew into Moscow, but they did not report to Oleg. They did not report to his office, nor to his big apartment in the city, nor did they come out to the dacha to see him. Finally, Oleg picked up his cell phone, called Piotr's cell phone and then his house, but he would not answer. Piotr let the calls roll to voicemail. Inquiries were made, and he was told Piotr went to Bratsov's flat. They found some women to abuse, got drunk, and stayed drunk. To Oleg, the Vor, his father and their Boss, those were not only abominations and insubordination, they were grave sins requiring punishment.

He assumed Evgeni came back with his older brother and was also at Bratsov's. It was later the next morning that he received a phone call from the consulate in New York telling him Evgeni was dead, that he had been shot to death in North Carolina in America. Now, Oleg knew why his older son was not answering his phone calls. When Piotr rebuffed his next call, he sent Dema Kropotkin to fetch him and Bratsov to the dacha. He told Dema he need not be polite or gentle. Bringing Piotr back conscious enough to speak and bringing Bratsov back alive would be adequate. Dema could be a force of nature when he wanted, and this was one of those times.

It was 10 p.m.. Oleg sat in his study at the back of the house, slumped in his black-leather desk chair behind his mahogany desk, fingers knit together, staring out the window into the woods, waiting. There was almost nothing on the desktop – no paper, no pens, not even a telephone, only a 9-millimeter Makarov pistol in the center of the desk. He had liked this room the minute he saw it, Oleg remembered. It had rich, dark wood paneling and a large fireplace. It was a warm and friendly room, even in winter, or it used to be. He had done some of his best thinking in here. He must do so again because the next few days would be decisive.

Finally, he heard a car approaching on the gravel driveway. It stopped in front of the house. He heard car doors slam and odd noises, followed by groans and several loud shouts and curses. After a moment or two, he heard the front door open and scuffling in the hallway. The voices became more distinct until something crashed hard into a wall and was dragged across the floor. Finally, the door to his study flew open. Dema Kropotkin tossed Piotr into the room like one would toss a large, floppy rag doll. He stepped in, dragging a battered and bloody Pavel Bratsov behind him by the back of his collar. Piotr lay on the floor for a long moment and finally rose to his knees, head down, bleeding from his nose and mouth. His clothes were a mess, and he refused to look up at his father.

"Get up," Kropotkin ordered Bratsov, who lay on the floor, moaning. "Get up!" he generously told him a second time before he kicked him in the ribs. Normally, Dema never repeated an order. Even with Bratsov's muscle, it was easy to recognize the sound of ribs snapping. He groaned again and rolled away until Kropotkin followed and was about to kick him again. Bratsov raised his hand to stop him and managed to push himself to his feet, wobbling back and forth. One look at him told Oleg that the former weightlifter had already absorbed a substantial beating from Kropotkin.

Oleg rose to his feet, looked over the desk, and stared down at Piotr, growing angrier and more bitter. "Look at yourself! Get up, I did not raise a coward!"

Slowly, Piotr also rose, shakily, his head still bowed and his eyes on the floor.

"Look at me!" Oleg growled.

With that angry outburst, Piotr's head snapped up, and he looked at his father, eyes red, skin pale and puffy. Oleg understood defeat and failure. He had seen it hundreds of times on the faces of men over a long lifetime. Each was different, but they were all the same, and he knew exactly what cowardice and failure looked like. To see it on the face of one of his own, his eldest son, was the cruelest defeat of all. At his age, with one son now dead and the other defeated like this, everything he had worked for and built over a lifetime was finished. All of it. Even so, he would never give up without a fight and not without exacting a price.

"What happened to Evgeni?" Oleg asked, trying to remain calm.

"He is dead," Piotr finally whispered. "They killed him."

"I know that! How did he die? I want to know how he died!"

Like a boxer on his last legs, Piotr retreated to the ropes. He turned his eyes away from his father's withering stare, trying to escape, but the old man would not let him and chased him into a corner.

"No, you sniveling coward! Here! Look at me. Look at me when you tell me."

"There is nothing to tell you, Father. We went to North Carolina to put an end to that fellow Burke, the one with the contract business who got in our way, the one who hit our office in Brooklyn. We had two dozen men with us, to hit his house, kill him, and burn it to the ground, but he ambushed us."

"And you permitted your little brother to go with you? You allowed Evgeni to go?"

"I could not stop him! He refused to stay back in Brooklyn. They had taken his laptop and you know how he is…"

"I know how he *WAS!*" Oleg flared angrily.

"You are right; you are right. How he was… I made Evgeni stay with the vans, with all the other men. I thought he would be safe there, while Bratsov and I took a crew through the woods to attack the house from the side. But when they attacked the house, he wouldn't stay put. He wouldn't listen to his crew chief. He charged the house with an RPG, and…"

"And you and Bratsov walked away? Unharmed…?" Oleg accused him.

"It wasn't like that, I…"

"You are cowards, both of you. When I was in New York that night, I told you to take care of him. He was only a child and didn't know any better. You did! You should have… both of you… and now he is dead!"

Oleg picked up the Makarov and pointed it at Piotr, who took a deep breath, expecting it to be his last. He stood up straight and appeared to pull himself together for this last time, staring back at his father like a man who knew he was already dead. But he wasn't. Piotr closed his eyes, waiting, but his father swung the pistol to the right. He pulled the trigger and shot Bratsov in the face, spraying blood and brains all over the wall behind him and bowling Piotr's bodyguard over backward onto the floor.

Piotr flinched at the gunshot, but when he realized he was still standing there, he opened his eyes and saw his father place the pistol back on the desktop.

"I will not kill you, Piotr, at least not yet. My sources tell me your American nemesis, this man Burke, arrived in Moscow this afternoon. He brought some of his men with him and has some renegade Red Army officers and Moscow police to help him. They are relatives of that police lieutenant with the Ministry of Internal Affairs we had to eliminate last year. The fact no one stopped them at the airport means he has 'official permission' from the Kremlin to come after us – to kill us, you and me – which means he is coming here."

"Burke? He's coming here?" Piotr asked incredulously.

"Why else would he come to Russia?" Oleg stared at Piotr, his eyes boring in. "It appears you have been given another chance to redeem your honor and your manhood, Piotr. He killed Evgeni. He destroyed our business. And he is coming here to kill us. Dema brought some of our best men here earlier to protect us. He will put them in a position to stop them, but you will kill this Burke, Piotr. It is your last chance to avenge your brother and show me you are still a man."

CHAPTER FIFTY-ONE

The Dacha

They waited until well past 1 a.m. to move. Night had fallen, to the extent night ever falls at that latitude in late spring, allowing them limited freedom of movement for perhaps the next two hours. Ivan's men learned one of the other dachas a quarter mile up the road was empty, so they drove there and parked the cars to get them off the road.

"If they have twenty men in there, we need to know more about how Oleg plans to employ them," Bob said.

"I doubt that would be Oleg," Ivan told him. "It would be Dema Kropotkin."

"Time to find out. Let's squeeze them a little. I'd like you and your two policemen: Anton and Sergei, to close the road. Park your police cruisers across it a half-mile each side of the entrance and turn any traffic back. Say there is a power line down and let me know if anyone tries to get by."

Bob then turned to Volodya Rostov. "I'd like you, Jefferson, Stephanie, and Sergeant Major Volek to block the front gate. From there, you should also be able to bring fire to bear on the front of the house and the front door. You and Stephanie will have the Chukavins, the others will have the AK assault rifles, the RPGs, some hand grenades, and anything else you think you'll need. I can't imagine anyone escaping through all of that. When we hit the house and the rats take off running, that's where they'll go. Your job would be to block, put down a base of fire, and then advance down the road later. If Kropotkin has stationed men at the gate or at the front doors to the house, you'll be in a good position to take them out."

"Excellent plan," Rostov nodded, so Bob turned to Theo Van Gries. "Theo, you and your two men take the right side, Ace and I will take the left. We need to stay in touch and figure out where he placed his gunmen."

"Yes. Paul and Franz are skilled at infiltration and silent killing. I would suggest we send them into the woods inside the perimeter wall on the right side and then in the rear for perhaps thirty minutes. They can 'thin the herd,' if you will, and take out sentries. That should give us a clearer picture of Kropotkin's defensive plan."

"Excellent idea, Theo," Bob nodded. "At the same time, Ace and I will work our way around the left side of the wall and see if we can determine if he has men on the roof or at the doors and windows. Our rifles all have sound suppressors, and when we are finally ready to strike, we can take those people out in quick succession."

"If I were them, I would have the front and rear doors protected, with men on the roof and perhaps at the upper windows as you suggest. I would also have roving patrols through the woods and around the building and grounds, perhaps even in the adjacent property. So be careful out there. Remember, we have no friends in there. Anyone inside those walls carrying a weapon is the enemy, a Mafia criminal, and a legitimate target. We have noise suppressors, so take the shot and eliminate them. There will be no repercussions."

"Everyone has an earbud radio," Bob added. "Stay in touch."

"And I forgot to mention, Bob, but my son brought some plastique, enough to blow the gate at the appropriate time. He also brought several anti-vehicle mines which we can place in the driveway, and we have the RPGs. I do not expect Shurepkins, Bratsov, or Kropotkin to run. I think they'll fight us to the bitter end. But I doubt their supporting crews have much loyalty. I think they'll make a run for it. Normally, I would not fire on a retreating enemy. The sooner they get away the better. But these people deserve no such courtesy. They can all go to hell."

Dema Kropotkin prowled the house and grounds like a lion in a cage, continuously checking the doors and windows and making sure his "soldiers" were where they should be and doing what they should be doing, which he rarely found was the case. Too many of them were merely beefy weightlifters on steroids who had spent far too much time in the Moscow club scene drinking and partying. They were accustomed to strong-arming shopkeepers over protection payments, kicking the crap out of gamblers on losing streaks, and beating up drug dealers late on payments. They had no concept of warfare, no respect for their opponents, and it was easy for them to think they were invincible. Dema had been a soldier in the Speznaz, Russian Special Operations, and he hoped he was wrong; but he knew what professionals could do to arrogant amateurs. From Bratsov's comments when they drove here from his apartment, Kropotkin understood they were facing very formidable men tonight.

Kropotkin had been an enlisted man, sergeant, not an officer. He was not as well versed in strategy as an American West Point or Ranger School graduate like Burke, but he had gone through long months of brutal, sadistic training and understood small unit tactics. He rose through the ranks to sergeant because he was the toughest man in the unit and could beat the crap out of everyone else. That was how one earned promotions in the Russian army. But he could also lead men. He could fight, was well-trained in fire team and squad tactics, and he was a bull of a man who knew no fear.

Bob Burke was half right about how Dema Kropotkin would position his men. He had twenty, counting himself and Piotr. The dacha had enough pistols and AK-47 rifles, even a machinegun, some RPGs, hand grenades, and tactical vests to equip a small army. Unfortunately, this wasn't an army. He didn't have many trained soldiers, but they were on the defensive. The building and grounds would be a difficult place to take; and he intended to make it impossible.

First, he concentrated his men who had some Army skills at the most critical locations with two or three of the "thugs," as he called them, assigned to each. They were to be little more than cows with loud bells around their necks to make noise if they were attacked and shoot back. He stationed two of them at the front gate and two each at the front and back doors, where they would be visible. In all likelihood, they would be the first to draw fire and probably die. Tonight, that was their function: to tell him where the enemy was attacking from. He sent four other men to patrol through the woods in two-man teams, constantly circling the house. They weren't soldiers. They weren't trained in stealth techniques and hadn't been trained to move quietly through the woods. Real soldiers could take them down one by one and rather quickly if they hadn't already taken themselves down by stumbling over fallen trees and getting hurt first. But they would be invaluable in providing intelligence; if nothing else, by letting him know when the attack started.

Months ago, he talked the old man into stocking the dacha not only with weapons and ammunition, but with some rudimentary communication equipment. They were older two-way walkie-talkie radios, not the high-tech tactical sets he wanted, but they were better than nothing. He carried one, Piotr carried one, one sat on the old man's desk, he gave one to each of the teams on the roof, and he gave one to each of the teams patrolling the woods.

When he handed them out, he put one man in charge, under strict orders to report in every five minutes. "Do you understand!" Kropotkin got right up in their faces and growled. If there was one thing he understood, it was how to project power and intimidate men. "Check in with me every five minutes, or they will be your last!"

Sufficiently motivated, he then sent them off to their assigned posts.

The building itself was easy to defend. Fortunately, the dacha had three sections of flat roof hidden behind low parapets. One of them was on the front of the house over the main entry, and one was on each side. This was where he would place three of his men who had some army training and could shoot. At least they knew which end of the rifle the bullets came out of. He would put them up on the roofs, but he was a realist. Best case, they might actually hit someone if they fired enough bullets. Worst case, they might chase Burke and his men away before they got to the house. He would position the rest of his thugs inside on the first floor or second floor to guard the building's windows and doors. Finally, he would keep the three most useless men inside near Oleg, in reserve.

From what the old man was able to learn, Burke was coming with far fewer men than Kropotkin had, perhaps only eight or ten. The Americans would be much better trained, so Kropotkin was willing to trade. If he could take enough of them off the board, he might be able to handle the last few, especially Burke, and live to get away. He learned the man had been in the Delta Force. Having Piotr take on a man like that was absurd. Burke would swat him aside like the pest that he is. Dema Kropotkin believed that he could kill Burke. He was supremely confident in his ability as a fighter and believed he could kill anyone, but why should he? Burke and the others wanted Oleg and Piotr Shurepkin, not him. So did Putin. Dema Kropotkin was merely a bodyguard, but above all else he was a survivor.

CHAPTER FIFTY-TWO

The Dacha

Theo Van Greis was the master of understatement when he said his two men, Paul and Franz, were skilled at infiltration and silent killing. Whether they were French, German, Russian, or American, special operations training in the elite units of the world was more similar than different, and those two young men had elevated their skills to a murderous level. They climbed a tree along the outside of the wall, went out on a branch and dropped silently onto the other side. Dressed in dark sweaters with blackened faces, they moved between the trees carrying thin, Fairbairn-Sykes commando knives, the favorite killing blade of special ops soldiers worldwide, Beretta M9A3 9-millimeter pistols with sound suppressors in shoulder holsters, and short, stockless Heckler and Kock MP5 submachine guns slung across their backs.

Silently taking down the first two Russians on patrol in the woods proved pathetically easy. The Russians were noisy and inexperienced, crunching through the leaves and twigs, smoking, talking, and paying no attention to their surroundings. Paul and Franz came up on them from behind with their knives and it was over quickly and quietly with both Russian thugs lying under the trees with their throats slit. Easy, professional, and very cold-blooded. That was nothing either man took any pride in. It was easy. Too easy. But that was their assignment. It was what they did.

Paul quietly reported in, "Two down. We have their radio. Old walkie-talkies."

"Copy. Things are about to start, so let me know what you hear on the radio," Bob told him. "When the shooting starts, use one of your plastic flex cuffs to 'key the mic' by keeping the 'send' bar pushed down. Put a stick or a rock under it. That will block their frequency."

"Roger that," Paul acknowledged.

Three minutes later, Dema Kropotkin looked at his watch and got a very bad feeling. Something was wrong. The team on the far side of the dacha and the men on the roof and doors had reported in, but Bobritskoi and Malkov, two of the idiots he pulled out of the brothels the Shurepkins operated in the city, had not.

"Bobritskoi... Bobritskoi... Malkov... where the hell are you?" he called to them over the radio but heard nothing in return. "Bobritskoi...?" he asked again but knew in the pit of his stomach that he wouldn't hear from those two again. Burke was here. He had struck first, and he was on the move.

"Theo, Volodya, Ghost here. I see two men with rifles on my side of the roof. What do you have?" Bob asked over his tactical radio net.

"Ghost, same here. Two on the roof on our side," Theo reported.

"Ghost, this is Volodya. There are two out by the road standing at the front gate, and two more back at the front door to the house, crouched down behind planter boxes. The others are mostly exposed, but those two will be hard to hit from here."

"Copy. On my mark, Theo, let's take them all out: the guards on the roof, your side and mine, and the ones at the front gate, Volodya. If you or Stephanie have a shot at the ones behind the planters, go ahead and take it. Then you can move your group forward to the gate, see how they have it secured. You have a better chance of keeping an eye on the guards at the front door from there if you couldn't get them. Theo, after that, you go over the wall, join Paul and Franz, and swing around to the rear door, ready to take out any guards back there. Ace and I will go over this wall and eliminate any roving patrol over here. Copy?"

"Copy... Copy... Copy..." He immediately heard back from the other three teams.

Ace already had his head over the wall, studying the targets on the roof through an infrared spotter scope. "Ready," he said as he brought the Chukavin SVC sniper rifle to his shoulder and put his eye to the night vision scope. It was a pathetically easy shot with a superb rifle like this at such a short distance, with the targets back-lit against the dark-gray, twilight sky. It wasn't daylight by any means, but there was enough light to see the figures clearly.

"On my mark..." Bob said into the radio. "Three, two, one, fire."

Human targets are not like paper targets on a rifle range. A sniper knows when he hits and kills a man. There is little uncertainty about it. He can see it, hear it, and even feel it in his bones as the .300 caliber Magnum bullet strikes dead center on the man's chest. The model of the rifle and the caliber of the bullet matter little with a clean shot. The same is true with the effect that has on the shooter; and that has been the same, regardless of the war or the weapons, going back to men firing arrows at each other or even throwing rocks. When Ace fired, Bob saw the guard's arms fly out to the side and he collapsed behind the parapet wall. In an instant, Ace rotated the rifle barrel about 10° to the right, lined up on the second guard, and dispatched him just as easily. Both men were probably dead before they hit the roof, and the only sound he heard was the muffled bumps and thumps of their bodies and rifles landing on the thick layers of tarpaper up above.

"Ghost, Theo. Two confirmed on my side," he heard, followed by, "Ghost, Volodya, confirmed. "Both are down at the gate. We'll move forward and take up new positions there."

"Copy," Bob replied. "And two down over here."

Bob and Ace quickly scaled the wall, dropped on the other side, and waited, but they heard nothing. Slowly, they moved through the trees toward the rear of the house. Halfway there they saw the silhouettes of two men with rifles hanging from their shoulders standing together talking at the edge of the wood line.

Over his headset, Bob heard Franz say, "Ghost, the guy in charge is making another round of status checks with his guards on the walkie-talkies. He seems to be missing more connections than he is making, and from his voice, he's beginning to panic."

"Roger that," Bob replied. "Time to make him even more nervous."

Coming from the deep shadows under trees, he and Ace were almost invisible as they crept silently toward the two men and came up behind them. Rather than kill them, which would have been criminally easy, he and Ace pulled out their pistols, wrapped their left forearms around the Russians' throats, and pressed the pistols into the sides of their necks.

The word, "Silence!" is understood in almost every language, particularly when there is a gun jabbing you for emphasis. Bob and Ace pulled the two men further back into the woods, took away their weapons and radio, hogtied them with plastic flex-cuffs, gagged them with their handkerchiefs, and left them lying in the leaves with the warning that if they made a sound, they would die.

Using some quick arithmetic, Bob figured they had already taken down ten of the sentries around the perimeter of the building, perhaps half of Oleg Shurepkin's men or more. The rest were inside or on the front and back doors, but it wouldn't be long before he realized he had a problem.

"Sit rep," Bob quietly asked over the radio.

"There's two sentries outside the rear door," Theo answered.

"Copy," Bob replied.

"And two on the front steps plus two more on the front roof," Rostov added. "They are in a strong position up there, and we have to eliminate them and the two by the door before we can open the front gate."

"We took out the two rovers on this side and we have their radio. Theo, you and your men work your way to the back of the house and take out those rear guards," Bob said. "Volodya, Ace and I will work around through the woods to the front-left corner. We'll see if we can take out the two behind the planters at the front door. Can you get the two up on the roof?"

"Stephanie and I have our crosshairs on them now. That should leave the men inside the house."

"Copy. Then we'll figure out how to smoke them out. In the meantime, Paul, if you and Franz see any targets inside through the windows, engage when ready."

"Roger that, Ghost."

CHAPTER FIFTY-THREE

The Dacha

Dema Kropotkin stood in the kitchen staring at his two-way radio, growing angry and frustrated, when Piotr walked in. From the expression on Kropotkin's face, it was obvious something was very wrong with more than just the radio.

"Dema, we cannot stay here," Piotr said. "Burke's coming, isn't he?"

"No, he is already here. They have already taken down half my men."

Piotr went wide-eyed. "Half? But... I have heard nothing."

"And you won't, not until Burke steps up behind you and slits your throat." As he said that, he saw Piotr turn his head and glance back over his shoulder. "Or perhaps he is watching you now through the scope on his rifle."

Piotr stepped back away from the window, trembling as he said, "You must get me out of here, Dema. I don't care what my father says."

"You made a bad choice of enemies, boy."

"I am no match for him. He will kill me for certain."

"Yes, I believe he will, or your father will, or Putin will," the big man said, unimpressed. "So, what difference will it make? You will be soon dead just the same."

"Think, Dema, Burke doesn't want me; and he doesn't want you, either. It is my father he has come here for."

Dema looked back at him, disgusted. "You are reaping what you have sown. All your stupidity, your carelessness, your women, your alcohol, and your drugs. You are the one who brought this down on us, so why should I care if he kills you?"

"Because I will pay you to get me out of here. I will pay you."

"You?" Dema laughed and turned away. "You cannot afford me, little man, I am way out of your price range."

"A million dollars, Dema?" Piotr stepped closer. "I'll pay you a million dollars... no, I'll pay you two million. Just get me out of here."

The big man's head slowly turned, and he studied Piotr for a moment. That second number got his attention. "Dollars?" he asked.

"Yes, dollars."

"Where can you get money like that?" Dema scoffed, but he continued to stare at the younger man. From the confident smile on Piotr's face, Dema finally caught on. "Your father's safe, of course. You know the combination, don't you?"

"Yes! And there is a lot more than that in there, lots more. He has diamonds and gold, too. Two million of it is yours. Now will you help me?"

"Your father's safe, the one in his office?" Dema smiled as he thought about it for a moment, but then shook his head. "That old Zek will die before he lets you or anyone else touch it. That safe is his nest egg, his last reserve. You know that. You must kill him to get him to give it up. Are you prepared to do that, Piotr? Can you kill him?"

Piotr's eyes turned as cold as a Siberian night. "You take care of Burke. I'll take care of my father."

"Then we must hurry," Dema answered as he looked down at his radio, now all but useless. "The only way out of here will be through the front gate."

"We can take my father's car. It has bulletproofed glass and steel in the doors."

"All right, you go to his office and get the gold and diamonds. He has two briefcases near his desk. Fill those and meet me by the front door. We will need a diversion to get out of here."

No sooner had Dema said that, than they heard gunfire break out in the front of the house and he heard more shooting and glass breaking on the right side, followed by a scream. "Looks like we will not need to create a diversion after all. They created one for us. Now go, or it is your father I shall be driving out of here, not you."

3.

Vladimir Rostov crept forward to the tall, wrought-iron gate carrying his Chukavin, flanked by Jefferson Adkins on his left. Stephanie Goss and Sergeant Major Volek approached the gate from the right side. He and Stephanie carried the long sniper rifles, while the others had AK-74 assault rifles slung over their backs. Volek also had three small anti-vehicle plate mines in his arms, while Adkins carried two RPGs.

All three went flat on the ground at the corners where the wrought-iron gates were attached to the heavy brick columns of the gateway. Rostov rested the barrel of his Chukavin in one of the decorative iron curves in the gate. He put his eye behind the telescopic scope and saw it was a good height and angle and provided good stability to engage the men on the roof. He looked over and saw that Stephanie had already done the same thing on the other side. As he was settling in, he heard Burke's voice in his earpiece,

"Volodya, you and Steph have the longer shots, give us a countdown when you are ready."

He looked over at the American woman. She smiled and nodded back at him before she turned and settled down behind her own scope. The Russian colonel got comfortable behind his, took careful aim, and counted down, "Tri, dva, odin, Strelyat!" Three, two, one, fire, and both he and Stephanie did, almost simultaneously. This time, the targets were better hidden. She hit the gunman on the left side of the roof. He screamed and toppled forward, falling onto the low stoop in front of the front door below. Unfortunately, as Rostov squeezed off his shot, his target moved, and he missed. He fired twice more, but the man was safely below the parapet. From that high vantage point he could see them at the gate at the far end of the driveway and returned fire.

Rostov was as familiar with the sound of a Kalashnikov as any man alive. Until now, he heard it as a shooter, not as a target. Fortunately, the remaining gunman on the roof was not particularly skilled. He fired off a long, undisciplined burst of poorly aimed shots that were not accurate and missed wildly. Rostov and the others immediately rolled behind the safety of the brick columns. As his mother once told him, "Volodya, even a blind pig finds an acorn every now and again," and with an automatic rifle, volume can often make up for accuracy. In quick succession, a dozen rounds flashed past them. Some clanged off the wrought-iron, while others smacked the brick column or skipped off the gravel in the driveway. That was when he heard a heavy grunt to his left and, "Ah, shit!" to his right. Rostov did not let that stop him. He took careful aim again. This time he put three bullets into his target in a "tight shot group," as they called it at the rifle range, and the second gunman disappeared from view as his rifle clattered down the short roof and fell onto the concrete below.

Only then did Rostov make a quick check of the others. To his shock, one look told him that Nikolai Volek, his treasured Sergeant Major and right-hand man for so many years, was dead. From the angle at which he was lying, it was clear he had taken two bullets in his upper chest, which had penetrated deep. From his eyes and lifeless expression, it was clear he was already gone. Rostov turned the other way, toward Jefferson Adkins, and asked, "Are you all right, my friend? Are you hit?"

Jefferson was cradling his right arm to his chest and said, "Ah, don't sweat it. The little bastard got me in the hand, but it was through-and-through. Hurts like hell and it's bleedin' like a 'som-bitch!' but I'll be okay."

"Probably, but I shall get you a bandage and compress," Rostov said as he turned back to Volek's body. He carried the first-aid bag around his waist. Rostov ripped it open and quickly examined Adkins's wound. He quickly applied a large compress on each side of his hand and taped them in place. "I will be surprised if you do not have some broken bones in there, Jefferson, but that should do until we get you to a doctor."

Rostov looked over at Stephanie Goss, who was back behind her rifle and carefully scoping out the front of the house, looking at the windows for more targets. "Excellent shooting, Sergeant First Class Goss. In my Army, women have always been some of our best snipers. The Germans learned that on the Eastern Front during The Great Patriotic War, to their eternal regret. So did Stalin. He said it was because the women had more patience than the men. So, I think you will do well against Major Burke and Master Sergeant Randall."

Bob and Ace worked their way through the trees and around the left front corner of the house, finally crawling forward to where they hoped to have shots from the side at the two men hiding behind the planters at the front door. Unfortunately, one of them was partly screened by the other, which was why he let Rostov take the first shots. As they took aim at the two men, Bob said, "I'm going for the one to the back before he moves. As soon as I shoot, you take out the front one. Does that work?"

Ace smiled. "I guess we're about to find out, aren't we?"

It was a very tight shot, only a few inches between the concrete planter and the guy in back, several hundred feet away. Bob took a breath, eased into the shot, and slowly took up pressure on the trigger. With the sound suppressor on the end of the AK-74's barrel, the long gun made little more noise than a child's cough as Bob hit the gunman farthest away in the side of the head and blew him sideways onto the front stoop. The second man had knelt behind his planter. He leaned forward, resting his rifle on the large concrete flower box. A split second after Bob's shot, Ace fired two rounds from his AK-74 and hit that gunman in the side, in the ribs with each. He also toppled over to his left, as dead as his companion.

CHAPTER FIFTY-FOUR

The Dacha

When Piotr burst into his father's study from the front foyer, his father was no longer behind his desk, where Piotr had left him. Now, the old man sat on the floor at the corner of one of the two outside windows, a field of broken glass lying around him on the carpet. The once proud and fastidious old man looked like a skid-row derelict now, clothes in disarray, jacket off, and hair mussed. He leaned forward and peered around the window frame to peek outside. His tie was down, his eyes sunken, and the lines on his face scored even deeper. The flying glass must have got him, Piotr realized. Blood from a dozen cuts on his face ran down his forehead into his eyes and onto his shirt. Still, the old Zek appeared undeterred, as usual. He had his Makarov in his hand and fired two shots, trying to locate his attackers in the shadows around the trees, and quickly drew back before he took another peek. He fired another shot and quickly pulled back again, fighting his own battle with the gunman in the woods outside his window.

That was when Piotr realized that Dema was right. The old bastard would never give up that safe as long as he had a breath left in his body.

When Piotr had left the office only ten minutes before, he was unarmed and being shoved out of the room by Dema. This time, he carried a short-barreled AK-74 assault rifle hanging on a strap from his shoulder and had a 9-millimeter Makarov pistol in his hand.

When Oleg realized Piotr was standing in the doorway looking down at him, that only made him angrier. "What are you doing?" the old man raged. "Take the other window and shoot at them. Shoot at them!" he ordered as he fired two more rounds out the window. When he turned back, he realized Piotr had not moved. "What are you...?" he sputtered until he saw the automatic rifle hanging from Piotr's shoulder. "A Kalashnikov?" he pointed at it. "Give it to me, you fool. I am almost out of bullets. Give it to me!"

At first, Piotr wasn't about to do that. Give the old bastard his submachine gun? Better he run out of bullets. Then, he realized it was the perfect way to keep the old fool busy. Let him shoot it out with the Americans. Maybe they will kill him and save him the trouble, Piotr thought, so he slid the AK to his father across the carpet. As soon as Oleg had it, he turned back to the window and began firing bursts into the trees, giving Piotr the opportunity to duck down, run across the room, and dive behind his father's heavy oak desk. The old man's thick-walled German safe sat against the wall. It had been made by Krupp in its Essen steel works. Piotr remembered hearing someone ask the old man how he could stand having a Nazi safe in his house that was probably made from melted-down Russian tank parts. Oleg appeared offended. "That is my money in there. I play no favorites when it comes to my money."

Piotr slid across the floor and got closer to the safe. He put his pistol on the carpet and immediately set to work on the dial. Several years before, his father had fallen gravely ill with a severe case of pneumonia, a difficult illness to survive in the dead of a Russian winter. Oleg hated doctors, did not trust them, and as usual he refused to allow the family to send for one until it was almost too late. In a weak moment, when the old man was weak and delirious, Piotr convinced him that the family would be ruined if no one could open the safe.

"Do you want the government tax collectors to come in here, blow it open, and take all your money? Is that what you want? To end up penniless in the pauper ward of a wretched public hospital because we couldn't get any money to pay the bills?" Only then did his father give him the combination. Piotr memorized it, knowing a day like today would eventually come. The old man couldn't live forever, he thought; yet there he was, still sitting at the window exchanging gunfire with the unseen American killers out in the trees. Piotr spun the badly worn dial and entered the combination, but it didn't work. Nervous and tired, with bullets flying around the house, it took him three more attempts before he was able to correctly enter the numbers and open the heavy steel door.

He looked inside and blinked. It had four shelves, stacked with wrapped packages of American $100 bills. There were also small one-kilogram gold bars and red velvet bags which he knew were filled with diamonds, more than even he ever dreamed of. Piotr didn't wait. He turned his eyes away and saw two black leather briefcases sitting in the well of his father's desk, pulled them over, and dumped the contents on the carpet. He filled the first one with the red velvet bags full of diamonds, taking them all, and filling the rest of the space with the gold bars. He stuffed the second briefcase with stacks of American cash and the rest of the bars. Still, even with two briefcases, he was unable to put much of a dent in the safe's contents. Like a child finding himself alone in a candy store, Piotr stuffed more stacks of currency into his jacket and pants pockets. Desperate, he looked around for another briefcase or bag to carry still more, when he glanced over and saw his father slumped against the outside wall of the room.

Oleg's legs were splayed in front of him. He wasn't looking out the window. He was watching Piotr with cold, angry, unforgiving eyes. Slowly, the old man raised the AK-74 and pointed it at his son. "What are you doing, Piotr?" he demanded to know, more to hear the lies he knew would spew from the younger man's mouth, now that he was caught, than from any truth he would learn in return. "What do you think you are doing?"

The old man didn't look well, Piotr thought. He appeared weak, pale, and sweating. That was when Piotr saw what appeared to be a bullet wound in his father's shoulder. His suit coat was dark, but the blood was wet and shimmering as it ran down his chest and arm. With the blood from the cuts on his face, it was all dripping onto the carpet now. Piotr knew the old man was hurting, but it would take a lot more than one bullet to finish off the old bastard.

"You are an embarrassment, Piotr. Instead of standing by my side and fighting them with me, instead of redeeming your honor by killing this American who murdered your brother, you sneak in here to steal my money? Is that why you came back?"

"Yes! What do you expect me to do? Stay here and die with you? Well, I am not going to do that, Father. We must get out of here. The Americans are all around the house and they will be inside in another minute," Piotr said as he snapped the two briefcases shut.

He glanced over his shoulder through the open doorway into the front foyer. Dema Kropotkin was in the house somewhere, but where was he now when Piotr needed him? He thought of making a run for it, but his father still held that damned submachine gun and it was pointed at him. He might be growing weak and he might not be steady, but he was still his father. Would he really shoot him? That question remained unanswered as more bullets smashed through what was left of the office windows, forcing Piotr to duck back behind the desk. They even made his father lean away from the window and cringe, long enough for Piotr to grab his own pistol lying on the carpet near the safe. Enough, he thought. His father would never leave, and he would never give him the money, Piotr knew, leaving him no choice, as he turned and raised the barrel of his own pistol toward his father.

That was when Piotr got the answer to his questions.

Oleg's old, tired eyes had never left his son's, and the old man no longer had any reservations. His son was trash. All he wanted was the money, HIS money; so he pulled the trigger. The AK-74 was a heavy and powerful weapon to fire on automatic with only one hand. The old Zek was exhausted and fading, but his hands remained as powerful and steady as they were when they chipped gold ore from the permafrost all day long. He pulled the trigger and the first three bullets from the Kalashnikov ripped into Piotr's chest. The barrel rose as it will do with the recoil, especially held in one hand, and two more bullets hit his son in the throat and face, bowling him over backward on the floor. His trigger finger seemed to have a mind of its own and wouldn't stop. It continued to fire until the magazine was empty, tearing up the wall behind Piotr, but they no longer mattered. Piotr was dead.

Oleg lowered the weapon and looked across at him, now sprawled on the floor. "Stupid boy," he mumbled. "Stupid, stupid boy."

Using all of his strength, Oleg rolled away from the window and rose to his feet. He stumbled over to Piotr's body, picked up one of the black leather briefcases by its handle and then the second one. His shoulder screamed in pain as he tucked them against his chest, and it took all of his strength to reach down and pick up Piotr's pistol. With a look of grim determination on his bleeding face, he stumbled out the office door into the front foyer where he almost collided with Dema Kropotkin.

Kropotkin had seen the old man in many conditions and situations over the years, but never like this. It took a second or two for him to even recognize him and take it all in. Then he quickly smiled and said, "I've been expecting you, what took you so long?"

"What took me so long?" Oleg repeated with an angry edge on his voice as he stood wobbling back and forth.

"Here, let me help you," Dema said as he reached for the briefcases in Oleg's arms, but the old man turned away and grasped them even more tightly. Dema smiled as he remembered. "Interesting. I told Piotr earlier that you would die before you allowed him or anyone else to touch that safe of yours."

"He was a stupid boy," Oleg seethed, but their conversation was cut short by a burst of gunfire back down the hallway near the rear door in the kitchen.

"We must leave here, now," Dema said, as Oleg looked around helplessly.

At the rear of the house, Theo, Franz, and Paul had their hands full. Theo and Franz positioned themselves in the deep shadows between the trees where they had an unobstructed view of the back door, while Paul continued a running battle with someone in one of the side rooms. It soon became apparent he could not dislodge that one gunman, and he would be more useful at the rear. There were two men on the roof hiding behind the parapets, two more on the rear stoop behind the posts that held up a small roof over the door, and they could see two more inside the kitchen. Franz had a clear shot at one of the men on the roof and put him down. The posts did not provide much cover to the two gunmen, but they required the shot to be precise. Theo fired on one of them and hit him in the leg. As he bent over in pain, he exposed his upper body and Theo got him with two more shots and put him down, too. That left one on the roof, one outside the door, and two more inside. Paul's arrival made the odds more sustainable.

Exchanging bullets with a well-shielded enemy was not a good way to prevail in a firefight, Theo would preach to his new recruits. Either move them or move yourself, but do not remain static. "Franz, you have the best arm. Do you have a grenade or two?" he asked the younger man two trees to his left. Franz held up one finger, so Theo rolled one of his over to him. "Paul, you are on the oblique, you keep the guy on the porch busy. I'll do the same with the one on the roof, while our young German friend shows us what kind of arm he has."

Paul fired a burst along the porch while Theo chipped holes along the top of the parapet wall on the roof. With those two gunmen busy, Franz stepped from behind the tree and threw a hand grenade onto the porch. It landed, bounced twice on the concrete and once off the door before it rolled behind the pillar. At that point, human nature took over. The Russian standing there forgot about the men with the rifles and backed away from the grenade, exposing himself to an easy shot from Theo.

Unfortunately, after making such an outstanding toss, Franz was exposed. The Russian on the roof didn't hesitate and fired a long burst that hit Franz. He fell to the ground next to the tree just as Theo raised his gun barrel and returned fire, killing the Russian. Theo rolled across the leaves to where Franz lay and put his fingers to the young man's neck, trying to find a pulse, but there was none.

Theo hated losing men, but he knew all too well it was the nature of their business and the risk they all took. However, losing one of his best men like this when the mission was almost finished was infuriating. He turned his AK-74 on the kitchen windows that flanked the rear door and vented by raking them with an entire magazine. He then waved to Paul, and they rushed the rear door.

Two of Dema Kropotkin's men remained inside the foyer by the front door, one on each side, taking quick peeks outside around the doorframe and firing the occasional shot down the driveway. The gunfire had largely stopped, but the door and windows continue to be peppered by some large caliber rifles from the front, by the gate. Behind them, Dema suddenly heard gunfire at the back of the house, followed by an explosion. Hand grenades! That was when two more of his men quickly retreated up the hallway from the kitchen, looking back and firing at the rear door.

Dema grabbed one of them, spun him around and forced him into a doorway. It was obvious the Americans were coming through the rear door, would soon be in the kitchen, and coming up the hall. He couldn't let them do that, not if he wanted to get away.

"You! Where do you think you're going? To see the ones outside the *FRONT* door? Stay here and stop the ones coming in the back, while the Vor and I take care of the ones out in front. Then you can follow us," Dema lied as he held the man by his shirt collar and pulled him closer. "All you have to do is fire a few rounds down the hallway every so often. That will keep them back. Once we get outside, you can come too."

When a man as big and powerful as Kropotkin tells you to do something up close like that, face to face, it must've seemed believable; because his gunman remained in the doorway, giving Dema time to help Oleg Shurepkin escape out the front door behind him.

Outside the front entry, Bob and Ace had disposed of the two gunmen behind the planters outside the front door, and from what he could see, Volodya Rostov terminated the two on the roof. Bob was about to stand up when Ace touched his shoulder and pointed down the driveway. Even in the dim light, they could see Rostov working on the other two men: Jefferson Adkins and Sergeant Major Nikolai Volek.

"Sit rep," Bob quickly asked over the radio.

"I'm afraid the Sergeant Major is gone. Two bullets to the chest. They also hit Jefferson in the hand. It is serious, but not dire."

That was when he also received the report from Theo Van Gries. "Ghost, we cleared the rear entry and Paul and I are going in the rear door. Franz is down."

Casualties like Franz and the Sergeant Major were always a possibility, but you learn to deal with losses afterward, not during the heat of battle. "Roger," he told Theo. "We have the front blocked, so see if you can herd the rest of them this way."

"Volodya," he told the Russian Colonel. "I'll work my way around toward the driveway entrance to give you support. Ace will stay here on the side. That should give us better covering fire. What's with that damned double gate? Is it chained? Or locked?"

"I think it's electronic, with a remote opening mechanism like a garage door opener or a keypad," Volodya answered. "We have Semtex and I can blow it open if you wish."

"Not yet. I'll be joining you shortly."

CHAPTER FIFTY-FIVE

The Dacha

Dema Kropotkin knew time was not on his side. He was down to five men now: the two behind him guarding the hallway to the kitchen from the doorways and three more "thugs" from their operations back in Moscow who were by the front door. One he recognized. He looked slightly more intelligent than the other two, so Kropotkin grabbed him by his shoulders and locked onto his eyes. "You are Sergei, that's your name isn't it?" Between the gunfire and Kropotkin's overbearing presence, the man was so terrified that the big man could swear he heard his head rattle.

"Yes... Yes, Sergei," he stammered.

Dema pulled the keys to Shurepkin's armored limo out of his pocket and jammed them into Sergei's hand. "We'll provide you covering fire. The Vor's car is parked outside to the left. Get it and drive it up here to the door as close as you can get. Do you understand, Sergei? Go!"

Kropotkin turned to the other two and said, "We're going outside. I want you to get behind those planter boxes and start shooting at the front gate. Have you got that?" He did not give them time to think about it before he opened the heavy front door and shoved them outside. It took a second or two before there was any reaction, but then the gunfire started up again in both directions.

It never ceased to amaze him how fast a man can run when his life is at stake and gunfire is going off around him. Sergei ran, stumbling and bouncing off a pillar, but the driver side door of the big limo was only thirty feet away and the car door wasn't locked. He pulled the heavy door open and got inside, slamming it behind him, astonished to realize he was still alive. His hand was shaking so badly it took him three tries to get the key in the ignition, but he managed to start the engine. The car was a special order with a powerful engine. When he dropped the transmission lever into gear and tromped on the gas, the engine roared and the car suddenly sped up, sending dust and gravel flying. He barely got it back under control and had to stomp on the brake to get the car stopped in front of the dacha's front doors.

"Keep firing!" Kropotkin shouted at the two men behind the planter boxes, who were now coming under fire from yet another gunman to their right, in the woods. Oleg was a large man, but nothing compared to his younger bodyguard. Even with the two briefcases weighing him down,

Dema grabbed Oleg under the arm and shoved him out the door toward the limousine. He grabbed the door handle, jerked the rear door open, and shoved Oleg inside while he ducked behind the steel plate in the rear door. It was a good thing he did, as he felt two bullets smack the other side of the door and one on the bulletproof glass window.

The old man landed hard on the floor on top of one of his briefcases, which knocked the wind out of him. He stayed there on the floor, gasping, while the other briefcase bounced off the far door and split open, scattering gold bars and stacks of money all over the rear floor. Now in a daze, Oleg began reaching for the wrapped stacks of $100 bills, cursing and mumbling, as he tried to put them back in the briefcase.

Dema turned, raised his pistol, and fired off three shots toward the gunman in the woods at the right as he opened the passenger side front door and jumped inside. He looked over at the driver. All it took was one look at Sergei's terrified expression for Dema to see this would not work. He reached across the young man, opened the driver's door, and shoved him straight out onto the driveway. Sergei landed on his ass in the gravel and rolled head over heels backward, while Dema slid over, took his place behind the wheel, and slammed both front doors shut behind him.

If his two gunmen by the planter boxes thought they were coming along, they were sadly mistaken, Kropotkin thought as he tromped on the accelerator and spun the steering wheel. Oleg's limousine was a big, heavy car, with a powerful engine designed to carry extra weight and get its owner out of difficult situations if they ever arose. This was one of them, and exactly what it was designed for. The car fishtailed down the driveway in the gravel and Dema was barely able to get it under control as it headed toward the front gate. As it accelerated down the gravel driveway it kicked up a thick, choking cloud of rocks and dust that served as a smokescreen, blinding the gunman in the woods to the right, allowing them to get away from him at least.

That did not solve the problem of the enemy gunmen by the gate, so Dema turned on the car's headlights and switched them to bright. It wasn't that the enemy marksman couldn't shoot, but with bright lights in their eyes, he hoped it would throw off their aim.

The control button for the electronic gate was on the dashboard above the radio. From a distance, it appeared to be made of delicate wrought-iron tracery; but the brick columns on either side were made of steel-reinforced concrete, and the gate's frame was solid steel. Dema reached out and pressed the button, but he didn't back off on his speed or wait for the gate to open. It ran on tracks at the top and bottom that went back into the columns and then into the walls. When they closed, the gates met in the center where they locked with two powerful electromagnets. It would take a small tank or a large army to get them open without the control box. Dema had run the driveway many times before and knew he needed eight seconds for the gates to roll open wide enough for him to shoot the gap, so he kept the accelerator pressed to the floor, counting off in his head: eight, seven, six, five,...

When Bob Burke saw the limo accelerating away from the front door, fishtailing, and kicking up dirt and rock, he knew exactly what the driver was doing. He'd be heading for the gate, hoping to open it or to burst on through, and Burke wasn't about to let them do either. He picked up his Chukavin rifle and began running down the tree line, firing bullet after bullet into the side of the car. He stayed abreast for a while, but quickly fell behind.

The big car's headlights illuminated the heavy steel gates. He saw them begin to open, revealing Volodya Rostov standing in the center of the opening, slowly raising an RPG-7 to his shoulder as the black limo raced straight at him, picking up speed. Clearly, the driver saw him too. He wasn't slowing down, and Rostov wasn't moving.

"Volodya! Volodya!" Bob screamed into his microphone. "Get the hell out of there."

Dema Kropotkin saw the man standing in the center of the gate and cursed. As hard as it was to believe, he recognized the stocky figure and chiseled features of that damned Russian Army Colonel, the father of the Ministry of the Interior Detective Captain who interfered in their business the winter before and had to be eliminated. Tasks like that, Dema reserved for himself, because he never trusted "lower-level management" to finish such things properly, not without it all blowing up in their faces. Now, here was that bastard's old man again, standing right in front of him. Stubborn? Dema saw where the detective got it from.

"Dema, we are trapped! You must get me out of here," Oleg Shurepkin screamed at him, always trying to tell him what to do, always ordering him around, the big man thought. The old bastard had crawled forward on the floor of the bouncing car and had now appeared over the back of the front seat, his head next to Kropatkin. "Who is that?" he pointed through the front windshield and demanded to know.

The gates had opened halfway and were still widening. A bit more, a bit more! Finally, Dema saw they would just make it through, and smiled.

Then he saw that damned Colonel raise something to his shoulder and point it at the car. What was it, he wondered?

"What is he doing, Dema?" Shurepkin yelled at him again.

In that split second there was a flash of light in front of him. He didn't have time to explain to Oleg, who was leaning over the front seat, his head next to Kropotkin's, looking out the front windshield. Shurepkin might not know, but Dema knew; and he knew something serious was about to blow up in their faces.

There are statues and bas-relief monuments all over Russia: in the forests west of Moscow; along the roads south and west of St. Petersburg, formerly called Leningrad; and west to Volgograd, formerly called Stalingrad. They show valiant, roughhewn Russian defenders holding various weapons in their strong hands with expressions of grim determination as they hold back the Nazi invaders. None of them look as roughhewn, valiant, or grimly determined as Colonel Vladimir Rostov did as he raised that RPG-7 and fired into the front grill of Shurepkin's onrushing limousine, now less than 100 feet away and accelerating.

Today, most Russian weapons were initially designed during World War II and have been steadily improved and enhanced decade by decade ever since. The two traits they shared were that they worked, and they were simple enough for an uneducated peasant to operate. That was true of the Kalashnikov rifle and it was true of the equally simple, ubiquitous "Ruchnoy Protivotankovy Granatomyot," the "hand-held anti-tank grenade launcher," or RPG. The sleek and efficient RPG-7, rolled out in 1961, is the pride of every liberation and revolutionary movement around the world since Vietnam.

Oleg's car had armor plating in the doors and bulletproof glass, but there was nothing in the front grill. The threat was from bullets and the car could only carry so much weight. Shurepkin's mechanics no doubt figured that the oversized engine block was thick enough to stop bullets from the front, not that it mattered that night. An RPG-7 packed enough explosive punch to slice through an armored personnel carrier, a bunker, or even a light tank. The limo didn't stand a chance, which was exactly what Colonel Vladimir Rostov was hoping.

He squeezed the trigger on the top of the tube. There was a burst of white smoke, a roar, little recoil, and a trail of white smoke out the back of the pipe as the rocket flashed across the short distance. As with the rifles he fired, Volodya's aim was impeccable. He did not miss.

Bob Burke continued to run as fast as he could along the tree line and slowly curved over to the road. He could have been an Olympic sprinter, and he still would not have caught up with the big limousine. In the end, that was a good thing.

Shurepkin's executive limousine was a very heavy car. With even the limited armor plating, it weighed two-and-a-half tons or around 5,000 pounds. That is a lot of steel, but when the RPG-7 hit its engine block and the shaped-charge warhead exploded, it stopped the big vehicle dead in its tracks as if it had hit a cement wall. The RPG blew the engine block and transmission back into the passenger compartment, blew the doors and windows off, blew the hood and roof up into the air, and blew the tires and a myriad of car parts all over the front yard of the dacha and up into the trees. The mismatched pieces of the car's chassis and engine were elevated five feet off the ground. Everything seemed to hang there in midair for a long, loud second, until it all crashed back to the ground. There was nothing left of its burning carcass that even resembled an automobile.

The explosion also knocked Bob Burke to the ground. Although none of the flying metal hit him, the explosion left him stunned and unable to hear, with a loud ringing in his ears. He sat there in the middle of the gravel driveway shaking his head as Ace Randall ran up next to him.

"Geez, you okay, Bob?" Ace asked. "That was really dumb!"

"Say what?" he squinted and shook his head again.

"Dumb!"

"Yeah, well, we won't mention it to the girls anyway, will we?"

"You got that right," Ace agreed as he looked him over, feeling his arms and legs. "I see nothing missing and no bleeding. You got anything that hurts?"

"Just my head and my ass where I landed."

"Interchangeable parts, you'll be fine, but we better see what the others look like," Ace said as he pulled him to his feet and the two men stumbled over to the gate. When they got there, they found Volodya Rostov and Jefferson Adkins lying on the ground on their backs, patting each other on the shoulders, roaring with laughter.

Bob and Ace looked at each other and then down at them, until Bob finally asked, "Are you two all right?"

"Yeah, but don't ask me how," Jefferson Adkins replied. "Did you see that thing go up? Boom! I've never seen anything like it. You sure know how to show a guy a good time, Volodya! Boom!"

"Boom!" The Russian repeated, and they both fell back to laughing and pounding.

At that point, Bob heard feet running towards them from the house. He turned and pointed his automatic rifle in that direction until he saw it was Theo van Gries and Paul running with him. And from the left and right on the road outside he heard more running feet and saw Ivan Rostov and his two policemen converging on the scene.

Bob turned to Theo and asked, "Anyone else back there?"

"No, but we have to go back for Franz's body," he answered as he looked down and saw the Russian Sergeant Major lying dead on the ground. "It looks like we have two casualties."

Ivan Rostov said, "Leave all the weapons here by the gate. We'll take care of them and the two bodies. But the rest of you need to get out of here. I think we made enough noise to wake up half of Moscow."

"Boom!" his father roared as he slowly got to his feet, leaning on Jefferson Adkins.

"Boom!" Adkins repeated, and the two men started laughing all over again.

"Concussions," Ace said to Ivan as he shook his head.

"But they are having so much fun, I hate to interrupt them," Ivan agreed as the other two Russian policemen drove up in the Range Rover and they piled inside.

CHAPTER FIFTY-SIX

Sheremetyevo Airport

The plan was for them to arrive back at Sheremetyevo Airport comfortably in time for the 6 a.m. flight to Frankfurt, not too early and not too late. Things deteriorate if you give security people too little time or too much time to worry about minor things, especially with people looking over their shoulders. But from their appearance, none of them were in any condition to make an international flight without raising major questions. Ivan Rostov had a quick solution. He ran them all to his divisional police station, where they could quickly shower and change back into their civilian clothes.

That worked for most of them. Volodya Rostov should see a doctor and be checked for a concussion, but he wasn't leaving. A handful of Tylenol was enough for him to get them through security at the airport. Jefferson Adkins needed a handful of Tylenol too, plus an x-ray, a talented hand surgeon, stitches, and a cast for the bullet wound in his hand, but most of that would have to wait. They redressed his wound at the police station and doped him up enough not to care until they got back to the States. Bob would personally deliver him to the emergency room door of the big, red brick Womack Army Medical Center at Fort Bragg, where Jefferson would say it was a hunting accident. The others all had scrapes, bumps, and bruises, except for Franz. Somehow, Ivan Rostov and his father produced a coffin with proper stamps and approvals, and export papers to allow them to put the body on the flight to Frankfurt with the rest of the group. Theo would take care of him from that point on.

As expected, when they reached the security checkpoint for the international concourse, FSB General Simyon Kuznetsov was there to meet them with a small contingent of his men, armed, but looking as disinterested and bored as a squad of basic trainees. Bob saw no OMAN, the particularly brutal Russian riot police or the SOBR Rapid Response troops hiding on the upper concourse, or armored military vehicles on the street outside. That tipped Kuznetsov's hand. The Russians weren't expecting to scuffle with a band of international terrorists and war criminals and weren't looking to pick a fight.

Volodya Rostov, now wearing his Army green dress uniform complete with his full complement of medals and ribbons, walked up to Kuznetsov and rendered a smart military salute. Kuznetsov was wearing a nice civilian suit and the salute must've caught him completely off guard, but he quickly recovered and returned the salute.

"Right on time, my old friend," Kuznetsov said as he looked at his watch. "With five minutes to spare."

"I know how much you always appreciated punctuality," Rostov smiled. "Besides, nothing else to do. The gift shops are all closed at this hour."

Kuznetsov cocked his head and studied Rostov more closely. "You know, Volodya, if I didn't know you better, you look a bit stiff and sore. Perhaps age is catching up with you, after all," he said, and then pointed to a darkening bruise on the Colonel's cheek and another on the back of his hand.

"From a game of football with my grandchildren," Rostov answered.

"They say old men like us should avoid contact sports, you know."

"Truer words were never spoken," Rostov admitted as he waved the others around the checkpoint and down the concourse toward the gate.

As Bob walked past, the General reached out, caught his sleeve, and stopped him. "You know, Volodya, I understand we had some unusually violent weather last night to the west of the city. I do not know if you were awake and watching, but there were reports of a great deal of thunder and lightning."

"Truly?" Volodya asked, sounding surprised. "But it is that time of the year, late spring, is it not?"

"Yes, but I suspect the season for storms is over now," Kuznetsov smiled. "In fact, I happened to speak with the President on my way over. He commented on all the violent thunder and lightning too. Apparently, it woke him, but he also thought the storm was passing and that would be the end of it."

"I am certain it was," Rostov agreed, looking at Bob, who also nodded.

The General turned toward Bob. "The President said he hoped you and your friends had a pleasant visit here in our country."

"Oh yes, we had a memorable time, although it was entirely too brief."

"And I understand you savored our unique Russian cuisine at a nice country inn. On your next trip you must try our specialty vodkas and our world-renowned Russian tea."

"The food was indeed wonderful, and I did have the opportunity to drink some of your marvelous tea, zavarka, I think you call it, with lemon, cinnamon, and cloves, with the boiling water from the samovar," Bob replied. "Unfortunately, the timing wasn't appropriate for us to drink vodka."

"How unfortunate," Kuznetsov sighed. "The President is well aware that you are hurrying back home, but he wanted me to give you his personal assurances that if you ever feel prompted to return to Russia, he will definitely make time to meet with you... personally."

"I'm sure he will," Bob smiled and turned away. As he did, Ivan Rostov approached him accompanied by two of Kuznetsov's security men who were accompanying an older Russian woman wearing a long black dress, a colorful babushka tied over her head, and a large black purse clutched to her chest with both arms. One of the security guards had what appeared to be a fresh black eye. He was carrying a small, cheap suitcase, presumably hers, while the other security guard held her by the elbow and was attempting to steer her toward Burke without much success. She frowned, fussed, and argued with the two men in Russian, while they were doing everything they could to keep their distance or at least stay out of swinging range of her purse.

Ivan said to Bob, "Major Burke, this is Ludmila Kandarskaya from Bryansk. You told my father, who told the General, who had his people bring her here and get her a passport and exit visa, so here she is, and here they are," he added as he handed Bob her papers. "You may need to do some explaining, because she wasn't very happy about this."

The two security guards happily set her suitcase down and walked away.

Bob turned and smiled at the old woman and asked Ivan, "Since I don't speak any Russian, can you tell her my name is Burke, I am taking her to Sasha, and our plane's about to leave?"

Before Ivan could even say anything, her face lit up in a big smile. "You Boss?" she asked, pointed down at her suitcase and said, "You bring, we go before they change minds." Bob grabbed her bag and did his best to keep up with her as she took off down the concourse.

CHAPTER FIFTY-SEVEN

Sherwood Forest

Lufthansa pampers its passengers in the First Class cabin with luxury service, but all the caviar, champagne, and personal movies the German airline offered couldn't make its flights one minute shorter. From Moscow to Frankfurt to Atlanta, and finally on to Fayetteville, it was one long, exhausting flight after another, after a long, exhausting week. Bob intended to spend most of the next one letting his various bumps and bruises heal up, relaxing, and getting back on Linda's good side by tackling her already long list of honey-dos which no doubt doubled as a result of the attack at Sherwood Forest.

The carpenters were refinishing their repairs on the front door, windows, and the scattering of bullet holes in the front façade of the house. The wreckage of the four white vans and their scattered parts had finally been removed from the driveway and front yard. Restoring the grass and landscaping to some semblance of normal would also require professional help and take all summer. He phoned Maryanne while they were waiting between planes in Frankfurt. She passed on that the repair work was now well underway on the Toler TeleCom building in Schaumburg. Final approvals on the construction drawings and finish work would require a trip to Chicago, one he would try to put off for another week at least. For the moment, Bob was looking forward to sleeping until noon for a couple of days before he set to work on her long list of chores.

Naturally, that did not happen.

Upon arriving home at 5:30 p.m. that afternoon after many hours of travel, they were eagerly looking forward to seeing Sasha reunited with his mother after nearly four years. They took a shuttle van from the Fayetteville Airport to Sherwood Forest.

As they came down the driveway and parked in front of the house, they saw Sasha standing at the foot of the front stairs, smiling, arms wide open, waiting as his mother got out of the van. She turned and looked at him as he rushed forward and then whacked him on the top of his head with her purse. She chased him around the van two or three times, yelling and whacking him on the head again and again.

His fellow Geeks, Ace, Linda, Ellie, Dorothy, the rest of the staff, and even Crookshanks the cat had come outside to watch the reunion. None of them understood Russian, but it wasn't hard to figure out the gist of the very one-way conversation. "You never call, you never write, you run off without a word. And look at you! Your hair is a rat's nest, you have grown fat ..." and so on and so on.

After the first lap around the van, the others were in hysterics, laughing. After the third lap, Ludmila had finally whacked herself out. She stopped chasing him and Sasha stopped running. They looked at each other and ended in an open-armed embrace in front of the van.

For the next three mornings Bob managed to sleep in until noon. On the fourth morning, however, at 10 a.m. Linda tromped into the bedroom and asked, "Were you expecting a really big box from Russia?"

"A really big box?" he mumbled, with his head still under the pillow. "Define a 'really big box,' please."

"Well, I guess it's more like a crate, a really big wooden crate, and even the FedEx guy is curious. He brought two helpers to carry it inside and he wants us to open it and make sure it's okay, 'Because,' he said, 'if he has to take that damned thing back...' "

Bob raised the pillow, looked up at her with one eye, and frowned. "A 'really big' wooden crate, you say?"

"Is there an echo in here?" she asked him, hands on hips, looking around the room. "Yeah, it's a 'really big' wooden crate."

"From Russia?"

At that point, she pulled the sheet off him and said, "Come down and look for yourself if you don't believe me," and stormed out the bedroom door, leaving him no choice but to follow.

By the time he pulled on a T-shirt and shorts and pattered his way down the staircase to the front foyer, a sizable gaggle of onlookers had gathered, all staring at the 'really big' wooden crate, which it was. It stood perhaps five-and-a-half feet tall and was over four feet wide and deep. In addition to Linda and the FedEx driver, the Geeks were there as well as Sasha's mother and Slava, Ellie and her cat Godzilla, Ace and Dorothy, and two carpenters who were finishing the trim work on the front windows. They were all staring at the wooden crate, especially the carpenters, who marveled at the joints and woodwork.

So did Bob.

Linda pointed to the shipping label. "$427, Bob. And that's just the FedEx Freight charge. What on Earth did you order?"

"A new wife. The kinder and gentler model that lets you sleep."

"Inflatable? You don't need a box this big for one of those," she quickly answered. "Well? You gonna open it?"

"Easier said than done," Bob immediately deduced, looking at the 1 x 4s along the edges and the precisely cut cross-bracing. He turned to the carpenters and asked, "You guys got a hammer and pry bar?" He took a long look at the paperwork and the labels. It had come from Moscow. "It says it's from Account 292, FedEx, Tverskaya Street, Moscow." Bob looked at the FedEx guys with a puzzled expression."

"Nobody at our end knows either, Mr. Burke," the FedEx driver said. "Our office manager sent a text to the Fed Ex office in Moscow, but we've got no answer so far."

By then, the carpenters were back with their tools and Bob and Ace set to work on the crate. It took them ten minutes just to get the top off; after which, they backed away and stared at the box.

"These guys know how to build a box!" Ace said. "Solid wood, big nails, and look at those perfectly cut joints."

They set the top aside and looked inside. Whatever was in there was wrapped in thick mover pads with Styrofoam peanuts filling all the gaps for further protection. Bob and Ace looked at each other again and set to work on the front and side panels. Finally, they had the box disassembled, by which time there were electrostatically charged Styrofoam peanuts all over the floor, sticking to everything. They drove Godzilla the cat crazy as he attacked them and chased them around the foyer, but everyone else stared at what was inside the crate. As they carefully unwrapped the thick mover pads, what emerged was a huge, brightly polished, antique brass urn with intricate metalwork, delicate curved legs, decorative engraving, a brass top or hat, handles, and a spigot at the bottom.

"What on earth is that?" Linda asked.

"Oh, Mizzus Boss," Sasha stared at it. "That is Russian samovar! Biggest samovar Sasha ever see. Antique. *VERY* expensive."

At the bottom of the crate between the legs of the samovar, Bob saw a case of what he could tell was Russian vodka from the few Cyrillic letters he could read.

Sasha knelt down and looked closer at it. "Boss, that is Beluga Noble Gold vodka," Sasha added, wide-eyed. "Is what they serve in Kremlin for big official events… Unavailable, except for special parties on third floor."

Linda turned and eyed Bob suspiciously. "Who do you know?"

Bob stared at the samovar and shrugged. "I guess Volodya Rostov sent it."

"No, Boss," Sasha laughed. "Russian Colonel may be nice guy, but this big samovar and that vodka? Colonel don't make that much money in a year, not even a crooked general can do that," Sasha said as he took the delivery papers from the FedEx delivery man and read them.

"Most of that's written in Russian," the FedEx guy said.

"Da," Sasha answered as he flipped the pages, until he got to the last page and his hands began to shake. "Boss, crate comes from Kremlin. From Special Events Office in Kremlin. Says that in teeny, tiny Russian fine print. Comes from Account 292."

"What's that? Is there any name on the papers saying who sent it?" Linda asked.

"Mizzus Boss…" Sasha patiently tried to explain, "Kremlin. Does not need name."

"Putin?" Ace piped up, as surprised as the others. "Bob, I think it's a 'thank-you note' for that $75 million. What do you think?"

Bob stared at the huge brass urn. "You think we should send him one back? For our $33 million?"

"Say what?" Linda asked as her jaw dropped open. "Our thirty-three million…?"

"We'll discuss that later. Meanwhile, the samovar is about to assume a cherished place right here in our foyer… as a permanent reminder of a place it wouldn't be smart to go back to."

"Oh, come one, Ghost," Ace laughed. "When were we ever smart?"

XXX

If you liked the read, kindly go back to the ***Burke's Samovar***

Amazon Page and post some stars and a few comments. It really

helps with their marketing algorithms and for people to find the

book. Just copy and paste this link into your browser and click

on the gold stars:

https://www.amazon.com/dp/B08HG8YJ11

Also, if you'd like a FREE copy of another of my

fan-favorite thrillers, *Aim True, My Brothers*, with

4.6 stars on 252 Kindle Ratings, copy and paste

this link into your browser:

https://dl.bookfunnel.com/3uu04iwhsd

Preview and Sample Chapter

The Undertaker

If you haven't already read the first three Bob Burke books,
by all means go and do that. Great reads all. But if you have,
try *this one*, a snarky, at times funny and scary
domestic suspense thriller starring my
reader's favorite couple: Pete and Sandy.

CHAPTER ONE

Boston: where California meets New Jersey

I knew I was in trouble when Gino Parini shoved that .45 automatic in my face and made me read my own obituary. I'm not talking about something vague or California-cosmic, like the San Andreas Fault will turn Nevada into beachfront property, or those McDonald's French fries will seal my arteries shut, or second-hand smoke will give me lung cancer. I'm talking about my own honest-to-God black-and-white obituary ripped from page thirty-two of that morning's Columbus, Ohio newspaper:

> *TALBOTT, PETER EMERSON*, age 33, of Columbus, died Sunday at Varner Clinic following a tragic automobile accident. President and founder of Center Financial Advisors of Columbus. Formerly of Los Angeles, a 1999 graduate of UCLA and a lieutenant, US Army Transportation Corps...

Hey! That was me. I was Talbott, Peter Emerson, 33 years old, and formerly from Los Angeles. I had graduated from UCLA and I had been a lieutenant in the Army. Coincidence? I didn't think so. There was only one of me and I didn't die in the Varner Clinic or anywhere else last Sunday. I was an aeronautical software engineer and I had never been to Columbus or heard of Center Financial Advisors much less been its President. Still, when somebody points a .45 automatic at your chest, it is hard to argue the fine points.

But I'm getting ahead of myself.

That day began normally enough. For the past two months, I had been settling into a new job as a systems designer and software engineer with Symbiotic Software in Waltham, Massachusetts. It was one of a hundred programming shops in those big, mirror-glass office buildings that dot the Route 128 Beltway around Boston. You know the kind: no hard walls, no doors, just dozens of low, pastel-colored cubicles filled with a mixed bag of grungy 20-somethings in every size, shape, color, orientation, and gender. My cubicle was like all the others, except for the cheap plastic nameplate that said "Peter E. Talbott, Senior Systems Engineer" hanging at the entrance. Inside, the wall behind my chair featured a framed poster of Eric Clapton, signed by The Man himself, ripped-off from a LA record store back in my younger and much crazier days. On the wall across from my desk hung a beautiful Air Mexico travel poster: a color shot of a beach at sunset near San Jose down on the Baja, with a thin, solitary young woman in a bikini walking away down the sand. That was where Terri and I were supposed to go that last fall, but she got sick and we never made it. Other than the simple 8" x 10" photograph of her sitting on my desk smiling up at me, the Baja beach poster was easily my most prized possession.

It was already 5:30 PM. Headset on, I stared at my big, flat-screen computer, pounding away at the keyboard, dressed in my treasured, but badly faded, Rolling Stones 1995 Voodoo Lounge World Tour T-shirt, blue jeans, and a worn-out pair of Nikes. Like the shoes, I was a tad older and more scuffed than the rest of the hired help, so clothes helped me fit in during those first awkward weeks after I moved there from LA. Anyway, I had just finished a crash project and was slowly coming back down as I listened to the last tracks of a two CD set of Clapton's Greatest Hits. When I really get into a problem, the building could go up in flames, and I'd never notice unless my monitor went blank.

I leaned back in my chair, eyes closed, playing air guitar riffs along with "Tears in Heaven," when a cold hand lifted one of the ear pieces and whispered in my ear. "Earth to Petey, you are going to have the sub-routines done by tomorrow, aren't you?"

"You said "tomorrow", as in "close-of-business tomorrow," not "tomorrow-tomorrow," or "tomorrow morning", or "today-tomorrow," I answered.

"I know, but I've got a problem and "tomorrow" just became first thing tomorrow."

Looking over my shoulder was Doug Chesterton in his "harried boss" costume: a wrinkled white shirt, a cheap necktie with soup stains, and a pocket full of pens. It read MIT all the way – smart as hell, but dumb as a rock.

"Douglas," I smiled. "Having anticipated that you'd be a completely disorganized and unreasonable asshole..."

"And your brother-in-law, your boss, and the magnanimous owner of the company."

"They're done. I e-mailed them to you twenty minutes ago."

"That's why I brought you here, big guy," he said as he gave me a big bear hug and planted a disgustingly loud, wet kiss in my right ear, tongue and all. "You're like a bloodhound when you get the scent, Petey, you're fucking relentless."

"Relentless with a wet ear, you moron."

Doug leaned in over my shoulder and looked at the screen. "Then what the hell are you still working on? Wait a minute. That's the Anderson job I gave Julie, isn't it?"

"Don't get pissed at her; it was my idea. She had some meetings at school with her kids, so I said I'd help her out."

Doug laid his hand on my shoulder. "I'm not pissed. I'm glad. I know it's been hell for you since Terri died, but you moved here to get a fresh start and Julie is drop-dead gorgeous. She's divorced and she's exactly what you need."

"Julie? Oh, come on, I'm just helping her out, I wouldn't..."

"No, you probably wouldn't, but she would. Trust me. The faithful widower? Half the secretarial pool wants to take you home and mother you, and the other half wants to have your baby. They think you're a saint."

I looked over at Terri's smiling photo. I knew he was right, but that wasn't what I wanted or what I needed. He saw me look, too.

"She's gone, Pete. It's been a year now and it's time you moved on. She was my sister and I loved her as much as you did, but that's what she'd tell you, too."

"I know, Doug, I know." The truth was, Terri did tell me that, almost every day at the end and almost every day since. That was where Doug and all the others had it wrong. I wasn't alone. I still had all my memories of Terri, and my life was full, so full I didn't have anything left to give to anyone else. Someday, maybe, but not then."

"Look, I didn't come out here to bug you," Doug said. "But accounting keeps gnawing on me about your social security number. The IRS still has your account blocked."

"I've called them three times. They keep mumbling something about a "numeric anomaly."

"It's no anomaly. They've got you mixed up with somebody else with the same name and they think you're dead. So, if you want to see a paycheck anytime soon, get the damned thing fixed."

I shrugged and put it on my list of things to do. Maybe it was number fifty-nine, but it was there. Besides, Doug was right. He was boss. More importantly, he saved my life.

I was born in Los Angeles -- a child of the Golden West, raised on a steady diet of hard rock, fast cars, Pacific beaches, and the trend-du-jour. After UCLA, I went to work at Dynamic Data in Pasadena. It was Terri who introduced me to her MIT techno-nerd brother. We both bounced around Pasadena, going from one hot software shop to another, doing what we both loved and what we were good at. I was smart, but Doug was always smarter. He sold his old Porsche and moved to Boston with his three mangy cats, sinking every dime he could beg or borrow into his own start-up software company, which he named Symbiotic Software. The title was just vague enough to let him take on all sorts of work. However, trading the beaches and sun of Tinseltown for a long, gray winter of snow and ice in New England wasn't my idea of fun, so I stayed in LA. Shows what we knew. Doug's little company found a niche and he never looked back.

Back then, LA was the "land of milk and honey," where the growth curve only pointed to "UP" and "MORE UP." Like the white rabbit told Gracie Slick though, "one pill makes you larger, and one pill makes you small." Gracie had no idea how small. Outsourcing was a new word to us "left coasters." Layoffs and downsizing were something for the Midwest autoworkers and the steelworkers in Pittsburgh with the beer guts and lunch pails to worry about. This time however, it was us smart guys with the white shirts and the glasses of Napa chardonnay who found ourselves on the chopping block. Yep, ask not for whom the HR manager tolls, he tolls for me and for thee.

I became a WOOWCP-WFP as we Southern Californians called ourselves -- or at least the ones who still had a sense of humor. That's a White-Out-of-Work-Computer-Programmer-With-Few-Prospects. The big aeronautical engineering firm in Glendale that I was then doing software design for was spinning off people faster than an Oklahoma tornado. Half of the parking lot was empty and the signs on the executive parking spaces had hastily painted-over names or no names at all. We'd been downsized and out-sourced to India and Pakistan and most of my friends were now calling themselves house-husbands, shoe clerks, the Orange County Militia, or alcoholics. My defense mechanism had always been a cynical black humor, but even that gets real old, real quick. So does the weekly humiliation of the unemployment line, a McJob that wasn't worth going to, or sharing my afternoons with Oprah. When Doug phoned me from Boston and offered me the job, I packed the Bronco, did a reverse Horace Greeley, and headed east. Why not? Terri had died of cancer the year before and there was nothing holding me in California anymore. All I had left were my memories of her, but I soon discovered they were surprisingly portable. I could take her with me anywhere I went, and she never complained, not once.

Terri and I met at a Bruce Springsteen Concert in Oakland when we were young and Bruce's liver was a lot older. She was a reporter for an on-line weekly e-paper and rock blog in Mendocino, a stringer actually, all bright-eyed and serious, hoping to catch the big break with an in-depth retrospective piece on the inner meaning of Springsteen's lyrics. Me? I had cut class for the week and hitched my way up the coast from LA, hoping to catch the music and some fun with the tailgaters and groupies in the parking lot. Don't ask me why, but for some strange reason we stuck. The unity of opposites? Who knows, but we had eight incredible years together and a lot of good times, right to the bitter end. When it came, I was left with a lot of pain and a gaping hole where someone else should be -- a hole I thought could never be filled. Fortunately, I had all those good memories of her too. Memories. Without my memories of Terri, I would never have made it. They were the parts of her I could tuck away in the back corner of my mind and pull out whenever things got really bad, when the hurting parts of me ripped loose and started to fly away. Those were the times I needed something firm to hold onto until I could pull myself back together. That was why they could kill me if they wanted to, but I refused to let them hi-jack my memories of Terri. They were too precious. I owed them everything.

There's an old saying, "that which doesn't kill you makes you stronger," but it's not true. Things can maim and hurt too, and leave you an emotional cripple. I've got to hand it to Terri. She fought the disease for many months and as she did, she taught me what real determination and courage were all about. When she finally did die, I fell into a black hole. I couldn't help it, but I had had more than I could stomach of doctor's offices, hospitals, medicine smells, denatured alcohol, pill bottles, flowers, funeral homes, and the musky smell of freshly turned dirt. Funeral homes. I swore I would never enter one again, not on my feet anyway. Even today, the smell of cut flowers and organ music can push me right over the edge, and all because of one tiny little lump, a growth no bigger than a pea.

I was numb at her funeral. When it was over, I piled into my Nissan 350-Z and headed south to Mexico, determined to drink them out of tequila. The next three weeks were a blur. Like Jimmy Buffet, I ended up with a blown flip-flop, an unwanted tattoo, and vague memories of too many barroom floors. I'm still not sure where I was or what I was doing, but they say my 350-Z hit a semi head-on out on the main highway. The Mexican cops found a charred body inside. Everyone assumed it was me, but it was probably some poor, dumb Mexican kid having the time of his life in a drunken gringo's Japanese sports car. Whatever, they packed the crispy critter back to LA and buried him next to Terri, and I'm told they threw me one Hell of a funeral. Coming right on the heels of Terri's, our friend's worst problem was to make sure they wore a different dress or a new tie. They didn't even have to ask for directions. It was sympathy squared, with tons of tears and an instant replay for those who missed the first show.

Whatever, the crispy critter wasn't me. I saw a copy of the Mexican death certificate and the florid obituary that somebody wrote for the Pasadena newspaper. The eulogy was so stirring; they said Doug never did stop crying. When they finally let me out of the drunk tank in San Jose and I talked my way back across the border a few weeks later, it really pissed off a lot of people. Talk about your emotional pratfall. All those tears wasted, all those interrupted vacations, all the schedules that had to be rescheduled -- how rude.

That was their problem. Me? I had hit bottom. No, I had crashed through bottom and landed in my private little hell somewhere below the sub-basement. Funny though. Even when I sank to the lowest point I could get, after mopping up half the bars in Baja, Terri didn't abandon me. I saw her face staring up at me from the bottom of every tequila glass I downed. She was watching me from the dark shadows in the corner of the filthy hotel room I crashed in. Whenever I paused to raise my blood-shot eyes to the puffy, fast-moving clouds in that high, blue Mexican sky, I saw her face up there on the clouds looking down, watching over me. No, Terri had not deserted me. She would always be there, but I knew she was not very happy watching what I was doing to myself.

When I got back to LA, they put me on medical leave. They called it stress, but the place was shutting down anyway. Four months later, they locked the doors and I found myself standing at the end of the unemployment line like everyone else. Let's face it, there was nothing left for me in LA and I was ready for a change of scene. I'd proven I couldn't in fact drink all the tequila in the world no matter how hard I tried, and that there were easier ways to kill myself if that was what I really want to do. But I didn't. Terri was up there watching me. I couldn't put up with her frowns and unhappy looks any longer, so I got myself dried out. No AA or twelve-step method, I simply took a good look at myself in the mirror one morning and stopped cold.

Two months later, the phone rang. It was Doug, desperate for a systems programmer. He didn't need to ask twice. Most people wouldn't look forward to a five-thousand mile drive all by themselves, but it didn't bother me one bit. I'd spent most of the year practicing being alone and had gotten good at it. Besides, it was easier for me to drive across the country for a week than to spend another night alone in LA.

In a way, I came to enjoy those long days in the Bronco. My first choice would have been to have Terri in the front seat next to me, anytime and anywhere, but out on the open road I had our music and our memories to keep me company. The truth was, I still had her. Every now and then, even cold sober, I heard her speak to me. Not always in so many words, but I understood what she was telling me. And I would get those looks. She was up there in the clouds looking out for me, as she did down in Mexico. She was worried about me, not that I could blame her. If I had a brain in my head, I'd be worried about me too. I understood what she was saying. It was the same thing she said to me that last night in the hospital before she died. She wanted me to get out of LA, she wanted me to make a new life, and she wanted me to find someone I could be with, for my sake as much as for hers. If I didn't, she told me she would haunt me forever, and we both knew what a single-minded pain-in-the-ass Terri could be when she wanted to.

It was shortly after 9:30 PM when I finished the stuff for Julie and switched off my computer monitor. The old Chinese janitor who was vacuuming the aisle glanced up at me as I walked by. He was probably wondering why the Barbarian was working this late. My back and legs wondered too. I was bleary-eyed and in a computer-induced fog as I grabbed my empty thermos and headed for the door.

Outside, I looked up at the night sky, as had become my habit in the past year. Just checking in again, I told her as I took a few deep breaths. After a long day in air conditioning, the warm, damp evening air felt good. I guess there were a couple of dozen other cars scattered about the parking lot, not that I paid them any attention as I trudged toward my dirty red Ford Bronco sitting in the middle. It was a grizzled veteran of the commuter battles on the LA expressways. Our friends jokingly referred to it as the "OJ Simpson" model. It didn't get good mileage, but it had a big gas tank and the cops could chase you all day in it.

I pulled out my remote key and pressed "unlock." Totally brain dead, I heard the doors pop open and got inside. I tossed the thermos in the back seat, pulled the door closed and fastened my seat belt. I stuck the key in the ignition and was about to crank the engine when the passenger door opened and very large guy slipped in next to me. His slick, jet-black hair was pulled back into a stubby ponytail and he had a weight-lifter's body that stretched the seams of his sharkskin sports coat. He wore a dark-red silk shirt open at the throat and a half-dozen gold chains around his neck. More importantly, he held a chrome-plated .45 caliber automatic pointed at my chest. Having spent two years in the Army, I knew what a .45 could do to on the pistol range. I didn't want to know what it could in the front seat of my Bronco.

"You Peter Talbott?" he asked, glaring at me.

"You want the Bronco? It's yours."

"No, I don't want the freakin' Bronco."

"It's yours, really," I told him as I reached for the door handle.

"Look, Ace, this ain't no carjack, and if it were, I'd pick something better than an old piece of shit like this," he said as he raised the .45 a few inches higher and I stopped moving. "Now, you Talbott, or not?"

"Yes, yes, I'm Talbott."

"Peter Emerson Talbott? 33 years old?" I nodded, ready to agree to anything. "From California? Went to freakin' UCLA? UCLA?" His eyes narrowed as he repeated the name of the school. "You know, I lost two large on those dumb bastards in the NCAA tournament last year. I oughta ..."

"Yeah," I kept nodding. "They're real dumb bastards, really dumb."

"But you weren't there then, were you? Says you graduated back in '98." More nods, wondering where this was heading. "I guess I can't blame you then, can I?"

"Uh, no, I wouldn't."

"Shut up! You were in the Army and then you went to work for something called Netdyne out in LA. Right?"

"Yeah, software and aeronautical engineering computer stuff," I kept nodding as the feeling of stark terror was beginning to wear off. After all, he hadn't shot me yet.

"You moved here to Boston two months ago and you're living in that little suck-ass apartment over in Lexington? So where's your wife?"

"Where's my wife?" Now it was my turn to get pissed. I sat up and glared. "She's dead. She died a year ago back in LA."

"Yeah? You freakin' sure about that?"

"Yeah, I'm freakin' sure about it!" The .45 or not, I'd had enough.

"Okay, Ace, then how do you explain this?"

He reached into his shirt pocket, pulled out a bad Xerox copy of an old newspaper story, and dropped it in my lap. One glance and I knew exactly what it was:

> *TALBOTT, PETER EMERSON*, age 33, died last Tuesday in a tragic automobile accident in Baja California. A 1998 graduate of UCLA and former lieutenant in the US Army Transportation Corps, he was a software engineer with Netdyne Systems in Long Beach and the husband of Theresa June Talbott who preceded him in death here last month following a lengthy illness. A memorial service will be held at the Montane chapel in Long Beach at 2:00 PM on Thursday.

"Oh, not this again," I laughed and shook my head, recognizing the old obituary from the LA Times.

"You see something funny, smart guy?"

"That obituary, it was all a big mistake."

"A mistake?" He raised the .45. "I'm all freakin' ears."

I tried to explain to him about the trip to Tijuana, the 350-Z, the semi, the dead Mexican kid, and the memorial service in Long Beach.

The guy sat and listened, as he said, he was all ears. When I finally finished, he sat there for a minute as if he was studying me. "Okay, then how do you explain Columbus?"

"Columbus?"

"Yeah, Columbus. In Ohio. You never heard of it?"

"Sure, I've heard of it."

"So what were you doing there? Having more funerals for the hell of it?"

"I don't know what you're talking about. I've never been there."

"Never?" he glared, looking deep into my eyes. "What about that dip-shit accounting office of yours down on Sickles?"

"Accounting office? I'm a software engineer, a computer programmer; I don't know anything about accounting. Look, whoever you're looking for, I'm not him."

"Okay, if that's the way you want to play it, how do you explain these?" he said as he dropped two other slips of torn newsprint in my lap.

They were two more obituaries. I picked the first one up and read:

> *TALBOTT, PETER EMERSON*, age 33, of Columbus, died Sunday at Varner Clinic following a tragic automobile accident. President of Center Financial Advisors. Formerly of Los Angeles. A 1998 graduate of UCLA and a lieutenant, US Army Transportation Corps. By authority of Ralph Tinkerton, Executor. (See also TALBOTT, THERESA JUNE, wife, accompanying). Funeral services for both at 2:00 PM tomorrow, Greene Funeral Home, 255 E. Larkin Road, Peterborough, Ohio. Internment, Oak Hill Cemetery, following.

"You making a fuckin' hobby out of these?" he asked, but all I could do was stare at it. Coincidence? How many 1998 graduates of UCLA were there? How many were thirty-three years old and from Los Angeles? How many of those were alumni of the "Fighting" Transportation Corps, "an officer and a gentleman by Act of Congress" named Peter Emerson Talbott? Only one that I could think of. I had never heard of a company named Center Financial Advisors, much less owned one, and I had never heard of the Varner Clinic or a man named Ralph Tinkerton, either.

Worse still, I looked at the other one. It was the companion piece for Terri:

> TALBOTT, THERESA JUNE, age 33, of Columbus, died Sunday at Varner Clinic following a tragic automobile accident. Loving wife of Peter. (See also TALBOTT, PETER EMERSON, Husband, accompanying). Formerly of Los Angeles and a 1999 graduate of Berkeley. By authority, Ralph Tinkerton, Executor. Funeral services for both at 2:00 PM tomorrow, Greene Funeral Home, 255 E. Larkin Road, Peterborough, Ohio. Internment, Oak Hill Cemetery, following.

This was no mistake. That couple in the newspaper was supposed to be Terri and me, no doubt about it. It was a lie and in that instant I got very angry. They could do what they wanted to me. My name and my reputation meant nothing, certainly not after Baja, but when they dragged Terri into it, something inside me snapped. This was worse than identity theft. It was memory corruption. They were stealing her, stealing my memories of her, wrapping their greasy fingers around them and warping them. Something snapped inside me and I knew that was something I couldn't let happen. I didn't care about this Bozo with the Soprano suit and the .45, and I didn't care about the odds. I was going to stop them. It's funny how when you have nothing to lose, as I did back then, it's easy to think stupid thoughts like that.

He stared at me. "You look like you saw a ghost."

"More than you'll ever know. Where did you get these?"

"This morning's Columbus <u>Daily Press</u>."

"Today? I don't get it."

"Yeah, neither do we. You ever heard of Jimmy Santorini?"

I shook my head.

"How about Rico Patillo? Bayonne? East Orange?"

"In New Jersey? You're kidding, right?"

His eyes grew hard. "Do I look like I'm freakin' kidding? I don't suppose you ever heard of Ralph Tinkerton either?" He stared at me, trying to read my eyes as I shook my head again. "Ah, shit," he finally said in disgust, then opened the passenger side door and started to get out. He turned and looked back at me, pointing the .45 at my old blue jeans and the Rolling Stones Voodoo Lounge World Tour T-shirt. "Freakin' California. Ain't you a little old for that outfit?"

I looked at his gaudy chain and the sharkskin "lounge-lizard" jacket and replied, "Freakin New Jersey. Ain't you a little young?"

"A smart ass, huh?" he answered with a glint of humor in his eye as he got the rest of the way out. "I like that, but you be real careful, Ace. Keep both hands on the steering wheel, drive straight out of the parking lot, and don't look back until you reach that "suck-ass" dump you're renting in Lexington. You got that?"

"But what about..."

"Forget about it. Tinkerton may have made one mistake, but he won't make a second one, and neither will I. So get out of here. Forget all about everything I told you and forget all about me. You got that? 'Cause if I see so much as a brake light come on, you'll get a slug through the rear window."

I did what he said. I drove away and I didn't stop, not that I thought he really was following me or that he'd shoot that big cannon at me, but there was nothing to be gained by finding out. I drove to Lexington, pulled into a parking space next to my little "suck-ass" dump and turned off the motor. Too bad I couldn't turn mine off. It was just getting going. Screw him, I thought, as I leaned over and opened the glove compartment. I pulled out my dog-eared Road Atlas. That was when I noticed the three newspaper clippings lying on the floor. The grease-ball had dropped them there. He wanted me to have them. I had to give him credit; he was pushing all the right buttons and there was nothing I could do to stop myself. Not that I really cared what kind of scam they were pulling or what they were using my name for, but they had crossed the line when they began messing with Terri. She was out of bounds.

Columbus, Ohio. I opened the Road Atlas to the mileage table on the back page. My finger ran down the left hand column until I found Boston column, then ran it across to the Cs until I found Columbus. It was 783 miles from Boston, about a twelve-hour drive in the Bronco. I looked at the clock on the dashboard. It was 10:17 PM. Plenty of time to run inside, make a fresh thermos of coffee, throw some stuff in an overnight bag, and make it there my funeral at 2:00 PM tomorrow. After all, I missed the one in LA and I would feel really bad if I missed this one too.

Looking back on it all, if I knew then what I know now, the smartest thing I could have done was exactly what the grease-ball told me to do -- forget about it. But if I had listened to him and went home and went to sleep, I would never have made it to Columbus or Chicago, I would have never met Sandy, and my life today would be infinitely poorer.

***

If the sample chapter interested you, you can go to

The Undertaker Kindle book page and purchase one.

Just copy and paste this link into your browser:

https://amzn.to/30TzgGL

***

Also, if you'd like a FREE copy of another of my

fan-favorite thrillers, *Aim True, My Brothers*, with

4.6 stars on 252 Kindle Ratings, copy and paste

this link into your browser:

https://dl.bookfunnel.com/3uu04iwhsd

ABOUT THE AUTHOR

With the addition of <u>Burke's Samovar</u>, I'm the author of fifteen books now available exclusively on Kindle. The first nine are mystery and international suspense thrillers, two are boxed sets of those, and four are my Our Vietnam Wars series of interviews and stories with Vietnam Wars vets about their experiences before, during, and after the war. Most are also available in Audible audiobook, and many in paperback.

 A native of Chicago, I received a BA from The University of Illinois in History and Russian Area studies, and a Master's in City Planning. I served as a Company Commander in the US Army in Vietnam and later became active in local and regional politics in Virginia. As a Vice President of the real estate subsidiary of a Fortune 500 corporation, I was able to travel widely in the US and now travel extensively abroad, particularly in Europe, Russia, China, and the Middle East, locations which have featured in my writing. When not writing, I play bad golf, have become a dogged runner, and paint passable landscapes in oil and acrylic. Now retired, my wife and I live in Florida.

In addition to the novels, I've written four award-winning screenplays. They've placed First in the suspense category of Final Draft, were a Finalist in Fade In, First in Screenwriter's Utopia — Screenwriter's Showcase Awards, Second in the American Screenwriter's Association, Second at Breckenridge, and others. One was optioned for film.

The best way to follow my work and learn about sales and freebees is through my web site http://www.billbrownthrillernovels.com, which has Preview Chapters of each of my novels, interviews, book reviews, and other links.

DEDICATION

First, I want to thank the best set of proofreaders a writer can have: my wife Fern here in Florida, Elisabeth Hallett in far-away Montana, Loren Vinson in San Diego, Reg Thibodeaux, also in Montana, Wayne Burnop in Texas, Ron Braun also in Texas, John Brady in Baton Rouge, Ken Friedman in Orlando, Sheldon Levy also in Orlando, and Craig Smedley, the farthest away of all, in Melbourne, Australia. It takes an infinite number of eyeballs to catch all those little e-glitches.

I also want to thank Todd Hebertson at My Personal Art in Salt Lake City, for the outstanding cover art he has provided for my books.

As you can see, it takes a very geographically diverse village to produce a book these days.

COPYRIGHT

Made in the USA
Middletown, DE
30 January 2021